SHADOW OF THE THRONE

THE OBSCURED THRONE TRILOGY
BOOK 3

RUSSELL ARCHEY

5 PRINCE PUBLISHING
5PRINCEBOOKS.COM

Digital ISBN: 978-1-63112-393-1

Print ISBN: 978-1-63112-394-8

Cover design by Marianne Nowicki

First Edition 01142025 vII040225

For more information about this title, visit:

www.5princebooks.com

To my wife and children, who put up with me and my weird imagination.

ACKNOWLEDGMENTS

Thank you so much to Bernadette and Cate, who put up with my writing process.

SHADOW OF THE THRONE

PROLOGUE - THE NIGHT THROUGH THE THRESHOLD

Nicholas' pen scratched in a slow rhythm on the page before him. His current missive was intended for the quartermaster, and he asked for his week's supply of bread. He kept stalling, hesitating to ask for a bit more as winter was on its way in.

There was little difference in the seasons anymore, but it would get noticeably colder, and going outside was something Nicholas wasn't overly fond of. His desk faced the window of his home on the third floor of his building. Staring out his window was basically a hobby. He liked the chill air that flowed in, although the smell left something to be desired.

His view of the city consisted of the rooftops spread out below him all the way to the city wall. Thankfully, he was far enough away to never see outside the wall. One might have thought rooftops were dull and made for a poor view, but it was nothing compared to the wretched vistas of Alda. In the distance, a temple's spires stood out from the usual rooftops. Little happened there, and Nicholas never went close enough find out much about it. Much like wandering outside, finding out about the cult that ruled over the city wasn't something he was fond of.

Not many of his neighbors were, either. They belonged to the caste of the Uninitiated; civilians in a sense. The initiates of the Black Gnarl went without names; their worth was yet to be judged. So what was someone to them who refused to join their secret, cloistered order, then? The Gnarl left the citizens alone for the most part, but their version of order and law was questionable at best. Nicholas was well-read. Books were one of the only things he used to pass the time. History was his favorite of all the bountiful pages stacked on his shelves. The way the old world worked had its faults, but it seemed like a paradise compared to what the people of Godscorn had. Some of the books told of despots and tyrants that sought to keep those beneath them, especially the peasantry and other commonfolk, in the most ignorant state possible. They felt this prevented their subjects from learning, thinking, and growing. This would keep the ruler in power and the lesser people in their place.

This thought always unsettled Nicholas. The Black Gnarl didn't care how much you read or what you learned. So long as you didn't cause trouble for them and stayed out of the places forbidden to all but those of their order, they let everyone be.

Of all the things distasteful about the city of Godscorn, they were the second worst, after what lay outside the walls. Even on the most oppressive of days when the land itself seemed to urge the living to remain indoors while the world moaned and writhed in pain, black robes wandered about and conversed in small clutches. No one else in the city moved so freely and with such unnerving indifference.

Once, Nicholas was on his way to have his glasses repaired when he saw a haggard-looking man stab another, then rifle through his clothing and run off with a handful of coins. A black-robed woman, her hair trailing down the front of her robe from beneath her cowl and partially covering a silver chain and pendant around her neck, turned to look at the situation as she passed. The two other Black Gnarl with her—subordinates, Nicholas assumed, judging by the way they flanked her and walked two steps behind—did the same. They did nothing to stop it and seemed utterly disinterested.

This was one of the first experiences Nicholas had with the Black Gnarl. His parents, before they died, had kept him relatively sheltered. At that moment, he knew why. The Black Gnarl ruled Godscorn. They created it, built it, brought others here, and took in those who arrived until outsiders stopped arriving. The Black Gnarl oversaw likely the last city on Alda, and they knew that rebellion or even revolution was unlikely. Such things required hope. One look outside the walls of the city, and all such frivolities like optimism and courage were lost.

All residents of the city took every morsel of solace from their daily lives. For some, that was their next meal; for others, a conversation with a friend. There were no grand dreams in Godscorn.

Nicholas was happy here at his desk, writing his own observations and thoughts. Perhaps when he passed on, the next occupant of his simple home would find some entertainment in them. He'd read through the books in his own personal collection multiple times. Those he'd borrowed had been returned, and fewer and fewer companions or associates were available to borrow from. He took up painting for a while, but the supplies became incredibly expensive. He apparently had some talent in the area, as one of the Black Gnarl purchased one of his paintings. The Gnarl buying his work was bad enough, despite his need for money. Drawing their attention was problematic.

What unnerved him about the sale and served as a tertiary reason to quit the hobby was the reaction of the black-robed acolyte, for they gave their name during the transaction, thus meaning they were actually allowed a name and could provide it. A name meant the Gnarl member was an acolyte, accepted into their branch of the order via whatever foul rites they performed. Nicholas and his civilian ilk weren't privileged to such information. He only knew this much because of certain connections in this besotted community. In this particular portrait, Nicholas had painted the night sky. He looked out his window and painted what he saw, save for a few creative choices in brushstrokes.

The acolyte mumbled excitedly about the stars, moon, and coloration of the sky. Nicholas couldn't quite make out all the words, but the description left him unnerved. It wasn't long after that he stopped painting. Another black-robed individual came some days later asking about any other work available to purchase and sneered when informed there weren't any and no longer would be.

Nicholas blinked; his eyes had gone dry. He tended to stare when his thoughts became too deep. He rubbed his eyes and refocused on the view outside his window. The white and purple haze behind the stars was very entrancing. What lay outside the bounds of their own sickly world called to him. He wished he was like the archmagi of old, with powers that would let him traverse the globe and possibly even beyond. He would make it his life's effort to find a way to do so. For now, all he could do was write and read.

Hours passed. Nicholas chewed on what remained of his week's rations of bread and cheese. The bread had grown stale, and the cheese had become dry. He'd need to finish this missive or risk going hungry. He'd had no luck in getting a few additional rations. The quartermaster explained that the harvests were getting smaller, and the animals producing less.

Nicholas thought about taking a walk to the hinterlands to see the farms for himself, but that meant a long foray outside. It was already dark, which had become Nicholas' favorite time. The light of day was a red-and-purple-hued haze of twilight that made shadows seem all that much deeper. Even during the midday hours, the darkness cast by buildings and people seemed to be living things all their own. Nicholas didn't see how farmers and laborers could stand it. He was happy to make use of the assets his parents managed to hold on to during their life, maintaining the meager existence it provided until it was gone, at which point he'd likely just jump from the window. The only work for someone of his intellect and low physical ability involved working for the Black Gnarl, and that was out of the question.

He traced a circle on his chin with the feather of the quill. In his head, he counted the number of remaining months he had before all his collateral, remaining funds, and possible charitable goodwill ran out. Unless something came up, he'd be stepping over his window's sill by next year. Nicholas finished writing up the request, making sure it sounded more complimentary than usual, with just a hint of urgency. After rolling up and tying it with some loose string, he went to bed for the night, thinking of the stars.

The next day, Nicholas walked swiftly to the quartermaster's residence. Godscorn had grown quickly in the first days of its existence, but the island had only so much room. Farmland had to be maintained, so instead of growing out, the city grew up. Steep roads and countless stairs wrapped around buildings that shot up in stone-masoned columns. One could walk by a window on the street, not knowing if it was the first floor of a newer structure or the third floor of an older one. Bridges and walkways hung like slack threads all around the city. Yet, the interior was so cloistered it became claustrophobic. The sickly light of the sun peeked through spaces between towers and columns, but torchlights were always needed, whether day or night.

This was still preferable compared to glimpsing what lay

beyond the city walls. Woe be to those who worked and lived on the outer edges of Godscorn and had to look upon such tragedy every day. Even Nicholas' planned flight to the hereafter would land him on the stone steps of some poor sod's doorsteps within the confines of the city's shadowed innards.

The quartermaster's residence was one of the first places designated during the city's construction. As such, it was located on the first layer of Godscorn. It was located near the outer streets, but thankfully close to the wall, so the only view one had was of those first old stones from when the city was young.

He knocked on the door, but no reply followed. After a few moments, he tried knocking again and met a similar lack of response. Nicholas tried peeking through the windows, but the curtains were drawn, and it looked dark inside.

The quartermaster must be gone, he thought.

Next to the door was a small iron hatch that swung downward and revealed a chute. All requests and mail were deposited there for when the quartermaster returned. Nicholas pulled it open and deposited his request, listening to the hinges squeak and squeal the whole time.

He spent the day wandering the streets, much to his chagrin. He didn't feel like painting or writing. Conversing with the city-folk often provided interesting information or, at least, entertaining gossip. Today provided neither.

His return walk was uneventful. Night was falling, and the air grew chill. Sometimes, Godscorn gave the impression of a city abandoned. Some evenings emitted a presence of ill foreboding, and nearly every citizen reacted like a flock of birds to a predator, turning in ominous unison to flee; in the case of the city's denizens, retreating indoors and leaving the streets clear. Nicholas felt like the only living soul in the area on these nights. His shoes clacked against the cobblestones all the way back to his home.

Back inside the comforting embrace of his own walls, Nicholas made some tea and sat next to the window. The smell of smokestacks mingled with the ever-present pungent odor of the world outside Godscorn and what remained of the Wailing Ocean.

When night fully came, and darkness' hold was at its peak, Nicholas stared longingly out the window once more. Something looked different. Once again, he felt his eyes dry out and rubbed them. He took another drink of his tea and squinted out the window again. It took some time, but he finally realized what it was that made the night sky look so strange.

The stars had changed.

Rather, the stars he could see remained the same, but some of the hazy cosmos beyond was gone like a layer of stars had disappeared from one of his paintings. Something within him stirred. Something in the primordial part of his mind that couldn't explain what he saw but knew it to be of ill omen. His mind raced. Perhaps he was tired and only seeing things. Beyond several rows of rooftops, the peaks of the temple stuck up like horns against the strange sky. The glow of a multitude of lights lit the area around it just below the surrounding rooflines. A ceremony or celebration of some kind was occurring. Nicholas felt a lump in his throat.

He finished off his tea and tried to go to sleep. His thoughts continued to swirl in his head, fear and logic battling one another for dominance. Nicholas decided to wait. If strange phenomena in the night sky continued, he knew someone who might have answers to his questions. He could go see him if need be. However, that meant Nicholas would be within sight of Godscorn's horrible surroundings. Time would tell if such a decision was required. He would wait. The night sky outside was his one comfort. He wouldn't let such fearful imaginings win him over so easily.

A DEAD GOD'S BLESSING

Victor woke to a dull ache in his side. He sat up from his bedroll, smelled the smoke, and heard the crackling of a freshly-made fire. A strip of orange light promised the sun would soon rise over the low hills on the horizon. He blinked, trying to remember where he was and what he was doing. A figure sat next to the fire, reading a book.

Lyra, he remembered. *She's awake.*

Through the shadows dancing on her face, Victor saw a slight smirk curl on one side of her lips.

"You were mumbling in your sleep," she said, feigning annoyance.

He looked around, his brain still foggy and unable to grasp reality. A strange beam—solid black flanked by a cold white glow—drew his eyes to the west of the rising sun. It shot up to the sky and beyond the stars. This woke his fumbling mind with a start. They were near Carnelia, making their way to the source of that fiendish beacon. It radiated an ominous, terrible energy even at this distance.

Victor slowly crawled out of his bedroll, his body heavy and slow to move. His mind was blank, though he knew he had been dreaming. He sat next to Lyra by the fire and felt its warmth seep into him. The fire flickered and mesmerized him. Echoes of forgotten dreams plagued his mind; sights in the fire flashed and were then gone. Voices mingled with the crackling of the logs and faint sounds of the flames.

"Have trouble sleeping?" Lyra asked, her voice soft and empathic.

"Yeah," he said. His voice cracked. His throat was parched.

Lyra leaned over and reached into the rucksack next to her. She pulled out one of their canteens of water and handed it to him. He took a few small drinks and felt better rather quickly. After the water settled in his stomach, the cold sensation moving down his chest into his gut, he took a deeper, longer drink. He felt his body relish the water and thanked Lyra before handing the now half-empty canteen back to her.

"I know I was dreaming, but I can't remember any of it. That —" he paused, his brows pulling together, "aggravates me."

Lyra's head lowered. She closed the book on her thumb, marking where she had been reading. Her lips pursed. He'd spoken multiple times since their first meeting on the importance of dreams, at least in his experience. A prophetic dream had led him to her, after all. She must have known this disturbed him.

"I know," she said. "I've been experiencing the same thing. My dreams have been hazy, too."

The closer they drew to the pillar of black light, the stronger their dreams had become. Lyra shared about some that she'd had, not knowing what they meant or if they meant anything at all. Trying to puzzle out the images in his own head was difficult enough. Adding another set of pieces only complicated the puzzle spread out before him. Victor had a suspicion this was the Fifth Magic trying to speak to them, help them find answers to stop the spread of the Inheritors' influence, and banish them and the Obscured Throne from Alda once more.

Victor rubbed his eyes, stretched and groaned as his joints cracked and popped, and then let out a heavy sigh. All he had were broken pieces of an old mural that weren't fitting together. Too many holes and jagged edges prevented him from seeing anything resembling a finished picture.

"What are you reading?" he asked Lyra, his voice muffled through the hands clasped in front of his face. His elbows rested on his knees, and his eyes stared at the fire.

"One of the diaries we found at the last village. Just seeing if there's anything useful in it."

"And?"

"Apparently, the writer liked growing tomatoes," she replied in a flat tone.

Victor groaned. The village Lyra mentioned was just the decrepit remains of an old hamlet, long empty of anyone living. The hearths were cold, and the fields dead. No skeletons or other signs of former inhabitants remained, so they assumed the villagers had abandoned the place in search of greener pastures. They hoped so, at least. If some tragedy befell the place, they'd never know.

Diaries, stories, and any sort of record-keeping were their best hope for such information. The libraries and archives of the sanctum and the towns they'd visited held information about the time before the Rupture, things Victor had read many times over. They needed rumors, legends, or stories passed down from the generations after the sky opened.

Victor's eyes drew to the dark pillar on the distant horizon. It appeared almost peaceful, a needle of subtly-pulsating shadow shooting into the sky and disappearing beyond sight. It mocked them, daring them to figure out a way to stop the encroaching doom in Alda's future. Victor grimaced and puffed a frustrated breath out of his nose.

A clinking sound drew his attention back to Lyra and the campfire. She was tapping a ladle on the side of their small cooking pot. Scavenged from an abandoned building, the crude cookware had seen much use in their time on the road. They often rested in small thickets when they couldn't sleep in one of the abandoned or ruined houses dotting the countryside. Avoiding the forests was the safest option. If they were lucky, they'd only be bothered by wolves or the occasional bear. If they were unlucky, something less pleasant haunted them. Such experiences were so frequent as to be expected anymore. They slept in the open if they had to, but never again would they go near the woods or cities.

Lyra poured a helping of hot stew into two tin dishes. The steam curled and carried the fragrance to Victor's nostrils. His stomach called out to him. He rose from his bedroll and pulled on his boots. Sitting beside Lyra, he took the dish from her and offered thanks. She handed him a small, tarnished spoon, and they ate.

His mind wandered, debating once more if they should continue directly to the strange pillar of darkness on the horizon or prepare more for such an encounter by continuing their agonizing search for information. Of course, the pillar itself would provide some information on its own, but he'd learned to take nothing lightly. His time had been divided between reading what they found in the ruined settlements and studying and practicing his magic. There was only so much he could do on his own.

Their options were running out. Once they passed through this region, the former sovereignty of Carnelia, they'd be in the sparsely populated region of Kalthav. Cold days and rocky plains awaited them. Their best hope was there.

Victor knew much about the history of Carnelia from his days at the Trifold Sanctum. Though Felkirk had a larger population overall, Carnelia's people lived in more densely packed cities. Their scholars and academies were more prestigious; their cities were focal points of education, philosophy, and the arts. Victor had hoped, and he explained as much to Lyra, that when the Rupture occurred, and people fled from its unleashed terrors, those learned men and women would be among those taking refuge in the countryside. It was those literate and thoughtful individuals whose written memories he'd wished to find.

"We may have to try something desperate," Victor said, his eyes narrowing.

Lyra scraped the remains of her meal from the edges of the dish and finished her last bite. "We're not already?" she said after swallowing.

"Compared to what I'm thinking, no."

She sat her dish and spoon on the ground next to her. A sigh escaped, and she rolled her neck in a wide circle, a slight cracking sound coming from it. "What are you thinking?"

"None of my ideas have been exactly fruitful. If any place had recollections and written accounts of the Rupture, it should have been here. Carnelia was the educational capital of the world."

"But we're not in Carnelia itself, only within the boundaries of its extended territory," Lyra commented.

"I know. That may be the problem," Victor said with a dark edge to his voice.

Lyra turned and looked at him. Her eyes shadowed, and her tone dropped. "Victor, you can't be thinking—"

"We have to go to the city of Carnelia itself," he interrupted. "Certainly, we'll find something there."

"You're insane," Lyra nearly shouted in aggravation. "Have you forgotten Felkirk? I certainly haven't. You told me about the Broken City. Do you have any other horrific, near-death experiences you're choosing to ignore?"

Victor grew silent and pensive. He remembered every moment of Felkirk and the Broken City, formerly the city of Giranta. At least, those moments his fragile mind recalled of Giranta. He'd never been to the city of Carnelia, but some rumors and documents existed about its fate. Like any other grand capital, Carnelia was no stranger to the horrid tales. It was difficult to discern what exactly had taken place, as the opening hours of the Rupture's vicious corruption had driven people from the city in a panic. The stories from Carnelia were far more varied than others. The city was also the farthest from the Trifold Sanctum, even more so than Kalthav. The magi who survived the few trips arranged to Carnelia brought tales of numerous horrors, but the dead black eyes that opened in midair were the common denominator.

"The Fifth will protect us," he finally said in a low voice. "You and I have both personally faced one of the Inheritors at Felkirk. It couldn't harm us directly. And at Giranta, I feel the Fifth is all that prevented my fate from joining the rest of the former occupants."

Lyra shuddered at the memories. Two years passed, and the emotional scars of that time still throbbed. "It felt very direct to me," she commented wryly.

"This is our last option. I guess it's a sort of a do or die situation?"

He tried to be nonchalant, but the words came out grim.

He continued as Lyra fidgeted uncomfortably with her gloves. "When we reach the edge of Carnelia's territory, we come to Kalthav. It was far less populated in the old times, and the weather was less than ideal on the best days. Traveling will become harder and possibly slower. It's also home to the Wilted Groves. My instructors at the sanctum said that the forest is one of the most haunted areas on Alda that they've discovered and is utterly devoid of people. Beyond that, the Shattered Peaks. Rumors of a valley inhabited by living vegetation and dreadful ghouls were all that my brethren could come back with. That's the direction we have to go to reach that pillar."

He looked at the black line on the horizon, and Lyra's eyes followed his.

"Does that sound any safer? Or more hopeful? In Carnelia, there are libraries, guilds, and repositories that are unlike any other in the world. If we find nothing there, we won't find anything anywhere else. We'll make straight for the pillar."

Lyra's eyes remained on the dark needle stretching beyond the sky. She breathed in deeply and released a heavy sigh. She then scooped up her dish and spoon in one hand and leaned over the pot still sitting on the fire.

"If I'm going to die, then I'm having extra portions."

Victor chuckled. He walked over to Gil, the greatest horse that ever existed in Victor's opinion, and pulled a dark-colored bottle from one of the rucksacks. Sitting back down next to Lyra, he pulled the stopper from the wine bottle after a series of squeaks from the cork. He took a drink and offered it to Lyra. She gratefully accepted.

"The only good thing we've found in these abandoned hovels," he quipped, referring to the wine.

They wasted little time after eating. They finished the wine and then cleared the camp. The horses whickered softly as the bedrolls and cookware were stuffed back into rucksacks and secured. Clouds hung in the sky like a heavy blanket, setting a dour mood. Thankfully, there was no smell of rain, only a soft wind behind their backs to urge them toward the once-great city of Carnelia.

To LYRA, it seemed the world died more and more each day. It had been a week since they decided to make their way directly to Carnelia, an idea she still thought was suicidal. But Victor made a good point, as he often did. And as he'd said, the Carnelian countryside was mostly empty. Dense towns—devoid of life with buildings crumbling and desolate—appeared like clusters of mushrooms at intervals along the overgrown cobblestone road. In the old times, before the Rupture, this would've been interesting. Despite the decades and, in some cases, centuries of decay, there were still signs of each town's individual charm. The buildings were slightly different or arranged uniquely. Now, they all shared a dreadful commonality: neglect. One and all, they had been abandoned. Any food had long rotted away. Brittle skeletons remained within some of the walls, their fates unknown, and the stories brought to an abrupt end. One town had several remains, some whole skeletons and others merely skulls on pikes, adorning the walls of the town. It appeared empty from Lyra's and Victor's shared vantage point, but they gave it a wide berth all the same. Lyra never took her hand from her sword until the grotesque walls disappeared behind them.

In another town, Victor called out to her from within one of the empty buildings. It sounded urgent, so she ran across the street from where she'd been scavenging for food and found him standing next to a wall. He stared at a piece of yellowed paper hanging there, a thin knife holding it in place against a wooden beam. Lyra came up behind him and put her hand on his shoulder.

"What is it?" she asked.

"It looks like a sign of where the people in this house went, at least," he replied, his tone thoughtful.

Lyra looked at the paper. It had a rough map showing the road they had traveled and where it branched off to the east a few miles ahead of them. A port town was marked on the coast of the Wailing Ocean with a straight line drawn to a small island far into the ocean's waters. A note also read:

TISHA AND FAMILY,

THE BLACK-ROBED ONES *told us of a safe harbor. A city is built on an island away from all this. If we help with the construction, we are welcome to live there. Bring yourselves and any others to the town marked on the map. It's called Nightshore, and boats will be there regularly to take people to the island. We may have finally found safety.*

~MARIANNE

LYRA HAD PUT her hands on her hips, and Victor had crossed his arms. She looked over to see him frowning. She lowered her head, and her eyes narrowed.

"Victor, what's wrong?"

"The black-robed ones. I know who they are."

"Should we go there instead? Maybe that's where all these townsfolk have gone to."

Victor shook his head sternly. "The Black Gnarl. That's what they're called. I've run into them before. I fought with one in my earlier days out of the sanctum. I've avoided packs of them near towns and seen from a distance the locations they've claimed as their own. There is a stench of the Fourth Magic wherever they linger. After my first encounter with one of their members at a town called Summer's End, I learned more about them. Some books came into my possession, but they were magically sealed. I could only decipher so much of the writing."

Victor let out a sigh and closed his eyes. Lyra couldn't tell if it was the firelight playing with her vision, or if he'd actually gone pale. "Attempting to read those books," he continued, his voice weaker, "was trying. I still have them, but I hesitate to open them again. I felt a little piece of myself wither away each time I worked to remove the spells obscuring the writing."

He turned to her, and Lyra felt her throat close just slightly at the look in Victor's eyes.

"The Scourge of Felkirk. That's one of the beings they worship. I'm sure the other Inheritors are a part of their vile reverence. We stay our course. I won't go to that island, ever."

"And do I have a say in this?" she asked in a half-jest.

She almost flinched when he took her hands in his.

"Please," he asked in a voice full of sincerity. "I ask that you trust me on this."

Tense and frightening situations were not uncommon for them in their journey these past few years, though these moments were filled with long periods of dreary and depressing emptiness as far as their environment was concerned. Lyra did recall a few things that stood out. There were times when they'd visit the remaining towns and settlements that Victor grew abnormally quiet. He shuttered windows or closed curtains if there were any. He'd say it was time to focus on their Fifth Sect meditation. She didn't think much of it at the time, but now those memories were illuminated anew.

"We've come across them before, haven't we?" she asked.

Victor nodded. "Yes."

Lyra replied with an edge to her voice. "You were protecting me from them, weren't you?"

Victor squinted and pursed his lips. She knew he'd instantly regretted where this conversation was going. She'd always voiced her appreciation of his training and taking her with him on this journey; however, she made it very clear that she was not to be coddled. Alda was no place for the meek or timid. She would have to fight, or be devoured. They both would. Every living thing had this choice. She also understood that there were forces out there that were better to hide from than confront. It was painful to admit, but they were rabbits to the dreadful Throne's wolves. Less than rabbits, actually. Rabbits could flee their hunters; the people of Alda were rotting fruit to be plucked from their withering tree, clawed fingers pressing into their fleshy rinds and then smashed beneath an indifferent boot or gnashed between hateful teeth.

"I'm not saying we have to run and face down all things head-on; just be honest with me, ok?" Her voice softened, and she placed her hands around one of his. "You're the only person I have left. I don't know how long we have anymore, but that time is better spent without hiding anything from each other."

Victor cleared his throat. She thought for a moment that she saw him blush, but he turned away and said, "I apologize. I'll never sugar-coat anything again. You're right. You, of all people, deserve the truth."

"That's all I ask," she said, releasing his hand and feeling it slide slowly out of hers.

He nodded and offered a small smile before turning back to the street. She grinned and followed him, then caressed her horse's nose before climbing on her back. Tula, the dappled stallion, was eating alone. She didn't seem to care for Gil the same way Lyra cared for Victor.

After bringing their horses alongside one another, they left the crumbling town behind them and continued on toward Carnelia. Upon cresting a small hill covered in grass flowing like a lazy tide in the winds, the dead city came into sight. It sat on the adjacent summit like a morose mausoleum. Outside the city gates, a number of houses and small villages gathered like flies around a corpse.

The horses refused to go any further once the town came into sight. They stamped and whickered, with Gil nearly throwing Victor from the saddle.

"Whoa, Gilfoyle!" Victor shouted. Using Gil's full name drew the horse's attention every time. Gil didn't like it.

Guess we're walking from here," he sighed. He dismounted the nervous, complaining animal, and Lyra followed suit. Both animals followed their riders to a nearby tree. Victor and Lyra used rope to secure their harnesses to a branch, hoping no one came along to steal them. They had both learned in their travels that if the horses don't want to approach a place, their minds are made up. They will throw you. Then they will leave you.

The two gathered supplies into back packs and pouches, loaded themselves up, and walked the long-forsaken road to Carnelia side-by-side. The cobblestones that once rattled the wheels of constant merchant caravans and traveling visitors now only echoed the soft footsteps of two weary survivors. Not a single stone was uncracked. Many were missing altogether, and weeds and tiny wildflowers poked up everywhere like clumps of hair on a mangy animal.

As the city grew closer, it became more of a somber sight rather than a frightening one. The shrouded sun cast a shining edge on the fat white and gray clouds sitting lazily from one horizon to another. They drew nearer to one of the villages. The stone houses appeared to cower in the shade of the largest clouds, covered in rotted and deteriorated thatching from the roofs. Vines and bushes reclaimed much of the streets and alleys.

Lyra looked over to see Victor squinting, his eyes focused beyond the street to the remaining stretch of road leading to Carnelia. When she looked back to the decrepit town before them, she suddenly stopped him with an outstretched hand against his stomach. He startled, his whole body flinching. She gripped her sword and moved forward, her firm hand holding him in place. She wasn't sure what had caught her eye, but the hair on her arms and neck prickled. After a moment, she saw it again. As filthy as its surroundings, a body sat against a pile of collapsed barrels and the wall of a building. Its legs curled up against its chest, and one arm draped over it, the other laying limp on the ground. The head was tucked into the arm, and long, straggly white hair fell across the legs.

"A body," she said in a low voice to Victor. "It looks fairly fresh."

Victor grumbled when he saw it. "It does. That's disconcerting."

"Should we bury them? Or, at least see how they died?"

"Both, I suppose," he replied, nodding.

Lyra felt a pang of sadness in her for the poor soul curled up in a corner, facing death dirty and alone. She wondered who they were, what led them here, and why they were alone. All the questions emptied out of her mind like water from a shattered vase when one of the legs moved. Slowly and quietly, the gaunt appendage pulled against the other. The hand draped over the side of the raised knee clenched its fingers.

She drew her sword, and Victor raised his hands while moving to the side to flank the person. At least, they hoped it was a person.

"Go away," a hoarse, weak voice said to them.

Lyra and Victor could only manage to breathe. No words escaped their stunned lips.

A weak wheeze came from the emaciated body. "Go ..."

"Are you human?" Victor asked, his voice firm. "Elf-kind or dwarf?"

No answer came. The gnarled fingers curled up even more into a weak fist.

"Are you hungry?" Lyra asked, trying a different approach. "We have food and water."

She pulled a chunk of dried meat from one of her pouches and tossed it towards the person. It landed on the ground a few feet away from them. The matted white hair, stained gray and brown from filth, raised slightly to reveal a set of jaundiced, incredibly hollow eyes. After a moment, the person darted on all fours like a beast to the food on the ground. It clutched greedily at it and returned to the corner to eat. The two jumped back, and sparks danced between Victor's fingers. Lyra motioned with her hands for him to back away.

"What's your name?" she asked gently, putting her sword away.

The wet, sickly eyes stared back at her. She felt like a cornered animal was watching her, waiting for what came next —be it mercy or violence. The person was male, wearing only the tattered remains of some cloth pants that barely held onto his skeletal hips. The rest of his body was exposed, grime coating his thin arms and bony chest.

Lyra noticed a broken ladle sitting on the stoop leading into the building opposite the barrels. She removed a canteen lashed to her belt and approached it slowly.

"It's just water," she said. The eyes followed her until she reached the old ladle cup and filled it.

After she backed away, the man scooted agitatedly over to

the water and drank it down, barely spilling any as he turned the makeshift cup up to his face. He sat the ladle-cup back down surprisingly gently, its soft clink echoing in the tense silence.

"Harden."

The word came out raspy and low like he hadn't spoken in years. It was highly possible.

"Your name is Harden?" Lyra repeated.

He nodded. "Put your magic away," he said, glancing at Victor and covering his face.

Victor put his hands down, the sparks disappearing, but he remained alert nonetheless.

Harden's voice was cracked and strained but agitated and hissed like a wounded snake. One of his hands slowly lowered. revealing the deeply wrinkled and gaunt face beneath. His mouth hung slack, and each breath came with hard effort.

"How long have you been here?" Victor asked, each word drawn out in disbelief.

Victor and Lyra looked at one another, and Harden's eyes darted between them. Lyra looked back at Harden, who continued his labored breathing. His glare never wavered. He chewed on his cracked lips before finally answering: "Years. Decades, maybe."

"Did you once live here?" Victor asked.

Harden shook his head slowly.

"Are you … from Carnelia? The city?" Lyra added.

"No," Harden replied flatly. "My mates and I came looking for a place to live. Been on the road all my life."

His words lacked any emotion. He stated them as rote as possible like he'd repeated them countless times. His dull eyes looked up at them from tired, hooded eyelids and eyebrows thick as caterpillars.

Without turning her head, Lyra spoke to Victor. "Let's get

him some food. The poor man looks starved. We can talk when he has more energy."

Harden's eyes lit up at the mention of food. He shuffled his limbs and squirmed slightly where he sat but didn't move from his spot.

"Let's find a house with a pot and fireplace still intact," Lyra said soothingly to the grimy man, putting her hand out to him. "We'll make you some hot food, and then we can talk more."

He stared at her with an intensity that made Lyra halt in her steps. Fear filled his yellowed eyes, and his lips tightened. "I don't go in houses no more."

"Ok," Lyra replied, "we'll find one and bring it back to you. We'll check this one right here, in fact."

"I'll stay with him," Victor said firmly. Lyra nodded.

She entered the home that Harden leaned against. Inside, the house appeared ransacked, but a hearth in the kitchen still appeared usable, and an overturned pot was nearby. She prepared it for cooking and used some of the shattered furniture to start a fire. She pulled her backpack off and removed what she needed for a meal: a large canteen of water, venison wrapped and salted for preservation, some herbs, and some still-edible vegetables. She heard the distant rumble of thunder on the horizon. The crackling fire would be welcome in a few hours. Harden might change his mind, then. She and Victor wouldn't be going any further today. The time to get to Carnelia would put them at risk of being caught in the storm, assuming they could find safe shelter when they got there.

The food cooked and steam carried a savory aroma throughout the abandoned home. Outside, no conversation had taken place the whole time. She'd looked out the window every now and then and only saw Victor, his arms crossed, occasionally looking up and down the streets. Harden was out of sight, likely still curled up against the wall and the barrels.

She removed the small bowls she and Victor used for eating and filled them with the stew. Then, she sighed when she realized there was nothing Harden could eat from. The bowls in the house were all destroyed—shattered at worst and cracked from top to bottom at best. She put the two bowls down on a table and stepped out on the stoop. She leaned down and slowly retrieved the broken ladle from earlier. Harden's eyes watched her carefully, but he didn't try to stop her. He probably smelled the food.

Back inside, she filled the ladle full and took it and Victor's bowl out to them before returning to grab her own. They ate quietly while heavy gray clouds rolled in. A stiff, chill breeze sent a shiver up Lyra's spine. She noticed Victor pull his cloak tighter.

"I haven't had decent food in almost a year." Harden's voice suddenly broke the silence. He didn't sound pleased or happy, only stating a fact.

"What have you been living on?" Lyra asked sympathetically.

"Wild vegetables. Plants. Rats."

Harden continued to eat at a measured pace for someone who had eaten so poorly for so long. She'd be inclined not to believe him if his body didn't look like it had crawled straight out of a grave.

"Harden," Victor said abruptly. It sounded like he wasn't addressing the man but rather saying his name out loud in thought. "You look starved, but eat your first decent meal in a year like it's your average fare. You talk to us, somewhat, rather than run away or hide. What *are* you doing here?"

He may have meant to ask out of sheer curiosity, but Victor's tone did have a touch of the accusatory in it. His eyes were quizzical, however, and his face wasn't stern or apprehensive. From what Lyra could hear while she had prepared the meal, he hadn't questioned Harden at all while they were alone.

Perhaps he was trying to gauge Harden's character during that time.

Harden was quiet and didn't eat any further. His sickly, sunken eyes stared at the ground while his mouth hung slack. It closed, his dirty white beard and mustache sealing together and covering his flaking lips.

"Nothing to wait for but death. Why rush?"

Harden's monotone answer was followed by the sound of him slurping the last of his food from the ladle. He tossed it aside, and it clanked against the stoop, rolling in a lazy half-circle before coming to a stop.

A clap of thunder echoed in the distance once more, and clouds, darker than earlier that day, cast a shadow over them all. The temperature cooled even further, and the breeze stiffened momentarily.

"We really should get inside before the storm comes," Lyra commented.

"Yes. That house there," Victor said in reference to the one where Lyra had cooked for them, "should suit us just fine."

"I don't go indoors."

Harden's words landed heavily among them. It was the loudest and boldest he'd spoken. His tone suggested he would not be swayed. He folded his body up, and his fingers wrapped around his knees with a white-knuckled grip.

Lyra grimaced. "Victor, why don't you go inside and find us a spot to sleep?"

They looked at each other, and she nodded at Victor. He blinked, his lips pursed, and he nodded back in understanding. He went without another word up the stoop and into the house. There was nothing left but the chill wind, the smell of incoming rain, and uncomfortable silence.

"Harden, I have some more stew left. And some clothes. Tell me your story, and I'll give you both."

He stared back at her and squinted, a look of distrust wrinkling his face.

"I promise."

"What does it matter to you?" his gruff voice was nearly a whisper.

"My friend and I haven't seen anyone in quite some time. We're on our way to Carnelia—"

At the mention of the city, Harden's head quickly turned to the side. He made a gruff, guttural whimper and shifted uncomfortably where he sat.

"Something happened to you there, didn't it?" she asked with sympathy.

His breathing grew shallower, more distressed.

"Harden? What happened in Carnelia?"

His hands started shaking, and a tear fell down his cheek, almost lost in the wrinkles and grime.

"I'd describe it if I could," he answered, his voice shaking.

"Try, please, Harden—"

"It's a city of demons! Of black blood and torture and eyes that open into a freezing hell!"

Harden shouted at the top of his lungs. He spoke so quickly his words nearly ran together like he'd vomited them out after years of hiding them away. His voice cracked, and he began coughing. The fit caused him to begin hacking, and he fell onto his side.

Victor had appeared at the window above where Harden sat as soon as the screaming had started. His eyes were wide, and his body curled up, ready to spring to action. Lyra held up a hand, and Victor tried to look out the window to where Harden lay curled up, coughing and crying.

"I can't remember ... I can't remember ... never go back ... stay outside ..."

Harden couldn't be broken from his rambling state. Lyra

called to him over and over, but he continued to repeat the same phrases. She smelled something strange; a pungent odor filled the air. She looked down and saw that Harden had pissed himself, the dirty cobblestone darkening beneath him.

Lyra gave up and went inside, bringing the ladle with her. She told Victor what little she had learned and what she promised Harden. After getting a spare shirt and pants from Victor's belongings and filling the ladle-cup with the remaining food, she took both out and sat them on the stoop. Harden remained where he was, though the manic chanting had softened to a whisper.

Victor was already warming himself by the fire when Lyra returned inside. He took a drink from a water canteen and glanced her way as she sat down next to him.

"That was … something," Victor remarked.

"I wonder what happened to him." Lyra watched the flames wave lazily in the fireplace.

"I can venture a guess," Victor replied. "He doesn't remember how long he's been here, but I think he was part of a group that ventured into Carnelia, and he's the only one that survived. He's been living here in this village, barely clinging to sanity, since then."

She shook her head in pity. Her mind flashed with images of possibility and conjecture, all surrounding Harden's experience. The idea of him being the lone survivor sparked a memory of something Victor had explained.

"Do you think it's because of the Fifth Magic? Could he be touched by it?"

"That or he was very lucky, if all the others died."

"Is there a way to find out?"

Victor thought for a moment. He squinted in his usual way when churning ideas over like he was trying to spot fish in rolling waters. She found herself smiling at this habit of his recently. She first noticed the habit outside a village they eventually decided not to enter. It looked like he was trying to see into the dark windows and cloistered alleys, but then Lyra realized he was thinking. Then, he began doing it over smaller decisions. The habit made him seem more bookish, like a mage from the stories.

He shook his head and took another drink. "Only through training. That's the only way I know of. If he shows no potential, then you know for certain."

Lyra sighed. "I know he won't go for anything like that."

"Not that it matters," Victor replied, his shoulders drooping slightly. "The Fifth Magic is the most likely scenario. He looks like he's lived off weeds and rats for years. Only someone with a connection to the Fifth could survive in such circumstances. Those with stronger connections tended to live longer, healthier lives."

"Like elves," Lyra commented, parroting one of the lessons Victor taught her during their time together.

"Yes. And if my theory's correct and what remains of the Fifth magic is coalescing into the few survivors still connected to it, Harden is living well beyond what he could survive otherwise. If the legends of Carnelia are true, it's the only way he could have possibly survived going within the city."

Lyra grimaced and looked over at him, staring intently. He looked very casual for someone who said such an ominous thing about the very place they were headed.

"Is it too late to change my mind about going?" she said in half-jest.

Victor chuckled, a smirk making his mouth crook on one side. "If our connection to the Fifth helped us survive a direct confrontation against the Scourge of Felkirk, we should be fine."

"Should be?" she echoed in concern.

"We'll be fine," he replied curtly, taking another drink from his canteen but not looking in her direction as he spoke.

The winds blew harder and brought cold rain to the village. The heavy pattering started suddenly and grew stronger with each passing hour. Lyra and Victor were forced to shutter the windows. The fire kept the inside of the building warm and sent Lyra's thoughts back to the bone-thin old man sitting outside, exposed to the elements.

Lyra stepped out to beckon him inside once more, but he continued to remain curled up against the stone foundation. She no longer heard his ramblings due to the storm, but his mouth continued to move frantically. She returned to the comfortable confines of the house's walls, her clothes already soaked through.

Victor was shaking out the second bedroll and glanced back at her with an expectant look on his face after the door shut. She grimaced and shook her head. She locked the door, feeling guilty about leaving Harden outside, but they had tried all they could to bring him in out of the elements. Victor removed his cloak and boots and sat them neatly next to one another by his pack. Lyra put her hands on her hips.

"Is there a reason we're using those bedrolls and not the perfectly good beds?"

Victor looked down at the bedrolls, rolled out and waiting expectantly like they had so many nights before. It must have become such a habit he didn't even think about it. When he looked back up at Lyra, it was with a dumbfounded expression.

She smiled and shook her head. After they packed the bedrolls away, they each chose one of two beds in the next room. The home was cozy, with a single bedroom split among multiple family members by the looks of the layout. Even if there had been multiple rooms, they would have dragged mattresses together into one location, a protective measure even when sleeping indoors.

Lyra looked over at Victor, who'd turned his back to her to sleep. She figured they'd be much warmer if they shared the bed, but shook the thought away. She sighed.

"Goodnight, Victor."

"Sleep well, Lyra."

So formal, she thought to herself. *Are all magi so intellectually ... annoying?*

Victor had changed lately, though. Normally, he would have tried much harder to help Harden. She took the lead this time, and Victor seemed almost disinterested in the man's well-being, especially for a person suspected of having Fifth Magic potential. Maybe he was troubled about their journey to Carnelia more than he was letting on. Her stomach tightened. She was terrified of it; only his confidence kept her from forcing him to turn away from that hellish place. She'd driven him to go beyond his comfort zone plenty of times before. However, this felt different. Her gut was telling her to stay away from this city. Meeting Harden and seeing the continued change in Victor only made it worse.

"You did all you could for him."

Victor's soft voice came to her from behind, muffled by the storm outside and his back being turned. The howl of the wind and rhythmic beat of sheets of rain continued.

"I felt there was nothing we could really do for him. Perhaps I should've done more. You did more than enough, though. His mind is gone. Broken. We can leave him some food and clothes when we depart, but I doubt we'll get much more out of him. The Fifth Magic can't work miracles."

There was regret in Victor's voice. Lyra smiled softly. She felt very sorry for the old man outside in the weather but hoped he gathered himself enough to find shelter. Victor's last words suddenly hit her, though. He made her believe that the Fifth Magic *could* work miracles.

"Victor, the Fifth Magic *has* worked miracles. It brought us together, protected us, and gave us purpose. If we're going to risk our lives going to Carnelia, I need you to believe that. Otherwise, what have we been doing all this time?"

She hoped the doubt that touched her heart didn't carry into her words. She heard Victor stir slightly before he spoke.

"I'm sorry," he said in a low, gruff tone. "I've been doubting a lot recently. Forgive me."

She heard more rustling. Victor rolled in bed to look at her. His smile made her cheeks flush slightly.

"Tomorrow, we'll see if Harden has changed his mind, then we'll keep going. We'll find a way."

She thought about what he meant.

A way.

A way to live. A way to keep the world going. A way to lock Alda safely away again.

She reached her hand up and placed it gently on his.

"Thank you," she said.

"Thank *you*," he replied, followed by more rustling as he turned back around.

The stifled sound of the storm raging outside, combined with the warmth of the fire and Victor's presence, lulled Lyra into sleep. As the calm darkness overtook her, she saw a mingling of light and shadows in her mind. She was aware that she was dreaming, but the images continued as she watched impotently. Within the darkness were scaled and prickly things, crawling over and among each other. Their mouths were without number, their teeth crooked and sharp. Then, they were wiped away by overlapping strands of light, glistening like diamonds. The darkness returned, roiling and spreading like oil upon water. Within these fresh strands of darkness were fire and bones. Large hands grasped at the remains of humans, elf-kind, and dwarves, snapping them in a balled fist like dried tinder. Once more, the light wrapped itself around the darkness, and the black, oily strands disappeared in puffs of smoke. However, the strands soon became orbs, surrounded by the darkness but slightly brighter than the strands had been. In the dark pool dotted by the quickly dimming orbs were things her mind could not, or would not, recognize. The other terrors had been palpable to her brain, things she could recognize. But the new sights were things her mind's eye recoiled from. She focused on the light, staring only at the winking orbs, but whispers and worse filled her ears ...

LYRA'S EYES OPENED. Her face was covered in a cold sweat. Her body felt fleeting moments of panic as her surroundings materialized around her. The sound of the fire-spitting feebly reminded her she was indoors. The storm outside had calmed, but only slightly. The wind came in frequent gusts rather than incessantly battering the house. The rain was now heavily drumming instead of being blown in sheets.

I'm dreaming now, too. She thought. Lyra stoked the fire, feeling the heat swell. Perhaps Victor was right. The power of the Fifth is being concentrated into those still living and connected to it, and that number continued to grow smaller, resulting in the esoteric magic speaking to her in dreams, as well.

Something felt off to her. The realization hit only moments after she woke. Lyra pushed herself up quickly. Victor's bed was empty. Her heart raced, and she looked around the room. There were no signs of violence, and his sheets looked like he simply crawled out of them. His boots and cloak were missing.

Lyra haphazardly kicked her sheets off, hastily donned her

own boots and cloak and strapped on her belt that contained her blade and sheath. She took off for the door and suddenly stopped. There was water on the floor there, glistening in the firelight. She opened the door and let the wind take it, banging it against the house.

"Victor?" she shouted into the storm. "Victor, where are you?"

She looked over to where Harden had been curled up. He was missing, as well. A pit formed in her stomach, and she drew her sword. She called for Victor again.

Stepping off the stoop and onto the streets, she looked for any sign of where Victor or Harden had gone. The heavy rain washed away any traces of travel almost immediately. Her feet sloshed through puddles and gutters as she walked quickly through the streets, calling both men's names.

She constantly swiped her own drenched hair from her face. Her clothes were soaked through once again, and she began to feel the chill despite her anxiety-driven alertness. A clearing opened in the densely-packed houses where a low wall surrounded a cemetery. The wall was collapsing in places with holes and loose stones all around it. A statue rose in the middle of the small, once-hallowed grounds. A single wrought-iron gate had fallen from its hinges and was lying on the ground.

There, protruding from within the wall and lying amidst the rubble and the rusted bars, were a pair of booted feet. Lyra didn't need to inspect anything further to know who it was. Victor's cloak was partially visible.

"Victor!" Lyra screamed as she ran toward the cemetery. Her hand continued to grip her sword tight, ready to end whoever or whatever was responsible.

She stepped around the fallen clumps of stone and saw Victor lying face-down on a weed-choked cobblestone path. A small pool of blood formed next to his face, red rivulets running along with the draining rain water through the gaps in the stones. A stone from the collapsed wall sat near his head, blood spattered on one side. Someone had struck him with the intent to cave his skull in.

Lyra felt her eyes grow warm despite the chill, and tears mingled with rain on her face. She cried out Victor's name, but he didn't respond. She sat her sword down and shook him gently, begging him to wake up.

He still did not respond. She grabbed him under the arms, grunting as she lifted him, and sat him next to the wall in a sitting position. She put her ear next to his mouth. Faint warmth kissed her skin, and she nearly gasped in relief. He was breathing, but barely so.

"Stay here, Victor," she said aloud and ran her hand through his hair, looking at the bleeding wound on his head. She ripped off a part of his cloak and wrapped the injury.

Lyra heard a noise behind her, a pattering distinctly different from the rain. It was heavier and slower but purposeful. Before she could turn around, she felt something thin around her neck digging into her flesh. It closed so tightly she couldn't cry out. She couldn't breathe.

A wild cry, that of a man gone mad, pierced her ears. She tried to pull against whatever was wrapped around her neck but couldn't get her fingers around it. Her hands clawed and grasped at fists made of gnarled fingers.

"You can't go! You'll bring them back!" a voice shouted. It was raspy and breaking. Through her pain-choked mind, she recognized Harden. His legs wrapped around her and forced her to her knees. Despite the starvation and exposure, he was still somehow very strong.

"And food! *Food!* You'll both feed me for a long time ..." he howled again, summoning his strength to choke the life from her. "Meat ... meat ..."

Hearing those words spoken in ecstatic joy made Lyra's blood run hotter. She choked out the closest resemblance of a shout and forced herself to try and stand. Harden struggled and squirmed, throwing her off balance. She fell back purposefully, letting all her weight carry them backward.

Harden screamed in pain. Lyra thought she heard something crack, but he still didn't let go. They fought and wrestled. The garrote loosened for the briefest moment, and she managed to take a quick breath before it tightened again.

"Food," Harden gurgled. He giggled with menacing joy and wrapped his legs even tighter around her. Lyra managed to roll over onto her stomach and push herself onto her hands and knees. Harden grunted and squeezed tighter. Lyra expected whatever he had around her throat to begin cutting into her. It hurt immensely, and her head began to swim. Her lungs screamed for air, and all she could hear was the sound of rain and rasping laughter.

Her hands groped blindly as her consciousness began to dim. She felt something familiar, and a brief flash of adrenaline sparked in her. Lyra's fingers closed around the hilt of her sword. She fumbled with it, barely able to focus, and turned the blade backward, resting it against the side of her cheek. Then, she let herself fall.

The laughter stopped, and she could feel the sting of cold air flow into her lungs. She breathed, choked, and breathed some more. Her eyes watered, and her nose ran. Her vision slowly began to clear. Her lungs ached, and her heart pounded. A gurgling sound came from beside her. She crawled back quickly to put as much distance between herself and Harden as possible. When she could focus, she saw him quivering on the ground, his limbs twitching. The blade ran through one eye and out the side of his head. She pierced him through by a mere inch or so.

Lyra stood on weak legs, her knees threatening for a moment

to give out. Glaring at the pitiful creature before her, she gripped her sword and yanked it free. A garbled gasp escaped from Harden's open, bleeding mouth. He continued to twitch until, with an angry cry, Lyra brought her sword down and separated his head from his neck. The twitching stopped. All that remained was the uncomfortable relative peace of the falling rain.

Lyra stumbled to where Victor was still sitting, leaning against the wall. His chest rose softly in a more regular breathing pattern. She practically fell when she sat next to him. She grabbed his hand and let the exhaustion wash over her with the raindrops. Her head lolled to one side, and darkness came back over her.

"LYRA …"

Her name came to her from a distance. Some place far away.

"Lyra …"

It sounded deep and masculine but weak.

"Are you alive?"

She heard a soft, incessant buzzing. Slowly, she recognized the buzzing as the sound of rain. Her eyes opened, heavy as coffin lids, and the gray world around her came into focus. She forced herself to lift her head and look up in the direction from which she heard her name come.

Her eyes fell on the bloodied face of someone familiar. His hair fell along his forehead in wet strands. Red-stained water trickled down his clothes onto the ground, forming a mingled pool of water and blood. Lyra suddenly felt the cold begin to seep in.

"You're alive …" the man in front of her said. He sat beside her, his arms limp at his sides, and his head lolled towards her.

His voice was weak. She looked into his gray, half-open eyes. Memories returned to her.

"Victor, you're alive, too." She said, relieved. Her voice came out strained and soft, her throat aching.

Victor turned his head forward and leaned it back, catching some of the rain in his mouth. He swallowed, then said, "House ... we need to get indoors ... get warm."

He put his hands on the ground and tried to push himself up. He made it to his feet, his knees still bent and back against the wall for support. Then, his legs buckled, and he slid back down, one leg extended and the other curled up against him in a losing fight to stand.

"Stop, Victor," she protested weakly. Also, using the wall behind her as support, she managed to get to her feet without falling. Her strength slowly returned, but her throat screamed in pain, and her body ached. However, she could stand; Victor had suffered a terrible head wound and needed aid.

She reached down and helped him to his feet, attempting to wrap one of his arms around her shoulder. He grunted as he struggled to get up.

"I can walk," he said.

"No. You can't," she replied sternly.

They stumbled their way back to the house where the fire and bandages waited. Victor could barely hold his own weight. Blood still dropped onto the pavement, only to become lost in the rain.

Lyra brutishly slammed the door to the house open and led Victor to the bed. He collapsed onto the mattress. Lyra elevated his head and made him as comfortable as possible.

Lyra went to their packs and retrieved bandages and wild healing herbs found along their journey. She crushed them in her hands and stuck them out in the rain to gather a bit of water. After mixing them into a paste, she spread it on Victor's wounds.

He grunted in discomfort and then was quiet. Lyra wrapped his head in clean bandages and let him rest.

The fire had continued to burn, and the inside of the home was quite warm. The sounds of the wind and rain turned from threatening to soothing within the confines of the walls. She fell to her knees, exhausted, and didn't remember laying down before darkness reclaimed her once more.

WHEN LYRA'S eyes opened again, they saw rays of sunlight coming through the shutters. A stiff but weaker wind blew outside. There was no longer any sound of rain. She realized she was laying on top of her bed, still in damp clothing. A few burning embers glowed in the blackened remains within the fireplace. She leaned up, her throat sore from thirst and strangulation. Her side and leg hurt; she'd fallen asleep on her sheath. She fumbled for her canteen and drank deeply from it.

Victor.

The image of him in bed, bleeding and unconscious, suddenly struck her. She stood, nearly tripping over her own feet, and walked with heavy steps to the bed. Victor was sitting on the edge, holding a wad of bandages to his wound, canteen in the other hand. The red-stained mass of cloth against his head was made of those that once wrapped around it. He'd taken them off.

"What are you doing awake?" she asked with a hint of annoyance.

He grunted as he replied: "Fifth Magic. It was once considered a healing magic, remember? Learn to focus it, and you can help heal your own wounds, too."

She plopped next to him, gently rubbing her throat. "Yeah, you'll have to teach me that."

They sat quietly for a moment when Lyra asked, "What happened last night? Why did you leave?"

Victor didn't reply immediately. He pulled the wad of bandages from his wound, checked them, and then tossed them haphazardly into a corner.

"I heard Harden calling out. I thought I was imagining it at first, that the wind was playing tricks on me. Then, I knew for sure it was him. I went outside, thinking he was in trouble. I should've known better when I heard his voice getting further away."

Victor paused and took a drink from his canteen, then shook his head in irritation.

"I saw the statue in the cemetery come into view, then pain, then I woke up against a wall with you next to me and Harden lying on the ground without a head. Then I passed out again, and here we are."

"Passed out again?" Lyra said, confused. "You don't remember us stumbling back here in the storm?"

Victor gently shook his head. "I thought you actually carried me," he added with a chuckle.

"Gods, no," Lyra replied curtly. "I could barely stand myself."

"So," Victor continued in a low voice, "Harden. What happened?"

Lyra looked at the blood-stained bandages in the corner. "He must have snapped. He tried strangling me with something and kept raving about food—meat, specifically. He was going to eat us."

"Gods," Victor whispered.

"I guess being connected to the Fifth Magic doesn't make you a decent person by nature."

"I suppose not. We both learned something today."

"Perhaps we should let you heal for today, then onward to Carnelia?" Lyra asked.

"I'm fine now," he replied as he stood to his feet. "There's something I need to do before we continue on."

"What is it?"

She saw Victor staring at her weapon. Her hand went to it, her fingers wrapping around the worn sheath.

"What's going on, Victor?"

"I've been thinking," he said, still looking at her blade.

"Aren't you always?"

"The storm was disorienting," he continued, as though he hadn't heard her, "but when I was looking for Harden as he called for me, I felt a magic resonance at the cemetery. Fifth magic. It was there I felt some sort of ... connection. One I haven't felt before."

Lyra saw his face darken as his eyes narrowed.

"It was like a ... conflux of the Fifth magic but intermingled with a sense of desperation. Me, the residual magic at the cemetery, and Harden."

Lyra nodded. "So Harden *was* connected with the Fifth."

"Yes, and his connection combined with that of the cemetery was possibly enough to protect him here for so long; however, even his connection to the Fifth didn't spare his mind the horrors of Carnelia. We've spent all this time avoiding places like that, but now that we're heading straight into the demon's mouth, we'll need more protection."

"What did you have in mind?" she asked tentatively.

"Let's pack up, and I'll show you," he replied, turning away toward their belongings, which were now scattered on the floor after last night's events.

They changed out of their damp clothes into dry ones they carried in their packs. They strung the others up to dry by a fresh fire Victor had teased out of the embers in the fireplace. He said they'd need some time before leaving so they could let their clothes dry in the meantime. They packed the rest of their belongings up and left them with their clothes.

Victor led Lyra to the cemetery, where the headless body of Harden remained lying in a pool of bloody water. Lyra felt a sudden urge to kick the son of a bitch—corpse or not. They removed the body out of sight, just around the corner of the walls. They had neither the time nor inclination to bury him or his head. The scavengers would feed on him, just as he fed on others. Victor said Harden's presence would disrupt his work, as well.

"What work?" Lyra pressed, still unsure of Victor's purpose for coming here.

Victor nodded toward the statue in the center of the cemetery. Lyra looked over at the statue and saw it in detail for the first time. The sculpture was of a beautiful woman dressed in a simple, flowing gown. She looked downward as though to gaze at those around her, with a look of sympathy and love on her face. Her arms were both outstretched with elbows tucked in towards her. One hand held an ornate bowl, now filled with rainwater slowly dribbling from wide cracks on the brim, while the other held what looked like a long, delicate cloth of some kind.

"That's Sheemra; she was worshipped in the old world as a goddess of healing and forgiveness. I don't know what other activities or magic were used around this cemetery, but her image is the source of the resonance of Fifth Magic. I can feel it."

Lyra nodded. "Now that you point it out, I can too. It's peaceful. Pleasant."

She said the words as though she had trouble believing them herself.

"I'm going to need your sword for a bit," Victor said. "I'm going to try using Third Magic enchantments to focus the power of the Fifth into the blade. My hope is that it will be more effective against whatever we may encounter in Carnelia. Or at least give it pause before interacting with us."

Lyra recalled Victor's explanation of Third Magic. She'd never seen it used and was curious how it worked, but handing over her only weapon, even to Victor, caused her to hesitate.

Victor turned to her, and there was a sparkle in his eyes. "It's fine; even if the enchantment doesn't take, it won't damage the blade."

His small smile eased her doubts, and she unstrapped the sheath from her belt. She handed it over to him. He took the weapon from her and sat it on the base of the statue. Both his hands contorted into gestures that Lyra didn't recognize but looked undoubtedly ... magical.

Victor knelt down and traced over the ground and spoke in words that stuttered and punctuated. Brief, staccato syllables were followed by longer strings of vowels and melodic words. She hesitantly stepped back when ciphers began to glow on the ground where his hands and fingers had been tracing. He stood up, took a breath, and turned around to grab her sword. He was standing in the middle of a large, arcane symbol.

"We've been traveling together for years, and I've never seen you do anything like that before ..." she said, amazed.

"Third Magic isn't my strong suit," he replied casually. "I'm hoping this works. It may take some time, so I'd appreciate it if you could keep watch for me. It might get a tad boring, so I apologize."

Lyra shook her head. "I've had enough excitement," she groaned as she walked over and leaned against a nearby wall.

Victor sat cross-legged in the middle of the symbol, her sword unsheathed and placed across his knees. He looked to be meditating. Lyra simply waited.

The wind picked up at times, rustling the leaves of the trees around the cemetery. Every now and then, her thoughts would go to Harden, lying butchered beyond the wall. She looked at the statue of Sheemra, goddess of healing and forgiveness, and shook the images away. At one point, she yawned but tried to hold it back lest she disrupt Victor, who still sat in a meditative state, back straight, and face emotionless. The sun moved across the sky, and he never flinched or wavered. Her back and muscles began to ache, and she realized she was trying to remain still this whole time herself.

The breeze suddenly stopped. It felt as though time itself had halted for a brief moment. The symbol on the ground was gone, and Lyra breathed more heavily, as though her lungs had stopped functioning for several seconds.

Victor opened his eyes and looked down at the sword. Lyra stared at him, her mouth open as her mind tried to grasp the few moments prior. Something felt different about the cemetery.

"Did you feel that?" she asked, seeing Victor lift the sword in both his palms, rotating and inspecting it.

"No, what happened?"

"I don't know ... something just now ... the cemetery feels different."

Victor looked up, then looked around with squinted eyes. He dropped his head, his brows furrowed, as he stared off into nothing. He looked like a cat that had just woken from a nap.

"Yes," he said softly. "Here," he said, lifting the sword for her to take.

She gripped it by the handle and lifted the steel in front of her.

"Notice anything different?" he asked.

"It feels lighter," she said, rotating it. "No—there's more."

As she twisted her wrist, rotating the blade, the light caught it differently. There was a shimmer to the light that reflected on the blade. It wasn't blinding, but even when the sunlight shot straight into her eyes, she could see through it;

saw the glint of countless diamonds in the otherwise natural sheen.

"Fifth Magic has been imbued into the blade. Unfortunately, this has weakened the presence of the Fifth in this area."

"So, you were right about that, as well."

"Yes," Victor said somberly. "I'm beginning to get tired of hearing that."

Lyra smiled at the sight of the enchanted blade. She read about them in stories but never thought she would ever hold one. "Thank you, Victor. Don't be offended, but I hope I never have a chance to find out what it can do."

He chuckled. "None taken whatsoever."

They returned to grab their belongings, their wet clothes now dry and warm. On the outskirts of the unnamed town, they saw the outline of the doomed city of Carnelia. It called to them like a dying man. The overgrown road before them told of centuries of abandonment. Unhallowed grounds were now haunted by memories of death and evils too horrible to name. Just as she'd stepped out of the warmth of the house into torrential rain to follow her missing friend, Lyra felt the peace of the Fifth give way to a pall of dread that seeped into the deepest parts of her being.

VICTOR WAS glad the enchantment worked. Every step in the vicinity of Carnelia felt heavier. The air here was weighed down by something malicious. They walked slowly until they could see the windows of the buildings on the outskirts of the capital city. Walled like any other great city, finding a way in would be their first objective. However, neither wanted to enter as the evening approached quickly. They made camp near a small rocky outcrop. They decided to take turns keeping watch that night. The campfire burned dimmer and colder, causing them to huddle close. Their minds turned every small noise into something sinister.

"This place feels wrong, Victor," Lyra said. She should have been asleep as Victor was on watch, but the constant sounds of her turning in her bedroll said otherwise.

Victor rubbed his eyes. He was incredibly tired despite being able to sleep during his turn at watch. He told Lyra she could take a few extra hours as he couldn't sleep, but apparently, neither could she.

"Yes," he agreed groggily. "Felkirk. The Broken City. Other places we've been have all been bad, but this ... this is different."

He placed his hand on her shoulder and felt the tension ease. "We'll leave in the morning when the sun stokes our courage a little more."

"You're quite optimistic," she said with a smile in her voice, though her back remained turned to him.

"You came with me, remember?" he said, his tone a lighthearted accusation. "I told you of the things I saw on my own. Not all were terrible, I suppose, but those were the exceptions rather than the rule. The elf-kind port town was very unique. The peaks of the Brindlecrag at sunset were quite a sight to see, as well."

Victor spoke of memories he'd nearly forgotten and sights he once didn't give much thought to. He was well aware of the purpose of his journey and the home he'd never see again. The people, and one person in particular, that he'd been forced to leave behind. The memory of the Archmage of the Trifold, the elf-kind with auburn hair, left a bitter ache in his heart.

Nethara.

He still remembered her name, at least. He looked down at the strands of blonde hair falling out of the bedroll and smiled.

"Then came Felkirk," he said. "One of the worst places I've encountered. But it did bring me you."

Victor hesitated. The memories of travel with Lyra sharpened as they flashed through his mind.

"You've made the last few years much easier. I'm sorry for what happened to your family, but I'm glad you chose to come with me. I don't know what I would've done without you."

He expected some kind of reaction, but none came. Had he offended her? He opened his mouth to apologize when he felt her shoulders rise and fall steadily. She was asleep. How long had she been so? Victor smiled and sat there, leaving his hand gently where it was. He felt drowsy but no longer as fearful of the night as he had been.

VICTOR OPENED his eyes to sunlight cresting on the horizon. A blanket lay over his shoulders, and he panicked for a moment, fearing he'd fallen asleep on his watch. He then hazily remembered Lyra waking and urging him to get some sleep before sunrise. He looked over to see her sitting at the campfire, observing her sword, rolling it, and watching the light of the flames dance on the steel's smooth surface.

After preparing for the road once more, the two of them left the security of the outcropping, and the looming, dreadful sight of Carnelia once more came into view. Their eyes never left the walls and structures that showed the corrupted beauty of the city, once considered a bastion of science and academia in the old world.

"What was that?" Lyra asked, her low, brief question cutting the silence between them.

Victor looked over and saw her staring at the sky above the city. Her face was pale, and her jaw clenched. This was the largest place they'd been since they'd met. No doubt this reminded her of Felkirk.

"Did you see or hear something?" Victor asked, also quiet.

She slowly shook her head. "I … I don't know. I thought I saw something in the sky just above the city—" her words died in her mouth, and her head darted away from Victor. "There it is again! Just within my peripheral vision; I swear I can see something."

"Let's keep moving," Victor said, placing his hand softly between her shoulders. A look of fear mingled with anger curdled Lyra's beautiful features. Her steadfast confidence, almost to the point of obstinance, was visibly shaken. It made Victor a little queasy to see Lyra, someone who had seen such fierce horrors as he, so frightened.

They passed through the looming southern gate of the city, long collapsed into rubble and choked by weeds, wildflowers, and patches of grass. The interior of the city showed decades of abandonment, but it didn't seem to be as dilapidated as one would think.

Time works differently around Them.

If the presence of the Inheritors was strong enough, they could spend a few days here, and a year or more could pass outside. And there was certainly a malign, lingering impression here. A potent and palpable hate, like the gaze of a spiteful throng, weighed on him. He heard a deep sigh come from Lyra and knew that she felt it, too.

"I really don't like this place, Victor," she said quietly. He saw her eyes darting around as though they were surrounded. Perhaps they were, from what he'd heard about the city.

Victor tossed a decision back and forth in his mind. He could become a locus for the Fifth, a central beacon to draw it around the two of them and see if it protected them, but he feared that it would also show their presence to whatever haunted the city and only attract the worst kind of attention.

Damn it. Either way, we're vulnerable.

The air thrummed with residual magic—bleak, black energy that stifled the breath and chilled the bones. It caused their hearts to shiver and nerves to fray. It induced a feeling of panic within the deepest corners of the mind, where the subconscious huddled and shivered like a cornered rabbit. The people of this city were likely helpless against such a primal urge. As the stories said, the people of Carnelia disappeared. Not even memories remained. Only the screams of their ghosts were left to echo in the wind that blew through the ruined streets. Victor and Lyra found accounts of the refugees who fled the city and they all mention a similar phenomenon: People forgetting their family and loved ones, asked questions about people they should have known but could not recall. That, and the strange, black blood that oozed from the walls of the buildings.

"Let's find what we need and get the hell out of here," Lyra whispered harshly, snapping Victor out of his morose thoughts. "Do you know where we're going?"

He looked up and pointed toward a building at the end of the wide main avenue. Its white walls and statues, once ornate and magnificent, were now broken and covered in ominous dark stains.

"That's the Carnelian Hall of Studies, the largest academy in the world—with the largest collection of books in the world."

"Good, let's get there and get this over with."

"We're not going there," Victor retorted.

Lyra's face swirled toward him. Her aggravation was clear in every wrinkle on her furrowed brow and scrunched mouth.

"Then what are we doing here?" she growled.

Victor looked around, his eyes taking in the details of the buildings and the layout of the streets. His eyes stopped on a plaza down one particular avenue. One of the descriptions he recognized.

"We've scoured libraries around half the world at this point. I was thinking of how we would get the best results for what little time we would have here. We won't have days to go through the thousands of books in the academy. Besides, no one—*no one*— was prepared for the Rupture when it occurred. Not even the largest gathering of the smartest men and women in the world. I realized on our way here that the academy isn't going to give us anything we don't already know."

"So what will?" Lyra asked, her words heavy with exasperation. Victor bade her to walk with him and turned down the avenue with the familiar plaza. She followed, and Victor explained.

"All the professors and lead scholars lived near the academy, where we are right now. The Trifold where I grew up had registries and maps of all the city-state capitals. I didn't go on the sojourns of the other magi; I was still honing my skills, so I worked with those researching the areas the magi went to in order to help prepare them. Two men, in particular, stood out in Carnelia: Corwin Syriell and Jermiah Colwerth. Both were prominent scholars of archaic magic and arcane history. Both dropped off the daily academy registry at around the same time. Not long after that ..."

Victor's voice trailed off. He'd thought it over many times, but saying it out loud struck a different chord.

"The Rupture occurred." Lyra finished his thought.

Victor nodded and continued. "They both lived in houses on this plaza ahead, on opposite ends. We'll start with Syriell's house first since it's closest."

The avenue opened up into a large square devoid of life. Several benches and a broken stone sculpture were all that remained. The design included no greenery. It felt very stiff and professional. Perfect for academics. These things all belonged here, broken though they were. It was what didn't belong that made Lyra cover her mouth, and Victor's breath catch.

Like the rest of the city, there were no bodies. But the patterns and sizes of old blood staining the stones were too many and varied to count. The silence, broken only by a whistling breeze now and then, amplified the malign atmosphere.

"Syriell lived over here," Victor said. It was all he could muster the courage to say. His hands trembled, and he wanted to be away from the stained plaza as quickly as possible.

Their footsteps fell heavier on the stones here, echoing louder than they should. Each step gave the impression it was a gift, a blessing, to be appreciated and relished. Victor's eyes wanted to dart among the dark spaces between the buildings and the open sky above them, watching them like a sorcerer peering into a scrying bowl. Despite these urges, he kept his gaze on the door of the former professor's house. His peripheral vision caught glimpses of shadow and movement; whether it was real or imagined, he wasn't sure.

It felt like hours passed in the few hundred steps it took to reach the front door. It was less time-worn than expected, speaking once more to the strange temporal fluctuations that surrounded Their presence.

Victor reached out and gripped the tarnished handle. Time felt as though it had slowed. He pushed, and the hinges complained because this was the first time they had been used in ages. Inside, he expected the worst. From the look on Lyra's face, she felt the same. However, the inside of the home was rather plain. Dust covered the bookshelves, couches, tables, and other furniture. Books and papers lay in haphazard piles and strewn about every available surface.

"There are no cobwebs or rodent droppings," Lyra observed, her head moving around, searching the corners of the home.

"Nothing living remains here; not even pests would return to this place."

"What does that make us?"

"I'm still mulling it over."

Lyra sighed. "Let's start checking all these documents and get this over with."

"Agreed. But we stay together. No separating into different rooms."

Victor saw her face grow a shade paler. Perhaps fear and a sense of danger tinged his words a little more than intended.

They went room by room, side-by-side, each checking documents, books, ledgers, scrolls, and anything else of interest. They found old lesson plans, texts on magic that Victor took a personal interest in but pocketed for later if the document was salvageable, and also interesting correspondence dated on the days leading up to the Rupture. The majority of this confirmed or provided a few clarifying details to Victor, but nothing of key importance.

Upstairs, however, they came to Professor Syriell's private chambers. When Victor pushed the door open, a stale breath greeted them. This room was so filled with piles of books and scattered papers that it couldn't be helped but to step on them. At the opposite end of the room, sitting in what was once a luxurious wing-back chair, behind a dark-wooden desk, was a desiccated figure in the robes of Carnelia's grand academy. Victor had no doubt who it was.

"Professor Syriell," he said under his breath.

"Was he that important?" Lyra asked.

"He was a notable scholar in the last days." Victor looked around and took in the chaos of the man's last moments. "He must have seen the Rupture coming. Or, at least, he had a great inclination that something was coming."

"Let's find out." Lyra took the lead and walked toward the skeleton's desk, documents crunching beneath her boots like dead leaves.

Victor followed behind, both of them once again picking up pieces of old parchment and reading, tossing aside things that weren't of interest. The pages in the books within the private chambers of the professor were filled margin to margin with ramblings that grew increasingly frenzied. There was a noticeable difference to those found in the other rooms of the house.

"It looks like he was slowly losing his mind," Lyra said, a page full of scratched and messy writing in each hand.

Victor pulled a book from under the bony fingers, the skin itself mimicking the old pages on which they sat. The book was open. In a macabre display, one of the skeletal hands detached at the wrist and fell against an inkwell, tipping it over. It clinked harmlessly on its side, the contents long dried. Lyra's nose curled, and she turned back to sifting through other documents.

Victor read the open pages, and his heart quickened. He turned the page and found them empty. This was a diary. He turned a few pages back and continued reading. He saw a chair stacked with more books and pushed them out of the way. They toppled over noisily as he took his seat and continued reading feverishly.

Lyra put down the papers she was holding and gave him a worried look. "What did you find?"

There was concern in her voice, and she came over to him to see what he was reading.

"This ... it's Syriell's diary. The last entry is dated on the very day of the Rupture. But before that, Syriell began theorizing and discovered something. He'd been researching ancient magic all his life."

Victor left a finger on the current page and flipped back to the beginning of the book. His eyes darted over the pages, finding nothing of note at first, until he came to an entry:

WE LIVE *in such days of wonder. Miracles of magic and engineering both provide stimuli for the busy-minded. Our world is rich in history and mystery. And yet, so often do the two meet. My cohort, Jermiah, and I have decided to cooperate on a joint venture. He enjoys the study of archeology, old cultures, and the origins of Alda's people. I engage in the more esoteric: not just the history and origins of magic but its meaning. Its purpose. A manner of 'archeomagical study,' if you will. We feel that our studies will complement each other, and so we have begun a new intellectual journey together that will take us around the world to seek out these tantalizing answers.*

THE NEXT ENTRY was dated nearly a month later.

WE HAVE RECENTLY RETURNED *from our voyage to the southern elf-kind kingdom of D'y'leth'glen. Rumblings of war are brewing among the gossipmongers in Gallancrest. Our way through Monte Virl into the elf-kind lands spoke of the same. Their troubles with Weldenbern are growing. This is the very reason I prefer to study and reason than solve my problems by bashing another man's brain in.*

Barbaric.

In more positive news, the elf-kind are studious people and a boundless source of information. They are fragile of build and light of frame, but their minds are rich with lore and history soaked by the experiences of their long lives. I knew of some of the elf-kind pantheon, but to hear it from their own mouths is a different experience. Their prime goddess, The'ya, is believed to have created the elf-kind people alongside the dwarven and human gods. Her companion, K'yus, is their patron of study, intellect, and music. They gave birth to the rest of their pantheon, of which one can, and many have, written entire books on their details. But their people have always lived in the forests, at most hedging the outskirts with what they refer to as Edgelanders. Some live among humans in their cities, like my friend Theolinas, but there are no current accounts of any choosing to live among the dwarves in their caves and stony hills. I could go on forever, but I had to write down my excitement immediately.

VICTOR NOTICED Lyra had been listening. He skipped a few entries and continued on to another, which was dated almost a year after the previous one.

WE HAVE VISITED MANY PLACES, so many I never thought I'd see in my lifetime. This time, however, we had to leave before I was truly ready. Jermiah insisted, as we were studying in Kalthav and the winter months were drawing near. I suppose he's right, though I regret not completing as much research as I'd like on the gods of the northern humans, who worship warrior kings nearly as much. Their grasp of magic was not as thorough as the elf-kind, but Jermiah was delighted at some of the old tomes he'd discovered in some of their oldest ruins.

MORE ENTRIES FOLLOWED, all of them speaking on Jermiah's findings regarding ancient cultures, particularly the connections between the gods of each culture, and Syriell's revelations of how magic developed over the millennia. There was also mention of Jermiah's disruption of Syriell's own work. Victor read another entry another year later into the diary:

.   .   .

THIS SHOULD BE *a time for celebration—of both our separate experiences had and the collation of the same. There truly is a link between all the gods of Alda's people, the origins of our world, and the magic that binds it. I just haven't been able to put the final pieces together. And Jermiah has become a substantial liability. The last several trips, I have been approached by members of the local academic societies or even the constabulary with unsettling reports of my companion's dealings. He finally spoke to me about the ordeal on our return trip and the threat that I intended to end our collaboration. He told me that, during our travels a few months prior near the ruins of Metodias, a centuries-old monastery reputed to be the site of the worship of forgotten gods not of the modern pantheon, he met a group of like-minded individuals studying the origins of magic, like myself, but also the foundations of the world's "truest culture." They called themselves the Black Gnarl. They worked in all areas of magic, including the publicly banned and ostracized Fourth Sect, which is what drew the ire of their nay-sayers. I informed Jermiah of my intense disappointment, but he rebutted that his archeological studies often uncover unsavory practices no longer acceptable by modern society but once considered commonplace. I couldn't, in intellectual honesty, argue with him; however, my confidence in him is no less shaken. I look forward to our next outing to the southern dwarven kingdom of Meibion Tan.*

"THE BLACK GNARL? Those people you were speaking of?" Lyra asked.

"Yes," Victor replied, an edge to his voice. Then, he read the next entry.

I HAVE CEASED ALL further work with Jermiah. He is no longer the man I once knew. After arrival at the gates of the mountain kingdom

of Meibion Tan, he disappeared almost immediately in a rush. When I
next saw him, he was returning from a trip into the belly of the mountain. A black-robed individual, marking them immediately as one of
those Black Gnarl, escorted him. They departed in the direction of our
lodgings, so I accompanied my hosts to another location, where we
continued our own discussions. I was graciously offered to lodge for
the night in a room nearer to them.

On the day we were due to return, I waited for Jermiah at the
coach. He arrived late, looking unapologetic as though I should have
expected him to be behind. He carried something wrapped in cloth,
holding it close to his chest. He never once relinquished it during our
return home. On that trip, I tried to discuss with him what he had
discussed with the Black Gnarl. He never denied the identity of those
mysterious individuals. He was focused on something else, though,
something he never shared. He refused to open the book in front of me,
but during our trip, I caught glimpses when he thought I was otherwise ignoring him. The things I saw in those old pages were
deplorable beyond description, even with the basest of words. I could
not interpret the language in which it was written, but there was no
mistaking the dark fluid in which with which it was penned. The
illustrations, even just glimpses, cut to the darkest parts of the soul.

I knew of this book; I possessed a copy myself. Though, I would
never have told anyone about it. Its purpose was strictly for study, but
I always felt a pang of the offensive, the malicious, whenever I worked
with it. I never knew the title of the work, only that it was dangerous
and forbidden. I recall a time when my own son snuck into my office
and found it. I reacted ... less than favorably. I always became the
worst version of myself when I worked with that book. It led me to
want to know more about the oldest magics of Alda, but I eventually
put that book away, no longer desiring to look at it. Perhaps its influence never truly let go of me.

I know this was the book Jermiah now held onto so obsessively. It
would bring him nothing but misery. I tried to tell him without letting

on that I possessed such a thing this whole time, but I never in my wildest dreams thought this was what he was looking for. We spoke not a word upon our return, and I haven't spoken with him for several days now.

VICTOR SWALLOWED before moving to the next entry.

SOMETHING ILL SWEEPS over our city. Weeks have passed since Jermiah and I returned to Carnelia, and we haven't spoken a word to one another. I haven't seen him since. Colleagues at the academy whisper among each other about him like he's a felon. He certainly isn't allowed back on academy grounds. The leadership of the academy hasn't revealed what it is he's been accused of, but I have no doubt of its source. I've taken it upon myself to research Jermiah's newfound friends. My initial discoveries are not pleasant.

VICTOR FLIPPED the page with the slightest hesitation, slowing his hand. Lyra placed her hand over her mouth. The following pages contained more entries, and the second page was also spattered with droplets of dried, ancient blood. Victor continued reading, his mouth dry, causing his voice to crack here and there.

TERRIBLE.

   Terrible.

   Jermiah has forsaken all things sane and pursued studies of the most taboo sort. Every kernel of knowledge I uncover is hard-fought and harrowing. My former colleague remains missing, though I still hear whispers among the other faculty. I spotted one of the black-

robed ones yesterday and tried to follow them, but they slipped from me like shadows beset by sunlight. I think they knew I was following them. Jermiah's home has been locked, and no one has answered no matter how loudly or frequently I knock. He lives just across the plaza, and I have never seen him. I grow more tired every day. I feel I've aged significantly. My wife has taken our youngest son and left. My eldest stayed behind, though we speak little these days. I've nearly forsaken all for the purpose of discovering more of Jermiah's work. He's taken a profound interest in ancient magic, and I certainly outclass him in this regard.

THE FOLLOWING entry was more difficult to read. The handwriting was more haphazard.

JERMIAH SPOKE WITH ME TODAY. I thought it would provide more closure or comfort than it did. He tried to assure me that the Black Gnarl were merely students of a different sort. They study what others fear, and so they must do so in secret. They ask for basic financial support from their members in their endeavors and nothing more.

I didn't believe a word of it.

Jermiah looked old and haggard. He was old. We both were. But I feel confident in stating that we still retained a level of handsomeness in our aging, studious frames. Now, he looked like an ancient sage, lines as deep as canyons marring his face. The color in his eyes faded. His voice haggard and raspy. He left after a short explanation of his circumstances and offered for me to join him. His eyes had the look of a man pleading, but his voice didn't betray any such emotion. I asked him many questions, and all were answered in the vaguest of terms. I finally dismissed him, telling him I wanted no more of what he had to offer. He sounded quite disappointed when he left, possibly heartbro-

ken. *A friendship lost is no small thing, but he was heading down a path I refused to follow.*

VICTOR READ the third entry as best he could. The writing became smeared like the author was in a hurry to get their thoughts down and smudged the ink.

MY LAST ENTRY was months ago. Has it been so long? I thought I had found not only a way to bring Jermiah back to his senses but something that would set me among the intellectual elite of the city. Perhaps my wife will return. My eldest son will understand. I only need a little more time! A book was delivered to my doorstep today.

THE NEXT ENTRY saw the smeared ink punctuated by droplets of blood and even more difficult to decipher.

THIS ISN'T RIGHT. Why did Jermiah seek such knowledge?
Can't eat.
Can't sleep.
I saw Jermiah leaving the city through my window. Headed west. He had an apprentice with him. A young woman from the looks of it. Poor thing. She has fallen to Jermiah and his new masters. He's likely headed to a cabin atop a hill where we used to study. I used to take my family there. My family ...

Dark thoughts assail my waking eyes. Note. A note was left under my door this evening. It said that 'their' work was solely in the interest of discovering the truth, nothing more. They wished no harm against any person or being. Alda's greatest truth is all that interested them.

No signature was provided. Only a strange shape: the barbed diamond that also adorned the cover of that wicked text. I know where the note came from. I know. And they know where I live. I'm running out of time.

VICTOR FELT Lyra's hand squeeze his shoulder. The final entry was equal parts ink and blood mingling on the page. As Victor looked at it a second time, here with Lyra, he recognized the pattern. The droplets lay on the outside of an obvious arterial spray, which splashed on the page while the ink was still wet.

I'M SORRY.

I have failed. The world has failed. Jermiah, the Black Gnarl deviants found out something, but he took such knowledge with him. The pieces are still missing for me. I will write a final letter to Edwin. I can feel something coming. Feel it in my soul. I cannot bear it any longer. It tears at me like dying men trapped in a bloody pit.

The Black Gnarl lied. We let them in.

VICTOR RETURNED the diary to the desktop. He looked at the shriveled corpse and now saw the crease along the throat. Syriell took his own life rather than face what Jermiah and the Black Gnarl unleashed.

"What ... what do you think they found?" Lyra asked, her voice shaky.

"Jermiah's secret work. We need to go to his house and see what's there. We're close; Jermiah discovered something that brought the Inheritors here. He's the key."

Victor steeled himself for one more thing he needed to do in this chamber of nightmares. He rifled through the papers on the desk until he saw it. As old parchments fluttered to the ground like ancient feathers, the fiendish cover of the Dread Praises stared back at him. It lay just out of reach of a mummified hand, as though the book itself refused Syriell's touch in his dying moments. Victor's mind thrummed. A hundred demonic hornets screamed at him inside his head.

"What is that?" Lyra asked in a whisper, as though afraid the book would hear her.

Victor's mouth felt dry. "The Dread Praises. The book the Black Gnarl hold sacred."

Lyra approached him slowly. He noticed her hand rested on her sword's handle. "I don't like it," she said.

"And well you shouldn't. This isn't an original. But it's no less despicable."

"That cover ..." she remarked pensively.

"Leather. Human, most likely."

"Gods ..." she replied, a gag escaping her mouth as she covered it with her hand again.

"Inked in blood and bound in magic so dark as to not to be spoken of. Or so the legends say."

"It looks real enough to me." Her words were saturated in disgust.

Victor reached out to the book when Lyra spoke up, sharp with alarm, "You're not going to open it, are you?"

His hands wrapped around the binding, his skin crawling at its touch. "I'm taking it with us. I've only had notes and historical writings about this book. Unfortunately, we may need it."

Lyra scowled and backed away. "I'll follow your lead."

The plaza remained silent and chill when they exited Professor Syriell's home. The feeling of countless eyes on them intensified the moment they stepped onto the cobblestones. Their footsteps echoed and stalked them like sinister whispers all the way to the door of Jermiah Colwerth's former home.

The door moaned as they entered, and the sight in front of

them stopped them in their tracks. Victor nearly dropped the book gripped between his arm and left side. Lyra gasped. A cold knot constricted in Victor's gut.

The inside of the home was built of stone, like the others in the plaza. The mortar between every stone had turned black. A substance oozed between them and bled down the walls. It was dark. It may have been blood, but if it were, it wouldn't have come from a human. The air smelled like burnt animal fur and tingled the nose.

The floor was mercifully spared from this gruesome phenomenon. They stepped inside, avoiding the walls as much as possible. The house was otherwise in order and far less chaotic than Syriell's. This dwelling only had a single floor consisting of a living space and kitchen that were immediately visible. Two other rooms lay beyond closed doors.

Victor approached the door further to the back, hoping it was some sort of personal chamber or workspace of Jermiah's. As they drew near the door, it brought them uncomfortably close to the oozing walls.

"Victor," Lyra said, leaning toward him. "Whatever this is ... it's still wet."

She sounded understandably revolted. Victor took a closer look and saw the light from the open door glistening off the dark substance. At this distance, it became clear that the substance was thicker than blood and a deep blue. Almost black, but not quite. It was also the source of the smell. Victor recoiled as a strong wave of the scent hit his nose. He turned to the door, and his mouth curled into a grimace.

"Are you going to open it?" Lyra asked.

"I hesitate to touch anything in here," he responded grimly.

"Here," Lyra said, putting her hand on his shoulder and moving him aside. She stepped back and then lunged forward with a grunt, kicking the door near the frame. A thunderous crack preceded the door flying inward and slamming against the wall on its hinges.

"That was loud," Victor commented wryly. "Hopefully, nothing was within earshot."

"Anything that's here is already well aware of us." She replied ominously, stepping aside and gesturing for him to enter.

The door had disappeared behind a wall of darkness. The empty portal before them grew ever more threatening in light of its surroundings. Victor held a hand out palm up and muttered, *Lumos*.

A ball of white light, edged by a yellow halo, appeared in his hand. The room beyond lit up, and Victor was grateful to see that it was a private chamber. A bed, bookshelves, writing desk, and other expected furniture adorned the space. The dwelling made up for the lack of a second floor by providing spacious rooms, apparently.

Their inspection of Jermiah's private chambers was disappointing, save for the unsightly substance on the walls glistening in the orb's light. Books and such as parchment and writing utensils were missing from the shelves. The bed was unmade, and the armoire was light on clothing. Victor recalled Syriell's entry of seeing Jermiah leaving town. He must have packed what he needed and left with his apprentice.

"Looks like we're headed west," Victor said, as much to himself as to Lyra.

"Good. I can't wait to get the hell out of this place."

They exited the bedchamber, and both stopped immediately when they turned to the door. Someone was standing there, the light behind them obscuring their features. After a moment of shock, the strangeness of the person before them stood out. They were tall, over six feet, with arms and legs too long for a human. Their hands had long fingers ending in clawed appendages absent of fingernails. Their face radiated a feeling of malice, but Victor couldn't make out any features. That's when the horror settled on him. It wasn't the light of the doorway behind them that obscured the strange person's features. They simply didn't have any. Their body was black as pitch, lines of musculature giving off the faintest glimmer like it reflected cold, distant stars.

The sound of Lyra drawing her sword came from behind Victor. He raised a hand, his eyes fixed on the entity standing there unmoving. He drew in the essence of fire and focused it in his palm. Something about the figure gave off the impression of an impossible cold, one far beyond the limits of their world. So, Victor planned to set this thing alight, even if they had to flee from a burning building as a result.

Once the flame burst to life before his palm, caged within his fingers and waiting for release, the creature stepped to the side and disappeared. There was no flash, no smoke, or crackle of magic. It simply stepped sideways into nothingness.

The Dread Praises shuddered in his hands like a living thing squirming in protest. Victor nearly dropped it, but his glance at the book led him to see a black void open next to Lyra. Ovular and lit from within by some hidden, bluish light, the void sent a shiver of primal terror through Victor. His eyes locked onto something beyond that empty hole. Something was seen in his psyche, not with his physical eyes. No mortal eyes could hope to see what lay in that space somewhere between reality and unreality, where things go to be unmade.

The book in his arm reacted once more to the presence of that *something*. It shook Victor from his paralyzed state and he grabbed Lyra by the arm, who was just turning to see one of the entities reaching for her from within the void. She cried out in surprise as he threw her to the floor away from some unknown and horrible fate. His hand, still containing the fire aching to be free, came round and let loose his spell. The fire burned out instantaneously upon crossing the threshold, but the void closed.

No longer paralyzed by that primal fear, he shouted, "Run!"

They bolted from the house and made for the main avenue. Victor led the way, knowing where they needed to go. Just before they reached it, another jet-black hole opened immediately in front of them. Victor tried to stop, but they were running so fast that his feet slid on the cobblestones. They fell and tried to roll out of the way of the yawning portal. He made it to his knees and turned to see if one of the creatures came for them but saw nothing there. He stood, catching his breath, when an arm and leg appeared, crawling out of nothing. He and Lyra instinctively began running, not waiting to see what followed.

They didn't flee at the same pace as before. If these portals could open wherever the entities pleased ...

Victor's thought was cut short as one of the portals opened on the ground. He had only a second to react and leaped over the hole. His foot caught a raised cobblestone, and he fell upon landing. As he went to stand, a dull pain shot through his calf as something fell onto him. He was prepared to fight for the rest of his likely short life. He scrambled, grabbing at whatever was attacking him, and realized it was Lyra. She'd landed on his leg and fallen on top of him.

It was her turn to stand, pick him up, and drag him along. More portals opened around them. He ran in a strange, painful scuttle. His calf ached, and he limped as fast as he could. Lyra was several paces ahead of him. She turned and looked back, worry mingled with anger on her face.

"Victor, come on!"

He clenched his teeth against the pain and ran faster.

"I thought the Fifth should protect us?" Lyra shouted as she grabbed his hand to pull him along.

"It likely is!" he shouted through gritted teeth. "These things killed Carnelia in less than an hour," he continued, watching as more portals opened. The sky appeared as though it had come down with a pox. Buildings and streets became afflicted with black sores, and the entities watched from each and every one of them. Some of them emerged, standing on the rooftops like dead marionettes rejecting the sunlight.

Another opened in front of them, and Lyra shouted reflexively. She fell sideways against a door, and it collapsed under their weight, the home being older and more dilapidated. Inside, the walls bled anew, small pools forming where the floors met them.

"Harden," Victor said, his breath coming in wheezing gasps. "Harden hated the indoors; we have to get back outside. We have to get out of the city!"

Victor learned why Harden was so terrified of the closed feeling of interior spaces. Multiple portals opened at once. Several of the entities leered at them, their torsos visible, and they all appeared at different angles within each portal. Victor felt his leg suddenly fall, and a pain outside of description shot through his leg. He screamed in agony and scrambled backward. No sooner had he pulled his leg out of the void in the floor than a clawed appendage appeared and grabbed him. Its hold was surprisingly weak, but he still couldn't shake himself loose.

"Victor!" Lyra screamed. She let out a hoarse cry and brought her sword down, both hands tight around the grip, and struck at the arm right at the wrist. A howl came from inside their heads, like a bull screaming into a metal bucket. The clawed hand let Victor go. Lyra had wounded it, as evidenced by the fluid escaping a black cut on the wrist. Spots of milky white blood were spotted on the floor.

Victor's leg throbbed, but with Lyra's help, he forced himself to stand. They ran, making their way for the western city gate.

He was baffled as to how one of the creatures could attack him. The Fifth Magic had always protected him against the Inheritors and minions of the Obscured Throne. What was different about these spiteful things? Were they Inheritors of some kind, as well? A collective of some sort?

Thinking helped take his mind off the pain. Lyra helped him stagger along until the gate came into view. Somehow, they'd entered a stalemate with the entities. They watched, glaring at Victor and Lyra as they made their way through the city. Some of the voids opened within arm's reach, but Lyra's brandished sword held them at bay. Now and then, she would take a swipe at them, grunting in anger and fear as the things watched.

They made their way through the gate, still open from the panicked flight of the townsfolk who tried in vain to flee from the hundred eyes of hell that claimed thousands on that awful day. They kept going until they could run no longer; Victor's injured leg had gone completely numb.

Collapsing on the road, Lyra pulled herself into a sitting position. Victor grunted in pain, trying to pull himself up, as well. She gently grabbed him and helped him, pulling him back into her lap. She grasped her sword and wrapped her arms around him, holding the weapon loosely and letting the blade sit against her thigh and the road. They breathed together, deep, gasping breaths that relished being out of those city walls.

Victor looked up. The city of Carnelia doomed and damned for centuries, still bore the dark voids of those that came for it like a cold disease. Something had happened that weakened the protective power of the Fifth Magic. The light in the east that reached up into the sky had to have something to do with it.

"My sword," Lyra said, now that she had caught her breath. "My sword didn't even take its arm off at the wrist."

"No, but without the blessing of the Fifth, it probably would not have done anything to them at all. You wounded it. That was enough to scare them or, at least, make them hesitate about taking us. Otherwise ..."

He didn't want to finish his thought. Lyra only nodded. They both knew what would have happened had Victor not enchanted her blade with the power of the Fifth.

A stalemate.

The tipping point would come soon.

"We have to find the cabin Syriell spoke of. Where Jermiah went. He left Carnelia just before the Rupture. That cabin is where we'll find some answers."

Lyra gently shook her head. Her eyes were red and heavy. "Are you sure we want to know?"

Victor continued to stare at Carnelia. His hand was holding onto one of her forearms. He squeezed it softly. "We have no choice. And we've come this far."

They took their time recovering from their horrifying escape from the city. Victor's leg stung, like he soaked his leg in ice-water. Eventually, it gave way to a dull, throbbing pain, which finally lessened to an incessant ache. When he could walk again, they continued up the road to the hills lined with sparse trees further west.

The land gradually inclined until Carnelia could be seen below them, spreading out like a giant walled cemetery. The terrible black voids were no longer there. The entities within them had nothing living left to torment.

"Heading west is quite vague for a direction to follow," Lyra commented.

"Yes, but at least we have *a* direction," he countered.

The cobblestones of the paved road, overgrown with weeds and sheet grass, transitioned to one of rough dirt barely recognizable beneath nature's reclamation. Victor did see something that pulled his eyes to the trees, though. A path, fully overgrown but recognizable as a notable gap between the trees leading off further away from the road, appeared up ahead and to the left.

"There," Victor said, pointing at the opening.

"I see it. Looks like an overgrown path."

"The kind that leads to a hilltop cabin?"

"Exactly."

The trail proved difficult to follow. They traveled through what was essentially an open space between trees as nothing of the original trail was left, save for the occasional ruts permanently marked by small cart wheels. The surroundings could be considered beautiful if Victor didn't know where it led. Gray clouds moved in and covered the skies, casting a shadow over the entire region.

They walked until the sounds of birds could no longer be heard, and the wind grew colder. Signs they'd both become long accustomed to. The cabin of Jermiah Colwerth's final destination was close.

The forest ended, and the path continued. A hill rose before them, fairly steep, and up top, where the ground became level, an old rooftop was visible. Something about the cabin in sight set Victor on edge, repelled him. While he felt the need to turn around and leave, the book under his arm thrummed once more, calling like a child to its mother.

Neither Victor nor Lyra spoke a word but continued forward by sheer force of will. Their boots crunched dirt and pebbles as they made their way step by step to the top of the hill. Victor nearly breathed in rhythm with his pace. He became acutely aware of it. His mind was rebelling against him, becoming its own entity. He thought he was hearing whispers—veiled sounds that still came from nearby. He wondered for a moment if it was his own voice, a separate version of himself trying to speak to him. It made his head ache and his skull throb.

They reached the hill's crest and, for a moment, were

grateful that the steep walk was over. The reprieve didn't last long. Atop the hill sat a cabin that cast only a shadow of its former rustic beauty. This was no hunter's shack but a place for respite. Now, it sagged and splintered. This paled in comparison to the profanity sprawled before it.

The hilltop was mostly stone and thin patches of grass. At the edge of the cliff, mere paces away from their feet, the sigil of the Black Gnarl sprawled from one edge of the cabin to the other. Dark, brownish-red lines formed the insidious barbed diamond. Worse yet, in the center lay the ever-dreadful irregular circle. However, it wasn't made of any dried, ancient blood. A hole the size of a wash basin stared up at the sky. It was pitch black, rejecting any light falling on it.

The air was heavy. The gray clouds seemed higher here, as though they stretched to avoid the gaze of that unblinking eye in the ground surrounded by blood. A foul air emanated from the black pit. Not an odor or gas, but a soft wind that made Victor's hair stand on end; the death rattle of a great god, belonging to an entire world.

They gave the old, profane sigil as wide a berth as possible. The taint of Fourth Magic was so heavy here it made Victor sick to his stomach. He tasted bile. His stomach gurgled, and his throat grew tight. The stark, sudden image of being buried in a thousand rotting corpses forced itself into his mind, followed by the sensation of falling as the corpses melted away and an uncountable throng of wailing spirits took their place.

Someone grabbed him and kept him from being carried away by the suffering geists. A feeling of vertigo swam over him.

"Victor, are you ok?"

It was Lyra. He looked over to her. She was holding on to his arm. He was leaning to one side like he was ready to fall over. She looked pale and sick, as though she were on the verge of vomiting.

"Let's ... let's get inside. Sit down ..." he said weakly.

"Ok," she agreed, her words equally as frail.

They made their way into the cabin, avoiding stepping across the boundaries of the sigil at all costs. Being indoors was a little better. It was enough of a relief on their besieged minds to let them focus for a moment and gather themselves. Enough to let them notice the corpse on the floor, a pool of dried blood beneath it.

Lyra drew her sword, but the sight, combined with the overwhelming presence of the wicked magic, overcame her. She emptied her stomach on the floor. Victor's knees weakened, and he fell back against the closed door. Lyra coughed, spit, and wiped her mouth. Then she shakily took a seat on the floor.

The figure on the floor wore black robes. Brown hair fell around the dried remains of a woman, a dead member of the Black Gnarl. No surprise, given what awaited outside. Did Jermiah kill her? Was she part of a sacrifice?

A sound, faint and horrible, sobered them both to a highly alert state. When they heard it again, Lyra screamed, and Victor pressed himself further into the door in a vain attempt to crawl through it. The corpse spoke.

"Who ... are you?"

The words were a rasping whisper, barely audible. The dried lips hardly moved. There were no eyes in the old sockets. The voice had only the hollowest echoes of once belonging to a young woman.

"Who?" it repeated. "Can't ... see ..."

"I'm Victor. This is Lyra," he answered with a quivering voice. "Who are you?"

"Can't ... remember ..."

Lyra and Victor looked at one another. Their eyes wide with horror; they were at a loss for words.

"Year ... what year ..."

A strained silence. Lyra was the first to answer.

"No one is sure. After the Rupture, most were just trying to survive. No one cares about that kind of thing anymore."

She spoke as though she realized the power of those words, the past and future meeting together and creating a whole new horrifying reality.

A pitiful groan escaped the cracked lips.

"The Rupture?" the poor woman wheezed.

"It's what we call the fall of the world, long ago. A phenomenon that is sometimes referred to as the 'sky opening' or 'bleeding.' We've been searching for more information—"

Victor's words cut short. He tried to move toward the speaking corpse. "What *happened* to you?" he asked, pity hanging on every word.

"Killed ... Jermiah ... stabbed me."

"That fucking wretch," Lyra said viciously. "Did he curse you to remain like this?"

"No. Don't know ... why ..."

"How long have you been like this?" Victor asked.

"Don't know ... pain in stomach ... went dark ... then woke up. Could ... could not ... move ... light ... thin light ... then I felt ... *alive* ... skin dry ... mouth dry ... eyes ... gone ..."

Victor looked at Lyra with shadowed eyes, and his jaw clenched. "The beam on the horizon. Maybe it called her back."

Lyra asked hesitantly, "Do you remember anything from when you were dead?"

"Darkness ... and ..."

They gave her a moment, but eventually, only another pathetic groan came.

"Why ..." the corpse gasped. "Why ..."

"I'm sorry to prolong your pain, but we must know: what happened here? The symbol outside looks like it was made of blood; the dot in the center is some kind of hole. Fourth Magic resonates here like I've never felt before."

"Seals broken ..."

The dead lips moved, quivered, and sometimes words came. Other times, it was only hollow breathing.

"Seals ... window for the ... the Throne ..."

Another gasp. This one sounded pained, agonized.

"Jermiah's blood ... the book ..."

"This book?" Victor said as he sat the copy of the Dread Praises on the ground. He gently took her hand, shuddering as she muttered the word 'warm,' and placed it on top of the cover.

"Ahhhhhh ... *ahhhhhh* ..."

It sounded as though the corpse was trying to cry out. It was a terrible sound. Victor removed her hand and reflexively looked at Lyra. Tears ran down her face.

"Nothing from ... that book ... but misery."

The hand lifted slightly, no more than an inch from the ground. It then dropped, all the corpse's strength spent.

"That book ... wretched."

Victor felt his own eyes welling, growing hot. "What's your name?"

"Don't remember ..."

Lyra put her hand on Victor's shoulder. "We have to put her out of her misery."

Victor was about to agree when the corpse-woman spoke again.

"No use ... souls ... wandering ... I ... I've seen them."

"Wandering souls?" Victor echoed in disbelief.

"Misery ..." the corpse muttered once more. "No death ..."

The occasional shallow breath from the poor woman on the floor is all that came for many long moments. Finally, Lyra grunted as she drew her sword and stabbed it through the woman's head. Her skull made a dry crunch. The breathing stopped, and a final wheeze escaped her lips.

Victor let out a sharp shout, startled by the sudden execution.

"Why did you do that?" he asked, a mix of curiosity and frustration.

"I was not going to leave her like that," Lyra responded with conviction. "Let's see what we can find."

Her voice cracked. The fate of the unnamed apprentice left her shaken and heart-broken. Victor nodded and rose to his feet. His eye went immediately to a writing desk by the window. A package sat in the weak sunlight filtering through the dirty glass. Its shape foretold what waited within. The tattered cloths loosely wrapped around it weren't near enough to hide its evil. Victor knew it was a book, and he knew what book it was.

He pinched the old fabric between his fingers as if the thing within was living and willing to bite. It was no less dangerous. He flicked the folded pieces aside until the book was exposed. Something inside him shivered. His blood went cold, and his heart sped up. There was no doubt this was an original. The black-bound volume of the Dread Praises at rest in Jermiah's cabin was one of if not the first ever created. The cover was black leather of hideous origin. The barbed diamond and its grotesque central punctuation carved on the top were surrounded by an ominous black scoring as though it had been branded. The pages were thicker than the copy Victor had been carrying. They were old, brittle, and fashioned of a material possibly belonging to the doomed owner of the fiendish binding, some fool or victim who gave their body to create this vector of damnation.

Victor picked up the book. It tingled in his hands. The hole in the center drew him in. He knew a magical geas when he felt it. Still, he couldn't look away.

He heard an awful sound.

Scratching.

Massive claws, sharp as razors, clawing at steel cords scraped in his ears. Images of dark, whip-like appendages covered with black-clawed fingers like some demonic vine lashing against a net of diamonds flashed in his mind. Except the diamonds were cracked. Their cuts imperfect, and their purity flawed.

The light reflecting off the diamond net came from within, for there was nothing but darkness surrounding it. The whipping tendrils coalesced from this darkness. They bit at the diamonds, sparks, and blood flying with each strike. Wherever the dark tendrils came from, it was angry and ancient.

"Victor!"

His name shrieked in his ear. The brilliant net tightened. "Victor!"

He felt like his eyes opened but didn't remember closing them. The dim light of the cloudy day seemed brighter than it should be. His breathing was labored like he woke from a nightmare. He was outside, standing within the sigil writ in blood on the stone ground. Before him, the hole in the ground sucked in all light and released a fetid air that reeked of death.

"Gods, Victor, what are you doing?" Lyra shrieked at him. He turned and saw her back at the entrance of the cabin.

"What ... what happened?" he asked, confused and dizzy.

"I don't know. I was looking through the cabin when I came for you, and you were gone. I saw you outside and came to get you, but you wouldn't listen to me."

She called out to him from the porch of the cabin. It sounded like she was far away, shouting from behind a thick wall.

"Get out of that thing!" she demanded, referring to the sigil.

Victor tried to move but found his body wouldn't respond.

His heart raced again, thudding against his chest so that he heard it in his ears.

"Get rid of the book, Victor!" Lyra said.

He tried to let it go, but his arms held it as though he were considering throwing away his own child. He gritted his teeth, fighting a losing battle against his own mind. Lyra must have seen his struggle. She came down from the porch and looked over the ground. Victor watched her as he continued to try and fight against the force controlling his body and stealing his will. Lyra grabbed a fist-sized stone and began hacking away at the ground, where a line of the sigil ran.

"You said if a magic sigil's shape is broken, it loses its power, right?" she asked through gritted teeth as she put all her strength into the blows.

He did teach her that once, long ago. A bit of hope bloomed in his chest. The image of enraged, night-black tendrils lashing and flailing covered his waking eyes.

Lyra's grunts of exertion became louder and faster, more agitated. "It keeps going!" she shouted in frustration.

Victor forced the violent, heart-shuddering images from his head. Lyra continued to dig at a small hole that was now in front of her. It was impossible for the blood to soak through the stones that far.

"Lyra ..." Victor said, his voice weak.

He felt cold. Sweat beaded on his forehead. He felt it drip down his neck. Every ounce of his willpower was going to fight the urges from the Dread Praises.

Lyra looked up, and her eyes went wide. Her chest and shoulders were heaving from her vain attempts to break the blood-made symbol. She scrambled to her feet and charged at Victor. Her arms wrapped around him. He felt her muscles strain. He couldn't force his body to follow her. In fact, he pushed against her efforts. His bones felt like they would break.

His mind began crumbling. The diamond net tightened, but the black claws bit and scratched more ferociously than ever. A thousand unseen mouths screamed in the darkness. The book rested in his arms, cradled like a precious treasure.

"Go, Lyra. I can't keep this up—I'm sorry."

"No!" she shouted.

She stepped back and drew her sword. Victor may have been seeing things, his mind in the state it was, but the blade caught some unseen light.

Lyra looked at him, her mouth open in unspoken worry, and her eyes held an unspoken apology. She swung the blade down, striking the book's binding. Despite the strength of her blow, it only bit shallowly into the cover. When she removed the blade, a thin black fluid dribbled from the cut onto the ground. They both looked down and saw the fluid drain toward the hole like wind-blown rain despite the flat surface.

She struck again, barely making the blade bite any further. However, the blow forced Victor to his knees as the Dread Praises refused to be released. Lyra kicked at the book over and over until Victor finally dropped it. He cried out as the final blow broke a bone in his forearm.

Lyra grabbed him under the arms and dragged him away from the light-killing hole and eventually out of the sigil. His body felt heavy until the moment he was outside the stained borders. Things seemed quieter, as well. He didn't notice until now, but within the bounds of the symbol, a constant sound of wind-drowned screams had pervaded.

He looked over to thank Lyra, but he only caught a glimpse of her disappearing into the cabin. Moments later, she came out with an oil lantern, lit with a feeble light. She hesitated when she reached the sigil, but her jaw clenched, and she walked swiftly toward the book, still spilling the thin, dark liquid. She slammed the lantern down on the cover.

The sound of shattering glass briefly proceeded the *whoosh* of lit oil. Fire danced on the book, but it refused to burn. The red and orange flames turned magenta and white—colors of flame that Victor had never seen before, magical or otherwise. A deep, rumbling sound came from all around them. It sounded like a giant, no, a god moaning in despair. A monotone rumble that set their deepest instincts on edge. Victor felt his stomach rise, and he rolled over on his arm to vomit. After coughing and spitting to cleanse his mouth, he looked up to see Lyra doing the same.

She screamed curses at the book, sitting on the ground covered in flames but still not burning. She kicked it, and Victor saw it fall out of sight. He leaned back against the wall and used it to stand, having sudden recollections of the cemetery days prior. Smears of the black fluid trailed into the hole. Lyra stormed past him and came back out of the cabin again with the other copy of the Dread Praises. She hurled it into the hole and stumbled back next to Victor. The dreadful groaning continued and then finally stopped as suddenly as it started.

The world was eerily quiet. The gray clouds continued to move lazily in the sky, ignorant of the horrific events occurring below them. The trees moved with a breeze that came in. The air smelled of rain.

They both sat on the ground next to the cabin's porch. Their breaths were the only sound either made. Lyra looked over to him.

"That makes two," she said casually, her voice tired.

"Two?" Victor replied, his eyes closed as he relished having control of his body and mind once again.

"Two times I've saved you, despite you having more experience with this shit."

"Oh," he replied, his voice much more tired than hers. "I think your sword, its blessing, saved us again. I saw visions ... I think it was the Fifth Magic protecting us against the Throne's influence."

"*That* was its protection?" her words sounded dubious.

"Something's happened. The Fifth has been weakened, as we suspected. Now we know. If it wasn't for our lingering connection ... I ... I don't know."

She sighed; it was more of a quick huff, a release of tension.

His eyes remained closed. He smelled the fresh scent of the incoming rain and relished it for a moment. Then, he heard the sound of rustling paper. Lyra's hand pressed a piece of paper gently against his stomach.

He took it and opened his eyes to read it. As his eyes scanned the paper, he felt his blood run hot again. He managed to stand. Out of the corner of his eyes, he saw Lyra's head raise inquisitively.

"Where did you get this?" he asked, his eyes still focused on the old letter.

"It was under the book. It's what made me come look for you. I haven't read it because that's when I saw you out here."

Her words hung in the air like she had more she wanted to say. She then asked, "What does it say?"

Victor read the contents to her.

IF YOU ARE READING THIS, *you have found something truly extraordinary. You should relish your fortune. The beautiful tome accompanying this letter is the original format of the Dread Praises. All other copies in the world, enough to be counted on a single hand, are but shadows of this one's magnificence.*

No other volume contains the same knowledge. One would have to possess all copies in order to have full insight into the revelations within this single book. The original founders of the Black Gnarl had to work in secret to save themselves from the ignorance of their detrac-

tors. *Unfortunately, this resulted in incomplete copies save for the one true original.*

No other book is bound with such potent sorceries nor made with such succulent sacrifice. The binding alone is one of a kind. It is made from a willing donation of one of the First Kin.

Yes, a member of the original inhabitants of this world gave of their own literal flesh and blood to create this tome of unutterable wisdom. Over time, the binding has blackened from those who have used it to study the secrets and powers of the outer dark, the place where the Obscured Throne and Its Inheritors dwell. Such exposure touches all who handle it, all who study it, even those who merely open it. As one's mind is initially opened to the broader ideas of nature, engineering, and mathematics, so is one's mind forever opened to the truth of the original Throne once a mere glimpse has been had.

This is a grand revelation that my cohorts refused to heed. They would not even hear me out. I was banished from the academy and Carnelia itself for my discovery. They closed their eyes. They sealed shut their ears. Both shall be rent open by the truth: there are no other gods but the Throne.

The First Kin were just as their moniker described. The original people of this world. They discovered the magic of this world, and a scant few became quite powerful with it. They became prideful, wanting to keep the world from the Throne and live without Its grand influence. Thus, they combined their arcane prowess and locked Alda away. The Throne has been searching for it ever since; for millennia has it been searching, growing more outraged at each passing moment. Its rightful treasure was taken.

The Obscured Throne created Alda, and the Obscured Throne wants it back. The false gods worshipped by Alda's people for so long were nothing but mortals, lifted up in stature by those who praised their deeds. Their potent magics certainly raised them to a higher pedestal than their fellows; of this, there is no doubt. Their initial discovery of magic led them to teach others, though none could ever match the skill of the original discoverers. So, their 'godhood' was born.

Pitiful. Mortals skilled in magic upheld as gods. But there was one among them who knew the truth. The first founder of the Black Gnarl. Man or woman, young or old, no one knows anymore. Their name mattered not. Only the knowledge of the Fourth Sect they wielded that drew the ire of their comrades mattered. The original magic. The purest. The other three sects were born of the world as it was created. The Fourth, however, is of the Throne itself.

The seals created by the First Kin 'gods' kept Alda hidden, but it was only because something unexpected arose due to their treasonous efforts. Once separated far enough from the Obscured Throne's influence, a new magic was born. Alda took on a unique, blasphemous existence. The Fifth Magic was born of this new life. A magic of abomination. Of an existence aborted. This new life was an antithesis to the Obscured Throne. The First Kin who discovered this magic were unaware of this. But the first founder, they knew. They knew that additional seals were created. Standards and methods of record keeping were primitive then, and full knowledge of the new eleven seals was lost.

But we will find them. The false gods are dead. Their seals breaking or broken. My journey ends here. My apprentice lost sight of that, unfortunately. But if you are to find this book—this treasure— do not waste it. In the end, it matters not. The window has opened. The Obscured Throne comes to claim Its lost jewel. Burn this letter. Hide the book. You will only cause a brief, inconvenient delay. And what is a few decades or centuries to One that is timeless?

~JERMIAH COLWERTH

. . .

VICTOR'S HAND held the letter limply. His arm fell to his side, and he gazed up at the horizon. Beyond the forest, beyond the graveyard city of Carnelia, a beam of light stretched into the sky.

"Do you think that's true? About the gods? The First Kin? The Throne?" Kyra asked in a flat, defeated tone.

Victor's mouth was agape. His mind didn't want to grasp it, but he knew it was true. "I don't want it to be. But I know it is," he answered aloud, voicing his unwanted conviction.

Lyra stood up, rising next to him. "The gods of our world were just the First Kin who discovered magic."

She sounded both disappointed and afraid.

"The Black Gnarl has been operating since the beginning of the world as we know it. If what the rest of the letter says is also true ..." she continued but didn't finish her thought. She didn't need to.

"Now we know," Victor said, his resolve hardening.

"Know what?" Lyra asked, despair soaking into her words.

"That the Fifth Magic is unique to Alda. It's the only thing that the Obscured Throne or the Inheritors are vulnerable against. Its weakened state has to be because of that," he pointed to the light rising like a needle on the horizon. "If a window was opened by the Black Gnarl and Jermiah's efforts to break the forty-four seals, then someone broke one of the remaining eleven in Kalthav. They cracked the door. No more detours. We make for that beacon."

"So that's what it is," Lyra commented.

"I'm sure of it. And we're going to put it out."

OLD GLORY

I've long rested in my wretched hovel. A stone sarcophagus fit for a pauper's burial. To soar in the skies once more; I dream of this night after night. The unnatural cold of the new world winds through the entrance of my cavern atop this lonesome peak. It chills me through, no matter the fires I light upon the stones themselves. The last time that I looked down upon the world from the sky is a fading memory, a waking nightmare.

Once, the shadow of my wings coursed over the vast forest of Athyl'glen. An endless sea of forest passed below me. The sun warmed my body. The wind lifted my wings. The cloud-crowned mountains were my own castle walls. The sharp peak jutting like a dagger with the ocean at its back was my throne, allowing me to behold the glory of my claim. I held elf-kind's respect. I stoked their fear. I inspired their awe. My sightings were not many, even then, but that was of my own choosing.

I am a dragon. I was among the greatest and fiercest creatures of Alda. A demigod. And a demigod among those demigods. All of Athyl'glen was my domain, and such had it been for hundreds of years. My kin ... creatures of legend made flesh. Elf-kind revered me. I held their art and song in high regard. I protected them from great threats in their past, or so I once did. They offered up the greatest treasures for my patronage, and I honored our arrangement. I held no ill will towards the lesser beings, but self-proclaimed heroes often sought my hide and horns as the ultimate trophies, cowardly sneaking through elf-kind lands and confronting me at the peril of persecution from the same. I never kept any of their bones as keepsakes. But now, perhaps I will claim something from Athyl'glen. Not from elf-kind, who are long dead or transformed by the otherworldly evil that still festers in their woods, instead I will take it from that very evil.

The sky ripped open and that gibbering boil appeared and infected the forest while I slumbered. Just the thought of such malicious cowardice sends gusts of flickering smoke from my nostrils. The brief wave of warmth is comforting.

I stirred when an ominous feeling of baleful intent wreaked havoc upon my hibernating dreams. The things I saw shook even me. How long I slumber, I never know. I do not worry about such trifles. Time makes no difference to the ancient. But, when I awoke and saw the wound in the sky, my old soul knew something cataclysmic had occurred. The forest looked different. It smelled different. It was foul and wreaked of bad magic. Old magic. Unfamiliar magic.

The sea of forests and large fingers of rivers now looked like a scabrous growth, veined with open cuts of dry riverbeds. My castle walls were broken and nearly brought to the ground. A foul odor emanated from their remains. My throne is intact, though storms rage on the seas more often than not, bringing cold weather and colder rain.

My investigations into the matter were swift and merciless. I recall crashing into the trees, sending them cascading like a wave of tinder, scythed down like so much chaff. My roar reached the very edge of the woods. The gray-skinned things flooded from beneath the boughs. They had the scent of elf-kind, but only vaguely. The pungent stench of that perverse magic poured from them. Something happened to these people, my charges.

I ignored the foul things that clawed and bit at me in the dozens. I flew straight away to the elf-kind capital. It had been transformed. The trees and marble that made up the city had turned to shades of gray and shimmering black, like it had been both burned and infected by some hideous mold, caught in some purgatory of partial decay. The marble crumbled, struck through with innumerable cracks and oozing a purplish substance that turned both my stomachs. What caused a growl to rumble in my throat and the heat of my blazing bile to rise was the blinking eyes bobbing in that gelatinous substance attached as though they were a part of it.

In the center of the city, where once a great and bustling plaza stood, the heart of the evil coalesced. These words do not describe the truest terror of that memory. A heart it was, beating and convulsing, but in no rhythm that was natural. The vile viscous strands covering it like a living, shining membrane stretched out and proved to be the source of the substance. It wasn't pouring out of the surfaces of the buildings but crawling into them.

This was no curse. It was an infection. A disease from beyond Alda, borne of magic and malice. No, more than magic. The power that seeped from this globulus mass of staring, empty, blinking eyes and quivering translucent flesh was a power greater than magic. It was a living energy that seemed as though it could create magic itself. This was something ancient, original, a dark seed from whence evil things birthed and crawled.

I swooped down, the wind tearing against me. I was set on rending this thing apart with fangs, claws, and fire. Perhaps its death would return some semblance of life to the rotted forest. Then, I would bathe in the ocean, in its cleansing and dark depths.

There was no hope of catching it unaware. So many eyes, looking in every direction, it would see me coming. I would strike with force and with fury. Give it as little time as possible to react. My old blood burned. My belly grew hot, and it rose up my throat. I would first strike with dragonfire, yes. I opened my maw, my fangs bared in the sneer that would precede this abomination's doom.

The first strike came to my chest. It stung like one of the behemoth jellyfish of the northern oceans that I tangled with once. Stung and bit and burned. Then came another across my throat. The pain caused the fire to retreat, and I roared in agony. My path was unabated, though the third strike was missed, and I saw what weapons it used against me. The slimy strands pulled from the ground and stretched from the marble surfaces like whips, the eyes closed and hard as stones.

The closer I came, the more of these lashing strands could reach me. They wrapped around me, squeezing and strangling. I tried to sweep the area in my flames, but my throat was constricted. My cries became pained. I could not reach the thing to kill it. To rend and eviscerate it. I managed to claw and pull at the whipping strands, which stretched like thin entrails and refused to break. With all the might I could muster, as one of the greatest dragons of Alda, I somehow managed to free myself. A scant few of the strands split between the force and sharpness of my teeth, a dozen swords at once barely breaking the black substance.

I retreated. My first assault was a failure. As I flew away, I heard a voice—deep as the earth, reverberating in my skull, slowly and purposefully stating: "I am the Black Heart. The

Blood of the Void. I *am* the seed that begets your torment and demise."

I returned to my throne. My broken throne in my broken realm. A broken king. I let my wounds heal. I contemplated the words of the otherworldly thing that had bested me. After some time, I know not how long, I took back to the skies.

Small havens of living forest still remained on the furthest edges of the Athyl'glen: to the south, near the coast of a new ocean, and to the west, near the remains of a stretch of human lands. Perhaps they noticed me, but I doubt it. I had business to attend to, and they would have to wait for me. I would bring them vengeance. First, I must consult with others of my kind.

However, in the months I traveled, I noticed many things. Many unfortunate things. A new ocean, the Wailing Ocean, I'd learned it was called, now took the place of nearly all of the central continents of Alda. Only a single island remained in the very center. There, a group comprised of mostly humans, elf-kind, and half-elves were constructing a city.

The rest of the world now consists of narrow bands of land in the northwest, northeast, southwest, and southeast. Roughly diamond-shaped. The vast majority of the old continents' land-masses were gone. It was strange, the new lay of the land, but I quickly learned that nothing was normal in this new world. Mountain ranges had crumbled. The aldyr trees were dead. Human cities vacated, and only small hamlets and villages remained of civilization.

Worst yet, there was no sign of my kin. I traveled to their domains and found no sign of them. Any potential to speak with the lesser beings was quickly stifled. Any sign of me, and they ran, barricading themselves in. I found a gathering of magi at an academy of sorts in the southwest—They called it the Sanctum of Requiem—and they had no information to provide. It seems even the magi were cast out after the strange event they were calling the Rupture. An odd name. The magical resonance it gave made it feel more like the magical fabric of Alda had been torn, cut open. But I couldn't dwell on this. More important matters weighed heavily on my mind, such as the well-being of others of my kind.

After months of searching, I found no sign of any other dragons. Any other that lived, I should say. I found the corpse of one. A fellow of the river dragons, judging by the bones and skull. resting on a plateau near the remains of Giranta. It was missing a leg and half of its skull. No other evidence remained, and I quickly gave up my interest in that unfortunate creature.

I left my final visit as the last for a reason. If she was gone, then there was truly no hope left for our kind. She was my mate, life-long and precious. A dragon's greatest treasure is the one who bears the next generation. Her lair rested near the Halgaroth Sea close to Carnelia. I flew above the never-ending whitecaps of this newly-born Wailing Ocean. I learned why it bore its name. Not just the incessant waves that sounded like the dreadful cries of millions of the dying carried up to my heights, but my sharp ears caught the sound of things more terrible. It was difficult for me to make it out. The lesser beings likely only heard it in their subconscious, the part of their mind that hears things that should not be heard. But I heard it. The calls of the countless drowned.

I listened to the damned moans for days as I flew. My hunger began to gnaw at me, and I dived for fish. They were sparser than I would have imagined. Unrecognizable species swam in the murkier parts of the depths. Just within that twilight of sun-pierced water where it grew dark and deepest, things stirred that my far-reaching eyes wished they could not see. I caught my meal and returned to the skies without hesitation.

I am powerful. I recognize my capabilities and my shortcomings. Magic annoys me to no end, but I can withstand it. Cold strikes me harsher than heat, but it cannot stop my wrath. What stirred within those depths, however, struck a fear in me I had not felt since I was a whelp. My mind wandered so that I did not recognize the coastline that drew close to me.

I circled once or twice before the realization came: this was a new coastline. Had I gotten turned around when I breached the surface of the cursed waters? I flew inland, not fully recognizing the landscape. Familiar territory graced my eyes. The city of Carnelia lay not too far to the northwest. Then, I began to ponder. I had not gotten turned around. So where had my precious mate's lair gone? I returned the way I had come, followed the coast, and stopped when I recognized the Blackwood. For weeks, I searched, flying over the Wailing Ocean until I could no longer deny it. Her lair was gone. Sunken beneath the waves. Hurled by the sentient hatred that came to our world into the cold oblivion of that dark water.

My rage turned in me. I so greatly desired to vomit white-hot fire. Instead, I turned my nose down and dove. I felt the force of the water hit my scales like stone against steel. The force of my descent cut me deep into the ocean before I had to swim, propelling myself with my great tail and muscles tempered by centuries of life.

Creatures from the smallest fry to the largest sharks fled my wake. The other things, those that came along with the new waters and coasts, waited for me. They did not flee. They squirmed and crawled in the water like an animal dying in midair. I no longer feared them. Fear had burned itself away in the furnace of my anger. These strange creatures did not give off the aura of power that the thing in the elf-kind forest did, however. These were lesser abominations. Good; I would take as many of them as I could before I needed to return for breath.

I could not see well; the dark of that abyss was unnatural, and my keen eyes were built to see in Alda's natural cycles of night. My maw clamped on something, however, and my tail and one of my legs were gripped by something else. I bit down, felt blood ooze between my teeth, and turned to rise for the surface. I would expose these creatures to the light as I killed them.

Alda is a world of many wonders and terrors, from the lowest goblin and orc to the fiercest manticores and sea-dwelling leviathans. These creatures, these lesser abominations birthed from the Rupture, made my innards curdle no less than the blinking monstrosity of Athyl'glen. Their sheer insult of reality and 'otherness' was beyond comprehension.

As I gnashed my teeth against spongey, deep-purple flesh in my mouth, rotund, shining tentacles rose and smacked against my snout in pain and protest. My eyes caught the sight of hundreds of round suckers of various sizes—except these were not the kind found on the typical squid or octopus. They were mouths. Mouths filled with rows of blunt teeth. The cacophonous screaming I heard came from these mouths. At the end of each tentacle was a humanoid head. Three small eyes, reflecting green light as they caught the Sun, sat above a black, triangular nose-like orifice. The mouth was missing, the chin leading to the tentacle where each head was given hundreds of mouths.

I couldn't see a central body. Only tentacles. Lashing, flailing tendrils of the deep that struck out in their death throes. Oily blood clouded the water, too thick to disperse and spreading in slimy strands in the dim light. I released that one. It was as good as dead. Sure enough, as it drifted back into the darker depths, its tentacles floated limp in the currents.

Another one had latched on to me with its sucker-mouths, too tightly to let go quickly. The teeth stuck in my scales. It was uncomfortably abrasive, but not painful. I saw the muscles around the shiny lips squeeze and try to take out chunks of my scales. They would have no success. Hundreds of teeth bit and pulled. Muscular appendages squeezed and pulled. The being writhed in pain from the sunlight; I could tell because it was trying to force me back into the darkness.

I saw for the first time what the tentacles were attached to. It wasn't a large head like one would expect from some other octopoidal being. They connected at a bulbous mass with no other appendages or orifices, only a trembling bag of lumpy muscle that I could only imagine housed its precious organs.

I curled around and sunk my teeth into it. The flesh was spongy and elastic. I gripped and pulled with my claws and chewed with my fangs. There was no breathing fire under the ocean's surface, so I bit and clawed and ripped and chewed.

I heard a sickening *pop*. The surrounding water once again filled with strings of thick blood and strange, yellowish, and green organs that appeared almost luminescent. The appendages released me immediately. The body continued to rip, torn by the ocean currents, until it sunk in pieces after its counterpart.

The last of the vile creatures made for the deeps. It tried to flee, being the last alive and witnessing the agony of those who had struck at me. I sneered, felt the strange blood rolling in my mouth. Tasted its foulness. I curled around and grabbed the head at the end of a single tentacle. It felt like it had more substance, some kind of bone or cartilage protecting whatever functioned beneath. I squeezed it in my claws and felt some-thing break and grind within my grip. Some of the black fluid leaked from the eyes, nose, and mouths beneath. I made for the surface, swimming as fast as I could with the added weight. When I breached the surface and the full force of the midday sun struck the creature, I heard a wail unlike anything that had come before. It came from every throat the thing possessed. With the buoyant safety of the water gone, the thing sloshed and flopped in the wind. I flew higher and higher, the smell of rotting fish and worse things overpowering the air. I roared, sending fire into the sky before me. It cleansed my mouth of the grotesque taste. It kissed the slick flesh of the creature in my grasp, making it quiver and groan in pain.

I slowed down, reaching a height where my momentum caused me to float in the air. I spread my wings. I opened my claws. Then, I watched as the disgusting intruder to our world fell. I watched as its countless mouths puckered and begged for breath, wanting to scream in pain without the ability to do so. Then, I saw it crash into the ocean, breaking apart like rotten fruit before sinking beneath the waves. A black spot, like a festering wound, spread on the ocean's surface. I waited there, my wings holding me aloft until all evidence of its existence was washed away.

Afterward, I returned home.

Now, I sit here in my hollow castle in the mountains. My empty lair devoid of purpose and life. My blood burning with infection. My bite killed the unwholesome things, but their blood is doing something to me. I feel my eyes and mouth grow colder and colder. The skin between my scales no longer hides the veins beneath; they show like black rivers on a pale map. My dreams are of deep places filled with ruins, bodies, and those tentacled beasts. They crawl over the remains of palaces and castles. They swim in the canyons and crevices that break apart the cities and plains of old. Worse still, they worship at the feet of some bulbous mass far larger than any single one of them. It groans like a whale and billows like an air sac. The ocean around it is devoid of any sea life, all having been consumed by the great tentacled demigod and its supplicants. I see them every night in my dreams. As the days and nights march on, I understand its groans more and more.

Within the realm of sleep, I feel reality and dreams bleeding together. I am both dreaming and conscious. I am aware that something speaks to me. The voice speaks of Its kin near

Giranta, whose call is much different, intended for the creatures of dry land. This One, whose supplicants I so gladly and utterly mauled, called to those of the deep. Consumes them. Changes them. Improves them. The voice calls to me. It says its name: Abultha, the Cursed Purpose. I feel its pull more and more.

I asked about the vile thing in Athyl'glen. The voice says the creature is the last of its kind. A thing brought from the worlds before, carried in the realms between with the Inheritors. A bauble that clung to hate and death so strongly it manifested those things in physical form. Some of the Inheritors were so impressed they brought it along to let it play. Their wicked toy ravaged the realm of Athyl'glen, infecting and destroying every man, woman, and child all the way to the southern woods, where its influence became weakened. Perhaps another Inheritor lay claim to that area.

I awoke with my chest aching as though I was holding my breath. My mind cleared of the fog that followed sleep and was quickly replaced by more rage. My cold eyes and clammy skin felt hot once more. I stood on shaking legs, my body still weak from slumber. I had one more battle left in me.

I launched from the rocky terrace of my broken mountain palace. My wings caught the rising drafts and carried me over the dead forest, nothing more than a layer of brown and gray and exposed boughs like the matted fur of a rotting animal stretched over exposed bones.

The cracked stone and marble of the elf-kind capital rose from the rotting corpse of its former kingdom. Some of those black strands I knew to be more than broken stone. I built up more speed and flew higher. Though it would break my body, a plummeting strike would serve best, I thought.

I then saw it: the pulsating mass of that quivering, eye-covered pustule. I snarled but repressed the growing urge to roar so loud as to stir the damned. I dove, tucked my wings against my side, and let nature throw me at the thing. The wind tore against my body, and the sound of my descent howled in my ears.

That sinister bauble still found a way to strike first. The black strands stretched and lashed at me. I held such a speed that they missed, one after another.

I opened my wings at the last possible moment. The force shot pain through my joints and threatened to rip the wings from my body, but I managed to slow my descent enough to crash into the gelatinous mass like a wrathful hammer. It was inelegant and crude, but the attack did *something*. I tore with my claws at the mucous-coated creature. Things churned and groaned inside it as my claws pierced the outer membrane, and all the eyes opened, all looking at me. If they had mouths, they would have been screaming, but I'd heard enough of that in recent days.

Something coiled around my ankles and body. My muscles flexed and pushed against my scales, the black-veined skin exposed in places. I lifted with everything I had. Every draconic strand of muscle, cartilage, might, and will went to my legs and claws. I lifted the thing and saw immediately why it was so heavy. The damnable strands that enrooted themselves around the city and sapped the life and soul of every living thing in Athyl'glen held the thing to the ground. Those slick tendrils ran through the ground beneath the mass like a thousand vines. They pulled against me, but I managed to lift it higher. I saw the tendrils flexing and squirming, a corded mass of nightcrawlers fighting to set the body back down. I bit into them. I filled my mouth with their foulness, and I bit down harder. Some gave way, some slipped between my fangs.

I chewed.

I chewed and gnashed my teeth until I'd swallowed some unspeakable substance pouring from the Inheritor's toy like water. Fighting the urge to vomit, I bit and I bit. The snapping sound of dead, slimy tendril-roots filled my ears. Then, I felt pain. Not all of the sharp cracks belonged to the life-giving strands beneath the creature. Many were from the dozens of tendrils that had been lashing at my body the whole time as I gorged on the bauble's suffering.

Weakness sapped my muscles. I looked down for just a moment and saw my own broken scales on the ground. My body was shredded down to the organs. I mustered enough strength to bite once more, and the force chewed through the last of the strands.

Many of the eyes began to roll back until only veins could be seen. Those that yet functioned continued to glare at me with nothing but hatred in their unnatural shapes. Then, the bauble stopped squirming. Its dead weight caused me to drop it; it landed with the sound of a wet sack. I could barely stand. I fell to my knees and saw the strands that stretched along the walls of the city and trees of the forest begin to pull back and fall away.

I roared, in both glorious victory and indescribable pain, and let the fire flow from my belly once more. My last gout went to the viscous mass on the ground. Nothing burns hotter than dragon fire. Even this spiteful outsider caught flame.

Finally, I fell. My body went numb, and my vision began to close in. It was too late for Athyl'glen. The Inheritor's bauble killed the forest. Mutated its people. However, I brought elf-kind justice, delivered in the manner only the dragons can. Sleep is coming. The eternal hibernation.

So passes the last of Alda's dragons.

PILLAR OF BONES

The order had failed before. It wasn't perfect. Not like the Throne and Its kind—those perfect beings that rightfully spite the imperfect creatures of Alda. What They promised was always delivered. The order had broken promises. The order had lost good people. The order was made of people who are inherently imperfect. Failure, to an extent, is to be expected. There would never be such a thing as a perfect city or perfect governing body, but The Black Gnarl sought to emulate the Inheritor's perfection as much as possible.

Lucien disembarked from the ship that had carried him to the round island in the middle of the Wailing Ocean. Surrounded by the drowned ruins of the old world, the island was the locus of the Fourth Magic, the closest one could hope to touch the true being of the Obscured Throne.

He scowled, his dark, handsome features marred by his utter disappointment. He pulled back his large, black cowl and walked a few steps inland, smelling the soot and ash. The charred remains of buildings sprawled before him. Scored stone with blackened bones of wood jutting at all angles. The buildings had fallen and half their remains reduced to rubble- and corpse-choked streets, the temple on the hill was readily visible. What remained of it, that was.

The roof had also fallen in on itself. The arches were broken, and tapestries burned or fallen to the dirt. The fountains no longer functioned, and Lucien saw their basins filled with gray, filthy water. The sanctum beneath, along with the long tunnels, likely caved in and destroyed.

The wind carried swirls of dust and ash into the air, causing dark plumes that recalled the night the city burned. The once-great Nel Aldyri now lay in ruins. A grand experiment. Ultimately, a failure.

More ships arrived. Their sails dotted the horizon like large, lazy birds. The next one to dock was larger than Lucien's, and the first person to set foot on the dock was another black-robed master like himself. This one was older, but not by more than a decade.

"Cornelius," Lucien said in greeting. "Are the other masters of the Order of the First Son with you?"

A narrow face jutted from beneath the shadows of the cowl like a pale knife. Cornelius smiled as he reached up and revealed a wide, thin-lipped smile. Lucien avoided his eyes, of course. The followers of Bac'thule were notorious for some of their more eccentric powers.

"They follow behind. I was given the glorious honor of bringing the untrained labor for our work."

Cornelius had the voice of a rodent trapped in a warren: guttural and nasal at the same time. He spoke in a constant whispering tone as though each word was a valuable secret.

"Untrained labor. The non-magical kind?" Lucien asked.

"Precisely. They'll begin working in the fallow fields in the hinterlands."

Cornelius came to stand before Lucien, who was taller by a head. The wiry man looked up at Lucien, and he returned the gesture by staring at Cornelius's forehead. The Bac'thule denomination master was likely used to it by now.

"You know the great pitfall of being a member of the order of Bac'thule, the First Son?"

"I couldn't imagine."

"No one looks you in the eyes anymore. Difficult to read someone that way."

"Are you trying to read me?"

Cornelius shrugged at Lucien's feigned aggrievance. "Your face is filled with disgust, that much anyone can see. Are you not happy with your assignment here?"

Lucien glimpsed over the top of Cornelius' head at the incoming ships, some of which didn't appear to have moved at all. They were all coming to further the Black Gnarl's goals. To reclaim this island of ash and bone; new pillars upon which to build their destiny.

People poured from Cornelius' ships, flanked by black-robed taskmasters. These were the untrained laborers he'd mentioned. Without magic, they would use machines and muscle to aid in the construction of the new city. Some were immediately redirected to Lucien's ship, where several years' worth of supplies waited to be unloaded.

The workers were divided into uneven groups led by a single Black Gnarl brother or sister. They'd likely been instructed while on their long ocean journey on what was expected of them. Given promises of a life better than the one they left behind on Alda's mainland. Lucien's lip curled. The masters gathering on this island would help no one. The laborers, the magi, the supplicants, acolytes, and apprentices—they could all build a city in a much more suitable location than a dead island.

"You're the newest member elevated to the rank of master, yes?" Cornelius asked, his voice cutting into Lucien's thoughts.

Lucien sighed before answering. "Yes. Just before embarking on my journey to take part in this wondrous undertaking."

A wry chuckle came from Cornelius. "Careful. You risk blasphemy. Your equals among our ranks are unanimous in this endeavor."

"I had no choice in the matter; my ascension came after the decision was already made."

"Then you are in for quite a learning experience," Cornelius said as he placed his hands before himself, both of them disappearing within his sleeves. He began walking forward in a manner that suggested Lucien follow.

They strolled through the broken, burnt, and gray-tone streets of Nel Aldyri, their direction consistently westward. A few times, they were forced to find a detour as fallen rubble blocked their path completely.

"It will take weeks just to clear the streets," Lucien commented.

"Days, perhaps, between the untrained labor and the magi."

"Years, then, for the completion of the city."

"Months," Cornelius retorted.

"Months?"

"The masters and the other powerful members of the Black Gnarl are all gathered in one place. The power of the Fourth Sect is growing year after year, and it all coalesces here. You didn't feel it as we drew near the island? The moment you set foot off the ship?"

Lucien's eyes dropped to the ground. He did feel a powerful knot of Fourth Magic focused on the ship. It did feel more potent on the island, but he assumed it was due to the presence of a significant temple, which was exacerbated by the deaths of several commanding members of the order.

"The powerful Fourth Magic resonance here isn't because the Black Gnarl came here once before," Cornelius explained, his tone like that of a patient teacher, "The Black Gnarl came here because of the power that was already present."

Cornelius' pace slowed as they reached an incline. Lucien looked up to see where it took them. He'd been so lost in thought that he hadn't noticed the blackened tendrils stretching into the sky above the hillcrest before them.

No ... he thought in disbelief.

At the crest of the hill was a cliff, dropping sharply to the fields that sprawled out before them. Dust and ash swirled in small whirlwinds created by the stiff ocean wind across the remains of the once-bountiful hinterlands. Farms pockmarked the land like blackened hearths, and the fields were a patchwork of death and ruin.

"As the master of the Order of Erysikthion, I imagine this would look unremarkable to you."

Cornelius smirked as he looked at Lucien from the corner of his eyes, whose own gaze was transfixed on the sight beyond the fallow, gray fields. A tree, larger than any he'd ever seen, loomed over the landscape. Its shadow crawled over the land before it like a wrathful, angry claw. Chunks of bark the size of house walls gathered around its trunk like shed scales. Black ash flew from its surface provoking the image of a thousand swarms of starving locusts.

His companion and elder was right: as the newly appointed master of the Order of Erysikthion, the Black Hunger, seeing such decay should have been nothing to Lucien. Unlike Felkirk, however, there was more to this site than mere consumption. There was a hate here that set his hands to shaking. A dread and sorrow that closed his throat. The two of them stood there, minute specks against the dead majesty of a vessel writhing with the essence of cosmic malice. Even the faintest residual presence of Bac'thule, one of the greatest of the Inheritors, was enough to induce a potent, terror-induced catatonia.

Lucien's frozen muscles reacted reflexively to a tickle on his hand. A flake of ash landed on the exposed flesh, and he wiped it off without even looking, creating a pale gray smudge against his dark brown skin. His eyes never left the charred bones of the world's last aldyr, bloated to grotesque proportions and burned by a paradoxical, unwholesome combination of Fourth and Fifth Magics. It still radiated an energy that promised lands far beyond the stars, far beyond reality, far beyond time. A land of things formless and sculpted, hateful and rapturous. A power he could not fathom. Cornelius spoke, but his voice was hazy, lost beyond a veil of barely contained insanity.

"Lucien, have you ever seen the corpse of a god?"

DAWN BROKE on the island of Nel Aldyri. Clouds hung heavy in the skies, and a chill morning breeze blew over stone streets, fallow stretches of field, and city ruins. The sounds of magic, incantations, and grunts of manual labor sounded like a morose overture to another day promising dreary construction and little else. Ash continued to fall, coating everything. The burned aldyr continued to shed, refusing to let go of the agonizing memory of fire.

The island was in as foul a mood as Lucien himself. His sleep since arriving had been unrestful at best, fitful and nonexistent at worst. Strange dreams assailed him. As a master of the Black Gnarl, he knew of their origins. Bac'thule claimed a hold on this island through the aldyr to break one of the evasive Fifth Magic seals while also becoming the window to which the Obscured Throne could ultimately arrive. He was forced from His vessel, His temporary prison on this level of reality, and His suffering and anger still lingered.

The followers of the First Son, as His members in the Black Gnarl were called, lamented this failure on the part of former masters Gideon and Helen. Everyone caught in the island's temperament was affected by the haunting wails of the banished god, a "dead god," as Cornelius said. But death is different for the Inheritors. It's a trivial term, the closest thing mortals could explain to the current state of the Inheritor's existence as they wait outside of reality to return and prepare Alda for the Throne's homecoming.

Cornelius and his ilk were too esoteric for Lucien's liking. Not as strange as some, but strange enough. Lucien and his supporters followed One known as The Cowled Feast. The Black Hunger. Erysikthion. Their lord, the Inheritor who inspired their worship, claimed the city of Felkirk as his temple. Such a sacred location was forbidden from travel. Lucien and a small entourage made an annual pilgrimage, but even then, being in proximity to their Lord Inheritor's chosen city proved too much for their mental fortitude. It was also known among them that coming too close to Erysikthion's mighty presence risked being consumed by it.

These things were known. As the flesh decays as the result of death, as the mountains erode and the flowers wilt, the Cowled Feast consumes all. Its power is witnessed every day. The followers of Bac'thule proclaim His superiority because He is the grand herald, the window and vessel. They spout platitudes and grand mysteries, but their god is no better than Lucien's. The moniker of the "First Son" was, to Lucien, an abomination. The Inheritors were not bound by something so profanely tangible as gender. He refused to even consider the disgusting practices of the followers of the Many-Faced Worm. Ultimately, all of the Inheritors bowed to the Obscured Throne. However, such was the Throne's incomprehensible greatness that only one who could survive all the trials and receive all the gifts of the Inheritors was fit to worship the Throne in all mortals' place. That was the role of the Crown of the Night.

Janesca.

She was currently indisposed to some task that only she was privy to.

Lucien's lord's work was certainly present here. The very vessel-prison of Bac'thule, the bloated tree, was subject to the Cowled Feast's consumption at this moment. The smell of the hinterlands, where half-burned animal carcasses yet rotted, filled Lucien's nostrils. He took comfort in his lord's presence.

The meandering path through the burned and ash-covered fields led inevitably to the base of the blackened aldyr. None of the workers had come here yet. The magi continued their work in the city, and the laborers continued to reclaim their immediate surroundings to make the land arable again. Here, only the scorned presence of *He* remained. A door closed. A window slammed shut. A vessel broken.

Lucien suddenly felt cold, like he'd been plunged into icy water. His skin prickled as invisible currents rushed over it.

Are You still there? he wondered momentarily.

"Impossible," he said aloud. The sound of his own voice was comforting. A human sound amid bouts of inhuman sensations.

Lucien turned and left. Massive roots pushed from beneath the ground like hills around him, dead, ash-producing hills that flaked off with every gust of wind. He tried to ignore the whispers surrounding him. He told himself it was that very same wind, coursing through the empty boughs and over the burned roots and keep-sized trunk.

The fallen city looked so far away. Lucien kept walking. Slithering things crept into the shadowed corners of his mind. Sharp pains pricked at his consciousness. Tiny pinpricks flailing weakly in the abyss. He kept walking, forcing each foot to step after the other until the sensations faded. It was a long walk back to the ruins of Nel Aldyri.

THE MASTERS MET THAT EVENING. A stone structure pulled straight from the ground by the most powerful of their Third Sect practitioners, their abilities to manipulate the physical world unmatched, served as their headquarters. A dark, craggy, bleak structure was a suitable location for the masters' dwellings and meetings. The stone was a deep gray, almost black, not from being burned but from the corrupted magic woven into it. Fourth Sect magic was also sown among the Third Magic incantations and runes.

The aura of that distant place, where their gods' true forms dwelt at the foot of the Throne, was felt immediately. The followers of the Black Gnarl relished it; the fear and revulsion were something they cherished. The newer, nameless initiates trembled with terror but knew this was a sliver of the Inheritor's presence among them. Those pitiful beings brought in for manual labor, however, knew little of what this unexplainable presence was. They cowered in their dormitories, many overcome and clawing at their faces as they cried out or curled into corners saturated in newly wetted clothing.

In that fiendish structure, a circular table of dark brown oak, carved with the barbed diamond on the top, sat in a round room lit by flickering torches and dozens of candles. The light deferred to the darkness, leaving even this low-roofed location crowned in a darkness that made the ceiling disappear and looked prepared to suck all present into its vacuous abyss.

The masters ringed the table like black-robed statues, wraiths preparing for some unholy rite. One of the faceless individuals placed a pale hand around a skull before them. The grisly item was embellished with sigils and items representing each of the known Inheritors whose master was present, for there were many of Their kind, and only some were openly worshipped. Cracked sapphires in the eyes represented Bac'thule. A crown of vines stained red with blood for Ygiddra. A crow's skeleton was carved in the back for the Cowled Feast. Four small rubies placed between the sapphire-filled sockets like a spider's eyes recalled the sight of the slavering children of the Mother of Screams. The inside of the skull was scorched black for the Baleful Forge. Screaming faces were tattooed between all these symbols, the most dominant of the Inheritors, and more. The skull itself was elf-kind, representing the death of the aldyrs and their caretakers. In the forehead, binding them all together, was the barbed diamond. Carved deep, the central dot was driven straight through to the scorched hollow within.

The pale hand clacked the skull against the table like a gavel, bringing their dark meeting to order. Each master pulled back their cowls. Each of them knew or had at least heard of one another.

"This will be brief," Cornelius stated. Since the island of Nel Aldyri was once in the control of the followers of the First Son, they retained a small level of seniority and superiority at these gatherings.

"Construction of the city has been slower than expected. We need options to expedite the process."

"Can we send a message for more Third Sect practitioners and manual laborers? That seems the most logical and obvious," one of the other masters suggested.

"It's already been done," another master replied. "The last of the migrants fleeing the mainland are already en route, but it will take months for them to get here."

"Perhaps more strategic use of our current magics?" Lucien offered up his own response. His voice was low and flat.

Cornelius smiled. His forefinger stroked the barbed diamond symbol on the front of the skull. "The master of the Cowled Feast's followers speaks. Ironic that the vicar of That

Which Consumes speaks of building up, not tearing down. What do you suggest?"

Lucien was quiet, his thoughts languid but with something stirring beneath. Something with tendril-branches and deep, whispered commands. "The aldyr. Or rather, what remains of it."

Cornelius' smile turned sour. "What do you mean? Why do you speak of something within the confines of my authority?"

"Then you're already aware the power remaining there," Lucien countered, unaffected by Cornelius' gaze that all refused to meet. "Your own god once dwelt within that ashen cage. Its power could still be harnessed."

"He may have a point," yet another master said in his defense. Her hair was cut short and dyed black, and four tattoos of gleaming red eyes on her brow and forehead gave away her status as the mistress of the Mother of Screams.

Cornelius' hand tightened around the skull. "Yes," he replied, as though agreeing with Lucien was painful and embarrassing. "As the authority on matters regarding the great Bac'thule, I will consider what options could be available among my vicars. We will depart at the conclusion of this council for the aldyr and confer on the possibilities. Another gathering shall be called after the representatives of Bac'thule have had time to discuss. In the meantime, longer shifts for the workers. Same for the apprentices and initiates. All are to be tapping every ounce of strength and power they have. Stringent punishment for those who fall behind. These matters are concluded." He clacked the skull again and other members brought up a handful of other topics. All mundane. All trivial and boring. A final clack of the skull and a shuffling sound filled the room.

Religious bureaucracy. The denominations were divided so that they could focus on their Inheritor's desires and purpose in the world. None could decide for that order what measures could be taken in their Inheritor's name. The last aldyr was a relic of Bac'thule. Cornelius and his fellows would have the last say and reserved the right to discuss it before bringing possible solutions to the masters' table. Lucien being involved in that process was incredibly unlikely, at best. At least they took his suggestion. Lucien saw Cornelius and his cronies making for the hinterlands that led to the aldyr immediately after the council had adjourned, just as the old man said they would.

STRANGE DREAMS VISITED LUCIEN AGAIN. He saw a city stretching up into the sky. Spires pointed up along the silhouette, climbing higher and higher. A glistening ocean surrounded it. Behind the city, the only source of illumination; an eclipse ringed by fiendish light. A low drone thrummed in Lucien's head. Fear set his heart to palpitating, his skin prickling. Within that horrible drone, sounds began to come together. A voice spoke to him, telling him of the city, the Inheritors, the Throne.

Was it the First Son, Bacthule? Or was it his own god, Erysikthion? Was it both? Was it *all* of them, all the Inheritor gods? He couldn't tell. He only knew that the voice was older than the stars that hid from the eclipse. The voice was the eclipse, or what lay behind the eclipse. Was there something behind the eclipse? An epiphany lay at his fingertips. He felt it. A blossoming spark of damnation that no other living being dared to know. It, too, came with the voice.

It spoke to him the way a master would speak to a dog. No. The way a nobleman would command a cur to move out of his way. It didn't ask or command. It spoke, and it would be obeyed. Lucien was too happy to oblige. Despite knowing he was asleep, he still felt himself falling to his knees. A million eyes and none watched him from all angles. The deep black of nothing thrummed around him. Living. Breathing. Dying then shuddering back to life over and over again, each breath the first and last. He felt himself vomiting, but as he looked around, there was nothing there. Nothing at all, not even himself.

His eyes hurt. He clutched at them, scratched at his brows and cheeks. He dug the heels of his palms into his eyes, and they only hurt worse. He dug his fingertips into the gelatinous orbs that aggrieved him, agonized him. Warm liquid ran down his face. The voice commanded him to see. Listen and do. Lucien screamed, but the sound was soaked up by the living non-existence around him.

He screamed more, and an image of a fiendish woman, teeth like knives and multiple breasts along her lithe frame like a mother to suckling beasts, threw its head back in ecstasy. He felt blood rush to his groin. It hurt and sent an ache through his legs. His silent scream reverberated like a song, tearing his throat into shreds. The presence of some long, writhing *thing* wrapped around him. Mouths of all sizes bit and kissed him over his entire body. Where their mouths made contact, he began to rot. Exposed flesh burned like nothing he'd known, soon to go numb and cold as bone was exposed. A dozen other sensations overcame him, unspeakable and unthinkable in nature. Where his flesh fell, a carpet of flesh-like grass grew. Ebon rock, reflecting a ghastly light of unknown origin, pushed through the ground like fingers through sinew. He saw all this despite a lack of eyes, both from his own perspective and somehow through that of the dream. An out-of-body, sixth sensation. The stones grew white hot. Even without a nose, he smelled his own bones begin to sear. It was a nauseating, unfamiliar odor. He felt like his body began to melt. Something was falling from him, a liquid or bodily fluid or something else entirely. The writhing worm-creature with the many mouths drank it as it fell and lapped it up from where it pooled on the ground. Those pools that remained untouched fed the flesh-grass below him. Vines the color of internal organs grew and wrapped around the burning, exposed bones—sizzling as they made contact. The stench was unbearable. The vines coiled around him and shot down his throat, which still hurt with phantom pain.

He could no longer scream. He could no longer move. He shuddered reflexively as his body was twisted and contorted by the tendrils of viscera. He felt every sensation once more, only now in reverse. The burning of exposed flesh, the kissing and biting of numerous mouths, the screaming song that rent his throat, the unbearable sensation in his eyes. He wanted to die. He wanted it all to end so badly that he could not express it in words; only in the yearning did he feel so deeply in his soul. The horrible image of his regrown body suppressed all hope he had. It was not over for him now, nor would it be any time soon.

Lucien woke in a quiet room, the sound of the nearby ocean softly echoing through his window. The chill air startled him and made him think his flesh was still peeled and exposed. He tasted bile in his mouth. His ears rang from the sudden cessation of the screaming, moaning, teeth-gnashing, and copious other sounds that filled his dream. The startling difference uneased him.

He threw off his blankets, suddenly feeling claustrophobic. His room was dimly lit by moonlight shining through the window. His nose curled. It took a moment, but eventually, he realized with extreme embarrassment, mingled with anger, that he'd pissed himself. He set his foot down on the stone floor and cursed harshly but quietly. He recalled in his dream, he felt himself vomit but couldn't see it. He still couldn't see it, but now he knew he did indeed vomit all over his floor.

Lucien used his soiled bedsheets to wipe off his foot. He threw it to the ground for the servants to clean. He tossed a silk robe around himself and made straight for the baths recently built in the masters' hall. Simple magic heated the water, and soap mixed with herbs and spices would help remove the smell. He cursed and grumbled the whole time. He was awake now, so after his bath, he had little to do but walk to one of the upper-floor balconies and stare at the dead, bloated tree in the distance, the stars themselves quivering at its silhouetted frame.

He stayed there until the sun rose. The light made little difference, with the presence of heavy clouds promising rain. They had moved in sometime in the night while Lucien watched the stars disappear above them. It was an ominous feeling, seeing the weak light of the distant celestial bodies wink out around the aldyr. The corpse prison of an unliving deity. His mind mulled over the voice that spoke to him. His body reeled from the memory of what he endured in dreams. He looked at his hands. It felt real. He opened his robes and looked at his body. Nothing had changed. The weak sunlight glinted off his dark skin and revealed nothing, but he knew what he felt. How he felt now. He felt like a prisoner, though empowered above other prisoners and charged with their duties.

The city below slowly came to life. Workers left their dormitories, and black-robed brothers and sisters gathered their charges. Lucien returned to his room and found his sheets removed, and a servant cleaned the floor. Neither of them exchanged words. They wouldn't have, regardless of the situation, but there was a special tension there now. The master's embarrassment and anger reverberated off the servant's fear-fueled assumptions. They wouldn't dare ask, however.

A wash basin and towel sat on Lucien's dresser next to his mirror. He went over and washed his face, splashing the cool water over his skin and taking a deep breath. When he looked in the mirror, his breath stopped. Caught in his throat.

His eyes had always been a natural yellow, the color of chartreuse tourmaline, and a point of pride in his sharp-featured handsomeness. Those same eyes he had tried to rip from his skull the previous night in his dream. Now, the eyes staring back at him were a dull blue. Not the milky white of blindness. That clearly was not the case. This was the blue of a cold sky. A living corpse.

Lucien pushed gently against the soft flesh below his eyes. Stretched the skin and turned his head. Nothing felt out of the ordinary. He closed then rubbed his eyes, pushing with his palms and massaging them. Still, nothing unusual.

He hastily left the room. Robes fluttering, his long, hurried steps carried him to the sacred chamber where the masters held a council. The most treasured of their vile texts lined up in alcoves in the walls. Lucien picked a book from among those present specifically for its contents on the rites and rituals of the various Black Gnarl sects. Particularly those involving initiations.

The rest of his day fell away as he devoured page after page. First, there was the initial book on rites and rituals, and then there was another book on a separate subject, and then there was another and another. A bell, recently added to a watchtower by the docks, tolled the evening hour. The sun would be beneath the horizon soon.

The candles of his room greeted him when Lucien opened the door back to his chambers. A cold dinner sat on his desk. He rang the bell outside his room, summoning a servant, who took the cold meal and returned with a fresh one. He hadn't eaten all day. He devoured the plate's contents and drank half a bottle of wine. Strangely, he didn't feel any effects from the alcohol.

He grabbed the bottle, gripping it angrily. The bottom faced the ceiling, and Lucien gulped down the wine as fast as it flowed. Or, rather, not quite as fast. The dark liquid spilled out the sides of his mouth and spattered on the floor. When nothing was left, he hurled the bottle at the opposite wall, hearing it break against the stones and fall in pieces, large and small, to the floor.

He stood and approached his bed, but before he could sit, his door creaked open. A thin-skinned, gray-haired old man stepped in.

"Allow me, my lord," the old servant said breathlessly. He'd run to Lucien's room the moment he heard the wine bottle shatter.

For the second time today, someone has had to clean my floors, Lucien thought.

He didn't motion for the servant to enter, so the old man stood at the door patiently for several moments until Lucien came to his senses. His mind felt rattled and unfocused. Try as he might, he couldn't collect his thoughts. When he looked up at the old man, he thought he was losing his mind.

It was difficult to describe what he was seeing. Lucien was a learned man. Very learned. But words wholly escaped him in this moment. Lucien saw and felt the servant's frailty around him. His life seeped from him like steam through a pinhole. Subtle darkness slinked across him like wine dregs, slowly tracing the spaces between the floor stones.

Lucien felt his eyes grow wide. What was this phenomenon? It had to be the change in his eyes. He rubbed them again and looked back, still disbelieving, at the servant. The old man wouldn't look him in the eyes. The servant had gone pale, shaking where he stood. He still didn't move without Lucien's order.

"Come in ... and clean. Clean this up," Lucien said, his words faltering. He lacked the stern tone he normally used when he gave commands.

The servant slowly came in, his steps mired in terror. After briefly surveying the mess, he managed to mumble, "I need to retrieve a mop and bucket. And a broom, my lord."

He turned to leave, the fastest he'd moved since arriving.

"Wait," Lucien called out, his voice tinged with desperation that he immediately regretted.

His hand shot out as he began to say something to the servant, but the words fell back on his tongue. The strange sensation, the cloying darkness he felt around the old man, reached out to him like thick, tarry hair standing on end. They shivered and stretched. The old man gasped. Similar strands stretched out from Lucien. His whole body was lined with them. They reached out to the same tingling fibers on the servant.

At his master's command, the servant stopped and turned, his eyes wide in terror. His lip quivered. The warm aura continued to seep from him slowly while the night-black fibers pulled and stretched outward. Lucien gulped, his throat dry. He used his knowledge of magic, the Fourth in particular, to call to those strands. His own fibers elongated, quivering in excitement. They touched somewhere between the two men.

"My lo—," the servant began, but the moment the dark strands met, they became one, and Lucien understood. The warm sensation seeping from the servant was his life essence. It would seep out until the time of his death when it would be extinguished. That essence utterly drained once the dark fibers connected. They simply ceased to be. A powerful, terrible feeling coursed through the Black Gnarl master. Feelings just like those painful, tormenting things from the previous night. All compressed into a moment, a flash of anguish.

Lucien passed out momentarily. When he woke, a gray stain, scattered ashes, splintered bones, and half a skull lay before him. He didn't know who they belonged to. Was someone in his room? Did he just defend himself from an intruder? An assassin? A hole in his memory gnawed at him. But, revelation washed over him like water, cold as the night sky. This was the Throne's essence. The Throne's purpose, if such a thing existed, for a being so magnificent. Time was nothing. Names were nothing. Only this.

Lucien stood, his panic subsiding. Washed away by the epiphany of the void. He straightened his robes and sat on his bed. He wasn't tired. He needed only to wait until dawn.

THE SUN BROKE over the isle, but none were blessed with its presence. Clouds blocked the light and left the chill wind and constant ash as a reminder that this place was not a paradise. Regardless, it was all that anyone would soon have.

Lucien called the other masters together. Some resisted, insisting their duties in rebuilding the city were too pressing, but when the other masters' messengers returned, shaking and wide-eyed with fear, they relented. Some of them out of curiosity, others out of anger.

The council chamber buzzed with the whispers and sighs of the Gnarl's various leaders. Lucien wasn't there, to everyone's chagrin. One of them remained silent, pondering this strange situation. Cornelius merely darted his cracked blue eyes around the room, searching for the missing one who summoned them.

Another shadow joined the many gathered there, slipping in unnoticed. Eventually, the others became aware of an additional presence. Their cowled heads turned to see a tall figure move silently among them, stopping at the edge of the table. Lucien pulled his cowl back. After a few moments, gasps, small and large, came from the gathered masters when they saw the change in his eyes.

Cornelius' forehead crinkled like folded paper. Lucien saw him out of the corner of his eyes. The older master stared at him, daring Lucien to look at those sharp blue eyes. *No,* Lucien thought and hoped it would reach Cornelius. *I am not a chosen of Bac'thule. I am much more, yet still much less.*

Lucien gave in to the bait and turned, looking Cornelius in the eyes. All others not devoted solely to Bac'thule would have turned away in pain. Lucien felt nothing. Truly nothing. Devoid of emotion, sensation, all of it. There was only one purpose now.

Cornelius' face shuddered, his lips quivering in surprise when Lucien simply stared at him without so much as flinching. The pale-eyed master didn't even smile. His eyes, now ghostly blue-gray, saw and felt each of their life essences, slowly seeping away as their mortal lives shortened. The dark fibers woven among them were stronger, though. Eager.

"It's time we stop with our worldly issues. We are building more than a city. This is the dais upon which the Obscured Throne will rest. The corrupted aldyr, the sign of this world's and its founder's defeat, is Its baldachin. The fires of welcoming to guide the great Malice here have been lit by The Crown of Night. We will be here to welcome It. All that remains living in this world will be here. We are Its gift. Our blood is an apology for our great sin. Our souls are forfeit."

A chorus of questions rang out. Lucien stood unflinching. A hand rose from the roiling sea of black fabric, followed by a guttural, nasal voice.

"And just what are you, now? Are you to be crowned along with Janesca? You look me in the eye with those pale ones of your own and feel nothing. Something has changed."

"Nothing has changed," Lucien returned flatly.

The room grew silent. A soft, ruffling whisper moved about the room in waves as many cowled heads turned to look at one another and the two men speaking.

Lucien continued. "Janesca has served her purpose. Her body and essence are powering the light that shines in the infinite cosmos, beyond the fabric of our reality and calls the Throne here. I am not the new Crown of Night. I am not some new grand master of our order. I am only here to serve the Throne, as we all are. And we have lost sight of that."

He put his hand to his chest. "The Master of the Order of Erysikthion."

Then, he gestured at Cornelius. "The Master of the Order of Bac'thule, the First Son."

Lucien went around naming each individual there and the Inheritor that their subordinates worshipped. "All of these titles. Our own order, The Black Gnarl. A lot of words with no meaning. No purpose. The Obscured Throne does not care about who is the master and who is the acolyte. Who is initiated, and who is not. Words. Words mean less than nothing in the face of oblivion. And our Master? It did not create oblivion. It *is* oblivion."

"Then, what would It have us do?"

Lucien turned to the woman who asked the question. The mistress of some order or another looked into his eyes, and he saw her expression give way to obedience. Something in his gaze must have shown her that he spoke truth.

"We cast aside titles, and we serve our purpose."

He turned his head back towards Cornelius. "Follower of the Void and Vessel, are you prepared to serve your purpose?"

Cornelius' brow furrowed. His reply came out firm but with an inflection of dubious curiosity. "Of course."

"Then we go to the aldyr."

All of the masters walked in a grim procession through the city. Acolytes and laborers alike turned and stared, though the laborers less intently. They passed the buildings slowly being refurbished, the gate to the hinterlands in working condition, and into the farmlands themselves. Here, Lucien stopped.

"Vana, gather Ygiddra's most devout. Bring the Sanguine Garden's portions of the Dread Praises here. Carve Ygiddra's praises into your flesh. Spread out among these fallow fields and let your blood enrich the soil. We cannot be here for the Throne if we die of starvation."

"Yes, we will do so immediately," she replied. Her voice sounded much like Cornelius' had. Determined but questioning.

"No. Tonight, after our business at the aldyr."

She nodded her head firmly, and the procession continued.

When they reached the aldyr, it appeared exactly as it had when Lucien and Cornelius last visited. Now, however, Lucien saw something encircling that bloated symbol of Alda's former glory that caused his heart to shudder. It wasn't the same as the fading life essences or trembling, eager strands of darkness. It was different. Potent and terrible.

"Cornelius," Lucien said, his voice practically a whisper. When no reply came, he spoke up.

"Cornelius, go to the aldyr."

"What?" came an incredulous reply.

"The aldyr," he repeated. "Go to it."

Slow footsteps grew louder behind Lucien until he saw Cornelius standing beside him. "This is ... unusual," Cornelius said in a low voice.

"Please do as instructed," Lucien replied, his neck craned to look up at the flaking boughs.

"What sort of asinine reason have you brought us all the way out here for, Lucien? This was a failed experiment by a man long dead." Cornelius' voice raised as he approached the immense trunk. He placed his hand on the burned bark and felt it. Lucien saw his hand suddenly recoil.

"Unusually cold. Just as I expected," Cornelius said. "Nothing has changed. You were right about that."

"I said our purpose hasn't changed. We only needed to find the right vector."

Lucien saw the countless night-black fibers, coursing like cilia, flow in grotesque waves toward Cornelius. The old master grabbed at his shoulder, where some of the fibers touched him. None could see this but Lucien.

"What's happening?" Cornelius asked, a touch of fear in his voice.

"Our purposes will be fulfilled. We are the pillars for this new seat of the Throne's arrival."

The fibers extended, stretched like strands of dark saliva until they engulfed Cornelius. He cried out in pain, then screamed when his eyes glowed with a cold blue light. A flash preceded a milky blue substance coursing down the wrinkled cheeks of the anguished master. The strands pulled and ripped at him, causing his body to collapse against the trunk of the tree, leaving only a gray stain and bits of splintered bone embedded in the trunk.

A collective sigh came from behind Lucien. He turned to see the masters staring silently. Some had faces hardened with resolve. Others tinged with fear. Some simply hid beneath the shadows of their cowls.

"We serve the Throne. The Inheritors are fractions of the Throne's power made clear to us. As the vines bear fruit and then decay for the worms to feast on, so does everything come back to the Throne. It is in us. It is in the world. We shall return from whence we came. This city will stand as the last testament to Alda's acquiescence to the Throne's will. We will nourish this symbol of penance," he said, motioning behind him at the tree, "until the very moment the Obscured Throne arrives to reclaim what It is owed. Where Nel Aldyri failed, Godscorn will succeed."

In the days that followed, numerous ships arrived in the rebuilt ports of the dark city of Godscorn. None believed ships could travel so quickly, and even the masters of the Black Gnarl wondered at what magic was afoot. It was Lucien who reminded them that the Throne was beyond time. The Throne created it, so the Throne controlled it. Every sacrifice at the morbid aldyr made the machinations of the Black Gnarl more potent. The Vessel provided power as it was filled and emptied.

The city grew, soon requiring buildings to be built upon one another, rising higher into the sky like long-dead bones reaching up for salvation but knowing none would come. What *would* come was the living malevolence that had shown Lucien the most terrible truths of existence. His mind shivered at the revelations, obscuring them for his own sanity. He worked toward that ultimate purpose, not fully knowing what it was or sometimes what he was doing, but it was better that way. It was work that had to be done, and he went about it in blissful, confident ignorance.

RECURRING NIGHTMARES

Pyotr couldn't remember the last time he cried. Even when he visited his family's graves, he kept the tears at bay. Every time the herald visited Kalthav and took another friend away, he covered his face with a somber veneer. This world preyed on those who cried. It was harsh and cruel. He tried to smile through it all. Bring a modicum of light into the darkness. Now, Alda beat that very last bit out of him.

Tears came slowly, falling into his beard and disappearing. He'd cried many times in the last few days. Years of bottled emotion were broken open by the force that leveled Kalthav. He looked back once more to see the strange pillar of black light that rose into the sky until it disappeared from sight. He saw the glowing sea that flickered to life as countless spirits gathered near the edge of the cliffs. They filled the streets of the city and lit them like ghostly veins. The windows of the long-abandoned keep on Storm's Pillar glowed from within with the same eerie light.

Annica was involved, he knew, but what actually happened just two days before was still beyond him. His home was gone. Everything he knew reduced to rubble on the streets and sitting at the bottom of the ocean. He and Hilna, his pack mule and last remaining acquaintance, were barely half a day's walk from the city when a tremor shook the land. He imagined one of the pillars collapsing into the frigid waters. Did the spirits fall with it, he wondered, or could they stand in mid-air on the streets where they once lived?

No, those thoughts would only feed into his depression. The last two nights were riddled with nightmares, visions of fallen buildings, and screaming, dying people. Pyotr wanted to leave it all behind. Again. He considered returning to his home village. He would live out his days next to the graves of his family, farming his own food and caring for Hilna. His last days were destined to be lonely ones.

He rubbed the snout of the docile animal, smiling at her bright, lazy eyes. She was his last friend in the world. Pyotr took a canteen from the packs, sipping from it as they walked slowly down the road. He'd have to make a choice soon.

The sun made its way down to the western horizon. Pyotr and Hilna stood at a critical point. He could head south, towards his old village. He could go west, towards Carnelia. Finally, he could go east to the Wilted Groves; his beard quivered at that thought. The weight of the decision made him even more tired. Heading west took him past the brigands. Pyotr had seen what they were capable of, and he was now alone. He'd picked up a weapon from a fallen guard on his escape from Kalthav but had no idea how to use it. Going south would be too close, as well. The old village was abandoned for a reason. That left only the Wilted Groves, long forbidden from travel and a nesting ground for fearsome myths. Considering the dreadful choices brought about a dark feeling to accompany the setting sun.

Hilna brayed and huffed, then laid down on the thin grass beside the road. Pyotr wiped the sweat from his brow and nodded.

"I agree, girl. Let's think on it for a night."

Pyotr unloaded Hilna, freeing her from her burden, and hitched her to a tree with a bag of the blue-gray wheat for dinner. He then found a safe place to make camp. A fire helped keep the cold at bay, but he feared the attention it could draw. He stacked as many stones around it as he could find to hide its light.

The night was quiet. The chirp of a brave cricket accompanied the only other sound: that of the weak, crackling fire. The occasional breath of cold wind rustled the trees and grass. Even Hilna was too afraid to make a sound. Pyotr's tent sat just behind him, but he feared to enter it. The closed-in space of the musty-smelling canvas wasn't as inviting as the fresh air and warmth of the flame.

He was also too afraid to sleep. Though his eyelids felt heavy and his head trapped in a fatigue-induced fog, his heart ached with fear. His blood streaked with adrenaline at every chirp of the cricket, every time the wind picked up. Every rock that settled or moved in his small light-trap.

After some unknown amount of time, when the minutes leaked away into oblivion, Pyotr fell asleep. He awoke with a start, his leg kicking at some forgotten thing lost to the fugue of half-sleep. The blanket he'd wrapped around himself began slipping, and his shoulder was cold. The fire was dwindling. He reached down, feeling his back ache from sleeping cross-legged on the ground, and grabbed a handful of large sticks to revive the fire and bring back the warmth.

Pyotr's head lolled to the side. His eyes forced themselves closed. When he opened them, he consistently found himself looking to the sky. There were no clouds. It was a clear, cold evening—like the waters of the Cold Stones itself. Why, then, were there so few stars? Usually, the great beyond was practically alive with twinkling lights and the vibrant, colorful haze of whatever waited outside Alda. But, now, it was unusually dark, with fewer stars shining in a deeper darkness. He fell back asleep, the blanket slipping once again, and he thought he saw, in that darkness, something more.

Morning came, and the chill felt even harsher. Frost rimed the grass. Low fog settled along the rocky outcroppings and trees. Pyotr felt the cold before he opened his eyes. When he did, the first thing he saw were black coals of burned-out firewood, faint orange embers the only sign of any warmth around.

"Gods, it's cold ..." he mumbled, rubbing his stiff arms with aching fingers.

The promise of hot tea helped his legs move. They creaked like old doors and popped like snapped twigs. Reviving the fire was easy enough. He put a pot on with water and tossed in some leaves and spices from his reserve. When the water was steaming, he poured it into his canteen, replacing the water. No room for luxuries like cups when you're fleeing for your life.

The tea warmed him, and he felt invigorated. The thought of leaving the campsite and finally deciding his and Hilna's destination quickly brought him back down. The question returned immediately.

South. East. West.

Marauders. Potential marauders. Or the unknown.

Pyotr'd heard the saying, "better the devil you know." He realized at that moment that whoever came up with that expression had never truly faced a devil of any sort. He turned and faced east, toward the Wilted Groves. His last experience was not pleasant. But it could have all been in his head. The beasts that inhabited the countryside to the west, those that tortured, raped, and murdered his family, over half the village, they were very real.

He cleared his throat and gathered his courage. Then, he fed

Hilna, loaded her up with packs and satchels, and prodded the stubborn beast into motion.

"East it is."

The familiarity of the route to the Wilted Groves quickly returned to Pyotr. It had been quite some time, but he had a mind for landmarks, no matter how mundane. An outcropping that looked like Hilna's snout. An overgrown trail with a particular strand of yellow wildflowers along the middle of a batch of white ones that looked like a runny egg. These told him he was on the right path.

Just as he predicted, the line of trees designating the boundary of the Wilted Groves appeared over the top of a particular set of hillocks. These mounds of earth and brown grass stood like sentinels before the infamous forest. A reminder of the stories that circulated among the inns, taverns, and travelers. Pyotr stopped for a moment after passing one of the cautionary knolls. The forest looked like any other, mostly; the line of trees ran thick along the boundary, like a riverbank. Within, sunlight was lost to the heavy canopy. He remembered. It was like stepping into another world.

This time, Pyotr decided against walking directly in at any random spot. He led Hilna along the edge of the forest, looking for a road or path that would perhaps lead somewhere. They walked for hours. No strange occurrences thus far. His heart jumped when they finally found it: a long-abandoned road leading into the Groves. Despite being choked by weeds and grass, the original shape of the road remained. It was small, not a main route. Perhaps it stemmed from another road further west or south, but this would work for Pyotr. He hoped to follow it through to the other side in search of other settlements. Any he found in the woods themselves would serve only for an overnight stay, at most.

Pyotr took a deep breath and gripped Hilna's reins so tight

he heard the leather screech. He gave a firm but gentle pull, but the beast refused to move. He stopped in his tracks, tugging on Hilna's reins. Even after working up the courage himself, the mule would prove to be his biggest hindrance.

"Let's go, girl!" he grumbled. Switching to both hands made no difference.

Hilna brayed in defiance and shook her head. Pyotr tried rubbing her muzzle and calming her before trying again. Still, the tenacious mule refused to move. She stamped and brayed, this time showing Pyotr her fear. He didn't know how long he tried to push, pull, coerce, and yell at Hilna to no avail.

"You ... big ... ass!"

Finally, he pulled out a piece of fruit and held it in front of her. She stopped fighting him and blinked her eyes. Her nostrils twitched, and her neck stretched toward him.

"Oh," Pyotr huffed, out of breath. "This got your attention?"

Hilna happily followed Pyotr at that point. Rather, she happily followed the fruit in his hand, never looking up from it. He used this opportunity to make his way directly into the Wilted Groves. Once past the threshold, that sinister feeling of stepping into another world seeped into Pyotr. He looked around carefully as the trees slowly passed him by. The grass, flowers, and weeds crunched under his feet on the road's old stones. His eyes were wide, and his mouth agape. Pyotr felt like he'd made his way into some dark fairy tale.

Something else gnawed at him, too. He couldn't quite place it, but some strange feeling made the atmosphere all the worse. Silence. That was it. It was completely silent within the Wilted Groves. No insects. No birds. Nothing made any noise at all. A wet smacking sound brought Pyotr back to his senses. He'd stopped moving, and Hilna had snatched the fruit from his hand. He was so caught up in the sense of foreboding that overcame him he simply wiped his hand on his clothes and continued to look around with a fear-widened gaze.

The canopy of thick trees allowed little light to penetrate. The pockets of sky he found looked different from this viewpoint. It was just after noon, yet the sky looked darker. Disquiet prickled his skin, giving him goose-flesh. He had the sudden feeling of a hare spotted by a wolf, a fly caught in a web. Instincts belonging to those in the presence of something higher in the food chain rang a bell in his subconscious.

"This was a bad idea."

Hilna finished the fruit and almost immediately began stamping in protest as though she had just noticed where they were. She began frantically braying and pulling against the reins in Pyotr's hands.

"Ok ... ok, we're leaving!" Pyotr said in an urgent whisper. The mule's complaints resounded like cracks of thunder in the silent forest.

His words came too late for Hilna, whose cries came incessantly as she tossed her head even more ferociously. Pyotr squeezed the reins and dug his feet in, but she pulled him toward the light that seemed so distant. His knuckles popped, and he grunted in pain. Finally, he simply let go.

Hilna reared on her hind legs and wheeled around, making a full gallop for the treeline. Pyotr rubbed his hands and gritted his teeth against his throbbing fingers. He took off in a stumbling gait. The mule quickly outpaced him, naturally, and both of them made a quick break from the blinding light breaking through the trees far in front of them.

A shape, shadowed and moving at frightening speed, shot through in a straight line among the trees like a black bolt. The beastly shape jumped, launching itself dozens of feet, and hurled itself against Hilna in a predatory strike. A wicked growl, familiar yet otherworldly, preceded the sound of Hilna's ghastly, pained braying. Her cries were brief, cut short by the sound of tearing flesh and breaking bones.

Pyotr's heart broke. His last remaining friend in this world was being torn apart before his eyes. He screamed for Hilna, knowing there was nothing he could do. The brightness of the daylight silhouetted the horrific scene in front of him. It looked like a wolf but was far too big; it was as large as a horse, at least. The terrible thing bit and gnawed, its immense muzzle disappearing into Hilna's unmoving body. Tendons and entrails stretched and snapped, blood flew, and all in flat black against the light of hope now cut off to them. Multiple eyes reflected that light, a murderous red, and Pyotr counted at least four. This creature was something corrupted.

Pyotr screamed again. The forest reacted. It reacted to his terror, to the hoarse cry that escaped him. The air seemed to tremble. He fell back, straight onto his buttocks, and kicked and screamed even more. The sight of the beast overwhelmed him. For a moment, he lost who he was. When he regained enough composure to stand, his body refused to do anything more than turn and flee. The sickening crunch and smacking of a feasting predator faded, but his legs continued to move. Painfully, they hurled his body further into the forest. His lungs ached, catching fire with each breath. He followed the road that became less recognizable the deeper he went in.

His foot caught on a raised stone or an exposed root. He was moving too fast to tell. His body left the ground and propelled forward. He landed with an outstretched hand and then onto his chest. Pain shot through his arm, and he screamed again, this one different than the sound of fear. This was the bellow of agony, made worse when he rolled over and saw his hand twisted at an odd angle.

The forest shuddered again, his vision rippling like the surface of a pond disturbed by a small stone. He'd felt this sensation once before. A drunkard at a tavern in Kalthav was known for his insatiable spitefulness once the drink took hold. Hearing his vile comments while in the same room affected everyone around him. It only lasted so long before he was tossed out on the street. That same sense of sadistic glee once more oozed into Pyotr's pores and settled against his nerves, prickling his skin. This sensation, however, was exponentially worse. It promised more and worse to come.

It's been so loooong ... a hideous voice cooed.

It was feminine. Husky. Sensual and sinister combined. It felt like it whispered right into his ear, causing Pyotr to reflexively flinch and wave away at the sound next to his head. But it also echoed in the woods around him.

A hundred stories, myths, and legends came to his mind all at once. Each of them from books, travelers, and drinkers' tales. Pyotr looked back, wanting to run for the outside world once more, but flashes of blood, glittering eyes, and a fiendish silhouette pushed away the tales and caused his heart to pound again. He scrambled to his feet, digging his heels and good hand into the dirt atop the old stones. His body powered itself; his mouth made fearful grunts and crying gasps, his eyes watered, his nose ran. He ran until he couldn't run anymore. Then, he walked. He simply couldn't stop.

Pyotr eventually passed out. When he regained consciousness, the light above the trees was dim. He couldn't tell if it was morning or evening. His muscles were sore, his broken hand throbbed in pain, and his stomach growled painfully. All his food was packed away in the bags on Hilna.

Hilna. His last friend in this world. Dead and devoured by some animal-demon. He cried even more, the sobbing sending shooting pains through his aching chest. He began to cough, and it hurt worse.

Water and food were his priority now, and in that order. He

wondered if the road eventually led to a bridge or even a town. He decided that was his best option. Despite sore muscles that screamed with every step and one functioning hand, he trudged on. The light through the canopy grew darker, and his stomach groaned louder. His lip split due to being dry. Following the road wasn't helping.

Pyotr left the path, wandering into the woods in a straight line to the south. If he didn't find water, he could turn back. However, without water, he may not have needed to travel back. He'd be a corpse lost in the woods, food for that 'thing.'

The sound of burbling water kissed his ear. It was faint, but he knew it wasn't a hallucination. He smiled and began trotting in the direction of the noise. He laughed in spite of his raw, aching throat at the sight of the small creek. It was clear water running amongst rounded stones, gathering in small, shallow eddies where thick tree roots and large rocks blocked its path.

He approached the creek and dropped to his knees. He scooped water into his mouth with his good hand, slurping mouthfuls at a time. It had no flavor—neither good nor bad. It was simply liquid that hydrated his throat and filled his stomach. It was also tepid, strange for the time of year. It should have been cold as the melted snow it likely came from. He didn't care, really. He finally drank his fill and could now focus on food. He'd foraged enough to know what was safe and what wasn't, though this forest was different. This was the Wilted Groves; who knew what grew here.

Finding wild fruit, mushrooms, and other meager provisions was easy enough. What was strange was the taste. Everything tasted bland and stale. Not that there was much to expect from mushrooms, berries, and wild herbs.

A rustling noise startled Pyotr. The shock made his muscles tense painfully and his legs gave out. He fell to the ground. His heart pounded, thinking the beast had returned. Then, he spotted a small shape moving hesitantly through the bushes. A large rodent with short, oil-sheened fur waddled a few more steps, creating the same rustling noise.

Pyotr's chest stopped hammering, the quiet woods becoming calm once more. He wondered if he could catch it and get a scant meal out of the creature, but he had no tools or weapon; it also looked very unappetizing despite his hunger.

He sat for a while by the creek, thinking about his options. He'd traveled so far into the forest along the road that turning back seemed impossible. Foraging would only take him so far. The hope of running into a town, village, or hamlet—abandoned or otherwise—was his best option. Pyotr didn't know how much time he'd lost to his thoughts.

Something felt wrong in his gut. Not a sense of dread. It was something physical. First, a slight rumble. Then, a shooting pain. He grunted, the discomfort taking him by surprise. It came on suddenly, and soon, his stomach was rolling like there was a wild animal in its death throes in his intestines.

He ran for the nearby bushes, barely getting his pants down in time. His whole body trembled as though he were freezing. Voiding his bowels was painful, his whole body spasming. When he was finished, he didn't even have the strength to take care of himself. He fell over in a fetal heap on the ground. His stomach continued to roll. Waves of stabbing pain rolled over his gut and into his back. He wanted to vomit, but his body wouldn't cooperate.

This continued for what felt like an eternity. Pyotr had no idea how much time had passed. Periods of debilitating suffering gave way to embarrassing bouts using a tree near the bushes to hold himself up so he didn't shit himself, to falling back to the ground when his strength gave out.

At some point, the pain faded. Pyotr waited and worried when the next bouts would come, but they didn't. He needed time to stand without shaking and falling back to the ground. When he could get to his knees, he cleaned himself as best he could. For the first time, he was grateful to be in the middle of the woods where no one could see him.

The food or water was what made him sick, he knew, but he wasn't sure which. With that terrible thought, he had to find some semblance of civilization quickly. With no trust in the water or food and shitting his weight in fluids, he was on the verge of dehydration.

His head hurt, too. Everything ached. Pyotr made his way back north to the road and then turned east, continuing his original route to some vague hope of salvation. He no longer looked at the canopy. He didn't care what time of day it was. There was an ever-present sense of twilight ever since he entered these damned woods.

It was getting darker, though. Night would be on him soon, and he'd have to stop. He had neither strength nor the means to make a torch. The darkness came, and with it came his will to keep going for the time being. He found some bushes and slowly, awkwardly crawled inside as far as he could with his one good hand to stave off the cold. He cradled his throbbing hand gently.

Surprisingly, the weather was fairly mild. Cold, but not too cold. Exhaustion eventually proved stronger than fear, and he fell asleep; however, it wasn't long until he woke to the sounds of rustling leaves.

His heart hammered in his chest again, harder than ever before. Pyotr was instantly awake but too terrified to move. He wrapped his arms tighter around himself. For a moment, adrenaline coursed through him, and he thought to run, but just the act of holding himself tighter had reawakened the pained muscles all over his body. His frightened reflexes did not take into account his broken hand, and it was all he could do to not cry out when he accidentally put pressure on it.

He closed his eyes and let a few tears fall. He was too weak and old to avoid being eaten alive. Is this how a deer or rabbit felt? His eyes closed a little tighter, but nothing ever came. The rustling stopped. Just as Pyotr was on the verge of falling asleep, he heard it again. This time, the noise stopped just as quickly as it started. Memories of the oily-looking rodents returned. Pyotr's nerves calmed down.

Stupid rodents.

He fell back to sleep and didn't wake again until rays of weak light reached his eyes. One in particular shined directly onto his right eye. He rolled his head away and blinked repeatedly. As his body woke, every cell screamed at him in anger and agony. He grunted, rolled out of the bush, and made a heroic effort to stand. His joints cracked in weary, half-hearted applause. His muscles burned like bad whiskey. His throat was parched, and his lips were cracked. He barely had the energy to stand, let alone move.

Fuck, he thought despairingly.

The only option he had was to move, no matter how painful. So, he moved. One painful step after the other. He staggered down the overgrown road, waiting for help or death to come along; at this point, he didn't care which. He was only thankful that the demonic wolf-beast hadn't returned. Perhaps it got its fill with Hilna and wouldn't leave her carcass to hunt for several days.

Stumbling, one foot in front of the other. His stomach burned. Joints ached. Muscles strained. One more step. One more step.

This rhythmic automaton built of pain and persistence continued until he couldn't even remember why he was walking in the first place. The trees slowly passed by; they looked like prison bars in his blurred vision. He thought something watched him, eyes peering from outside the bars, deep within the black trunks of the trees. It didn't matter, though. Let him die. Eat him. End it.

Pyotr started having more vivid hallucinations. A short way up the road, he saw what looked like buildings, but who would build a village so far into these horrible woods?

He blinked and swallowed, pain shooting down his dry throat. The slow, rhythmic trudging stopped. He wobbled on his feet, nearly falling over after the forced march made his body protest its existence once more. He blinked again, squeezing his bloodshot eyes tight. When they opened, the buildings were still there.

A low wall of stacked stones circled around it. The homes were more hovels, barely standing with poorly thatched roofs. No smoke rose from any dwellings or fires. Pyotr didn't see anyone milling about. Just another deserted collection of stones where life had once made a feeble attempt to go on, but had failed.

"Don't move."

The voice was stern, feminine, and coming from beside him somewhere. He grunted a half-hearted response, but his swollen tongue refused to work.

"Turn to me," the voice commanded.

He did as instructed, turning to his left where the voice originated. Once he did, however, he was startled at what he saw, his legs growing weak, and he nearly fell again. He gave a low, hoarse cry. A woman stood there, sword drawn and pointed at him. Her long blonde hair, tied in a ponytail, fell around her shoulders. She was younger than Pyotr, but her face began to show the beginning wear of middle age. She was probably in her mid-thirties and quite pretty. Her eyes were cold and hard, unforgiving. All of these were trivial details, even the sword she threatened him with. Her most notable quality was her translucency. Pyotr could see through her ever so slightly.

He pointed a finger at her and tried to call out, but he choked on his words. His fingers instinctively gripped his shirt at his chest as he coughed—dry, hacking, and painful. He fell back, landing on his ass, and felt a carpet of leaves thankfully break his fall. Somehow, he managed to wheeze out a few words.

"Ghost ... what ... are you?"

He worked his throat and mouth, every surface sticking together from dehydration. The woman's forehead crinkled, and something akin to a grimace appeared on her face.

"Not this again," she moaned. "I'm not a ghost. Something about this forest; it does something to those who dwell here too long."

Something thudded in front of him. He saw a canteen on the ground, nestled in fallen leaves.

"Drink and then tell me who you are."

Pyotr leaned over slowly, hoping the pain would magically disappear, and wrapped aching fingers around the translucent leather. Could he even drink from this? The canteen was as solid as anything else. He stood back up and opened the container. Remembering the results of the last water he drank, he gave the nozzle a cautious sniff.

"It's clean," she stated firmly. "I take it you've had an encounter with straight water in the Blackwood?"

No sooner had she said the water was drinkable than Pyotr was already downing it as fast as he could. The lukewarm, blessed liquid filled his empty stomach. His throat stung, but the pain was gone. His tongue and lips could move unhindered again.

"Straight water, is that what it's called?"

She nodded. "Water that hasn't been boiled. Purified. Straight from the source. Something about the water here, too.

It's been that way for as long as I can remember. You won't die from drinking it, but you'll wish you had." A smirk curled her lips. She stared off momentarily as if remembering something.

"Yes. Yes, I did." He said between heavy, relieved breaths. "I definitely thought I was going to die."

He held the canteen out to her. "I'm Pyotr," he said when he noticed her still watching him closely. "Do I look like I can hurt you? I'm half-starved and barely strong enough to walk. What's your name, ghost?"

The woman huffed and walked over to retrieve the water. She jerked it out of his hand and returned it to her belt. She took a few steps back.

"Grayce," she said. "I'm not a ghost."

"Well, now I don't have to call you ghost, Grayce," Pyotr said with a slight smirk in his voice. "This world truly has gone to a whole new level of shit if I'm talking with a real person; I can see through you like you're nothing."

"Or the forest has driven you mad," she offered, with no hint of humor.

He nodded. "Or that."

"You're not mad," she continued. "I told you, the forest does things to people. I noticed it once when travelers still came through once in a great while. They never stopped, always passing by on the road. Anytime we'd approach, they'd ride off faster, often never looking back. We assumed it was just the way things were or that no one trusted a small hamlet in the woods. I noticed something different, though, after I'd been the Sword-bearer for some years. They looked at us in fear. I forced one to a stop once. He nearly died of fright, I think. After getting him to talk, I learned he thought he'd trespassed onto some haunted land. He thought we were all ghosts, too. He didn't stick around much longer. He took off, nearly running me over. The Keeper and I looked into it as much as we could; however, we only had our guesses. *She* probably has more control over those who remain in her realm. Keeping us in some kind of ... dream-like otherworld. I'm not sure."

Keeper. Sword-bearer. Pyotr could only assume these were titles used where Grayce comes from. The way Grayce said 'she,' however, was unsettling.

"She?" he asked. "Who rules this realm? I come from Kalthav, and we thought these woods were abandoned for decades. Is there a manor nearby? Some countess?"

Grayce snorted—dry and mirthless.

"If only it were that mundane. Something owns these woods and all within it. Something old and powerful. She's called the Mother of Screams. We've also read that Her name is the Whisperer in the Womb. I don't know if she's a monster or a god. Or both."

"Both," Pyotr whispered. The last day the lightning came to Kalthav returned to his mind in an ironic flash. "I've seen things I can't explain, too. Been fleeing from them for a while. Lost my only friend to something just yesterday at the entrance to the woods. Seems there's no escaping the nightmares."

"I'm sorry," Grayce said with genuine empathy in her tone. "I understand that kind of loss all too well. What was their name?"

Pyotr smirked. "Hilna. She ... she was a mule," he chuckled. "As stubborn as an ass and as friendly as a horse."

Grayce smiled just slightly. It looked as though she hadn't done such a thing in some time, and her muscles were unaccustomed to it. "May I ask, how did she die? Was it a broken leg?"

"Some horrible wolf, bigger than anything I've ever seen. Couldn't have been a wolf, though. Those eyes ..."

Pyotr's voice faded when he saw the look on Grayce's face. She'd gone slightly pale, her jaw clenched. She lowered her gaze and stared intensely at Pyotr's feet.

His tone dropped. "What is that thing?" She must know, he thought, with a look like that.

"Her children," she replied. Her tone lowered, and Pyotr crossed his arms to ward off what felt like a chill in the otherwise stale air.

"They're not wolves of any sort."

"I could tell that much," he interrupted.

"They're called barghests. They're her personal demonic pets. She creates them, I think. If you hear their howl, you're done for."

Pyotr's eyes widened, and his gut clenched. "Just hearing them kills you?"

"Not right away." Her words hung heavy with sadness. "It starts with nightmares. Subtle at first. Then, worse and worse. Soon, you start seeing things. Sleep brings no rest. Only screams and visions of terrible things. You hear their howl more and more."

Pyotr saw fear take Grayce's features and twist them. It was as if some hidden hand gripped her face and wrenched it into a pained knot. Tears began to fall. He opened his mouth, began to offer words of comfort, and even thought of reaching out his hand for her shoulder, but she shuddered and spoke words that froze him in his steps.

"Then ... she visits you."

He didn't know how to respond to such a statement.

"I think it's only when I sleep, but sometimes I can't tell when I'm dreaming or not anymore." Her red, moist eyes looked up at him. "I questioned, at first, if you were real or not."

Pyotr swallowed, feeling the sting of his worn throat once more. He stepped toward her and put a hand on her shoulder. "Is there no one in your village who can help?"

She scowled. "No. They're all a bunch of pricks, anyway. They pretended to be kind to me when I was still the Keeper's daughter, but when I took up the sword from my mentor, they turned on me instantly and treated me like they did him. They had no idea ..."

"It's ok, dear," Pyotr said. He took her in a gentle hug that shocked them both. Though she looked older, Grayce reminded him of Annica in a way. He remembered the young woman's smiling face and the better times they shared with Lorna. "I'll help you figure this out."

He heard her sniffle, her muscles tightening in her arms. "You smell," she said.

Pyotr chuckled. "I'm sure I do. Let's go back to your village. Why don't you introduce me to this Keeper?"

She gently pushed him away and regained her composure. All traces of vulnerability disappeared. Her face hardened. "We can't. I'm sorry. You seem like a kind man, Pyotr. I wish I could've known you longer."

Pyotr wanted to ask why, to assuage her concerns as well as ease the rising anxiety in his chest. The look on her face betrayed more than sadness. There was a cold resolve in her eyes. Then, he noticed she wasn't quite looking at him but past him, into the woods at his back.

Pyotr spun around, hoping it was just his imagination. That she just couldn't look him in the eyes to deny him shelter. It was too much to hope for.

A shape stood in the shadows of the trees, completely still save for one long arm attached to a gangly hand stroking the fur of the creature next to it. The shape was womanly, lithe, and appeared naked. It was difficult to make out more than a silhouette. A black shape that sucked in the light around it, deepening the canopy's shadows even further.

The same could be said for the creature next to her, though its many sets of eyes reflected the weak sunlight. Its hair bristled. Its jaws slavered. Its throat growled. It shuddered under her touch, though from pleasure or pain, it was hard to tell. It was the beast, the one that killed Hilna and set him fleeing into the woods.

"It's Her," Grayce said from behind him. Her voice cracked with genuine terror.

"Who is she?" Pyotr asked in barely a whisper.

"The Mother. And her pet."

Realization began to set in on Pyotr, dawning like a blood-shaded sunrise. Did that thing set a trap for him? Did it wait to attack so that he would flee further into Her realm? If so, then She set the trap herself. The stories were true. The Mother stood there next to that awful beast, petting and stroking its rigid fur over and over. The barghest was large enough. She towered over the thing like it was a typical working dog.

You took them from me.

A voice burrowed into his brain, like maggots feasting on dead flesh. It revolted him and set his skin to tingling. Pyotr looked at his arm and saw the hair rising above masses of goosebumps.

"You can't have them!" Grayce shrieked, causing Pyotr to jump.

They're mine now.

"Lies!"

"Grayce, what's happening?" Pyotr asked, but he couldn't turn to face her. He could only look at the Mother, who continued to pet the bristling, growling thing at her side. All the while, her voice cooed in his mind.

Tell him.

Grayce made no reply.

Tell him about your lovely work. The way you pierced them in their sleep, one after another ... after another ... and another ...

Pyotr heard Grayce weeping. A quiet 'no' broke between her sniffles and muffled cries.

You denied me their screams. Denied Fang their flesh.

Pyotr turned and saw Grayce's eyes wide, filled with horror, her mouth agape.

"What?" she asked, the word escaping quietly from her lips.

It's ok. Mommy forgives you.

"Grayce ... what is She talking about? Where's your village?"

Gone gone gone

The words danced in his head, screaming, then whispering, then screaming again.

Can you still smell the smoke? Smell them cooking?

"I had to ..." Grayce said, but she sounded painfully unsure. "If I didn't, she would have—"

The barghest barked viciously, interrupting her. It growled, a sound like a tremor in hell.

Quiet, lovely. You will have both their flesh. Soon.

Pyotr looked back and forth between Grayce and the demonic pair of shadows. Grayce's silent, free-flowing tears contrasted with the unsettlingly still things in the woods. The Mother's arm still petting, petting.

"Fang?" came a shuddering croak from behind Pyotr. "Is that you?"

He looks much better like this. His human body was so frail; the flesh so soft. Now, he is strong. He serves.

The otherworldly growl came once more. In response, the long-fingered hand caressed the multi-eyed face of the beast.

Grayce began loudly weeping. Pyotr heard a thump and assumed she'd fallen to her knees, possibly even prone. He didn't know what to do. If he ran, the beast would kill him. If he stayed, the beast would kill him, or worse, what would this Mother do?

Shhhhhhshshshsh ...

The voice hushed like it was soothing an infant. Pyotr felt nauseous.

It's time.

His heart thudded in his chest. The barghest pawed the ground impatiently. Pyotr felt his leg muscles tense. He would run as fast as he could toward where Grayce approached him from. If he could make it to her village, whatever state it was in, he could possibly survive. He'd have to pull Grayce back to her feet if they were both going to make it.

A searing pain tore through his stomach. He cursed. Now was not the time for some bout of stomach problems when his life was in danger. What a comical death that would be. Run down by a demonic wolf-beast while shitting himself standing. At least he could spoil the creature's meal.

But then, he felt something running down his gut. The pain was also in his back, tearing through his entire torso. He tasted blood and felt his mouth become wet. He began choking. Every cough sent fresh pain through him. Looking down, he saw a dripping red blade poking through him. A steady breath caressed his ear, followed by a soft but resolute voice.

"She won't have you, either."

"Grayce ..." Pyotr wheezed. He couldn't turn around, but he saw the hand on the barghest's head clench.

Naughty child.

The blade pulled away, out of his back and gut, and a gout of blood shot through his throat and out his mouth. His vision began spinning. As everything began to go dark, Pyotr realized he couldn't breathe or speak. Stranger still, he could see his own body falling to the side and crashing on the ground.

GRAYCE SPAT at the Mother and clenched the sword tighter. The barghest unleashed its death-bearing howl and launched itself at her. The sound reverberated in her brain painfully, sending the vilest memories of her life flashing through her waking eyes. Images, some half-remembered and hazy as to if they were real or not, of blood and corpses. She winced.

Her leg exploded in agony. It felt like two planks full of nails snapped around her calf. The pain then multiplied a thousand-fold as she heard a rip, a snap, and felt her body propelled through the air. When she landed, Grayce saw the remainder of her lower leg being thrashed and then tossed aside by the barghest.

This one looked like the other two she and Fang had fought so many years ago. However, it had one significant exception: A streak of red ran along the carapace on the left side of its face.

The red line, your father called it. My children are all equal in my eyes, but this one is special. I decorated him for you. He is the best one so far. I will keep him for a long time. He still longs for you, so I will make you special, too.

The barghest charged her again. She tried to raise her sword, but her pain-wracked body moved too slowly. She brought the blade up in time to hit the thick plate on the beast's shoulder, but it careened off harmlessly. The blade fell from her hands and landed in the limp grass. The next moment, hot breath blew over her face, carrying the smell of decay and death. Grayce tried to scream, but too many teeth had punctured her throat. The only screams she heard were those of a thousand trapped souls, mingled with the moans and laughter of their grim keeper.

Fear not, child. You will not join them. You will carry them. Both of you. Together.

THE DEAD MEN

The ruins in the distance seemed to pull the wind toward them. The crevice in the rocks provided enough shelter to wait for game, but food was getting more and more scarce. Hobble didn't like journeying this far away from home to track deer and rabbits, but his father insisted. Since he was little, the trips had sent hunting pairs closer and closer to the old human town.

"I don't like it here," Hobble said as he pulled the hide blanket tighter.

His father grumbled. "You will be an adult soon. You'll have to head out with your own hunting partner. How about Gara? She's pretty."

Hobble sneered. "Mating is disgusting. Why do we need it? Just more mouths to feed."

His father sniffed. He always did that when he was preparing to say something he thought was profound.

"Because humans die, where goblins don't. Just look at those," he said, pointing at the ruins. "Humans lived there. Prospered. Warred with our kind for generations. Now they're dead, and we live on."

Hobble stared at the road a few hundred feet away. "You're just repeating what Great Grandmother tells us."

"She carries the stories of our past. It is why she is our leader. Respect her."

The wind blew a long, low dirge among the trees and stones behind them. The cold day wore on until the sun set, and they could finally go home.

The next two days were much the same. Waiting for game, catching few, and returning to their village that smelled of old leather and smoke. Eating thin soup most days and a few cuts of meat on good ones. At least no one went hungry.

Before leaving for the day with his father again, Hobble loitered around outside their home of brown bear skins draped over a frame of animal bones, all strapped together with strings fashioned from animal guts. He kicked the base of one of the foundation poles. They could pick up and leave within an hour and go anywhere they wanted, yet for years, they chose to stay here.

Great Grandmother said the ruins nearby kept them safe. Said the humans feared them. So why shouldn't they fear them? The Dead Men would always come. Shouldn't his people be afraid?

That night, Hobble and his father return from their hunt, and the old leader of their tribe called them together. One of their kin, hunchbacked and slow-moving, limped its way to the fire. All of the Flintscar tribe gathered, their thin shadows cast by the firelight against the dirt and patches of pale grass.

Great Grandmother's guide helped her along. They say magic is all that held her together, that she would be the last of the Flintscar to pass away, heralding all the souls of the past into the afterlife. The ancient goblin was older than Hobble's father, grandfather, and possibly great-grandfather.

It was all a waste of time, Hobble thought. Though he never

spoke such things aloud except to his father. And then, only rarely.

A shaking hand, draped in sheep fur, pulled back the fraying cowl covering her head. Milky white eyes gazed emptily into the flames. Her face looked like little more than paper-dry skin stretched tight over misshapen bones. When she spoke, it was so low the guide had to speak loud enough for all to hear.

"The winds stir with apprehension," he bellowed. Then, he leaned down to listen. Her thin lips moved, and he nodded his head. "The animals of the woods grow quieter. Something stirs across the veil of spirits."

A murmur moved through the gathering. Children huddled with their mothers. Warriors scowled. Hunters crossed their arms and shook their heads.

"Be increasingly cautious as you go about your business. My old heart trembles at threats unseen to my physical eyes but heard by my soul."

Great Grandmother then slowly and shakily pulled her cowl back over her head, shrouding her wrinkled face in shadow. The guide nodded his head slowly at everyone else, the sign they could all take their leave. He placed his large hand on Great Grandmother's back and walked with her back to her home.

Hobble did not read too much into the old woman's words. He looked at his father, though, and saw his thick eyebrows furrowed. The muscles in his jaws were tight. The last time Hobble saw his father like this was when they received news that his mother had been caught by Dead Men.

"THIS IS FAR TOO DANGEROUS," Hobble complained. He and his father were forced to cross the road this time in order to find game. They saw a deer, but it fled before they could attempt to take it down with their bows. They tracked it throughout the morning and turned back when they lost the trail.

His father didn't reply. He'd been unusually quiet this entire outing. Hobble, as his father so loved to remind him, was no longer a child. Being a male without a family, he was moved to the appropriate lodging until he found a wife. His father left the bonfire without saying a word, and Hobble hadn't seen him until this morning when his sunken eyes noted a lack of sleep. Those glossy eyes stared out ahead. It was likely his current state that cost them the kill. His steps were slow and clumsy. His gait wavered from time to time. Hobble walked a few steps ahead and, now being downwind, noticed something else: a faint, acrid smell.

"You drank last night, didn't you?" Hobble said with pointed accusation.

His father grunted.

"No wonder we can't find anything to hunt. You probably can't even see straight."

"I see well enough."

Hobble growled. "Damn it, what happened to you last night? After you left without speaking to me, did you go off and drink yourself to sleep? Is that it?"

A hand reached around and closed around his mouth. His father's hot, alcohol-reeking breath wafted across his ear and nose.

"Quiet," he whispered. "I see well enough."

An arm stretched along Hobble's other side and pointed beyond the trees to the road, which was far closer on this side of the clearing than the opposite, which led to their village. Humans again. Four of them walked along the road.

"—this shitty route was all your idea," one of them finished saying.

"Sod off. Every other town has been abandoned. The ruins

are right there. We can shelter for the night and maybe find some people to tag along with."

"Right, right. Whatever you say. Keep walkin'. I gotta piss."

Hobble's eyes widened. One of them separated from the group and walked in their direction. Two groups of humans in as many days, and one of them was heading right for Hobble and his father. What curse was upon them both?

The sound of his heart pounded in his ears. Hobble nearly jumped when his father put a firm hand on his shoulder. The weight suggested he crouch down further. Neither of them made a sound as they practically pressed themselves into the dirt.

The grunts and sighs of the human tromping through the brush drowned out any noise two goblins could possibly make. A shadow passed over them; the stranger was close. So long as they didn't move, the human would do his business and leave. So far, that appeared to be the case.

The boorish groan the man made as he relieved himself brought up the taste of bile in Hobble's mouth. He glanced over and saw his father still stone-faced, staring straight ahead and breathing softly through his nose.

Hobble closed his eyes in relief when he heard the man finish, his feet rustling as he turned around. Then, the rustling of moving feet was replaced by panicked cursing.

"Fuck!" the man shouted. The heavy thud accompanied by tousled leaves gave the impression he'd fallen. He was dangerously close to them. More cursing was followed by the sound of hands brushing off clothes. "Gods-damn it," he grumbled.

Oh no. The stranger had stood and began moving in a different direction. A heavy foot crushed Hobble's calf, and he yelped in pain. A hoarse shout came from the stranger as he stumbled backward. His father moved with surprising quickness.

By the time Hobble was on his feet, limping due to his

injured leg, the man had a rusty sword drawn, glaring death at the two of them. His father already had his bow drawn and aimed at the tall stranger. Hobble drew his skinning knife.

"Loose that arrow, an' my friends'll skin you alive," the yellow-teethed mouth growled. "You understand that, goblin?"

His father nodded. Hobble looked back and forth between the two. The silence and tension hung heavy in the air, congealed into a fear on both sides that dared the other to act first. After several uncountable moments, a far-off voice called, "You finished yet?"

The coarsely-bearded jaw moved as the man ground his teeth. His chest heaved with a heavy breath. Hobble's father still hadn't moved, and his arrow was still trained on the human. Hobble traced the path of the arrow; it was aimed directly at the man's heart.

"Goblins!" the man shouted.

The whistle of his father's arrow sounded just before the tell-tale thunk and grunt of a lethal shot. The man had time to gurgle before falling to the ground, his heart pierced through. They both turned to see the other humans already in the trees.

"Run!" his father shouted at him. He loosed one more arrow and hit another human in the chest. They collapsed, screaming in pain.

"No, father, I'll—"

His father dropped the bow and grabbed Hobble by the collar with a strength he didn't know the old man had.

"You will *run!*" he repeated viciously and threw Hobble backward. He landed painfully a few feet away.

The last thing he saw before turning around was the humans reaching his father, who'd drawn his own skinning knife. The old goblin bellowed and lifted his blade to stab at the front-most human, but the taller being was already in mid-swing with his hand-axe by then. His father grunted forcefully and bent over, blood spilling to the ground.

Hobble turned and ran, tears in his eyes. He could move quicker through the brush than the humans could, and they were busy with his father at the moment. His legs pumped and carried him across the clearing, where he swiveled his head in a panic, looking for any other men.

He ran until he reached the village. His head pounded with fear, adrenaline, and fatigue. He collapsed after he passed the palisade wall. Voices called out to him, but they were foggy and distant. He didn't know if they were real. Shadows flitted over his vision, and he barely recalled other villagers running by him. Shouts and cries, also foggy and far away, touched the edge of his consciousness. Hobble breathed and gasped for air. Finally, his vision cleared, and he regained enough feeling to know that his muscles felt like they were exploding.

Someone helped him to his feet. He recognized Lorg, one of the pig farmers. He turned to see those on guard duty gathered at the opening of the wall. A body lay on the ground, the arrows protruding from it, giving it the look of a dead tree. It was human.

"One of them got away," a guard was saying to Great Grand-mother's guide. The stoic goblin that aided the old woman listened, stone-faced, as the guard spat in a rage about the human who knew of their village's location. There could be more of them. The Dead Men could come. The ruins would no longer keep them safe. The concerns continued on until the guide turned and came to Hobble.

The guide stopped in front of Hobble and looked at him with cold, calculating eyes. "How many were there?"

Hobble's eyes darted about as he tried to think, his mind as exhausted as his body. He was still catching his breath. "Four, I think? Father," his voice broke for a moment, remembering that his only family was now gone. "Father killed one, possibly two. Two others began chasing me."

The guide nodded. "That leaves at least two more for the survivor to return to."

He turned and left, entering Great Grandmother's dwelling without saying another word. Hobble listened to the others argue and worry over the news when the flap of Great Grandmother's tent lifted, and the guide stepped out. With an arm raised, holding the thick, woven sheet up as he stood in the doorway, the guide made a motion with his head beckoning Hobble to enter. The guide then turned and let the flap drop.

Inside the tent, the smell of incense and dried fruit was almost overpowering. Other, more earthy and bitter smells were masked by the incense. Great Grandmother sat in a handmade chair of wood and bone. Hides and furs draped all around to cushion her old, fragile bones. Her empty eyes stared blankly at the opposite wall of thick leather. Several candles lit the room and created soft, dancing shadows amid a dull, orange glow.

Her guide extended his hand to an empty stool, offering Hobble a seat. Taking the offer, Hobble sat down and put his hands on his knees.

"Do you know how old I am?"

The croaking voice nearly made Hobble jump from his stool. It was soft, breathy but surprising in the still quiet.

"Um ... no, Great Grandmother," Hobble stuttered.

"You are still young. A new adult in our tribe, I hear. You could not fathom what over a century of life can mean."

He didn't know how to reply to that.

"I am not concerned about the humans. Do you know why?"

"No, Great Grandmother."

"They are still Dead Men. The Dead Men always seek the ruins. The Dead Men are cursed to seek them. They will not come for a village of our kind when the false hope of the ruins is reflected in their eyes."

Hobble nodded, forgetting for a moment that she was blind. But she continued as though she had seen his response.

"I went to the ruins once," she said in a voice lower than before. Hobble sat up when she said it.

"I was young then, too. Many more people walked the road then. Many more Dead Men. Our tribe had just come to the forest. We were looking for a place to call home after humans ran us out of our former one. They killed nearly half of us. I was sent with others to the ruins of man to see if it would suffice for us. I saw what the things there did to men and goblins alike."

Her voice began to shake. As did her hands. She trembled with the memory, and tears began to moisten her white eyes.

"I only saw it for the briefest moment. My vision went dark when I saw the things that came out of the buildings and streets and took the Dead Men and my own kind. My friends. I don't know why they did not take me, but I felt their presence. I fled, stumbling and falling, my knees and hands burning and bleeding from the scrapes."

For the first time, Hobble saw the scars on her palms and fingers.

"I cried out and ran in what I thought was the way home. Eventually, I heard familiar voices. They brought me home, and I told the elders everything. We never returned to the ruins, but we did notice something. Men found the ruins irresistible. Our scouts and hunters came back, telling us how humans have always sought out their city from the old days. It seems many of them ignored the warnings of their fellows if what we overheard was true. That is why we call them the Dead Men. They walk so eagerly to a death that defies explanation. A death that I can no longer remember, only that it was so horrifying as to blind me for merely witnessing it. I think my mind refuses to remember.

But we know that we are safe here because they will forever venture to the ruins like rabbits to a hunter's snare."

Hobble realized he was on the edge of the stool, and his mouth had gone dry from hanging open. Her story was both horrid and fascinating.

"So, we won't need to fear the humans coming back for us? They are still Dead Men?"

"Yes."

Her head turned slowly toward the guide, who leaned over and placed a thick but gentle hand over Great Grandmother's own. "I am tired. I'd like to sleep now."

"Yes, Great Grandmother." The guide replied obediently. "You may leave now," he said to Hobble.

"Go," the woman grunted as the guide helped her to her shaking feet. "Tell the others what I've said of the humans. They are Dead Men now as they always have been."

Hobble nodded nervously before remembering he needed to speak out loud for her to hear. "Y-Yes, Great Grandmother."

It eased the nerves of the other goblins to hear Great Grandmother's words. Tempers calmed, and fears faded. The tones of their voices changed, and they all suddenly agreed that there was nothing to worry about. Of course, Great Grandmother was right.

Hobble was paired with another hunter the very next day. Things returned to normal with no further sightings of the Dead Men, at least for a time.

HOBBLE HEARD a familiar voice waking him in the early morning hours. It wasn't calling for him directly but addressed everyone in the confines of their tents. He didn't recognize it at first because it was the gruff, quiet voice of Grandmother's guide, now shouting in the dirty streets of the village.

Great-grandmother had a message for them all. The guide was directing them all to the bonfire. It was burning fiercely when Hobble arrived. Other goblins were feeding it with whole logs, tossing them in as large embers shot out in great billowing clouds.

Hobble noticed many goblins looking at the sky. He followed their gazes to see a needle-black line stretching up and beyond sight in the northeast. It struck an unnatural fear in him when he saw it.

"Hobble," the guide said from behind him, "She wants to speak with you first."

Hobble only nodded, curiosity and anxiety making him wonder what she wanted with him.

When he entered the tent, the same smells greeted him but took him less by surprise. Great Grandmother lay on her bed, her chest raising and lowering slowly. He could tell her breathing was labored.

"Ah, you're here," she said weakly, turning her head towards him. Her hand lolled sideways, and her fingers curled, beckoning him over. She didn't have the strength to raise her arm. "Come. Come."

A stool sat empty at her side. The guide never came back into the dwelling. Either he was keeping the rest of the village calm, or what she had to say was strictly for him. He wasn't sure which one made him more nervous. Her fingers curled again, asking him to lean down for her to speak. She must have used most of her strength to call out to him when he entered.

"You saw the light?" she said weakly. So much so that it didn't seem like she had spoken at all.

"I wasn't sure what it was, actually, Great Grandmother."

Her dry lips smacked together.

"A light, calling out to something, bringing it here."

She had to stop, only able to speak in short bursts.

"I saw ... in a vision. A dream. A city ... in the ocean. This land is no longer safe. Take them there."

"A city in the sea?" he replied incredulously. "How will I know how to get there? Where will we get a ship?"

"You must ... find a way. Find a ship. Take them to the center of the ocean. A city rises in the sky there. Take them ..."

She repeated the last phrase over and over until she could no longer speak. Her last words flowed into a final rattle that saw her fingers stop curling, her white eyes go dim, and her mouth fall agape. Hobble sat there for a moment. He couldn't believe what she had tasked him to do. Take all the villagers to an unknown island in the middle of the ocean? How was he supposed to do that? And, again, why him?

The rustle of the tent flap made Hobble turn his head to the entrance. The guide was standing there, his face as stoic as ever.

"I knew it."

"Knew what?"

"She woke this morning, panicked. Her old body could no longer keep going. She rambled about a dark light until I finally gave in and went to see it for myself. That's when she told me to gather everyone and find you."

"She told me ..." Hobble hesitated. The responsibility continued to grow heavier with every minute. "She said we had to leave. Go to a city in the middle of the ocean."

"I see," he replied simply. "Then we go."

Hobble furrowed his brows. Shook his head. "Why? We should be safe here; there's no reason to leave!"

"Great Grandmother is always right. She spoke of the world growing weary and dark times coming. Then, the light appeared."

"We don't know anything about it," Hobble countered.

"Exactly. But Great Grandmother did. At least, she knew of it.

She's connected with it, somehow. She's far older than you know."

Hobble stood, his fists clenched. "How can we do this? We are not sailors. Has anyone in the village even been on a ship?"

"We will find a way."

"How?" Hobble persisted, his tone agitated.

"We take what belongings we can carry," the guide began, his voice calm and sure. "There's an abandoned human town nearby, on the river. There may be a ship there. We will find a way."

Hobble took a deep breath and closed his eyes. They would find a way. He would not be able to live with himself if he ignored Great Grandmother's dying wish. Her guide would probably go without him anyway.

"Very well," Hobble said, resigning himself to his new role.

The guide nodded.

They exited the tent to an expectant crowd of goblins. Some were scared, clutching onto their mates or their young. Others' eyes blazed with impatience, uncertainty, or both. The guide spoke to them, relaying Great Grandmother's last wish. The goblins would go to the city on the ocean.

THE WAVES of the Wailing Ocean lapped against the strange stones of the large island. Grunts, made in unison, came from several small boats filled with goblins making their way into the underbelly of the island alone in the middle of the endless waters.

The guide and Hobble sat in the foremost boat. Staring solemnly into the shadows of the water-carved caves, they mourned those who didn't survive the trip. Some had fallen overboard in storms or given up and tossed themselves into the seas whose waves sounded like the cries of countless dead. Some had become ill. Others had refused to even make the trip once they saw the ship and realized it would be their home for a long time, for the island was in the middle of the vast ocean.

The guide could still read the language of men, and a letter was found posted in the empty village. It spoke of exactly what Great Grandmother said. A city, a safe haven, in the middle of the ocean where all were welcome.

"All" wasn't exactly specified. Many of them took that to mean goblins, as well, but there were doubts, shared too by the guide and Hobble. They feared making the long trip only to be slaughtered once they reached their destination.

The ship they had found was in poor shape, required some repair, and then still left many feeling uneasy about the journey, but Great Grandmother had said this was their path. After repairs were made and those that chose to leave on their own trails were gone, the rest of the Flintscar tribe loaded into the hastily patched human ship and made their way slowly forward to this mysterious island. Moving down the river allowed them time to learn the workings of the ship, but in the ocean, things became stressful and frightening. They let the sails down and hoped the wind would carry them where they needed to go. Otherwise, they would be forced to take their chances wherever they landed.

Fate, it seemed, was on their side. The currents and winds all appeared to pull in to the middle of the ocean. After many long weeks, the survivors arrived at the island. Those who spent their time learning as much as they could about the ship dropped the anchor before they ran aground near some steep cliffs. This is where they piled into the smaller boats and disembarked to row their way into their new home.

Now, the guide and Hobble helped pull their boat onto the rocky shores of some caves beneath the island cliffs. Along the dark, slick shores, other goblins did the same. They meandered aimlessly, wondering what to do. The sound of wood shattering loudly brought Hobble's attention to the massive rock archways leading back out to the ocean. The rope holding their anchor must have snapped. The ship was tossed into the cliffs, and flotsam began making its way with the waves toward them.

The villagers began gathering what they could. Once dried, the wood from the hull and torn cloth from the sails could be used to build new, if temporary, homes.

The guide and Hobble walked together, scouting the area of their landing. The stones that made up the cliff and caves were dark, almost black. Strange, gray striations and deposits of some sort jutted from the wall. They were smooth to the touch.

Someone managed to get some torches blazing, along with a bonfire. Hobble and the guide took a torch each and continued into the caves. There were no signs of animal habitation. That was good. No animals this close to the rocky beach meant no predators for the time being. However, something very bad revealed itself shortly after.

The guide let out a low growl from his throat as soon as Hobble saw it. The gray striations led their eyes to skulls. Hundreds of them. Thousands. They were closer to the ceiling and dotted down along the walls like gray boils. Then, they both realized that the striations themselves were other bones. Human, elf-kind, dwarven. They stretched and twisted unnaturally as though they had become part of the black stone.

"Dead men," Hobble said in a low, breathy voice.

The guide nodded. "Not like those where we came from, but close enough, I suppose."

"We can't stay here," Hobble said, a hint of fear tainting his attempt at firmness.

The guide moved his torch from left to right, revealing more and more of the skulls that covered the roof like hideous egg sacs. Each pale and threatening to burst and unleash a host of fresh nightmares.

"We have nowhere else to go."

"What do we do?"

"We stay on the beach for now. No one comes here. We tell no one what we saw. You and I, we will continue to scout further into this blackness until we come out the other side. For our people."

Hobble nodded. Somewhere inside him, Great Grandmother's dying command echoed like a waking dream. This was their new home. And Great Grandmother was always right.

DARK

No regrets. That is the motto Celia's father had always repeated to her and her sister. Life was hard, but he never let that take away his smile. Sometimes, it was a sad smile, sometimes a smirk, but most often, a genuine smile that he shared with his daughters and neighbors. People said her mother was not as optimistic as her father, but nevertheless, she was a lovely woman, and they both belonged together.

This influence led Celia to enjoy every little thing that she could in her brief time in Alda. Their garden was as healthy as could be asked for. Carrots as long and thick as a thumb, potatoes that you could barely wrap your hand around. Even a watermelon or two would show up in their harvest. The farmers on the edge of town harvested almost half the wheat they planted, enough to make bread for everyone most seasons.

They were lucky compared to what they had heard from the few who had come through town now and again. Travelers always brought ill tidings. A collective sigh made its way through everyone when a small group or creaking wagon visited their streets.

Some wanted to join them. In the past, they were happy to

take in stragglers from the ruined outlands, but now they were full. All the homes and inn rooms were taken, and any other visitors were politely urged on their way. This always bothered Celia's younger sister, Serena.

"There goes more," Serena commented morosely. "I wish we didn't have to make them leave."

"We have no choice. We have a good life here and can't take on any more people. Where would they live?"

Serena crossed her arms as the small group of vagrants disappeared from the outskirts of town. "We can build homes, you know."

"Building homes takes time and resources. Where would they stay until then?"

"Why can't we build a few simple places before others arrive?"

That made sense, but that would also require people to stop what they were already doing. Everyone had their hands full, keeping the town in the shape it was in. Food required constant care to grow the way it did. Animals had to be guarded non-stop to protect them. There was too much to do to build more homes.

"Let's go see what the apothecary needs today," Celia stated, changing the subject.

Serena sighed and let her arms drop. She acted her age, which meant constantly annoyed, at nineteen years old.

The young woman knocked on the wooden door with the symbol of the goddess of healing carved on it. Slowly, Celia pushed it open, its hinges creaking. They were free to enter, but occasionally, Gregory, the apothecary, would have a visitor or patient in his entry room. The girls preferred to be polite and give him the chance to tell them to wait outside.

"Anything for us today, Gregory?" Celia called out.

"Celia?" an old voice rang out from behind another door.

Gregory came out from a back room with his hands covered in green. He'd been working with herbs all day, apparently.

"Oh, good," he said upon seeing the two of them. I am short on monk's hood. They should be in bloom on the west ridge. Could you two bring me back a basket-full?"

Straight to the point, as always. He turned back around and returned to whatever he was doing in the other room.

"Shall we?" Serena trilled.

The two sisters left and found Nolan, a city guard assigned to escort those leaving the town borders. Anyone going out to harvest, scavenge, or even go for a walk was required to take a guard with them. A few people had gone missing lately, and the number of disappearances had steadily risen over the last few years.

"The west ridge?" he repeated upon being asked. "I never liked it there."

Neither Celia nor Serena cared to ask why. Everyone had places they hated going. Celia's was the northern river. The last time she went there, she swore she'd seen people in the trees beyond it. She wrote them off as shadows, but no more than three days later, someone went missing. She reported it, but the subsequent search turned up nothing. Celia swore to never go back but knew that she'd have to at some point unless they wanted to start catching and drinking rainwater.

Her sister's trilling voice began to grate on Celia's nerves. She was flirting with the guard. Nolan was young and handsome, true enough. He smelled like leather and steel. The sword sheathed at his side clanked on his legs as they walked. The presence of an armed individual should have made her feel safe, but it was superficial at best. Everyone knew that anywhere outside the town was dangerous. The things that took people couldn't be fended off by sharp steel. No one had heard from a mage in decades. The people they sent off earlier that day were likely already on their way to some early grave. Everyone knew the cities were dangerous. Too many people drew attention to dark things. Too few people, and you likely couldn't survive long. Damned if you do, damned if you don't.

Celia wasn't a pessimist, as some called her. She just knew their reality. To most of the town, ignoring reality made things easier. Her father probably thought that way. That was how he kept smiling. Ignorance was infectious, though. He made those around him relax, including herself.

It took less than an hour to get to the western ridge: a patch of forest running up to a cliff's edge overlooking a small valley below. The river ran nearby and fell over the cliff's face, roaring into the same valley. You couldn't hear it from here, but she'd gone there once. No good foraging to be had and, according to the hunters, no good game, either.

Here, though, where the trees were thinner and more brush was present, grew several different batches of herbs and useful plants. It made Celia wonder if they'd been planted in the past by someone. Her dark imagination also went to the image of a former townsperson or traveler killed by something and their pack's contents scattered here.

"What are you looking for?" Nolan asked.

"Monk's hood," Serena said. She was already scanning the ground ahead.

"It has purple flowers," Celia added. "It almost looks like lavender from a distance."

"Ah, ok," he said. The guard made an honest attempt to help them look.

Celia found other useful plants and called Serena over. They'd both brought baskets, and Serena's was reserved for things other than monk's hood. Any extra they found could be bartered or used by them personally. She pointed out the bright yellow blossoms of evening primrose, and Serena happily plucked a handful for her basket. They also found fennel, flax, and wood sorrel. They had yet to find any monk's hood, however.

"I found some," Nolan called out. He sounded quite proud of himself.

Serena giggled when they walked over to him. She took the purple bunch from the guard.

"That's lavender," she said teasingly, slapping the stalks against him and causing small blossoms to fall.

"Oh," he said dejectedly. "So I'm looking for another type of purple flower."

"Yep," Serena chirped.

"Wait, is that it?" he asked, pointing to the flax in Celia's basket.

"No, that's flax," Celia responded.

"Gods, how many purple herbs are there?"

"Hyssop, sage, and sweet violet, to name a few," Celia replied, squinting as she tried to remember more."

Serena tossed the lavender into her basket. "How about bluebell?"

"Oh, yes."

Nolan's mouth curled on one side. "Why is it called bluebell if it's purple?"

"I didn't name them," Serena scoffed. "Oh, and dame's arrow."

"Dame's arrow is more pink, I believe," Celia said.

Serena rolled her eyes. "Fine, how about light purple?"

"Pink is light red, not light purple," Celia countered.

Serena chuckled, and then they both noticed that Nolan wasn't next to them anymore. He'd walked over closer to the trees.

"Nolan?" Serena called out to him.

He shushed them and held out a hand behind him, urging

them to stay. His other hand was wrapped around his sword's grip. Celia felt her heart beat faster. She looked over, and Celia's face was marred with concern.

"What is it?" Celia asked. Nolan was leaning from side to side, craning his head to see further into the trees.

"Thought I saw something."

"Probably just a deer," Serena said, though she didn't sound confident.

"You both wait there."

He took a few more steps into the woods.

"That's not a good idea, Nolan. We'll go look somewhere else," Celia suggested.

They both watched as Nolan turned around and offered a shrug. "I'm not going any further. Just right here."

The sisters turned to face each other. They continued half-heartedly looking at the brush to find the herb they'd come for.

"I don't like this," Serena whispered.

"I'm sure it's fine."

They searched for several more minutes when they finally found a small bunch of monk's hoods. They breathed a conjoined sigh of relief. It was time to get Nolan and go home.

Both sisters turned to where the guard had walked into the forest. Serena had just begun to call for him when her voice broke. He wasn't there. Celia grunted in annoyance.

"Where did he go?" she complained.

"Nolan?" Serena yelled, sounding worried.

"Nolan?" Celia echoed but in an aggravated tone.

"Should we look for him?"

"I'm not going in there."

Serena sighed. "Neither am I."

"Nolan!" Celia shouted. Her voice seemed to echo off the trees.

They agreed to wait for a little longer. When their baskets

were full and could not hold anymore, neither could Celia's patience.

"I'm leaving without him."

"Just a moment," Serena practically pleaded. "Let me go look for him."

Celia's mouth dropped open. "Absolutely not!"

"I won't go far, I promise."

"Serena—" Celia began, but her sister was already gone, jogging through the bushes to where Nolan had entered the forest.

"Damn it, Serena," Celia cursed aloud and followed after her.

"You don't have to follow me," Serena called over her shoulder.

"I have to catch you so I can throw you in the river!" Celia shouted back.

The sound of Serena laughing up ahead made Celia smile. That ridiculous girl. She was too much like their father.

Celia stopped. It became quiet. Serena's laughter no longer came from up ahead. The sounds of the insects stopped. The world was quiet, heavy, and somehow darker.

"Serena?" Her voice came out too low to do any good, but she was afraid to be any louder. "Nolan?"

Celia felt her body locked in place. The shadows of the trees were deeper than before. They looked like silhouettes of darkness against the backdrop of the rest of the forest. She saw things within those shadows. Things that were familiar but strangely twisted, like a face in a broken mirror or a disturbed puddle.

She still couldn't move. Fear fused her joints together. Froze her blood and atrophied her muscles. Her lungs felt like iron plates. Even when she wanted to run, she couldn't force her body to respond. Her physical and mental self belonged to those things in the shadows. She kept telling herself to run. She remembered her father's smile. Her sister's laugh. Her breath came back to her. She croaked out a pitiful scream. The things in the dark made promises and threats. Celia felt her legs give, and she turned and, finally, ran.

It wasn't until she fell into the bushes and brush that she remembered she'd passed something on her way back out of the forest. A basket on its side, herbs spilled onto the ground.

"Serena!" she screamed. She sat there on the ground, shouting for her sister over and over again. Celia rested her arms on her knees, and she sat her head on her arms and cried; a heaving cry that soaked her shirt and sleeves. Then, she waited.

When darkness began to fall, she stood and walked in a daze back to the village. Her basket remained where she left it: on the ground by the woods where Serena and Nolan disappeared. Her foot hurt. She looked down and saw that one of her shoes had come off at some point. Once she entered town, a trail of single, bloody footprints followed her home.

Celia entered their small home and saw Serena's door open. For a moment, her heart raced at the thought her sister had come home. When she saw the empty room, she remembered that Serena never closed her door. A fresh wave of grief came over Celia.

She sat in a chair at the dinner table. Her father's leather gloves, which he used in the garden, sat on a shelf. They never moved them, left them as a reminder of him. "I'll find her, Papa."

At some point, a knock rapped on the door. Celia didn't remember asking anyone to enter, but she must have said something. The door opened slowly. Gregory entered with two guards following him, both carrying torches to light the darkness both outside and inside.

"Celia, thank the gods you're ok," he said as he ran over to her. "Are you hurt? Whose blood is outside?"

Celia looked over at him, reality coming back slowly. "What? Blood?"

"The footprints outside your house; they lead all the way from the entrance to town." His words were urgent and worried.

Celia looked down at her bare foot, turning it over to look at it for the first time. It was crisscrossed with cuts and covered in grass matted with dried blood.

"We need to get this treated. You two, go find Serena," he ordered.

"She's gone," Celia said flatly. All emotion had left her. "Serena and Nolan are gone."

"Gods," Gregory whispered, "what do you mean 'gone'?"

"They went into the woods. Now they're gone."

The guards looked at one another and then back to Gregory.

The apothecary pursed his lips. "Let's get this taken care of before it's infected. Then we'll talk."

The guards remained inside while Gregory lit candles to light up the dark interior of the house. He removed the satchel carried around his shoulder on a wide strap. He opened it and pulled out one item after another as though he'd prepared for this injury beforehand. One guard brought a basin of water. The other some clean rags. Gregory cleaned her wounds, applied tinctures and ointments, and then wrapped her foot.

All the while, Celia sat there stoic and unflinching. Nothing ran through her mind. Her body and soul were numb.

"There. You two can leave now. I'll stay with her and find out what happened."

"You'll let us know, Gregory?" One of the guards asked.

"Of course."

When the door closed, the inside of the home was silent. Celia continued to stare, bleary and red-eyed, at her father's gardening gloves. Gregory pulled a seat over so he could look at

Celia as they spoke. Her eyes went past him. He took her hands in his. They were soft yet bony.

"What happened, Celia? Tell me everything," he said empathetically. His voice was low and warm.

Celia was silent at first. After a few moments, she managed to put words together. She told him about the herbs, about Serena and Nolan, and their young flirtations. She told him about Nolan going into the woods and disappearing. Gregory then interjected with a question.

"He left you two alone and walked into the woods?"

"Not very far," Celia added. "We could still see him."

Celia explained that she and Serena were both surprised to see him gone. Then Serena ran after him, and she went after Serena. Tears threatened to come back but never materialized. Celia told of how she'd passed Serena's basket on her way out of the forest. That her sister simply disappeared.

"What shadows?" Gregory asked.

"Shadows?" Celia replied in confusion. She'd never mentioned shadows.

"You said you saw things in the shadows? What things? Animals? Could that be what took Serena and Nolan?"

"I never said anything about shadows ..." Celia said hesitantly.

"Yes, dear, you went into quite the amount of detail. It sounded like you were quite traumatized."

Celia felt a twinge of that earlier fear. She swore she never talked about the things in the forest, but there was no hint of deception in Gregory's face or voice.

"I ... I did see something, but I don't know what it was."

Gregory placed the back of his wrist on her forehead. "You don't have a fever, that's good."

She wanted to protest that she knew what she was talking about, but that meant admitting she might have talked about something she didn't remember talking about in the first place.

Gregory checked her over and told her that she was fine, other than the cuts and bruises on her foot.

"Gregory, what happened to my sister?" Celia asked. She didn't know if he'd have any answers, but she wanted any comfort that could be offered. Even if it was just lip-service.

He shook his head just slightly. His head slowly rolled back until he was looking up at the ceiling. He put his hands in his pockets. "I don't know, Celia. But two guards are looking now, and one of their own is missing, as well. They won't give up."

No regrets. Celia would have to put her father's words to the test for her sister and for Nolan.

"IT'S BEEN OVER A MONTH," Celia said, her words filled with heated accusations. The worst part of all this was not knowing what happened to her sister or Nolan.

"We've been looking every day," the captain of the guard returned. She had to admit that his eyes appeared tired and empathetic. "Nolan went missing, too, not just your sister. We haven't given up on them."

"You haven't?" Celia rebutted. She sighed and put her hands on her hips. Then, she lifted one hand and rubbed her eyes with a thumb and forefinger. "I'm sorry," she said. "I don't know what to do. I've looked and looked. Went against everything my mind and body were screaming at me to not do and went back to where they went missing ..."

Her voice caught, and she felt her throat tingle with promised grief. The captain stood from his desk and walked around to her, his boots clicking on the stone floor. He put his hands on her shoulders.

"We'll keep looking. But you need to be prepared. At this point, we're most likely looking for their bodies, Celia."

He spoke without hesitation like he'd prepared them beforehand. They still came out coated in sympathy and care, though.

Celia nodded and sniffled. She wiped her eyes with the back of her hand and left the captain behind at his desk.

Outside, the first cool wind of autumn struck her, almost taking her breath away. It carried the weight of portent, and she shuddered at more than just the cold. She went home, refusing to come back outside. She built a roaring fire that evening, one that was sure to keep going long after she went to sleep.

"HOW ARE YOU DOING, CELIA?" the old baker's wife asked. She was a sweet lady, plump and rosy-cheeked, with a voice like a bell. It startled Celia from her thoughts, which had grown darker by the day. The previous night brought little sleep despite the fire. Autumn was approaching quickly, and the townsfolk felt the cold coming in. Talk of the incoming harvests buzzed amid rumors of early snow.

"I am getting better, Ms. Kindlin. Thank you for asking," she lied. Her tone probably was not convincing whatsoever.

A small loaf of bread slid into her view. "Here you go, dear," the bell tolled softly. "You should really eat more. It is going to be alright."

Celia gingerly took the bread in her hands and looked over at Ms. Kindlin, who smiled at her. Her eyes were sad, though, and Celia saw pity in them.

"Thank you," said Celia with as much genuine gratitude as she could muster.

She placed the bread in her basket along with the other

meager goods for which she had the strength to shop. Without her sister, she felt her resilience draining away. The mystery of her disappearance only made it worse.

After returning home, Celia took out the bread and the small jar of honey she had traded for. She managed a few bites before the tears and bile rose again.

"Damn it," she muttered, seething.

Celia got up and threw on her cloak. She grabbed a knife the blacksmith had given her—apparently, it came out "deficient," and she bartered for it at a large discount. All she wanted was something sharp. She hoped her anger could do the rest. At this point, she didn't even care if she came back alive.

It was still early in the day. If she left now, she would have plenty of daylight to search again. Maybe in a different area this time.

Regardless of her intentions or the plans made on her way out of town and toward the west ridge, she became lost in a storm of random thoughts and scattered ideas. Every time the wind blew, it came in quick gusts, plucking up shadows from the ground and causing them to billow up and out like flocks of ghostly crows.

Celia felt dizzy. She kept walking, forcing one step after the other. If she passed out here on the outskirts of town, who knew what would happen to her. The dark things ... they could come for her.

Her head suddenly cleared like the sun breaking through storm clouds. The actual sun blinded her with its brilliance. It felt like she'd walked out of a pitch-black room into midday. One hand reflexively went up and shielded her stinging eyes. The forest of the west ridge spread out before her, beckoning her. She didn't remember walking long enough to be this far.

It didn't matter. No regrets.

The forest looked different. All these years, it was intimidating to face the shadows and not know what waited in there—natural or otherwise. Celia always pushed that fear down, just like she did everything else. Life wouldn't care about her fears. No regrets.

But now, the forest looked mundane. It induced neither fear nor serenity, which her sister often felt the flowers invoked. It was a collection of wood, leaves, and blossoms. Tall grasses and creatures of various kinds. Nothing more.

She walked through the flowers and herbs and felt them crushing under her feet. The cool shade of the trees washed over her, nearly audible in the way it devoured the shining sun. Underneath the canopy, it was peaceful. No birds, no insects, no townspeople gossiping and haggling. It was cool and quiet.

Why did she hate it so much?

Oh yes—it had taken her sister. And Nolan, the poor guard.

Something caught her eye. Celia turned and saw a large discolored patch on one of the trees. It wrapped partly around one of the trunks. It was an irregular shape, and she thought that it was just moss or something similar at first. On closer inspection, it was some kind of stain. It smelled strange, so she turned and let it be, her nose curling at the stench.

The forest didn't seem as frightening, but it seemed lonely. Like nothing living other than the trees called it home. She saw more of the strange, discolored patches on other trees as she walked. A sound swelled up in her ears, like thousands of birds and insects chirping and chittering all at once. It had an echoing quality, as though the sound originated from deep in a cave. That's when she felt her blood chill again.

The shadows between the trees became darker, much as they did when Serena had disappeared. The black shade quivered and stopped, quivered and stopped as though it were some flexing muscle. Thin strands of the darkness snaked out on the ground, crawling towards her. Celia ran. No screaming or crying, only her legs pumping as fast as they could go. The darkness and its coiling fingers seemed to close in around her, but she broke into the blinding light of the field beyond the forest's edge and felt like she'd crossed a veil into another world. A safer one.

Her chest hurt like she'd been holding her breath for too long. Her tongue felt dry and swollen. Pressure built within her forehead and gave Celia a headache. She began walking along the treeline, heading east towards the river and the waterfall. Celia never entered the forest. She didn't have the courage. Walking didn't help her build any nerve. The interior of the woods appeared normal, but she feared what waited for the moment she stepped inside. Worse, she knew to some extent what waited. She walked until she reached the river, and the sun began to edge low on the horizon.

"I'll wait for you," Celia said aloud in a soft voice. Her sister was in there, somewhere. Serena's presence was there, just on the edge of awareness. Celia knew it.

All that was left was to return to town.

Days. Weeks. Months. They all passed, slow and lonely. Gregory offered advice and medicines for Celia's depression and sleepless nights. At least once a week, she had a nightmare about chasing after Serena, only for her to disappear once more. Her dreams taunted her relentlessly by replaying the heartwrenching moment over and over again.

Celia had tried returning to the forested ridge and searching for Serena. Every time Celia went, whether to gather materials for Gregory and other townsfolk or simply to continue looking for her sister, she could never once enter the cold shadows under that canopy. "No regrets," she repeated to herself, but her father's words held no more strength for her.

Thus, each day she spent in a misery-induced haze. She ate to sustain her strength. She used her strength to work and trade. She used her work and trade to be able to eat and sleep under a roof. All the positive words from friends and strangers alike did nothing to persuade her to move on. Her sister had been all Celia had. Her only family, her only real friend.

Things continued this way until a stranger, mysterious and unique, came to town. Their arrival prompted a wave of fresh gossip and concern among those in authority. No sooner had this stranger entered town than they were called before the town council: the mayor, captain of the guard, merchant lord, and judge.

People whispered about what they were doing here and why their interview with the council took so long. Some were excited. Others were cautious. Celia could not have cared less.

The one thing she took note of along with everyone else was the stranger's robes. They were very clean for someone who must have been traveling the roads. The hems were not torn or muddied, not even frayed. The material used to make them glistened but also seemed so black as to soak up the light. Black leather gloves covered their hands. Their heavy cowl covered their face in shadow so that no one yet knew if they were a man, woman, or even human.

When the stranger emerged, those present, Celia included, watched them depart with measured elegance from the wood-laced stone council building. Both hands worked to remove the leather gloves. The pale skin revealed them to be human, at least.

The hands gracefully rose to grip the sides of the cowl in a three-fingered pinch. After the shadow lifted from the face, the stranger was revealed to be a man. The cowl settled just beneath jet-black hair trimmed short. Gray eyes quickly scanned the surroundings. His brow was slightly furrowed, but his chin was up. He knew what he was looking for but not quite where to find it.

One hand ran through his hair and then slid over his clean-shaven face. A very handsome, clean-shaven face, Celia had to admit. She smirked. Women old and young had a sparkle in their eyes now. Some of the men frowned. She could tell by the look in their eyes that the merchants smelled fresh blood in the water.

Apparently, he found what he was looking for. His eyes stopped, meeting Celia's for a moment. She felt a touch of tangled nerves as his measured walk brought him straight toward her. Then, she realized he was walking past her. To the inn. His eyes met hers again for a moment as he passed her, and she felt embarrassed.

One of the old women smiled at her. Celia rolled her eyes and returned to what she was doing before. After finishing her chores and errands, she returned home. It was interesting seeing a new traveler in town; it was nice, if momentary, and a distraction from everything.

THE FOLLOWING morning was brisk and windy. It was getting colder by the day. Celia dressed in thick layers and could still feel a touch of chill through them. Gregory asked for a special batch of herbs today. It was an unusual request. He didn't typically need ingredients of this kind. Work was work, however, and it would take Celia back to the forest ridge.

She stood at the edge of town, holding her basket in one arm and pulling her scarf tighter with her free hand. She somewhat dreaded this trip. The cold, combined with going back to that place to once again be hurt and disappointed, left a sour taste in her mouth.

"May I join you?" someone asked from behind her.

Her brows knitted, and she turned. It was the black-robed stranger.

"Uh ... no," she said bluntly. "No offense, but I have no idea who you are. Why are you asking me?"

"Gregory asked that I assist you," he said with a hint of a disarming smile.

"And how long have you known Gregory?" she questioned sardonically.

"About fourteen hours." His reply was deadpan.

She scoffed. "Why did he ask you to assist me? I've fetched his ingredients for years."

"I'm assuming they're not his usual order."

"How do you know that?"

"Because I asked him for them."

Celia bit her tongue. She looked at him and tried to gauge his intent as much as possible. His gaze was soft but focused. The smile still lingered on his lips.

"No guard?" she asked.

"Someone of my talents doesn't need a guard."

"It's not for you," Celia replied pointedly.

"You don't trust strangers, I get that," he tried to explain. Celia raised her eyebrows.

He continued in his attempt to convince her. "Your council trusts me."

"After one day?"

"After what I told them? Yes." His reply was cryptic but resolute. "If it makes you feel better, he'll be there, too." The stranger pointed to a guard standing a few dozen feet back. Celia's eyes widened. She hadn't seen him there before; such was her distraction and surprise from the stranger.

Realization hit, and her face grew hot. "You were playing with me."

The stranger chuckled. "I was. Let's go," he said as he walked past her. The guard followed and grinned at Celia. Was the entire town trying to piss her off?

They began their walk to the ridge, across grass fading from summer green to autumn's golden colors. Trees began their transition, as well. The leaves shifted to reds and yellows that Celia once thought bright and beautiful. Now, their colors dulled in her eyes and gave the impression of blood and bile.

The wind kicked up, sending some early-fallen leaves swirling in the air and skittering along the ground. She wrapped her arms tighter around herself, the handle of her basket hooked through her right arm.

"Gods, it's getting cold," the guard commented. She never asked his name.

"It is," the stranger replied. He flexed his gloved fingers and began making some strange hand gestures. He muttered some words, unlike anything Celia had heard before. She recognized its source from stories, though—and from what followed them. She felt a warmth come over her as though a fireplace suddenly sprang up beside them. Her breath was no longer visible, and her eyes were no longer tearing up from the cold wind.

Celia rubbed her hands together one last time before relaxing her arms. Her muscles finally felt relief from tightening due to the cold. "I've never seen magic before. Honestly, I thought it was dead."

"Magic is never dead." The stranger replied, with a hint of a lilt in his voice. "If anything, it grows stronger. Well, most magic."

"Most magic?" Celia asked with genuine curiosity. She had only ever read and heard of magic as a practice. Most of the time, it was told from the viewpoint of possibly being what destroyed the world. Magi weren't looked upon favorably for centuries. If anyone in town knew how to use it, they kept it to themselves. She'd never heard of different kinds of magic.

"Magic comes in many forms. Like food. Hot, cold, savory, spicy, bland, sweet."

She glanced over at his dark robes. "What kind do you practice?"

"Most magi practice combinations, depending on developed skill and innate talent. There are five sects. I'm most adept at the First and Fourth."

"That doesn't tell us peasants much," Celia replied, grimacing.

He replied with a smile in his voice. "The First Sect is what you just witnessed. Harnessing raw magic to trap heat within a sphere focused on our location. A touch of the Second Sect was used to pull heat from the ground in order to warm us up."

"Oh, that's ... actually very interesting. And the Fourth?"

"The magic of death, decay, and entropy, for the most part."

Celia's footsteps slowed. She felt a sudden hesitation to ask more. The stranger must have noticed, because he turned to look at her before slowing his own pace.

"What is it?" he asked, sounding like he knew something was amiss.

"Death? Decay? I don't know what entropy is, but if it's associated with the others ..."

She glanced back at the guard. He didn't say a word, but warily watched the stranger in the black robes with a hand on his sword grip.

The stranger barked a quick laugh. "I'm not here to kill anyone for my gods, if that's what concerns you. Your council would've likely seen me hang in the square first, don't you think?"

Given her feelings about the council in general, she chose not to answer.

"Death is a part of life. Decay is the natural end for most things. Ultimately, entropy is a nice way of saying the ultimate destination of all existence is formless chaos. This is a natural progression, I don't intend to make anything unnatural of it."

"Like murdering us with your magic out in the woods?" The words came out reeking of brutal candor, but she didn't mind at all.

The stranger laughed openly this time. "If I wanted to kill people with my magic I could've easily done so. I'm no master, but I'm not a student, either. Trust me, this guard is here for your own emotional support. I can handle anything that comes after us—well, most things. Including him, if I wanted."

Celia turned to look at the guard a few steps behind them. He grimaced and his face grew red. She thought she saw a slight flash in his eyes, but if it was there, it passed quickly.

The warmth of the heating spell made her wonder if it was something to truly comfort her or put her off her guard. She didn't exactly let her guard down before, but she certainly kept it up even more so, now.

They continued their walk in silence until it was broken by the mage's voice once more.

"You know, I think part of the problem is that we haven't even been introduced."

There was a pregnant pause.

"I'm Cole." He said, attempting to be as friendly as possible.

"Interesting," Celia replied. Cole's eyes widened momentarily. Apparently, he wasn't a stranger anymore. "Did your mother name you that because of the hair, the robe, or your soul?"

He ran a hand through his thick hair. It looked like it had been taken better care of than her own.

"I didn't have hair when I was born. Or the robe. My soul is my own business, thank you."

Celia nodded. "Ok, fair enough. I'm Celia."

"Nice to meet you, Celia," Cole said, turning to her and smiling.

"I'm Glynn," came a voice from behind them. They both turned to see the guard give a curt nod to them both. Celia stared for a moment, having forgotten he was there.

"Nice to meet you, Glynn," she replied awkwardly.

"Now that we're friends—" Cole began.

"Don't get ahead of yourself." Celia interrupted.

"Now that we're friends, why do you come out here for the apothecary? Are you the only one?"

Celia pursed her lips. "My sister used to come with me. We gathered herbs and such for others in town. It's what we traded. Our jobs, more or less."

"I can see why. It's quite a walk. Useful, too, though." He added casually.

"Yes. We get by quite well. Well ..." she trailed off after the use of 'we.' She sighed and Cole looked slowly over at her.

"Gregory mentioned your sister." His tone was soft.

Her eyebrows knitted together. "Why? That doesn't make any sense. Why would he share something like that with a stranger?"

Her voice grew angrier with each word. Cole put a hand up.

"He said that you've been having a very rough time. You keep going out to look for her. When I mentioned I needed some unique ingredients of my own he wanted us to go together. He hoped my specialties would either help bring you some kind of closure or at least give you more information."

After his explanation, she calmed down significantly. That made sense. Gregory was looking out for her. She still didn't appreciate being sent out with a strange mage and one guard.

Not that anyone in town would know how to handle a mage, anyway.

"Well, you are about to find out. It's just up ahead." She pointed to the trees that hid the ridge up ahead. The land dipped then sloped back upwards to a dark green wave cresting underneath a gray, cloudy sky. Once more, she was back at the worst place on Alda. One familiar and strange. This time, she also had a death-mage with her.

"WELL, THIS IS DIFFERENT," Cole said when they arrived at the multiple patches of herbs and flowers in front of the ridge. "Is this typical here?"

Celia shook her head. "No. You won't find clusters like this anywhere else along the forest's edge. I think perhaps a shipment of herbs, plants, seeds, or some combination wound up deposited here; perhaps it grew and flourished over time."

"Couldn't have been a good thing that caused it all to be left here," Cole remarked.

"My thoughts exactly."

He smiled. "Well, let's see what I can find then."

"Do you know what you're looking for?"

His eyes scanned the colorful quilt around them. "Scarlet Milkweed. Some call it bloodflower."

She mumbled as she thought, then said, "That won't grow here. Too cold during the winters."

"Fairywand?" he asked.

"I've heard of it. Gregory doesn't ask for it, though."

"You know your ingredients." He said with a touch of approval in his voice.

"I told you, this is our ... my job."

"Do you know how to read?"

"Yes, I do."

"Ever thought of apprenticing for Gregory?"

Celia shrugged. "Never had much interest. I enjoyed coming out here with my sister. Not many people want to go this far for 'herbs and flowers,' or so they say. But they pay for it well enough."

The bushes and plants rustled quietly as Cole made his way slowly through them, watching the ground. "I bet they do. The use of magic and magic-adjacent practices have long been frowned upon."

It was quiet again but for the slight rustling of their search and the occasional yawn from Glynn the Guard.

"I'm sorry about your sister," Cole said, cutting the quiet. He sounded genuine. "I don't have any siblings, myself. But, I do have family."

Celia wanted to keep her thoughts off her sister as much as possible. This close to the forest, it was almost too much to ask.

"Then, why aren't you with them?"

It was a poignant question. She'd never leave her sister's side again if she had the choice.

"I, like you, have a job to do, as well. It takes me far from home."

Celia licked her lips. They'd gone dry from the cold. With Cole farther away, the heating spell must have followed him and left her behind. The chill had begun to seep in more and more since they began searching. She took her flask from her hip pouch and drank.

"Understandable," she replied after slaking her thirst.

Cole stuttered for a moment, then finally managed to get out a question. "Can you tell me what happened?"

Celia's breath caught for a moment, then she sighed heavily. "I've told the story over and over. Ask Gregory or the captain of the guard or one of the other damn council members. I am not repeating it again."

After a moment, Cole asked, "Please. Gregory wanted me to help you, too."

"I thought death was a part of life? Why should you pursue this anymore?" she answered curtly.

Cole crossed his arms. "I thought you insisted she was alive?"

A scornful laugh escaped Celia's mouth. "Gods, is there anything Gregory didn't tell you? Are you aware of my feminine cycle? Should we find some herbs to help with that?"

Cole pointed somewhere on the ground nearby. "Fennel." He said flatly. "It's ... supposed to help with ... that."

Her mouth gaped open, and her anger flared. "How d—"

Cole raised his hands as though he was conceding, but she knew it was also meant to apologize and try to calm her.

Puffs of air came in small clouds from her mouth as her mind floundered. She glared at him, but he merely stared at her in return, lowering his head slightly. His eyes were soft but resolute. His expression stern.

"*Gah*, fine. I refuse to think she's dead. No one has found her body or Nolan's, the guard that came with us. I felt her presence. I feel it *every* time I come here. I *know* she's alive."

A warm, wet sensation filled Celia's eyes. She didn't want the tears, but they came, regardless. Her lip quivered and warm streaks fell down her face, but she refused to weep.

Cole nodded slowly. He uncrossed his arms and looked around. She wasn't sure if it was an awkward gesture, but he lifted his chin toward the forest and called out.

"Well, look at that. Fairywand."

He walked over to the cylindrical clusters of tiny white flowers and beckoned her over. She helped him pluck them and begin laying them gently in her basket.

"Death is our destiny, Celia," he began, speaking tenderly and slowly. "We are grains of sand in a vast, unfeeling ocean.

Once we come to terms with that, it provides a level of peace. Even purpose."

Celia sniffled, in part due to the cold. She felt the heat of the insulation spell begin to warm her bones, though. "Is that what your gods teach you?"

"I don't worship gods," he replied plainly. "Our ancestors worshiped gods. Some people today still do, holding on to a hope that no longer exists. I live in reality."

The fairywand snapped as her plucking grew more intense. She felt a sermon coming. "I suppose you're going to preach to me now?"

A soft chuckle and sly smile. "No preaching."

They continued their harvest until her basket was nearly half full. "I need to stop with the fairywand. Gregory wanted some things of his own."

Cole wiped the beads of sweat from his forehead. "Of course. Lead the way."

They continued plucking and pruning until Celia had everything she needed and wanted. A few of the things she picked for herself would help her sleep tonight.

"You lied to me," she accused, quietly, as they both stood once they were finished.

"About what?" he replied in a tone indicating he was not worried about her claim.

Celia hesitated, pondering if she was overthinking. But she decided it was too obvious. "You said you came looking for fairywand. You acted like we were searching for it, but you walked straight toward it as you pretended to 'look.'"

"Well, damn," he sighed.

Glynn took a step toward them. A scowl caused his beard to turn crooked on his face.

"What do you want?" she asked. "Give a good answer before

this turns ugly. Not that there's much we can do to stop you, I suppose."

The arms hidden within the dark, glossy robes crossed across Cole's chest. "Gregory and I were discussing medicine. He asked about potions that could soothe nerves or ease heartache. He heard about magic that could do such things. I was curious and knew he wouldn't ask about such things lightly. The conversation turned to you. I wanted to help."

"You're still lying," Celia said, and Glynn stepped closer.

"It's getting late. Too late for what I really want to do to help." Cole regarded the forest. "You say she disappeared in there?"

Celia hesitated, the memory still painful. The wound still fresh. She nodded stiffly.

"We'll come back tomorrow. No harvesting. No gathering. We'll go in where you last saw her and investigate. Together."

"I've looked many times. Others have, too. Do you have some kind of magic that could help?"

He turned back to look at her. His gray eyes turned a shade darker. "Perhaps."

Despite being in the confines of the insulation spell again, she crossed her arms at an imagined chill.

"Being this close ... something is in there. You're right. About the shadows."

Celia wanted to be angry at Gregory and Cole yet again, but at this point she wasn't surprised that the apothecary shared that, too.

"I can feel it from here."

She took a breath that shuddered slightly. "We should go look now," she said, the words coming out before she could stop them.

He shook his head. "No. We don't want to be in there when the sun gets low."

"I thought there was nothing you couldn't handle out here?" she chided, with a hint of mockery.

"I said 'most things.' I am not toying with whatever that is when the sunlight fades."

"Ok," she acquiesced. "Let's return home, then."

The three of them gathered together to keep warm as the cold grew more intense. As they walked away, Celia turned to look back at the forest. It seemed to be even darker within the trees than before. She stole a glance at Cole, who looked straight ahead, his eyes still a darker shade of gray, like a patient storm.

THE CLOUDS HUNG like a gray blanket over the landscape the following day. Light winds meant less chill and Cole did not need to use his insulating spell for their trip. No guard accompanied them. Both Cole and Celia wanted to travel alone and she and Gregory vouched for the mage.

The whole walk there was rather quiet. Celia had assured Gregory upon their return yesterday that Cole had been helpful and they wanted to investigate further together. The apothecary and the mage seemed to share some sort of bond already, as Gregory looked to Cole when Celia said this and the mage nodded.

When they drew closer once more to the ridge, Celia felt pressed to ask, "Why do you want to help me? Is that all you came here for? Is it some magical thing?"

He smirked. "No, my purpose for coming to your town is a completely separate issue. In fact, I have to get back to said issue upon our return. I'm a people person, you could say. I noticed something different about you compared to the other townsfolk."

She still did not like how that sounded, but let it be. He could have done horrible things and worse to her and the guard yesterday, but he didn't. Celia tried to focus on the positive. Someone who, possibly, really could protect her if it came down to it escorted her to help her look for her sister. Someone who knew magic and might actually provide new information.

Eventually, the bleak, deep green spread of trees marking the forest on the ridge loomed before them. A hopeless weight settled onto Celia again. She prepared herself for more disappointment.

Cole's eyes once again turned a stormy gray. He stared into the woods. "Are you ready?"

His voice was grave and cold. Celia began to wonder if she really wanted to follow him. She clenched her fists until her knuckles popped. No regrets.

"Yes," she replied with gravitas equaling his own.

They entered together, side by side into the otherworld of the shadowed woods. Celia couldn't remember the last time she had felt this uncomfortable. Cole's presence may have played a part in it. It was the first time someone accompanied her to look for her sister since the first investigation by the captain of the guard. It was also the first time she'd been alone with someone in here. But there was something else. Some unease she couldn't explain. It was directly tied to Cole, this much she knew. He was a death mage, though. Perhaps he just exuded that sort of feeling inside the confines of a gods-forsaken forest.

"There's a lot of power here," he said in a low voice. "A lot of resonance of the Fourth Sect. Someone was busy here, long ago."

"This place is evil," Celia hissed. "This is the type of place you are familiar with, death mage?"

Cole scowled at the remark. "Priests often get caught with their hands in the temple coffers. Guards manipulate shop owners. Apothecaries sell fake medicines. There are those who mishandle their authority and power all the time. My people are no different."

She gave him a cautious look. "What sort of things could they have been up to? What is wrong with the forest?"

He stopped. The soft sound of rustling robes was the only noise heard. Cole looked around, his neck craning and heels pivoting as he took in the forest around them.

"Who knows. But the resonance is getting stronger."

He peered into the distance, squinting his eyes. Suddenly he began walking again and made straight for a particular tree. Celia followed and saw that it was one with the discoloration on the side. Cole sneered.

"What is it?"

He crossed his arms and looked over at her. An eyebrow raised and he appeared hesitant. He turned away, stared for a moment, then went to another tree. This one also had the discoloration. They continued to walk and found several more.

"Did you notice this the previous times you came here?" he asked, referencing the splotches.

"Yes. I assumed it was just moss or something. A discoloration in the trees."

Cole scratched his chin. "I'm afraid not."

"Then what is it?"

The rise and fall of his shoulders was the only giveaway that he let out a deep breath.

"What remains of a human being."

Celia's jaw dropped. She felt dizzy. It couldn't be. She couldn't have walked past these so many times and not noticed it was blood.

"It doesn't look like blood." Her voice came out weak and cracked.

"Blood. Some tiny viscera. Not very noticeable. Some of the stains are older than others. The trees should have grown over them, but that doesn't seem to be the case." His voice lowered as he leaned over and looked closer at one of the more visible patches. "These people were utterly disintegrated."

She put a hand over her mouth. Then, she turned and emptied her stomach all over the forest floor. Her face felt hot from the exertion and from embarrassment. She took a large swig from her water canteen and rinsed out her mouth.

Cole had a slight smirk on his face as he put a hand on her shoulder. "It's certainly not pleasant."

"What did this?" she asked, trembling after vomiting.

"I don't know. I'm not sure I want to."

"But—"

"Don't say anything about me being a death mage." He interrupted, his voice brusque. "I'm starting to find that particularly agitating."

"I'm sorry," she returned.

"Magi study. Not all magic is known to everyone, even the masters. I'm nowhere near that talented or skilled. Magic doesn't mean we can snap our fingers and find answers. I know the Fourth Sect is very strong here. I thought it was because of some practicing magi from times past. Maybe one of the Inheritors' offspring was attracted to the lingering magic or maybe it was the other way around and the magi came to worship or study the thing. I don't know. I do know that something resides in these woods and it is old and it is powerful. We need to leave."

"We were looking for my sister," Celia reminded him.

He put his hand gently on her upper arm. "I'm sorry, Celia, I truly am. But, your sister and the other guard—" he shook his head, "they can't have survived whatever is here."

Once again, her jaw fell. Her eyes felt warm and her throat tingled.

"I felt her presence," Celia said with a hint of desperation. "You are a magi, you know that has to mean something!"

His eyes darted around. Cole began to look visibly nervous. "I can explain that later, but you're reaching out with your own potential now. It can sense you, too. Your love for your sister is empowering it."

"I don't understand." Celia's voice broke. She pulled away from him. "Are you going to help me or not?"

"As much as I can," he answered, but his focus was no longer on her. He looked around, his mouth open and his hands apart as though he were going to grab something. "But the thing in these woods, the shadows you saw, they do not enjoy the feelings you have for your sister. We have to go, *now*."

That's when she felt it. The same sensation the last time the forest changed in her eyes and the shadows of the trees turned black as the night sky. She saw something in the shadows, but couldn't make out what it was. Despite looking right at it, her eyes refused to focus; refused to register in her brain what she was seeing.

Faster than she could comprehend, Cole shouted more of the strange, lilting words and his hands flashed in a series of short gestures. He grabbed Celia and they shot off like an arrow, her head snapping back. Branches flicked her skin painfully. The sound of black robes fluttering violently. The wind pulled at her hair. It was exhilarating and terrifying all at once.

Suddenly, she saw light and felt herself crash onto the ground. Cole was holding her tightly. Though they only fell a few feet, he'd grunted from the impact and groaned as they lay there on the ground. His robes fell around her and smelled of both earthy and flowery odors.

"That hurt," he grunted. Celia felt his arms relax and was able to make her way to her feet.

Both of them stood shakily. Cole slapped at his robes to remove leaves and twigs. Celia still felt her hands trembling.

Under normal circumstances, that might have been entertaining.

"Shit," Cole cursed, leaning forward and putting his hands on his knees. "That was close. Very, very close." He stood up straight. "You survived that on your own?"

His tone heavily suggested he didn't believe it.

"Yes," she replied simply. "Whatever 'that' was. What about our escape?" she asked, her voice rising with the question. "That magic was, well, impressive. Not that I have anything to compare it against."

"Survival instinct. I've never actually used the spell before. It is supposed to be an escape method for those of us who travel."

"It worked."

"Indeed it did." He sounded surprised with himself.

As her heart settled down, Celia began collecting her thoughts. A lot of words, names, and phrases were turning through her head. A lot of things that sounded absolute that she didn't like.

"Cole. Can you explain what is going on? You were describing a lot of things I'd never heard of. I think it may be time you do some preaching."

He pulled a twig from his robes, the sharp end taking a strand of fabric with it. He patted a few spots of his robe down and then ran a hand through his hair.

"What would you like to know about?"

Celia mulled over the possibilities. She didn't quite know where to start, either. But, it only took a moment to go with the obvious choice.

"Let's start with this: why are you certain my sister is dead?"

He nodded softly as if he understood perfectly why this was her first question.

"You really think she survived what we just went through? A town guard is nothing against that."

"I survived," she shot back quickly.

He sighed and shook his head. "That's ... that is a little different."

"A little?"

"You have something working in your favor that she likely did not." He spoke slowly as if he were carefully choosing his words.

"And what would that be?" Celia pressed.

"You have a connection with magic that may have helped you survive."

"I have absolutely no magic powers," Celia scoffed.

"Again, magic isn't something you snap your fingers to and make things happen. You can be tethered to a particular kind of magic and not have any talent to use it whatsoever. And if you don't know about your connection, then you certainly wouldn't. I've grown up around magic, but I am still aware that its practice is all but extinct in most parts of the world. I assure you, though, you have it."

"How did it protect me?"

He shrugged. "All I have is conjecture. I've heard the Fifth Sect can outright guard you against the Inheritors and their children. In your case, I can only assume it was curious about you since your connection is middling at best, and unrefined. It probably looked at you like a stray dog, perhaps."

She chuckled dryly. "That's flattering. What is this Fifth Sect I'm connected to?"

He raised a hand and frowned. "I wasn't finished explaining. You aren't connected with the Fifth Sect. You, like me, are tethered to the Fourth."

She grimaced and cocked her head. Celia waved the idea away. "I'm not connected with death magic," she concluded.

Cole rolled his eyes. "It's not death magic, Celia. There's more to it than that."

"How do you know about this connection?" she asked, her tone giving away her impatience.

His expression changed. It didn't harden, necessarily, but it did show further resolve. "I noticed it when I first saw you on the street. After I left the council chambers. It's one of my gifts and why I do what I do. I can sense magic auras. It makes the residual magic like what lies in those woods resonate even stronger for me."

Celia gritted her teeth. That was the look he gave her. He noticed this magical tethering.

"Anything else you're hiding?" she asked, with an edge to the question.

"I've never hidden anything."

He barely finished speaking before Celia said, accusingly, "Did you bring me out here as bait for that thing? Some kind of experiment?"

"What? No." he huffed in exasperation, "When Gregory told me about your sister, I was curious about the link between her disappearance and what you said you saw in the woods. I wanted to investigate with you, not use you to some other end."

Her response was cold. "How can I believe that?"

"Because I could have left you there to die. Easily."

Cole actually sounded wounded. Her accusations pierced him. Celia felt a tinge of regret but was still hesitant to believe him. Her father always said she was the more stubborn of his two daughters.

"You're saying my sister is ..." she could not finish the thought out loud, though Cole completed her thought as it echoed painfully in her brain.

"Dead, Celia. Just as you've been told. Her remains are right there. On one of those trees."

Tears fell freely down her cheeks. She couldn't stop them.

But Celia refused to let out any cries of anguish. That would be giving in. It still didn't explain one thing.

"I can still feel her. Even now." she choked out with all the strength she could muster.

"That could be the influence of whatever's in the woods. Your sister is gone, I promise you."

Cole's words were desperate, pleading. Perhaps he wasn't here for some sinister purpose. However, it didn't change what she had to do.

Turning sharply, Celia stormed toward the forest again. She made it a few steps before a strong hand grabbed her upper arm.

"Where are you going?" Cole asked.

"I'm done with this. Let go of me, Cole. I'm not coming out until I find Serena or I'm dead."

"You and I both know how that's going to turn out."

"We don't," she replied harshly, her voice cracking from lingering sorrow.

"Celia, I don't know what's in there, but I have an educated guess. This will not end well for you."

"You keep saying things like that, but none of it makes sense," she shouted at him. "Did your people do this? Who are 'your people?' What do you want?"

He released her arm and stepped back. A wry smile crossed his face. "I never got to preach, did I?"

Celia turned back to him, breathing heavily. She swallowed and nodded.

"I'm a mage. Not a cleric or a priest. But my order does worship very powerful things. I guess you could say we're a bit of both mage and missionary. The people of the old world worshipped gods and goddesses, both light and dark, and everything in between. Not all of them were wrong in doing so, actually. It's just that there is something greater. Something above the simple deities of man, dwarf, and elf-kind. Something above and beyond the limits of time and even reality."

Celia's muscles relaxed. Cole's words didn't sound practiced. They were genuine. His voice was soothing, and it provided a pleasant distraction.

"My order is called the Black Gnarl. Since the First Kin walked Alda, our order has been there. The founder was one of them. The Black Gnarl wants to return the world to its original Creator: The Obscured Throne. The First Kin stole Alda from its Creator."

"And the thing in the woods? What does that have to do with this?"

Cole looked at his hands, opening them palm up like he wanted to hold something. "Think of the Obscured Throne as a gardener with many gardens. One of Its gardens is Alda. The plants are the Inheritors. All different in ways pleasing to the Throne. Like herbs, they're different; some serve different purposes that may overlap with others. They're affected by their environment."

He gestured to the woods. "Things such as that dwelling in the forest are like the creatures attracted to the plants. Some are aphids. Some are bees, and bees sting."

Celia crossed her arms and frowned. "Bees sting. They don't devour people and leave nothing but bloody stains behind."

"Have you ever seen the bees further south?" Cole joked. Celia didn't respond, and he understood his poor timing.

"So what are we?" Celia asked. "Are we the dirt?"

He shook his head. "No. We don't matter enough to be the dirt. We're not even nutrients from the soil. We're the space in between the dirt, so inconsequential as we are."

Celia dropped her arms. "So why even bother with what you're doing?"

Cole shrugged. "A lot of people ask that of those who seek a higher power. Why should the gods notice anyone? And the Throne is above even the gods."

"I don't care about the Throne or the gods," Celia replied, turning her head to look at the forest. "But at least you explained the shadows in the forest. A little."

He gestured to the forest as he spoke: "That's not an Inheritor. Otherwise, neither of us would be able to do much of anything. It's one of the insects. More like a wasp than a bee. To get outside my analogy, it's more like a wolf. Now that it understands you and your Fourth Sect limitations, it won't hesitate to take you. I gave it pause, but barely. Your arcane connection is a stronger smell but also a bigger deterrent. When I became involved, it probably lashed out."

Celia walked back over to him. She stood next to Cole, and they looked at the forest together.

"Do you have any idea what it is?" she asked.

"No. The things that the Rupture brought into this plane of existence are sometimes very unique. I personally haven't heard of anything like this, but I'm not surprised. It could live in the shadows; it could be the shadows itself. As I said, the Throne and all things tied to it are above reality. Beyond understanding for our limited minds."

That was a much better explanation. This explanation left just as many questions but at least an understanding of the dangers of the forest on the ridge. For the first time, Celia truly felt afraid of what was in there.

"Shall we go home?" she said in a defeated tone.

Cole looked over at her. "Yes," he replied with sympathy.

IT WAS late afternoon when they arrived back in town. There was still time until evening, so Cole invited Celia to eat at the local inn. He'd traded goods from his home for a week's worth of room of board. She took the offer, being too exhausted to cook for herself.

Before their food arrived, she had another question for him. One that became lost in the emotions and memories and preaching.

"You never told me why you're actually here," she said as she sipped a glass of tea.

Cole took a drink of his wine, then another. "I'm here to visit with the people. Explain the situation. Convince whoever is willing to listen to come with me."

She was in the middle of picking up her cup once more when it nearly slipped, tinking against the plate. She must have misheard him.

"Come with you?"

Another drink of wine, this one longer and deeper. "The world outside my home is on borrowed time. I'm here to take back everyone I can. Godscorn is the safest place to be. Soon, the only place."

"Is this your convincing speech?" she asked dubiously.

He chuckled. "No. I think we're fairly familiar by now. I soften the blow more with others."

"And?" she asked with a sharp upward inflection. He certainly wasn't going to leave this kind of topic hanging between them.

"I told you I haven't lied to you. And I won't. The Throne is returning to take Alda. Others like me are on a pilgrimage to visit the towns and villages that are left to bring as many as we can to Godscorn before It arrives. The Inheritors are reclaiming the land as we speak."

His eyes lingered on her for a moment. There was a sadness there. "There's not much left, from what I've seen. Most places are abandoned at best. Haunted or possessed at worst."

She shook her head. The words came with difficulty. They

hung sour in her mouth before coming out. "And you worship these things?"

"Alda was stolen. Wouldn't you be angry if a precious possession was taken from you and hidden away?"

"I don't think I'd kill millions over something." Her mind thought back to all the people who died during and since the Rupture centuries ago. Most in horrifying ways.

"We're not unfathomable beings," he replied plainly. "I definitely am not."

Their food arrived, and both ate heartily. The meat was warm, the vegetables fresh, and it made one forget the cold outside and within one's heart. Celia drank the last of her tea and sat with both hands holding her mug, feeling the last of the warmth fade from it.

"Thank you for the food," she said. "I truly appreciate it."

"My pleasure," he returned with a smile. "I'm going to retire to my room. I'm quite tired after today. I'll come see you soon. I have work to attend to now that I've helped you and Gregory."

"Yes," she said, letting a silence hang in the air for a moment. "Thank you for that as well."

"Would you like me to escort you back to your home?" he asked.

"No. I'm fine on my own. You go get some rest."

He nodded and rose from the table. The sound of his footsteps and rustling robes faded. Celia was left alone, staring at an empty tea cup. A lone tea granule floated in the remaining liquid. She thought about her small town drowning in the events Cole described. He hadn't given her any reason to doubt him. This scared her most of all.

～

CELIA WAS content to remain within the borders of her town. Once again, she took other work instead of going to the herb patches near the forest on the ridge. Cole had warned her away, so she took his advice for now. She wanted to ponder what she'd learned and what Cole had said when they ate together.

They crossed paths at least once a day. It consisted solely of friendly small talk, Cole asking for directions, or if Celia knew this or that family. They shared lunch once, but the conversation remained normal. It was like he walked away from that dinner and left all the weight of the events prior in his wine glass. Maybe that in and of itself was a spell. She didn't know. She also wasn't sure how to feel about it. Grief and ignorance had left Celia exhausted for so long. Perhaps getting a few answers left her emotionally and psychologically relieved for the time being.

One night, about a week after Cole and Celia's dinner at the inn, a knock came on her door. She'd been winding down from a hard day delivering flowers for the miller. Her muscles were sore, and she looked forward to the fresh bread provided by the baker for her services. With a weary sigh, she stood and prepared a polite response for whoever waited at the door.

The hinges creaked as the door slid open barely an inch. Celia didn't care who it was; she wanted to hurry this person on their way. Her eyes widened when she noticed Cole standing there.

"Oh, good evening, Cole," she said, trying to keep the surprise out of her voice.

"Hello, Celia. May I come in?"

"Of course." She opened the door completely, and the mage stepped into her home. She didn't want visitors. Why did she feel the need to let him in?

"It smells good in here."

"Fresh bread from the baker," she replied.

Celia offered him a seat. She brought two mugs and a pitcher of water for them to share.

"Thank you," he said, taking a drink.

"I don't have any wine, I'm sorry."

"It's fine. I brought some." He said with a hint of cheeriness in his voice. He produced a small bottle of white wine from his robe, revealing it like a magician.

Celia smiled. He was nothing like his gods, for lack of a better term, or what his practice suggested he should be. He was kind and honest. Thoughtful, too.

"We'll have to make do with these simple things. I don't have any glasses."

With a simple word and a flick of his wrist, the cork on the bottle popped into his palm. "I only care about what's in this bottle."

They both drained the water from their mugs, and he then poured for both of them. The bottle was small, and the mugs fairly large, so they each received half of the bottle.

"I'm going to sleep well tonight," Celia commented. "No matter how good or bad it is."

"Ben Greensley insisted it was good."

"You don't know Ben Greensley," she scoffed.

They both chuckled.

Celia took a deep drink from her glass. It was fruity, tart, and sweet. "He wasn't wrong this time."

"No, he was not," Cole agreed as he took another drink.

"What brings you to my empty house?" Celia asked, taking another sip.

"Oh, I wouldn't say this is empty. It's quite comfortable."

"It used to be." Celia took a long pull from her mug.

Cole nodded. He almost looked chided.

"Tomorrow. It's time." He said in a low but confident voice.

Celia quirked an eyebrow and looked at him in silence.

"I'm returning to my home. Probably for the last time. The forays out into Alda are getting emptier and emptier."

"Ah," Celia said, a hint of sadness in her voice. "You're here to say goodbye."

"Quite the opposite. I'm taking people back with me, remember?"

"Yes, I remember." Her words still came out heavy. "How many are coming with you?"

She now thought of all the possible people who would be leaving the town behind. The world would be even emptier, especially for her.

Cole took another drink. "Everyone."

His tone was cheerful. Celia's heart sank.

"Everyone?" she echoed, somewhat in disbelief.

"Well, almost everyone," he clarified pointedly.

"Cole ... I don't think I can do that." She didn't sound so convinced even to herself. Doubt lingered within her. She rubbed her sore shoulders, wincing in pain at the muscle in her neck that she grabbed wrong.

"Celia, surely you won't stay behind by yourself? We're going to one of the last civilized locations in Alda. Most likely *the* last."

He stood and walked over to her. She still rubbed her shoulders. Cole gently put his hands on her shoulders and began rubbing the knots out of her muscles. It was heavenly.

"And, I cannot stress this enough; you have Fourth Sect potential. You are the only one I've found in my journeys in the last couple of years. You would not be any ordinary citizen."

Her mind was muddled by the wine and the massage. Her strained body and mind eased at the same time. She didn't want to think of such things right now.

"Cole, I need to think about this. And I don't want to think about it when I feel relaxed for the first time in months."

He gave one last squeeze and removed his hands, letting them slide off her shoulders. "I understand. I do."

Celia stood and turned to him. "Give me tonight, ok?"

He nodded firmly. "I will. I just want to give you one more thing to think about."

"What's that?" she gave him a thankful smile.

Gently, he took one of her hands in both of his, cupping it between them. His hands were warm. He looked her in the eyes and said, "I don't want you to come back *with* me. I want you to come back with *me*."

Her head lowered, and she looked at their hands, which were sitting between them. She looked back at him, a mix of anxiety, fear, and intrigue no doubt sparkling in her eyes and showing on her flushed face.

"Do you understand?" he asked.

She took a deep breath in and out of her nose. Their faces seemed closer. He seemed closer. Did he do that, or did she? Their lips touched, and once again, she didn't know who was responsible for what. It didn't matter anymore.

They kissed each other deeply, and she found her hands inside the folds of his robes. She ran her fingers over his body, which was quite unlike that of a scholar. He wasn't muscular like a soldier, but she could tell it was a strong, disciplined body.

His hands grabbed onto her, and they became lost in each other. Her heart raced in a good way for the first time in ages.

SHE HADN'T LET a man into her bed in a very long time. She hadn't joined a man in his in some time, either. It wasn't a priority for her. Romance. Marriage. Children. Especially children; she didn't want to bring anyone up in this world. Not a pet, or a child, or a lover. There was too much to lose.

So why was she laying here, under her blanket, nestled in

the arms of a death mage? Cole would hate if she said that again, but the name stuck with her. Celia felt his chest moving rhythmically with his breathing against her back. His arm draped over her and held onto her just beneath her breasts.

"Are you awake?" she whispered.

"I am now," he replied.

"Sorry," she apologized. She didn't even know why she asked. She had nothing to say, really.

He released her and sat up in bed. She felt like something more was missing suddenly. Cole got out of the bed and began to put his robes back on.

"It's ok. I should return to my own room and prepare for tomorrow. That and I wouldn't want any strange gossip to start," he finished with a smile.

"Too late," Celia groaned. "Any of the old women who saw you come already had their minds made up when the door closed."

"Well, at least we didn't disappoint them."

Celia smiled.

"Tomorrow morning, in the town square. I'll be waiting."

Cole took her hand and kissed it, letting his lips linger there for a moment. She looked into his gray eyes and nodded with a smile of her own.

The door closed a few moments later. The taste of the wine lingered in her mouth. She stood and let the evening air coming in through an open window caress her naked body. The water in the other room was room temperature and stale, but it worked for now. She drank a full mug to help with the lingering sweetness and then returned to bed. That night, she eventually fell asleep as her mind struggled between thoughts of her sister and Cole.

∼

CELIA ARRIVED at the town square to find half the town already there. Guards were creating convoys of the many gathered with all they could carry. Other families, small and large, continued to trickle in steadily.

The families of the council were in the front of the masses, while the figureheads gathered in a half-circle before Cole. He was talking to them, his hand movements making it seem like he was providing directions. Celia waited until he was finished. When the council turned to leave, Cole stood there for a moment, his head bobbling around as he took in his gathered flock. Celia began to walk up to him when he turned around.

He smiled when he saw her, but then his forehead creased. "Celia, did you not bring anything with you?"

There was no luggage of any kind on or with her person. She only wore a fresh set of clothes. The same one's she'd been wearing when Serena went missing.

"I'm sorry, Cole. I won't be going with you."

"I don't understand. You have such a good life waiting for you. You'll be a part of my order. We'll be together there, in the safest place on Alda."

The look in his eyes made her heart ache. He was telling the truth about everything. She would live well, and she would have him. But Cole wasn't family. He would never be the family she lost.

"My mother and father died here. My sister ... Serena ... I still don't know if she's out there."

"I told you, Celia, she's gone!" He sounded angry for the first time. Several heads turned and looked toward them.

He breathed and then lowered his head, calming himself. "I know it hurts, but you know, now. You know what happened. You can trust me on this."

She took one of his hands in hers, much like he did the night before.

"I do feel I can trust you, Cole. I really do. But, I feel if I leave here without Serena ... if I leave everything behind without doing everything I can to find her and know for sure she's gone, as you say, I'll regret that more than anything. Could I truly be happy with you, then?"

Cole put his other hand over hers. Then, he softly pulled away. He must have seen the determination in her eyes, as his face hardened with its own resolve.

"A day's walk from here, there's a town by a small river. It's abandoned and falling apart, but it has a port where my ship is docked. The captain waits there for me. I won't be coming back here—no one will—but if you change your mind, the signs by the town call it 'Eldensburg.' You'll have to catch up because I can't wait. I hope to see you there."

She gave him a genuine smile. Her eyes began to swell with tears. "Thank you, Cole."

And goodbye.

He kissed her on the cheek and returned to overseeing the townsfolk, preparing to leave.

BY EARLY AFTERNOON, the last of the townsfolk trailed off as the convoy made its way to the waiting ship. Cole was in the front and one of the first to go. He turned before leaving, giving her one last, longing look. She lifted a hand to wave goodbye and watched as he turned, downtrodden.

A few had stopped to say goodbye and asked if she was sure that she wanted to stay. She exchanged a few hugs and handshakes. When she could no longer hear anyone, she let herself cry openly. The town was truly empty. No one stayed behind. Now, she was utterly alone.

Celia found a bottle of wine that had been left behind, along with a few things to eat. After her meal, she turned back to the side of town facing the ridge and made her way there. The walk was cold without Cole's insulation spell. It made her long for him more. She gritted her teeth against the cold and the ache in her heart and pressed on.

The ridge came in sight. Seeing it made her angry. It had cost her so much.

She stood at the forest's edge and shouted into the darkness. She hated it; whatever it was in there, she hated it with all her being. Then, she calmed herself and listened. She could still feel Serena's presence. It was faint, but she felt it. The two had always shared a bedroom, even as adults. The feeling was like when someone woke up before you and was missing, but you knew they were still near.

"I'm coming, Serena," Celia said and made her way into the forest, where lurked the spiteful, ink-black shadows.

And she came to regret everything.

THE LAST CITY

Lucien sat in his designated chair, thinking. His ghostly eyes traced the barbed diamond symbol carved onto the large, dark wood table. His chin rested in the palm of his hand; his fingers curled inward against his mouth. The carving of the Black Gnarl's ancient symbol was deep and black, like it had been burned into the table's surface although no such practice was used to create the engraving. After it was made using a sacrificial knife belonging to one of Lucien's subordinates, the lines had sunk and decayed before the eyes of all in attendance.

The rest of the table was engraved as new information about their world arrived. The ambassadors, chosen for their unique skills and innate talent for persuasion and charm, brought back news and maps of their travels. The current continents of Alda, all its broken shores, lay before him. The last of the ambassadors were arriving in the coming months. It was no longer safe or necessary to send any further delegations. All that was left of the people of the world had come to him. To the Gnarl. To the Throne.

A question had been gnawing at him lately. A single word that started as a simple itch against his brain: *why?*

After his mind had wandered to distant places—dark and harrowing—for an unknown span of time, a knock came at the chamber doors. The sound resonated against the walls, echoing like a storm's dying call.

"Enter," he replied with placid authority.

A robed figure slipped morosely into the room. Their cowl was pulled up, creating shadows that covered their face. The room was dark enough, with only two windows, one to the east and one to the west, allowing light inside. With such ill ambiance, his fellow's visage was utterly black.

Lucien sneered inside. Everyone always had their cowls up, despite that inside these halls, there was no reason to do so. In this city, Godscrown, there were no reasons for them to hide. Over the last few years, the practice had gone beyond habit to one of vanity. A show of authority. Of power. Some legitimately felt that without such spectacle, the order could have lost influence. As though there were any other organizations left to work against them.

"Lower your cowl, brother or sister. I cannot tell which," he groaned.

Pale brown hands pulled the dark folds back, revealing the tired face of the Master Constable. Lucien could not place his name at the moment but knew the tired eyes and pinched mouth of the middle-aged man who pored over report after report in the lower floors of the Umbra Terra—the Black Gnarl's grand tower—in which they currently resided.

"What news have you?" Lucien asked plainly, avoiding using the man's name. A useless thing, anyway.

The tired eyes avoided Lucien's like a guilty child explaining themselves to a parent. He had nothing to explain; it was only Lucien's pale-eyed gaze that unnerved him. And Lucien understood. This man's life-fibers hung limp at their ends. They flickered once in a while with an unseen shock. All the other masters assumed Lucien had some kind of power granted him by those eyes, but none knew what it was. All those subordinates below the masters never even looked in his direction. He never gave them a reason to behave in such a manner; weak-willed and afraid, all of them. Lucien never raised a hand to any of them without dire need.

"Well?" Lucien asked, a touch of impatience in his voice.

"Master—" the other man started, but Lucien interrupted him.

"I'm not a master of anything."

The man stuttered, trying to figure out how to address his 'superior' until he finally gave up and carried on. "There have been some reports of an alarming rise in people, well, they're found on the streets. Dead from having jumped out their windows, apparently."

Lucien stood and stretched his back. He groaned from the physical effort and that of his mind working. Suicides. The world was harsh and getting worse every day. People choosing such a departure from this world wasn't wholly uncommon, but if it was becoming an issue to the point of the Master Constable making a personal visit, it must be a dire situation.

"And how many have there been to make this situation so remarkable?"

"Twelve. In the last two days. Nine civilians and three brothers and sisters of the order."

Lucien's jaw clenched. He had trained himself to withhold any expression of surprise, though little surprised him anymore. Twelve people killing themselves and members of the Black Gnarl included in their number was enough to illicit a slight shock. It caused his mind to race with possibilities.

After a few moments of heavy silence, Lucien dismissed the constable. He promised to investigate the issue personally and instructed that any further incidents be reported immediately.

A venture into the city streets was called for. He avoided these whenever possible. Though his robes were not adorned any differently than other members of the order, his presence was apparently felt by all those he came across. Be it his stature, his gaze, the powers imbued upon him by the Inheritors, or some combination thereof, Lucien cast a shadow across all he encountered. This time, he would take a different approach.

THE LARGE FRONT doors of the Umbra Terra groaned as they opened. Twice as tall as Lucien, braced with black iron and lacquered a deep crimson, the two doors spread like a demon's wings, sending the stale, fetid air of a dying world into Lucien's face.

His cursed eyes saw the life essence of everyone present, writhing like black strands of seaweed in most cases and twitching in the spasmodic manner of those closing in on the last years of life in others. Then, there were the other signs of life that he chose to ignore. Not the rats or insects, which floated tiny strands of their own, but the island itself. The very stones were tethered by inky threads. These did not weave haplessly back and forth like those of the people and pests. These flexed and pulled, stretching angrily upwards, then falling slack for a moment before rising again. That was the question Lucien always had: were they reaching on their own or by some other force? Either way, he had little doubt as to what they were reaching for or what was pulling them.

Lucien closed his eyes. He felt the raw, unfiltered Fourth Magic that comprised those fibers of the island. The fibers were more sharp-edged grass than lolling seaweed. He let his own essence, steeped in the Fourth, weave into those strands. He became a viper in the grass, unnoticed by those around him.

Care was still required. The melding only hid his presence

from the eyes, not his physical body itself. He could still touch and be touched. This would break the black glamour that hid him. Now, however, he could peruse the city as he liked without being disturbed. He was also more in tune with his surroundings as a whole.

The atmosphere of the streets did not seem unusual. Civilians went about their meager lives crafting, bartering, and living gaze-down one day after another. Black-robed members of the Gnarl stood out like dead stars, some in small clutches handling their own affairs. Lucien tried to eavesdrop on conversations. Those he heard were filled with tripe and told nothing of the mysterious rash of suicides.

He walked the streets of the city proper, spiraling down from the Umbra Terra like a giant tower of its own. The island itself was named Godscorn, and the city was only half of it. The other half consisted of the farmlands and rocky outskirts unfit for inhabitation. The Black Gnarl's plans for a grand city had succeeded far too well. The immigrants fleeing the dying continents of Alda poured off the ships coming into the harbor. The city was forced to build upon itself like creeping coral, reaching higher into the night sky as its borders swelled too large to continue outward.

There was no main street. No central road leading to important places or landmarks. There was no purpose for such a thing. So, he meandered through the streets and alleyways, careful to avoid bumping into anyone. The viper slithered through grass and seaweed alike, seeing people cast the occasional worried glance here and there as the fibers of their lives pulled toward him.

He heard a commotion at one point. The sound of gathered voices speaking in disbelief, then a scream. It took Lucien a few minutes to find where it had come from and make his way through the tangled web of streets to get there, but he knew by a gathered crowd when he'd found the right place. A man was vomiting in a gutter. A few women were weeping quietly while old men ran their hands through their beards and muttered in disgust and disbelief.

There was no way to get through the crowd, so Lucien had to make his way to the top of a bench and then the wall next to it. He held on to an iron lamppost and looked over the heads of the crowd to see. Knowing what he was searching for, the answer came as no surprise.

A body lay sprawled on the ground, limbs contorted in awkward directions. The woman was face down, but her head looked to be half-buried in the cobblestones. The pool of blood, viscera, and brain matter surrounding her explained otherwise.

"She just stepped off the balcony," someone said, their words garbled by shock.

Lucien stood by, unseen, as murmurs and whimpers circulated through the crowd. Speculation rose above the pathetic noises, but none present could conclude why this girl—unknown to him but obviously familiar to her neighbors—would take her own life.

It was one comment, spoken off-handedly, that clicked in Lucien's mind: "So many people leaping to their doom. Is it some sign from the gods?"

Lucien's eyes squinted. His mind sparked with an idea, pulling knowledge from deep within the dark crevasses of his brain. It was an interesting idea, but was it even remotely correct?

He left the grisly scene as a cart arrived to retrieve the body, no doubt headed for the breathing pit beneath the island where all the detritus of flesh eventually travels.

The door to the building where the dead woman lived was around the corner, according to bystanders. When he felt he'd found the correct place, Lucien let himself in. Everyone was distracted by the incident, which was good. He preferred not to draw attention by having a door suddenly open on its own to any eyes that may be watching.

Inside, the multi-family complex was unremarkable. The same wood and stone make up nearly all buildings in Godscorn. Meager furnishings, an occasional sickly-looking plant. Nothing that would make someone seem so eager to hurl themselves from a window or balcony.

His boots clomped dully against the stone steps leading upstairs. The close confines of the interior killed the echo and created a heavy atmosphere. At the top landing, pale light betrayed an open doorway. It beckoned him. No noises came from this floor, which was the same as the first. Either no one else was here, or they were cloistered behind the other doors.

Inside the room was a single-person's living space. Nothing special could be ascertained about its occupant. The woman was, by all evidence, another faceless member among the masses.

The door to a small balcony waited at the opposite end of the room from where he entered. Weak sunlight poured in, creating a dark frame around cloudy skies. The white and gray masses sat lazy and unmoving. Dust particles floated and swirled in the breeze that came through. The sound of the distant waves of the Wailing carried the sounds of the dead and damned.

As Lucien walked to the door, an ill feeling began to encroach upon him. It pulled and clutched weakly but persistently at his heart like a dying man grasping at air. The closer he drew to the door, the stronger it became. He found himself drawn inexorably closer to the balcony.

It felt as though he'd blinked and held his eyes closed for longer than needed. However, he knew he hadn't closed his eyes. Regardless, Lucien stood at the very edge of the balcony, his knees brushing the low guardrail. His breath caught, and for a moment, he was an unnamed initiate again. Fear and ignorance coursed through him, but it soon faded.

SEVERAL DAYS PASSED with no further incident. There was no foreboding feeling hanging over Lucien. He knew exactly the purpose of the Being's arrival. Lucien's eyes traced the barbed diamond on the table as he sat, again, alone in the central chamber of the Umbra Terra.

A knock came at the door, resonating throughout the room. His expected appointment had arrived.

"Come," he barked.

The tired, pinched-mouth Master Constable entered. His eyes were the slightest bit brighter today.

"You summoned me, Master?"

Lucien ran a hand over his face, squeezing at his chin and hearing his stubble scratch against his skin.

Fools never learn to not refer to me as 'master.'

The constable cleared his throat, possibly recognizing his mistake.

"There's been no news of any further suicides?"

"No, sir. Not one since your investigation. I didn't receive any report from you, and I don't expect one, of course."

"I handled it," Lucien replied with stale confidence.

"I am sure it was a fascinating thing to see. Did you bargain on our behalf?" the tired eyes lit up for a moment. Lucien sighed inwardly.

"Of course not."

"Then what was the source? Have we been graced by the presence of another of His Children?"

Lucien regarded him with patience as a parent to a questioning child. "You already know the answer to that."

"I must ask, mas ... uh ... sir, which one?" The constable did not attempt to hide his enthusiasm.

"You wouldn't know of it. It is one of the very few our order has no sect with which to worship it."

The other man's brows raised. "Intriguing. How did you come to learn of it?"

Lucien blinked his unnatural, pale eyes purposely. The constable nodded stiffly and remained quiet.

"The Being Beneath the Swells. It tried to claim me, as well. Evidence that I am master of nothing, like all of us," he added as an aside.

"But, the boon granted me by the Throne," he continued, gently touching the soft skin below one of his eyes with two fingers, "granted me a reprieve from the Being's purpose. The final stages have come. Send the Master of Logistics to me immediately."

"Of course," the constable replied, bowing and leaving to the sound of rustling robes.

WITHIN THE HOUR, the Master of Logistics came to Lucien as requested. A stiff, formal woman, he found her intellect and no-nonsense demeanor refreshing amongst the growing zealotry and pride of the other masters.

"You summoned me?" she asked plainly without ceremony or titles. Her brusque voice matched her stern eyes.

"I need to know if any ships are not docked at present."

She nodded and reached into a leather satchel she wore on a heavy strap around her shoulder. Inside were several tightly rolled scrolls with bindings and seals of various thicknesses, colors, and materials.

Lucien furrowed his brow. "That's new," he said in reference to the container. "It's unlike you to fancy anything that is not ... wholly utilitarian."

"My previous one had a hole eaten into by rats," she said with a hint of disgust as she closed the flap and unrolled a piece of parchment. "How could you tell?"

"The leather is an odd color." He did not include the fact that his eyes also perceived a strange aura to it.

"I didn't want to use the leather from what few cows we have in stock for a bag. It was made from some goblins found foraging in the hinterlands. Shall I report?"

He nodded, and her brown eyes danced over the paper. "One scavenging ship departed for the northeast eight months ago. The last message put them near the Weeping Tower. Overdue to return by one week. Ambassador Nyla's ship departed north to Kalthav nine months ago. Overdue to return by three weeks. Ambassador Cole's ship departed west for the Broken Ridge-lands ten months ago. Overdue to return by eight weeks. All are assumed lost."

"If they weren't, they are now," Lucien commented in a low voice. It was a great shame to have lost two ambassador ships. Who knew how many vagrant souls they had discovered.

The Master of Logistics stood as silent and stiff as one of the temple guards. She had rolled the report back up, but it remained in her hands and was placed in front of her.

"Any ships that are overdue are to be marked lost. It's impossible for them to return. No further departures."

She nodded and returned the scroll to the satchel. "How long until the restriction is lifted?"

"Never."

This made her head bob up from where she was buckling her satchel closed, causing her black locks to bounce. Her forehead crinkled, and he saw genuine concern in her usually stoic face. "Without those ships, Godscorn will stagnate. We can self-subsist with basic foodstuffs, but—"

She stopped when Lucien raised a hand. "As always, your candor is welcome. It is not an option, I'm afraid. Not yours. Not mine."

She looked into his ghostly eyes and pursed her lips. With a nod, her unshakable mask returned.

"No ships can leave this city. Make sure the constable knows that none are to try to stop those that do. They won't make it far."

"So, the time draws near," she said, with all the emotion of someone writing down a line of numbers.

"Yes, but you know as well as I that time works differently here. Those ships are a few weeks overdue for us and departed a matter of months ago. It could be years to them, for all we know. And in such times as these, Their influence only grows stronger. The rigid laws of our reality will only continue to see greater fluidity."

"The heads of the sects say we will take part in many grand things. I am deeply intrigued and look forward to seeing it."

You shouldn't. Lucien thought. The masters overseeing the various sects worshipping the Inheritors were the oldest roles among the Black Gnarl. The masters of the various civil duties that fell upon the order when Godscorn was founded were new roles headed by those with specific worldly talents. The Master Constable and Master of Logistics were but two of them. They knew as much of the Dread Praises as the rest of the middling echelons of the Gnarl, but the masters of the sects carried the deeper truths. Lucien was burdened with the deepest truth of all; it was terrifying and inevitable.

Another knock came at the door, and this one was unexpected. Rather than polite rapping, a fist pounded heavily on the door. The loud thuds shocked them both for a moment, and Lucien called out, "Enter."

The fellow member who walked through the door was a broad-shouldered, pot-bellied man with a beard that hung down to his chest. With his face shadowed, it gave the impression of a curtain of moss growing from a mountainside cave. Poignant for the master of the Ygiddra faction that replaced Vana after the Sowing, where she and her hand-chosen priests gave of themselves to the Sanguine Garden to fertilize the new fields.

The new master, Druug, worshipped the Timeless Garden in his own special way. The dirt and mud staining the hems of his robe were the marks of his devotion. In particular, Druug favored Miriamyn, one of Ygiddra's many "daughters", and bragged of his devotion often. Lucien preferred to keep his talks with the master short.

The stout man waddled up to stand next to the Master Logistician. He pulled his cowl back along the way to reveal a bald pate surrounded by long, messy strands of hair falling down the sides of his head like wet roots. His face was scarred and tattooed to resemble a knotted mass of brambles. He looked over at the woman, a stunning contrast to his foulness, and gave her a wide, brown smile. She rolled her eyes and turned back to Lucien.

"Why do you interrupt us, Master Druug?" Lucien said with tempered calmness.

"I thought you should know," he began in a voice that sounded like a drowning bullfrog, "that farmers are reporting some interesting sightings. Some of Ygiddra's pale children have been spotted roaming near the base of the broken aldyr. They're also complaining of large root systems pulling up in the fields."

Lucien sat up straight. The foul-smelling master brought worthy news.

"And by large, you mean ..."

"The smaller ones are the size of my ample leg," he chortled.

"I suppose you would be happy at this news," the logistician commented. "Ygiddra is among us."

"Ygiddra has always been among us," Lucien clarified in his usual flat tone. "Now, It is making Itself known. It is preparing the island. Converting Godscorn into a proper receiving hall."

"Should we contact the constable? To protect the farmers? The pale children are known to be indiscriminate in their choices of nutrients."

"As long as it bleeds," Druug said, smiling. "But they haven't so much as approached the farms yet."

"Yet." Lucien echoed.

Protection. Lucien chuckled internally. There was no protection from Them. Those Others they'd spent so long seeking. The pale children, the Inheritors, the Throne Itself ... they were beyond human understanding, let alone control. They would do as They wish. Especially here, where the Fourth Sect was woven into the very foundations of the island city both magically and physically. The power of residual magic grew stronger with time and use. The Fourth had been used in surplus on a daily basis. The fluidity of time here could mean decades, even centuries, of lingering augmentation. Their power here would be unspeakable.

"We do nothing," Lucien said, his command firm. "Things are progressing as they should. Continue as you are. Inform me of any change."

Both masters nodded and turned to leave. Druug held the door open for the Master of Logistics, offering her a hand. She neither thanked him nor returned his gesture.

"There will be much celebrating tonight," he said in a lewd voice. "Ygiddra's faithful will wrap themselves like the vines before the Garden's own roots and fleshy blossoms. You should join us."

As the door closed, Lucian heard the logistician reply, "Absolutely not."

He remained there for the rest of the day, circling the room, glancing out the window and still seeing there, below the surface of the Wailing Ocean, the Being. He traced the edges of the table with a finger. He was placid yet restless.

Eventually, night fell. The sky turned from a pale white to dull purple and finally a deep black. The clouds never let up, but the moonlight consistently broke through to reveal the silhouette of the island's various landmarks. The broken aldyr continued to reach into the sky like the skeletal hand of a cremated god. The jagged, rocky protrusions of the infertile and forbidden outskirts looked different. Those trees hadn't been there before, had they? Certainly not. A small forest had grown around the black crags and was now nestled among fiendish-looking trees that shouldn't be able to grow there at all.

His eyes caught the shape of a bulky animal's shadow stalking up the side of one of the large rocks. It looked like a wolf, but it would have to be twice the size of the largest one he'd ever seen. Then, Lucien realized all at once what it all signified: the sudden appearance of a wicked forest, the massive wolf-like beast, and the twitch in the back of his brain. The creature lifted its head and howled. Lucien thought it sounded like a dying man screaming. Then, a second one of the creatures came up beside the first. It joined in the ritual of macabre sound, but its voice came out as the wretched screech of a woman in agony. The two beasts rubbed their heads against each other and along one another's shoulders as though they were a mated pair.

Something tugged at the back of Lucien's mind. It threatened to pull him into the hollow of a dead tree, scratching his face with knife-like fingernails as sharp as dried thorns. It never fully claimed him. Would he be granted a reprieve from this, as well? If not, he would be joining many others for some sleepless and harrowing nights.

Why?

The question came up again. But he knew why. He knew all the answers. Only disciplined repression and succumbing to fatalistic apathy saved his sanity. He could share the grand truth with them all, but that would lead to absolute chaos. In-fighting, subterfuge, assassinations, possibly his own trial and torture. Surely, the civilians would revolt against them. That would destroy the purpose of what they'd done. It was the only thing he really had left. Not that such a thing mattered. He knew. Knowing was the worst of it all. He could share it with no one. He could only ask 'why?' And then answer his own question, over and over again, in the last city left in the world.

SHADOW OF THE THRONE

CHAPTER 1

Victor and Lyra took the longest route possible around Carnelia. At its closest, the city was a dark patch on the horizon. Even then, the winking eyes of oblivion still seemed to watch them. They could both feel them on their backs. The nights were sleepless, and the days passed in silence and persistent walking.

By the time they rounded back to Gilfoyle and Tula, the horses were gone. The part of the ropes tied to a tree now lay limp on the ground. The frayed end tormented Victor with thoughts of what had happened to his old partner and friend. Lyra had a hand over her mouth and her eyes glistened. There was no blood, but that meant little.

"Perhaps they're nearby?" Lyra said, with a notable lack of hope in her voice. He felt his heart clench. They could search the nearby fields, but he knew Gilfoyle and Tula were gone. They both decided to search for an hour before moving on. Together, they called the horses' names, checked the fields nearby, and walked along nearby streams. One hour turned into two and then three.

Physically and emotionally worn, Victor and Lyra knelt next to the burbling water of a wide and shallow creek. A tear dripped from his cheek. Lyra sniffled. Gil had been his oldest companion. Lyra and Tula were also as close as horse and rider could be. They were all each other had. The weight of a hand pressed on his slumped shoulder.

"We have to keep going."

Lyra's soft words both comforted and bit at him. She was right. They had to continue on if they were going to make it to the Kalthav region and find a way to destroy the beacon. They were so close to a resolution.

He wiped the tear from his face and stood. The sound of the water was calming. The cool shade of the scattered trees near the banks eased his tired mind and sore muscles. Lyra put a hand on his back this time.

"We are going to finish this," she said.

Victor nodded firmly. "I hope you don't mind the cold."

Lyra sighed.

AFTER TWO WEEKS of traversing the roads and countryside of Alda, one thing became clearer than ever: the world was in its death throes. Victor knew where groves of dead aldyrs were, as it wasn't the first time he'd been through certain regions. However, more and more of the forests around them were dying, like the aldyr groves, which became an infection that started to spread. Lakes bared low banks, covered in dead and dry algae. The rivers were much the same.

At night, they'd go against their best instincts and keep a strong fire going. Each night, the darkness felt more and more alive, as though it waited for the moment the fire would flicker out and consume them whole. Victor once looked up, surprised, to see a full moon in the night sky. Usually, these nights were alive with blue-gray shadows and a slight reprieve from the crushing blackness, but the light of that pale body no longer reached them. It floated like a white spot in an ink-black ocean.

Victor hoped that getting away from the cursed city of Carnelia would provide at least a modicum of freedom from the terrors of the Throne's influence. Instead, he and Lyra felt like they were being watched everywhere they went. Eyes in the dark. In the trees. In the sky. In the mountains far off in the distance. Eyes unblinking and unwavering. Sometimes, they felt a presence following even right behind them. Lyra would sometimes turn, ready to draw her sword.

The unending pressure of these unnamed presences taxed their patience and their very sanity. They became ill-tempered with one another and often found themselves apologizing after snapping for some small reason or another.

One evening, while preparing camp for the night, Lyra approached Victor as he was placing a series of large stones around their site. They were all roughly the size of melons. He had found them scattered around everywhere, a sign they were nearing the rocky lands of the cold north.

"What are you doing?" she asked dubiously as he plopped down the third stone so far.

He slapped his hands against his pants to remove the dirt. "Trying something."

"Are you creating a fairy circle?" Her tone was playful, if a bit sarcastic.

"I don't think I'd want to see what fairies look like anymore," he replied, leaving to retrieve a fourth stone.

"You're so dour," she muttered.

The next addition to the circle landed with a dull thud. Victor was sweating from the labor.

"I'm going to try something to protect us from all ... this," he made a sweeping motion behind him with his arm.

"Third Sect magic?" she asked. Lyra had traveled with him long enough to know what he was up to.

"Runes from the Third. Blessings from the Fifth. Empowerment from the First."

"Anything I can do?"

"Find me some honeysuckle and start a fire. I'll need the charcoal."

"Please?" she asked pointedly.

"Please. And thank you. And ... I'm sorry."

"That's better," she answered with a smile in her voice.

With the stones in place and the ingredients gathered, Victor began the next phase of his work. He asked Lyra to place a clutch of honeysuckle at the base of each stone.

"What is this for?" she called out to him from the opposite side of the camp.

Victor began carefully writing runes on the stones with the charcoal as he answered, "Honeysuckle is a strong conduit for Fifth magic. It's a key ingredient in many wards against dark magic."

"All done," she called out.

Victor continued on with the next stone. "Good, now please put on some water to boil. I need it purified."

He wished for some salt or silver, but they had only the bare essentials on them with Gilfoyle and Tula gone along with the bulk of their supplies.

After a few minutes, Lyra came to him with the steaming kettle just as he finished the last inscriptions. He took the water and poured it slowly over the stone, softly chanting a continuous mantra. As the purified water dribbled over the stone, the charcoal didn't wash away. The runes inscribed in a circle around the rock's surface burned with a soft green light.

He walked slowly, still pouring the water in a line, to the next stone. The water splattered as it hit the rock and the effect was the same. Now, though, the trail of water between the stones glowed a soft green, as well. This continued with each other stone marker around their small camp. The green light following him from one stone to the next.

When the final stone marker glowed and the circle was complete, he finished the continuous mantra with a final, closing phrase. There was a soft *whoosh* sound as the magic took hold, almost making his ears pop. The light faded and the inscriptions, once written in black charcoal, now appeared as a lighter shade of the stones themselves.

"We'll see if this works," he sighed. The combination of the magics, the chanting, walking, and pouring, all made him tired.

Victor went to a stump near the firepit and sat. He placed the kettle on the ground. Lyra grabbed it.

"Thank you for that. I hope it works so we can both rest."

He smiled and nodded.

"I found some mint while getting the honeysuckle. I'll go get some more water and make us some mint tea."

"Pretty sure it would just be mint water," he replied in jest.

"Close enough."

She left and returned shortly with another kettle full of water. After putting a handful of mint leaves inside, she placed it directly on the coals. Soon, they were sipping on mint-flavored water as the sun lowered and the darkness drew in.

THE SMELL of cooking meat roused Victor from sleep. He blinked, clearing the sleep from his eyes and his gaze fell on the sight of two rabbits spitted over the fire. The juices of the meat dripped and sizzled on the open flame.

"Gods that smells amazing," he mumbled.

"Found them this morning in the snares I set. I made up the spit and put them on for us."

Lyra sounded more high-spirited this morning.

She stood in front of the fire, facing Victor. She stretched, arching her back and weaving her fingers together high above her head. "I haven't slept that well in weeks. Why didn't you create these markers earlier?"

Victor stood, listening to his own joints pop. "Didn't have large enough stones. At least, not enough."

"We're taking them with us," she declared.

"Are you going to carry them?"

She closed her eyes and groaned.

"Besides, moving will break the enchantment. And it will grow weaker over time."

He walked the perimeter of the camp, keeping his eyes down on the faint line where the enchanted water burned a slight trail into the ground. He stopped, staring at one particular point. Lyra approached him.

"So we would have to perform that ritual every night?" She sounded disappointed.

"Yes," he replied vacantly. His mind was suddenly very distracted.

"Victor?" Lyra asked, concerned. "What are you looking at?"

She stood next to him and followed his gaze to the ground. The thin grass was matted. It looked like footprints of some kind, but nothing from a human or animal.

Lyra looked over to him and he looked at her. Their eyes met and he saw the sudden fear there. Something came to them last night while they slept and neither were aware. The ward appeared to do its job, but the thought that some unknown *thing* was right next to them, warded off by a thin line of enchantment, was horrifying.

They ate their breakfast despite a sudden lack of appetite, knowing they would need the energy to cover as much distance as possible. An old road helped guide them. It appeared in a shallow valley, stretches of the old paving stones appearing and disappearing amid worn and grassy sections like the back of a stone serpent occasionally cresting above a calm green sea. The road split in places, punctuated with worn and illegible signposts. They followed the path that appeared most likely to lead them onward to the pillar of dark light that remained ever ahead of them.

The weather grew consistently colder. Soon the days became colder than the previous nights, and the nights were a whole different manner of freezing. Victor used his magic as much as he could to stave off the chill. However, his powers were taxed. Since the night the footprints were discovered outside their ward, he found himself unable to sleep.

He still put up a ward with Lyra's help. Stones were readily available as they went further north. The campfire proved less and less effective, as well. They made it a little bigger, but would soon have to create a full bonfire to do anything against the cold.

"Is this normal?" Lyra asked, her arms wrapped tightly around her as she sat nearly on top of the flames. "Have you been this far north?"

Victor's weary eyes stared into the flames. He became entranced by them; let their dance work their way into his tired brain.

"Far enough," he answered. "This is colder than I remember. Much colder. Perhaps the beacon has something to do with it."

He stood, stumbling momentarily as his legs had gone numb, and walked around the fire to sit next to Lyra. He put his arm around her, hoping their body heat would help them. She moved closer and his heart skipped slightly. He smelled the earthiness mingled with a slight floral scent in her hair. They were both travelling non-stop and bathing had become something of a rush in the cold waters of this northern region.

Warming the water with the fire only helped so much. Lyra used any flowers she could find to freshen her hair.

"The next village we find—or outpost, tower, whatever—we should gather our senses and strength. Take a day to rest," she suggested.

That sounded nice, but Victor wasn't sure it was possible. Their journey took them in a northeast direction, and it felt more like they were fleeing the entire time. Lyra didn't appear to notice, and Victor did not want to point it out to her, but he sometimes thought he saw things crawling in the brush and near the rivers. Like the plants themselves were alive. Lyra never argued too much about not straying into the woods from time to time, and for that he was grateful.

"We'll see what we can find," he replied in a non-committal tone.

They spent the rest of the evening in silence, eating what meager food they had and drinking water summoned by Victor's magic, which always tasted stale but was otherwise safe. Afterwards, Lyra crawled into her bedroll and suggested he do the same. Victor knew the thought of their protective boundary being probed by unthinkable things was at the forefront of her mind, as well. But she had more faith in his magic than he did, apparently.

Victor stayed up for a while longer. He made sure the flame was suitably fed with ample logs to run through the night. It would not be an issue, though. If the last several nights were any indication, he would be awake to make sure the fire burned. He summoned one more cup of water. The lukewarm drink coated his throat which was constantly dry from the cold.

As the minutes and hours wore on, he decided to get at least a little rest before he inevitably woke back up. His bedroll was placed on the opposite side of the fire from Lyra's. He used his cloak as a blanket on top of the bedroll. He forced himself to look at the fire, let its subtle dance capture his attention. Behind the flame were Lyra's closed eyes, her mouth and nose tucked away beneath her cloak. Then, further, the faint green illumination of the protective border. The magic itself may have been what drew in the nightly visitations. They could not possibly sleep without it, though. Even if they took turns keeping watch, the things that seemed to harry them each moment, in the periphery of their vision and back of their minds, would have nothing stopping them during these times.

He focused back on the flames and tried as hard as he could to keep his eyes on them. Sleep would not be coming any time soon unless he could lose track of his own worries by staring into the fire, looking through it and letting his mind go blank and forget. Forget that beyond the subtle green of the magic ward, creeping and persistent things prodded the thin glowing line and slithered slightly up the invisible barrier it created—like swaying strands of thick wet grass or trembling, curious worms.

A COLD SUN began to rise over the treetops of the forest on the horizon. The land made its way upwards, rising to a hill that led to a shallow valley out of sight, and then on to the highlands of Kalthav. The temperate climate and broad-leafed trees were giving way to a cold, more unforgiving boreal realm of the north with its arrow-shaped and needle-covered pines. The black silhouette of the treeline was crowned by orange and purple bands, above which huddled a thick, heavy pad of clouds.

It looked almost otherworldly, but that could have been Victor's tired eyes finding something to focus on. He realized his mouth was also agape, his body dreaming of sleep while his mind resisted. He was so very tired, yet so very afraid to close his eyes.

A rustling noise came from the lump of bedroll and cloak that covered Lyra. The sound melded seamlessly into the crackling of the fire. Victor thought he heard whispers in that space between the two sounds, where the crackling and rustling met.

He summoned some stale water and splashed his face. Auditory hallucinations were a sure sign of sleep deprivation. Although, one could never be sure if it was a hallucination or something else, something terrifyingly real.

"You're up already?" Lyra asked, her voice heavy. She yawned after sitting up. As if by instinct she crawled out of her bedroll, rolled it up, and put on her cloak. She then walked the warding line near her before coming to sit by Victor.

"Gods, your eyes look like they're about to sink into your skull." Her voice was low but rang with alarm.

"I'm fine," he answered reflexively.

"No," she replied sarcastically, "I'm fine, because I'm getting *sleep*. You look like you've caught a wasting sickness."

"I appreciate the compliment," he replied with a smirk.

"I'm serious, Victor, you need to get some rest." Her words were pointed, but not without sympathy. It was not that he didn't disagree. He just couldn't bring himself to tell her about the things he'd seen while she was asleep. Otherwise, they would both be spending sleepless nights together.

He stood up and began gathering his things. "Tonight. I'll get some rest, even if I have to have you knock me out."

Lyra stood and chuckled. "I can agree to that."

They left the site behind and made for the verdant border of Kalthav. The sun had fully risen but only slightly warmed them. There was something off about the cold. It bit through their clothing. There was no wind; only the cutting, biting cold. Victor learned of an insulation spell that magi often used in these climates, unfortunately, he was too physically weak to keep it up for long and still be able to make their journey.

Lyra was right. He needed sleep. They were both suffering for it at this point.

They followed the road over a hillcrest, their feet practically numb. The valley below them was more a shallow basin of thin grass and rocks. A river ran nearby, leading into the forest. It sparkled in the sunlight and looked damningly cold.

The road led into the Kalthavian forest of dark pines and exposed stone crags. Typically, the cold would be somewhat abated within the natural shelter, but it remained ominously persistent. In the silence, Victor could hear Lyra's teeth chattering.

Keep moving, he thought. Keep moving until we find a place to rest. Then you have to sleep.

His legs felt sluggish. The exhaustion made the cold bite even harder. His mouth hung slack and his breath puffed out in front of him. He vaguely felt himself grow heavier, and then felt a pressure around his body. He realized Lyra had her arms around him.

"What's going on?" he asked, his words coming out slurred. Everything was blurry and his body felt like a crumbling tombstone.

"Your foot caught on a root and you collapsed, then you nearly passed out. You *have* to rest, Victor!"

"I ... I do," he agreed, relenting to her rising anger. She led him to a tree and he slumped against it, sliding slowly to the ground.

Lyra swiftly made a stone circle, practically punching the stones into the ground. She then gathered up kindling, tossed it in the middle, and placed a few large branches in a tent shape. After stuffing some dried leaves beneath the kindling, she asked him if he had the power to ignite a spark. He mumbled a weak affirmative, summoned enough heat from his body, and made the appropriate motions to ignite a spark to start the fire, but nothing came. He tried again, but his body was too weak for the spell to function.

"Damn it ..." he grumbled.

Lyra sighed and knelt beside him. She cupped his cheek in her hands and looked at his exhausted face. She smiled. "It's ok, your magic has been spoiling me, anyway."

She turned from the firepit and removed her pack. After digging around for a moment, she pulled out a piece of flint and a scrap of steel. The sound of the steel striking the flint resounded sharply against the dull quiet in his ears.

"Found this at an old blacksmith shop a while back," she commented, punctuating every other word as she struck the flint.

She huffed enthusiastically and the soft crackle of a young fire came from in front of her. Victor smiled. They could be a little warmer for now, at least. Lyra stood and grabbed a canteen from her pack. She placed the drink in Victor's hand, giving it a soft squeeze.

"This stale mage-water is going to be even staler, but drink it. I'll be back."

Suddenly alarmed, Victor nearly sat up, but now his vision was dimming despite the slap of concern against his chest. "Where ..." was all he managed to say before his head lolled to the side.

"To find a better place for us to rest. Don't worry. I won't be long."

His vision darkened and his heavy eyes won over. He saw her

draw her sword and walk into the woods. He wanted to call out, but exhaustion had already taken him.

THE CRUNCH of brown pine needles and leaves under her feet didn't echo as she'd expected. It was noticeable right away and made her very uneasy. The cold bit through her layers of clothing. The sky, despite being heavy with dark gray clouds, was darker than usual. It all felt and sounded unnatural. With Victor unconscious from exhaustion, she was even more on edge. He was lying to her about something. His intent wasn't malicious, she was sure, but he was being deceitful, nonetheless.

She came up to a tangle of branches blocking her way. Instead of walking around, she released some of her tension by taking two quick slashes at it, barely breaking her stride, and continuing on. The crunching sound of her walk was louder and her foot felt slowed down by something. When she looked down to inspect her feet, she found some of the chopped branches dragging behind her. They were attached by a white, thread-looking material.

Webbing, she deduced. *Gross.*

She tried to rub it off by scraping her foot against the ground, but it didn't work. Stubborn stuff. Then, she tried slicing it off with the tip of her blade. This effort proved successful, but some of the web stuck stubbornly to her blade.

"Ohhhh no," she grumbled. Her sword was precious to her. She tried wiping the edge of the blade against a tree and caught the webbing in bark. It pulled free and Lyra was finally relieved of the silky assailant.

She looked around, seeing if any more of the webbing was present. She didn't want to walk into any. Her skin prickled at the idea. She ran her hand through her hair and along her body, quivering in disgust. She'd seen the eternal suffering of corrupt nobles and had run from damned souls trapped in melting puddles of flesh. She had literally fought and survived against faceless creatures ambushing her and Victor from holes in reality. In the end, spiders still made her squirm.

There was, unfortunately, more of the sticky substance lacing the spaces between the trees. Her heart grew heavy at the idea of having to cut her way through. Something about the webbing caught her eye. It was larger than seemed typical. Her disgust gave way to caution. She walked with increased attentiveness. The ground below her felt somewhat spongy. When she looked down she saw the pine needles, leaves, and twigs captured in spider netting.

Sword at the ready, she looked for her best way out. To her surprise, there was a section of trees without any strands blocking the path. There were more beyond it. As she took the clear route, random as it was, Lyra felt confident she'd be out of the disgusting webs soon enough. She watched her head and body, making sure not to disturb any of the webbing and possibly attract any of the ugly things. This effort led her to an unwelcome surprise.

Her heart sank when she walked into another small glen, this one covered in more webbing than any before. It was draped around the tree limbs like blankets of lace, sparkling in the beams of sunlight that broke through the canopy. It would have been pretty if not for the disgusting peppering of animal bones everywhere.

The leather of her gloves creaked as her fingers gripped her sword tighter. Among the remains on the ground, a blanket of forest detritus and fuzzy white masses of webbing, were a few human skulls and other bones. She brought her sword up to the ready and turned in a small circle, keeping her eyes on the trees.

There they were. Multiple beady eyes reflecting the sunlight. Bulbous abdomens bobbing slightly on so many spindly legs. A few of them crawled slowly out into the open, using the tree limbs and webs that made them appear to hover in midair.

She suppressed a scream, but barely so. An image of them leaping from their perch and landing on her, pointy legs digging into her side and sharp fangs piercing her skin as poison ran hot through her body, flashed in her head. Cursing, she forced herself to focus.

Did these fucking things ambush me? she thought, seething.

Two of the dog-sized spiders skittered toward her. The movements were jerky and almost unreal. Their white bodies were covered in gray, splotchy patterns. Their legs, eyes, and fiendishly long fangs were jet black. Their approach began as one of hesitation—testing her, perhaps. When she didn't move, they struck out at her.

That's when she screamed. She brought her sword down, splitting the head of one of the creatures. Its death was soundless save for the hideous crunch of its carapace giving way. The second one, just to her left, was too close for her to regain her momentum. She kicked it in the face, right where its eyes were. The spider recoiled for a moment, but only long enough for Lyra to regain her balance. She wrenched her sword free and stomped on the other spider's head as it came back for her. Its legs flailed and stabbed at the ground as she held it there with her foot. The foot-long fangs bit and tore at the dirt and twigs on the ground. Lyra leaned in with all her weight, not daring to lift her foot. Another crunch, this one wet and drawn-out, preceded the gray-brown innards of the spider violently discharging out the sides of its head. She brought her sword down, stabbing the beast in the thorax and pinning it to the ground.

Some of the legs moved weakly, some not at all. She stomped it one more time, a disgusting squelch making the bile rise in her throat. A last leg was twitching weakly, but the creature otherwise stopped moving. Lyra pulled her sword from its body and sneered at the innards streaking down it.

A harried shuffling noise came from behind her and her eyes widened, nearly coming out of her skull. She swung her blade in a hard backward slash and spun around. Another one of them had come up behind her. It reared back, exposing its belly and lifting its four front legs in alarm.

Oh shit, it's going to spit on me, she thought, terror gripping her. *Oh shit, oh shit, oh shit.*

Lyra didn't know whether to attempt to dodge some sort of hideous acid spray or charge the thing and run it through. An awkward stand-off followed. Her heart thudded in her chest and the spider stood there, arms raised and nothing more.

When she realized that it was, possibly, hopefully, only trying to intimidate her, she rushed forward. The creature flinched backward, but then responded by trying to pounce on her when she moved too close. It was too late for the creature, though; Lyra brought up her sword and ran it through. Its marionette-like legs stretched out and curled in, over and over. She continued to push until it fell backwards and she was able to push her sword even deeper.

A sharp pressure pushed against her shoulder and Lyra screamed again. She let her sword go—a stupid, horrible mistake she immediately realized—and fell backwards, forcing herself away from whatever it was that touched her. To her chagrin, she realized that it was the spider's legs curling inward as it died.

She looked around and didn't see any more of the awful things, then took a moment to catch her breath. Her lungs burned with the exertion and cold. They filled with sharp, painful breaths until she got her nerves under control. Lyra stood and retrieved her sword, pulling it from the spider and groaning at the amount of monstrous guts that ran down her blade. She didn't look forward to cleaning it. Then, she blushed at the thought of her screaming like a child and falling backward.

It's a good thing no one saw that. She thought, knowing she was probably in the middle of nowhere.

"You are quite the swordswoman," came a voice from the forest.

CHAPTER 2

Damn it, was her first thought, then, "Who's there? Who are you?"

She'd brought her sword at the ready again and tried to find where the voice came from. It sounded like it came from the direction of the dead, curled up spider.

A flame blossomed in the shadows behind said spider. It danced out and lit the thick webbing in the trees ablaze. It burned away in a thin orange halo and three individuals appeared: a human woman preceding a female dwarf and another, male, human. They were all wearing black robes, their cowls pulled back to reveal their faces.

The dwarf was holding a torch, the source of the blaze, and her hands moved deftly, guiding a strand of fire to the webs and burning them away, leaving the trees untouched. Her curly hair was as red as the flames she controlled, while her facial features were round, almost bloated, reminding Lyra of the spiders' bulbous proportions. The dwarf went silently about her work, removing the webbing and carcasses.

The man that escorted the woman was taller than her by two heads. A rail-thin, looming creature, his skin gave off the appearance of pale tree bark with lines and creases covering almost every inch of his visage. Two sunken eyes scanned the web-laden grove. They were surprisingly bright and alert, deep brown in color. Lyra sarcastically noted him as the 'tree man' in her head. All three were wearing packs on their backs, though the tree-man's was larger than the other two.

"You dispatched all three on your own. I'm surprised you're still alive." The woman's voice was pleasant and youthful, but her demeanor betrayed that she was much older than she appeared. Her golden hair fell in long, silky waves around her shoulders, which looked slender underneath the robes. She came from somewhere that could afford the luxuries of consistently washed clothes, healthy food, and personal grooming. Or, it was just some damn magic, again. Her green eyes twinkled, but it did not make Lyra feel any more at ease. Her look was off-putting, despite her magnificent beauty.

The woman's pink-lipped smile failed to distract from one more detail that Lyra noticed: pointed ears visible just within the lustrous strands of hair. She was elf-kind.

"I thought your kind was extinct?" Lyra blurted out. She already had a sword trained on them, so the sting of her bluntness wore off quickly.

The woman chuckled, the sound of a giddy young girl mingled with the bemusement of an aged mage. "You speak your mind without any hesitation. I find that is quite common with mainlanders."

"Mainlanders?" Lyra returned dubiously.

"I am an ambassador from the last great city on Alda. We," she said while gesturing with open arms to her colleagues, "are attempting to rescue all we can from the dying landscape. No doubt you've noticed the sorry state of the land on your travels," she concluded, turning her head to take in their surroundings.

The woman dropped her head and lowered her voice, somewhat dramatically, Lyra noted, to emphasize her point. It was true, though. Something had been different since they began traveling to Kalthav.

"I am Nyla," the elf-kind said as she placed a hand against her chest. "This is Droman and this fiery-haired dwarf is Embla."

Lyra's eyes danced back and forth between the three of them. Droman simply blinked in greeting—a quiet, awkward man. Embra turned to look at Lyra and grunted with a nod, then turned back to continue clearing the webs. It must take great concentration to not set everything on fire.

Nyla sighed and put one hand on her hip. She then cocked her head and her hair bounced, a lock falling in front of her face. She moved it out of the way with a graceful swipe of her fingers. Everything about her was utterly, sensually, and confidently feminine.

"Don't be rude," she said, with an upward inflection intoning that she was trying to goad Lyra on. "We're three prominent magi. If we wanted you dead we could have done so while we watched you kill the frost widows."

"You watched?" Lyra nearly shouted. "You didn't think to help?"

Nyla shrugged. "We could step in if necessary."

"Could?" came Lyra's echo.

"You're alive and gave an impressive showing. Take the compliment."

The capricious elf woman approached Lyra and slowly circled her. Nyla's head remained lowered while her eyes looked Lyra up and down. Lyra felt like she was being gauged by some predatory animal.

"A little on the thin side. Nice, corded muscle, though. Hair's a bit rough." Nyla vocally checked off boxes as she made her round. "Very pretty face," she said with a smile. "Are you alone?"

"No," Lyra replied stiffly. She did not like being sized up like this. But what could she do? There were three of them. If this Nyla started to get any closer, though, regardless of what the other magi would do, Lyra would run her through.

"How many are with you?" Nyla asked, her tone becoming academic.

"Why?" Lyra spat the reply.

"We're looking for survivors. Last great city, remember?"

"Just one more."

"I see. You two just surviving the cursed wilds of Alda on your own? Why haven't the two of you settled down somewhere? Wait out the last days?"

"Not in our nature." The reply came naturally. It wasn't exactly a bluff.

That tinkling laugh again.

"I would love to meet your companion. Please take us to them."

The red-haired dwarf, Embla, and the tree-man, Droman, came and stood next to Nyla, who'd stepped away and had stopped circling Lyra. The fire of the torch still danced around Embla's twirling fingers.

"Is she always doing that?" Lyra asked with a hint of annoyance.

Nyla looked over at the dwarf. "You'll be grateful for her skill with fire in the coming days."

I have no doubt, she thought coldly.

"Follow me," Lyra commanded. "I may not be able to stop all of you, but try anything and I will kill at least one of you."

The three black-robed magi looked at each other. Nyla shrugged and they all began to follow their guide back to another waiting mage.

Please be better, Victor. Lyra felt anxiety course through her as she led the way.

VICTOR'S EYES OPENED SLIGHTLY, a slit of white light piercing the darkness. He couldn't count how many times he'd tried to wake only to pass out again. Each time, he was able to stay awake a little longer. He might make it to a few seconds this time.

A crunching sound echoed through the darkness that threatened to claim him again. Twigs, leaves, and pine needles crunching. It could have been Lyra, but she tended to move much more quietly. Either it was someone or something else, or Lyra was purposely making that noise.

Adrenaline made his eyes pop open. The fire was still burning. Lyra wasn't there. The noise came from his right. He turned to look and saw nothing but fog-laced trees. He stood—weak and unsteady—and placed an arm against the tree he'd previously slumped against for support.

The crunching grew louder and multiplied. There were several someones or somethings coming. Still slouching from weakness, Victor let go of the tree and raised his arms, preparing a spell to strike out if what came through the trees wasn't friendly. He would get one good spell before likely passing out again.

One figure appeared, silhouetted in the fog. They split into two, then four. Sparks crackled between his fingers. It was difficult to manifest the lightning with the moisture in the air. Ice would have been easier, but if these were native creatures of Kalthav, the cold may not work as well against them.

The first figure broke through the mist and Victor relaxed instantly. Lyra's face was a pleasant sight to behold. His arms dropped and he slouched even more, leaning back against the tree with his shoulder. Then, he remembered the other figures and his heart skipped again.

"Victor, you're awake!" she said with excitement. She ran up to him and hugged him, helping him stand. "You need to look strong," she whispered. "Try not to show how weak you are right now."

Her words pierced into him, spiking his adrenaline again. They were heavy with concern and a touch of fear.

Three other figures appeared, keeping their slower pace from before. Black-robed individuals walked out of the fog like specters of death, except the one in front who wore a confident smirk like it was a birthmark.

Black Gnarl. His mind screamed. Every part of his mind and body went on alert. He stood straight and tried to look as confident and strong as he could. He stared at them, trying to look suspicious without appearing hostile—which he certainly was.

The woman, no, the elf-kind he noticed, in the front leaned her head back and looked down her nose, her mouth smiling wide.

"You're not fooling anyone, Victor. I can see by your sunken eyes and wide stance that you are *quite* exhausted."

Victor gritted his teeth, but didn't reply. The elf-kind woman made a waving gesture with her hand.

"We're not here to hurt you or your lovely lady friend. Quite the opposite. May we sit?"

She mumbled a few words out of earshot and made motions with her hands that Victor recognized as belonging to the First Sect. Thick branches pushed up out of the ground. Wiry shoots curled around them and stretched into large, looping arches, forming five small chairs around the fireplace.

The three Black Gnarl cultists removed their packs and sat down by the fire. Without any command, the thin, rough-skinned man of the three reached into his larger pack and removed a small, lidless pot. He barked a short command and placed the pot just above the fire where it remained in place, hovering in midair.

"You both looked half-starved and even more frozen," the elf-kind said with concern. She leaned back in the chair and closed her eyes. After a moment, she reached a hand out to her side and left it there, wiggling her fingers. Suddenly, she snapped her hand closed, wrenched it like she was breaking something, and then turned her hand palm-up and waited. A lifeless, fat rabbit hovered slowly into her hands from the bushes nearby. She flicked her wrists and the skin and fur ripped in one large piece from the muscle. Another flick and it was hurled far away. She placed the rabbit over the fire and chirped the same command that the man did and the rabbit hovered there, beginning to cook.

The man removed a canteen and poured some brownish liquid into the pot. He pulled some leaves out of a side pouch and crumbled them in his hands before adding them, as well. Then, all was quiet.

"While our food and drink prepare—"

"How did you use First Sect magic without incantations?" Victor interrupted.

The elf-kind's eyes lit up. "I was going to begin introductions, but my, we have another mage in our presence."

"I'm Victor. This is Lyra."

"We've met." The elf-kind said with a smile. Victor noticed Lyra grimace.

"I'm Nyla," she said, placing a hand on her chest. "This is Embla and this, Droman."

Victor nodded at each of them in turn. He preferred not to provoke them or give away that he knew anything about the Gnarl. Given what he *did* know, the forced politeness would wear on him quickly.

"Now that we all have names," Nyla announced, "it seems you are as curious about me as I now am about you."

"I did ask first," Victor pointed out.

"That you did," she replied with that ever-present smile. "I am elf-kind, as you've probably noticed. We always did have a unique connection with magic and nature. I am particularly gifted in the First Sect. As such, manipulating nature with the First comes more naturally to me."

"Elf-kind were naturally gifted at promoting life and growth. You just broke a rabbit's neck and skinned it whole, if I may be so blunt."

Her eyebrows bounced and she glanced away momentarily. "Well, when I joined my order, I had to alter a few things."

Elf-kind trading off their connection to life to propagate death with the Gnarl. We are truly lost, Victor thought dourly.

"Now, my turn," she said, her eager personality returning. "Where did you learn magic, Victor?"

He thought about his answer for a moment. The Trifold was gone; anything of import either on his person or burned with the remains of the sanctum.

"A sanctum south of here. There's nothing left, if that's what you're wondering."

"Pity." She pouted. "We could always use more knowledge and recruits."

Over my dead body, he thought.

"Who taught you? Did something happen to them?"

"My old mentor, she's dead. She was elf-kind. Like you." He was surprised at how hard those words came. How much they hurt.

Nyla leaned in, almost shocking Victor into reacting defensively. She looked deep into his eyes, her smile faded.

"You loved her, didn't you?"

Victor's mouth dropped open. He glanced over at Lyra who looked uncomfortably into the fire.

He swallowed. "I did. It was long ago."

"I'm sorry," Nyla said, surprising him further. "It is something special to love an elf-kind. I'm lucky to still be alive after so long while all my kin withers away without the aldyrs."

"I'd like to know how that's possible, truly," he replied, with as much sincerity as he could muster.

For once, Nyla's face bore no hint of humor. "It is ... unpleasant. I'd rather not discuss it."

"Something to do with your order? What order are you from? I'm afraid I've been quite bereft of information without contact with other magi."

Her smile returned, though it had an edge to it. "The Black Gnarl. Are you interested in apprenticing?"

"It never hurts to ask."

"It can."

"My apologies, then." He sat back in the summoned chair. The thin shoots creaked and settled as he leaned back, providing a comfortable sitting position.

Nyla fidgeted with her hair for a moment then asked, "Where are you two headed?"

It didn't feel as innocent a question as she made it seem. Victor scoured his memory for any references of the area that didn't involve the city of Kalthav. Lyra merely continued to stare into the fire.

"There is supposed to be a valley near here. It's very green, from our understanding, so we assume people may have gone there. Established a settlement of some kind."

Nyla chuckled dryly. "Oh, it's very green. But you do not want to go there, trust me. Anything within that valley is not human, or not any longer."

An uncomfortable silence hung in the air. Droman stared at the cooking rabbit, and Embra tickled the air near the campfire, causing little tendrils of flame to curl out and dance.

"I would imagine you'd be interested in the light on the horizon?" Nyla continued. "It's awfully close."

"We've learned that curiosity gets you killed in the worst ways," Victor replied rather quickly, surprising himself this time.

"Hmm." Nyla hummed in response. "That's not untrue. Well, the food appears ready. Let's eat and drink, then we'll continue our conversation."

When the food and drink were being passed around, Victor and Lyra waited until the others had eaten and drank before taking part. This elicited another chuckle from Nyla. When the three Black Gnarl began eating and drinking, the two hesitantly joined in.

In the end, they all shared a meager but appreciated meal. The drink was a dark tea already brewed and then heated with spices that Droman had dropped into the pot. He also put some salt and thyme on the rabbit near the end of its cooking. He spoke for the first time, his voice deep and bored, to say that he specialized in Third Sect magic. The herbs were part of his magical assortment as well as used for cooking when he felt like it. Embra remained silent the whole time.

Nyla began a monologue about Godscorn, the city at the end of the world. She talked up the goals and aspirations of the Black Gnarl. The realities and possibilities. She emphasized the concepts of food and shelter followed by safety and purpose. She was very persuasive. It still made Victor sick to his stomach. He knew what the Black Gnarl was. What they were after. He had the benefit of being educated in a magi sanctum and personal experience with their order.

He taught Lyra everything he could, but she still came from a town surviving each day however it could. When he looked over at her, it pleased him to see that she only showed meager interest. Her face gave away no outward show of emotion—to those that didn't know her. However, Victor could see the suspicion subtly etched into her features.

After she was done, Nyla took a deep drink from her spiced

tea. She looked pleased with herself. Then, she outright stated her offer. They were, as she stated previously, ambassadors. The two of them were welcome to join other survivors waiting for her return at an old port town further south. There were a few more locations for her and her companions to visit and look for more, including Kalthav itself, but there were food and supplies waiting in the town.

"How many others have accepted your invitation?" Victor asked.

Her eyes, looking like burning emerald in the firelight, glanced up as her face pinched in thought. Her fingers tapped sequentially against her mug.

"Twenty-two, I believe," she smiled at him. "All that we've come across have taken our offer so far," she added with a wink.

Victor was silent for a moment. The Gnarl were going to Kalthav, too. He had to get rid of them. He shuddered inwardly at the choice he was being forced to make.

"I'm going to go for a short walk to think about this," he said, standing up.

Lyra looked at him, her eyes wide with concern. "You're going for a walk? Here?"

Victor looked down at her and gave a smile. "I won't go far."

He leaned down and kissed her cheek. He felt her twitch at the sudden and greatly unexpected gesture, but he needed to get near enough to whisper a warning without drawing suspicion: "Be ready for anything."

She gripped his hand in acknowledgment. "Ok, please don't go far," she replied, giving him a knowing look.

Victor sighed and turned, walking casually back into the direction they first entered into the Kalthavian forest. The trees were thinner here. It gave him a better view of the sky. He found a small hill and walked up it, stepping on the exposed rocks that jutted out like broken stairs. He was fully out of sight of the camp. Scattered clouds spread their dark fingers across the starlit sky. Moonlight fringed them in cold silver.

Remembering Nethara was difficult. He tried pushing her out of his mind, replacing painful memories of her with anything he could manage. Mostly, that consisted of Lyra. He felt guilty and wrong for doing so, but there was only so much pain that one could handle and keep surviving.

He honestly hadn't thought their time at the Trifold would end. She was elf-kind, too, after all. He expected to grow old and die long before her. He should have been the one making apologies on his death bed, not her. The apologies should have been, "I'm sorry for growing old and ugly while you will always be vibrant and beautiful in my eyes;" or, "My life's greatest joy has been learning with you and loving you." Instead, the world took her from him. The aldyrs died and with it her people's ageless vitality. He watched her wither away and she was the one apologizing for leaving him with an empty sanctum and warnings against a dying world.

The Black Gnarl took her from him.

A rustling noise came from behind him. He turned, a spell ready by reflex, and then he let himself relax. It was Nyla. Another elf-kind woman come to change his world. One who belonged to the Black Gnarl, itself. The diametric opposite of Nethara. Perhaps it was ironic. A cruel prank of fate.

"Your lover is right. You shouldn't wander out alone."

"I wouldn't exactly call her my lover," he replied coldly, turning back to look at the sky. Nyla came to stand beside him.

"Well, just wait," she cooed.

"I wanted to think. Alone. What do you want?" Victor asked pointedly.

Nyla was quiet for a moment. Her head slowly lifted, joining him in looking at the sky.

"I know you're lying to me, Victor."

His heart skipped. The corner of his lip curled and he clenched his jaw.

"How so?"

"I know you're not going to the valley further east. You were educated in a sanctum. The possibility of them not knowing what happens there is slim, even if it was just an educated guess that journeying there is fatal."

Her words were subdued, but calm and even. A striking difference from her usual tone. A hint of her playfulness was still present. It was as though she were a teacher patiently scolding a student.

"You're going to Kalthav. Just admit it."

"Why would we be going there? There's only two of us."

"I haven't quite figured that out yet," she admitted. "But, you're a trained mage. She's a skillful swordswoman. Back in the old times, I would say adventure was on your minds. There's no such thing anymore."

"You were alive during the old times? Before the Rupture?" he interjected.

Nyla slid her fingers over her face and gave him a smile. "800 years old. Elf-kind glory," she chuckled.

"Anyway, as I said, there's no such thing as adventure these days. Maybe curiosity because of the beacon? Thinking there may be some people left nearby? I don't know. Why don't you tell me?"

Victor looked over at her. The golden color of her hair caught the moonlight and shone like silver, instead. What did she do to retain her elf-kind powers with the Gnarl?

"I just want honesty between us, Victor. I meant it when I offered for you both to join us in Godscorn. Someone with your abilities? You would do so well there."

She put a hand on his shoulder and gave it the slightest squeeze. "And honesty never hurt anyone. I'm a more powerful mage than you, without a doubt. So, if I wanted you dead I would have done so already. You know that."

All of her words leaned more and more toward the seductive. She wanted to put him off guard and attempt to build rapport with him at the same time. Regardless, her touch made his skin crawl.

"What does the Black Gnarl want with the beacon? Why are you headed there?"

She left her hand on his shoulder and turned her head toward the north, where the beacon shot like a pitch-black needle into the sky.

"Honestly? Nothing. The beacon serves its purpose. We are genuinely out here to find survivors. Of course, with me visiting this part of the world, my elders wanted me to venture into Kalthav and report back what I find, for studious purposes.

"Of course," he echoed sardonically. "What is the beacon for?"

She turned back to him and flashed him a smile like he'd never seen. Her eyes glistened. It felt like he was being stared at by a panther.

"Such secrets are privy to those in the Black Gnarl. Another reason for you to come back with me, no?"

Victor looked over at the hand on his shoulder. He let out a long breath from his nose. He needed the concentration.

"Nyla, you've been very honest with me. And very accommodating to Lyra and myself. Now, I will be perfectly honest with you."

"Goo—" Nyla began, but her words were cut short.

Victor's own hand shot up and grabbed her by the throat. The sparks were already coursing through his fingers by the time they touched her flesh. Her hand tensed reflexively and grabbed his shoulder painfully. He barely noticed, however, and used his free hand to wrench hers free. He stepped back, leaving her at arm's length with his fingers wrapped tightly around her neck.

"I want you to hear this," he growled, speaking through his teeth. "This is just enough to keep you subdued."

Victor glared at Nyla. He felt her muscles twitching beneath his fingers. Her body was stiff from the electricity coursing through her. She would not be able to focus enough for a spell, be able to call for help, or even fight him. Victor wanted to be able to be honest with her.

"Your order is vile. Disgusting. It took everything from me. From millions upon millions of people. You opened the way. You tore the sky and broke the world. All the dark gods from the past could never hope to aspire to produce the suffering you and your Black Gnarl have caused."

He focused his anger, drew in the crackling power from the sky, from the air. Nyla yelped and stared at him with murder in her eyes, her teeth clenched and lips pulled back.

"We are going to Kalthav to learn about the beacon. I will find a way to stop you. I will find a way to hide Alda from the Obscured Throne *forever*. You are a more powerful mage than me, yes. But, I've dealt with the likes of you before. Your hubris is your weakness. That is why you will die."

With a final burst, Victor let loose with all the power he had summoned with his talent for lightning magic. Nyla tensed in his grip, her mouth making little more than seething, angry noises. Her eyes rolled back and with a final choking, gurgling noise, she went limp. He released his grip and she fell to the ground, her skin smoking and the hems of her cowl and robe smoldering with orange embers.

"Mala rak ecsil!"

The magical incantation set off alarm bells in Victor's head. He turned to see Droman emerging from the trees, hurling something in Victor's direction.

"*Tyryn!*" Victor barked, clenching his fist and summoning his arcane shield. Three small, sharp pebbles pinged off the swirling air in front of him. He remembered Droman was an expert in Third Sect magic, according to Nyla. The pebbles must have been enchanted, waiting for key words to send them flying at lethal speeds.

The lanky man pulled a length of rope from within his robe. It was only about a foot long and dark in color. To Victor's chagrin, he realized it was a cord of human hair. Droman gave another command and the rope of hair uncoiled, turning into a whip of a thousand tails. The hairs moved like snakes, seemingly at their controller's will.

"*Rivis ocmand!*" Victor shouted, motioning with his hands to empower the spell to intercept command of the enchanted item. "*Rivis Ocmand! RIVIS OCMAND!*"

Victor repeated the chant over and over, making sure his movements were sharp and confident. The hairs hesitated, some of them recoiling, but he couldn't gain full control. Several of them whipped out and grabbed one of his hands, wrenching it painfully in the air. A wicked smile crossed Droman's face, causing it to bunch into a near unrecognizable mass of wrinkles. More hairs circled Victor's neck and began to tighten.

Without his voice, First Sect magic was impossible. He could only rely on his one hand for meager Second Sect spells. He threw out an open, splayed hand and focused fire from his fingertips. The flames splayed over the hairs, snapping many of them. He drew in a breath, but more hairs replaced those that were destroyed. Then, more hairs grabbed his other wrist.

Victor cursed inwardly. He was helpless.

∼

THE SOUND of the strange language of magic reached Lyra's ears. She recognized it from times past with Victor. She thought of standing, rushing to his side, but remembered his warning.

No sooner had this thought crossed her mind, the dwarf near her stood. Embra's fingers were already working furiously and angry strands of fire began lurching from the torch she always carried. They combined with a few burning tendrils from the campfire and shot out at Lyra like spears of flame.

Lyra dropped to one knee and propelled herself forward. The orange spears just missed her and she felt the heat on her face, her cheek burning in pain. Ignoring it, she went for the dwarf without hesitation. In a single motion, she drew her sword and brought it up in a flashing arc, feeling the metal connect with flesh and bone. The torch fell to the ground, still in the grip of the dwarf's thick-fingered hand that was no longer attached to her arm. It thumped to the ground and the flames returned to normal.

Embra's eyes opened, tears already falling. Her mouth opened wide into a silent scream. Lyra stood and brought the tip of her sword up into the dwarf's gut. The blade protruded, dark and bloody, from the other side. Embra still made no sound. Lyra pulled her sword out of the dwarf and, with both hands wrapped around the grip, brought the blade down in a strong blow that sent Embra's head rolling. It stopped near the fire, where her red hair caught alight.

"Huh," Lyra said, breathing heavily. "So you were mute."

She ran to where she heard Victor shouting the words some spell. After clearing the trees, she saw Nyla's body crumpled on the ground. The tree-man's back was facing her and in his hand was an item made of nightmares: a rope that looked to be made of human hair stretched out and writhed like impossibly long snakes. The strands led to Victor, who was turning blue from being choked to death by the horrible thing. Both of his hands were also in their grip.

Lyra howled in rage and stormed up the small hill. Just as Droman turned his head to look behind him, she began to feel the tip of her bloodied blade rip through cloth, flesh, and the vital organs beneath. The blade pierced through Droman's heart, ending his life as quickly as the weak gasp that escaped him. The hair whip went limp, the strands retreating to their normal shape.

Victor fell to his knees, coughing and gasping for air. He put a hand on his throat and rubbed the red, bleeding cuts that appeared there.

"Are you ok?" she cried out, dropping her blade and grabbing him by the shoulders.

"Yesh," he gurgled. "Where ... dwoff?"

"Don't talk," she said soothingly. "The dwarf is dead. It looks like all three are."

He nodded his head in the affirmative.

"Let's go take care of your wounds. We can do something about the bodies after."

She helped Victor to his feet. They both walked back to the camp, her arm supporting him as he regained his composure. They walked past the two bodies of the Black Gnarl members, one still smoldering while the other bled onto the grass and cold stones.

VICTOR STIFLED a gag when they arrived back at the campground. The dwarf's head lay next to the campfire, burning and spreading the smell of cooking human flesh. He noticed a gray-skinned hand clutching a torch in the cold grip of death. Embra's body lay nearby with two separate pools of blood uniting beneath it.

"Gods, I'm glad you're on my side," he remarked, covering his mouth. The stench was powerful and nauseating.

"Never piss me off," she replied with a smirk and patted his check before taking her arm from around him.

They moved the body and its parts from the camp. There was little to be done about the blood, but they covered it with dirt and forest debris until it was no longer visible. The smell might attract animals, but the hope was that the bodies would prove more enticing.

"I take it you don't want to bury them," Lyra asked, in a tone that said she knew the answer.

"Let the wilds have them," Victor replied coldly.

Victor and Lyra pilfered what supplies they could carry from the three packs of the Black Gnarl cultists. Neither felt an ounce of guilt over it. Some dried food and canteens of water and tea were very welcome. Droman's pack contained many useful items like spices, herbs and other Third Sect-oriented components.. They also took some survival essentials like medicines and better bedrolls. They'd hoped for a tent of some kind, but had no such luck. Victor was also very grateful that no copies, notes, or documents of any kind related to the Dread Praises were present.

After helping themselves to the Black Gnarl ambassadors' supplies, they cleaned up the camp and prepared for the night. Victor began the process of setting up the warding ritual for the evening. A few ingredients in Droman's selection didn't make the process easier, but it did allow for it to be more potent. The green light emanating from the inscriptions and line of water was more vibrant. It gave off the slightest of residual magic sheen that shimmered in the air like heat off a flame.

The fire burned warm and bright. The bedrolls were soft and

not thin and frayed. They weren't hungry, their bellies still filled from the rabbit. The tea the two of them shared earlier around the fire had a calming effect. Victor slept well for the first time in weeks. He tried to tell himself it had nothing to do with ridding the world of a few more cultists.

A RUSTLING SOUND, followed by a series of snaps and crunches, woke Victor from his deep slumber. His eyes opened to the weak light of early dawn. The fire burned low, but still crackled and fought against the cold. More crunching. Victor leaned up on an elbow, concern driving him to wake up quickly. He saw Lyra moving slowly around the fire.

"What's happening?" he asked in a low, raspy voice.

"I'm going to relieve myself," she replied in a slightly offended tone. "Go back to sleep. There's no more bogeymen for now." This last part was thrown teasingly at him.

He could see the light of the ward still active, though weaker than before. It was still strong enough to do its job, though. He smiled and did just as Lyra asked.

THE NEXT TIME his eyes opened, it was brighter out, sometime in the morning when the sun was still low and not yet above the trees. Lyra was sitting in one of the summoned chairs. Apparently, it was a permanent enchantment; the chairs would stay here looking like green and gray wicker accompaniments to a long-abandoned campsite after they left.

He smelled food again. Lyra had made a makeshift spit while he was asleep and had the pot hung from it. Something bubbling inside smelled very good.

"Found another rabbit and some mushrooms," she said

cheerfully. Then her face hardened a little. "I killed and skinned it the old-fashioned way."

"I don't suppose you used some of Droman's goods in there, too?" Victor asked as he crawled out of his new bedroll.

"I did," she answered pridefully.

Victor chuckled. "Don't use too much. We may need it when we reach Kalthav."

"Don't start," she shot back sternly but playfully. "I wanted stew and I'm not going to have it ruined by your logic."

"Logic will do that," came his rueful reply.

THE ROCKY TERRAIN and constant upward slope of the land leading to the capital of Kalthav all but forced them to take the road that cut through the forest and crags. It was rough terrain and rough walking. Victor missed Gil dearly, but now he also painfully missed having a ride.

The temperature also seemed to grow colder and the day unnaturally darker with each step they took. Unnatural, Victor felt, because no stars accompanied this darkness. No orange and purple sunset. This was a different type of darkness. One that made his inner soul tremble and the deep recesses of his brain recoil.

"Do you think they'll come looking for us?" Lyra asked. Her voice made it sound like she was trying to distract herself.

"Who?" he replied. The Black Gnarl ambassadors were dead, so who could she mean?

"The ones waiting on the black magi." She said before cupping her hands and blowing into them in a feeble attempt to keep warm.

"Oh," he'd forgotten about those waiting at the port town. "I highly doubt it. I'm betting their fellows waiting at the port will return without them after a given amount of time."

The cold sapped away any other attempts at conversation. Victor wished he was more proficient at fire magic. He attempted an insulation spell, but there wasn't enough heat available for even such mundane invocations.

The closer they came to Kalthav, the more it became clear that other powers were at work. His magic was being dampened by something. A weight fell upon his being that was due to neither cold nor fatigue. Victor looked beside him to see Lyra, her cheeks and nose red from cold, focusing on the road ahead. One step at a time, like himself. Her eyes, too, were clouded with distracted concern.

A sudden wave of guilt washed over him. He had been so focused on the Black Gnarl that Lyra's well-being kept getting pushed to the side. He would never let something happen to her and would readily die to give her one more day to go on, but she deserved better than this world.

"I'm sorry," he said, still looking over at her.

Lyra returned his look while rubbing her hands against her arms. She looked surprised. "For what?"

Victor turned his head back to the broken road. "All of this," he replied cryptically.

"I don't understand," she replied with a tired voice.

"I've dragged you along with me on this journey of mine. Mission. Quest. I don't know what it is. And you've suffered so much for it."

She grimaced, and her brows furrowed. "Lest you forget, mage, I came along willingly. I *asked* to come along. I'm not helpless."

"I know ... I knowI just want better for you. I keep feeling worse and worse about what comes next. This darkness, this oppressive feeling that grows every day. I don't know what to expect."

Her face softened at the sound of his frustration. "No one

does, Victor. We were both luckier than many others. You lived your life among others like yourself. You're the only person I know who has some sort of idea of what we're up against and any sort of training whatsoever to fight it. I lived in relative comfort in Rainward, but our town was still just a scared bunch of people hoping to wake up the next day. How many empty towns and villages have we found? Destroyed farmsteads and hamlets?"

Victor's chin dropped slightly. His eyes lowered. It was too many to count.

"And how many of those yet bear the skeletons of what happened? Literally and figurately? That's only counting the ones we were able to get near. Others ..."

Her voice trailed off. There were too many places so cursed, so haunted, that they gave them a wide berth. Not counting their harrowing encounter at Carnelia.

"You've given me hope, Victor," she said with conviction. "More than I would have ever had if I'd stayed in Rainward—especially after I lost both my parents."

"Can we really say that? You've seen things with me that—"

"You know damn well that I saw far worse before we even met," she said, cutting him off, her voice shaking and on edge. "It may not be much, but it's still hope."

He felt her hand touch his. Their fingers twined together. For a moment, both of their hands were warm. Unfortunately, it quickly faded.

Victor's mind wandered to the conversation with Nyla. A city in the Wailing Ocean. Godscorn. It sounded familiar. He thought back on the maps that had been created from knowledge gained from returning magi. One had been created by overlaying a map of the old world over top of the Trifold's most up-to-date rendering of Alda. A spot stood out in his mind, and his stomach lurched.

Near the center of the map of the old world, a mountain peak was marked. It was long lost amid the destruction wrought by the Rupture. A nigh-sacred place called Godscrown where the largest grove of aldyrs grew high up where no other living thing could.

Victor seethed at the thought of the Black Gnarl making such a mockery of Alda's plight. He wasn't surprised. The black-robed monsters plotted for centuries—eons—to bring this about. His blood burned, and his heart stirred. Victor's conviction was invigorated. He squeezed Lyra's hand and saw her smile in return.

CHAPTER 3

On the last night before they reached Kalthav, Victor and Lyra were woken from their sleep. Their two bodies rose from their bedrolls nearly simultaneously. With groggy eyes, they looked at one another, and then both snapped awake as their instincts told them this was more than coincidence. Though they both felt the same strange tingling on their skin, Victor was the only one to recognize it for what it was: a powerful resonance of Fifth Magic.

He put a finger up to his mouth, signaling Lyra to remain quiet. She nodded, her wide eyes showing him she was ready and alert. Her head swiveled, looking for the source of the odd feeling. Victor did the same. Light snow fell softly in the silence, some flakes twinkling like fireflies in the light of the campfire.

Victor saw a soft glow coming from behind Lyra in the trees. The source of the soft, bluish-silver light moved. It was slow and purposeful, ever in one direction: toward Kalthav.

Victor rose as quietly as he could. Lyra did the same and grabbed her sword. She unsheathed it, slow and whisper-quiet, and they both began to approach the strange light. As they stepped outside the faint emerald light of the arcane ward, Victor readied a spell, and Lyra used both hands to grip her weapon.

They both felt calm. Whatever this was, it was imbued with the Fifth and kept them at ease. However, they didn't want to take any chances. It could be some other twisted form of Black Gnarl deception.

Lyra, as ever, walked far more quietly in the snow and brush than Victor. She cast a quick glance his way. He knew it was because he couldn't be any quieter. They continued moving in on whatever it was, Victor trying to move more slowly but no less noisy.

The light was just beyond the next few trees. Its glow cast sliding shadows as it moved past the pillar-like trunks. A loud snap caused them both to jump. Victor had stepped on a branch he couldn't see due to the darkness. Lyra sucked in a breath through her teeth and brought her blade up.

The light continued forward, unfazed by the sound. It acted as though it hadn't heard anything at all.

Lyra looked back at Victor, her mouth pulled into a tight line and her eyes begging him not to cause any more noise. He nodded, sighed softly, and focused on walking one step at a time. Lyra took long, low strides like she was hunting game. Victor did his best to imitate her.

Finally, they came to a particularly wide-trunked pine tree. Lyra reached it first. She put a hand behind her, motioning for Victor to stop. He did so immediately and watched as she took cover behind the tree. The light continued on its purposeful course.

Lyra stood slowly, and in direct correlation, her sword lowered until the tip touched the ground. One hand left the grip and slowly rose to cover her mouth. Victor couldn't help himself any longer. He made his way up to her as quickly and quietly as possible. He looked around the other side of the tree trunk and saw what had made her hesitate.

A person walked casually through the cold forest. Their partially translucent body glowed a bright silver, tinged with a shimmering blue the color of a midday sky. Their physical features were easily recognizable, and they were without clothing—utterly naked on the freezing night. Their stride was measured and casual. They seemed to be unfazed by the weather or the terrain, simply walking in a straight line toward Kalthav and the beacon.

Lyra pulled Victor back and mouthed the words, "What do we do?"

Victor, wide-eyed and caught by surprise, simply shrugged. The Fifth Magic radiated from this individual, so he assumed they couldn't be dangerous. They both watched the man for a few moments, following him in the forest. He never looked back or otherwise acknowledged them. Soon, Victor and Lyra stopped bothering with trying to be quiet. They simply walked along with the glowing, naked man, except their footsteps crunched loudly while his were silent.

Victor took a deep breath and said in a loud voice, but not quite shouting, "Where are you going?"

Lyra grabbed his shoulder, squeezing, and opened her mouth to share with him a few choice words but stopped when the ghostly figure stopped, turned, and looked right at them.

"I'm going to Kalthav," he answered plainly.

Lyra and Victor shared another wide-eyed look. "Why?" she asked.

The figure didn't answer. It turned around and continued walking. The two of them stood there, unsure of how to proceed.

"Do you have any idea what is going on?" Lyra asked in a low voice.

"Something involving the Fifth Sect is all I know."

"How? What about the Fifth Magic?"

"That ghost, or man, or whatever it is, is flush with it."

Her shoulders relaxed. "So, it shouldn't be dangerous, correct?"

Victor nodded his head slowly. "One would think. But don't forget Harden."

Lyra exhaled loud and nervously.

They ran back to their campsite, haplessly crashing through brush and limbs to reach the still-burning campfire. There was no time to waste. They packed up their things and ran together back toward the direction of the glowing figure.

They found him easily enough. He hadn't disappeared, and continued walking at the same pace as before. They followed him all through the night; excitement, curiosity, and fear mixing in a cocktail that kept them wide awake and with plenty of energy to keep moving.

Eventually, the ache in their muscles overtook their emotional drive. The being before them walked without urgency or need of rest. Victor and Lyra didn't talk out of fear of what would happen. The being could disappear, attack them, or worse. One thing was for certain: they could follow it all the way to Kalthav.

Traveling to the capital city took far longer at their pace. They ate what they could on their feet. Once in a while, they would rest for a few minutes and catch up to the being. The first time provided little rest at all. They were both so nervous that they would lose their quarry, and neither of them got much rest. After confirming that it didn't disappear on them, the next few breaks provided enough respite for their aching legs that they could continue on with little complaint.

After what felt like a week of trudging through the freezing pine forest, the road finally emerged onto a sweeping, downward slope of tough grass and exposed stone. Withered, gray-blue crops that appeared to be some kind of wheat were sectioned off into orderly fields. The familiar sight of an empty town lay at the base of the slope, huddled against a cliff bordering the northern ocean. Beyond, a massive bridge—collapsed in the center with broken pillars laying on the exposed remains—led across the cliff to a walled section where a once-magnificent castle rose from the back side of the enormous rock column upon which it sat. The thunderous noise of the crashing ocean waves filled their ears.

The city of Kalthav. As dead as all the rest.

Lyra and Victor stood on trembling knees. This was not out of fear or exhaustion but uncontainable awe. It was early afternoon, but heavy clouds hung black in the sky with only a slight gray lining, the only sign that the sun was still up. Covering the grounds of the city, though, all the way to the fallow fields of shriveled wheat, were figures like the one they followed. A glowing sea of ethereal beings: human, dwarven, elf-kind, goblin, orc, and every manner of humanoid imaginable. All were bare-skinned and exposed; there was no projection of their tastes, poor or wealthy, in this form. They appeared just as their bodies were upon death. If any of them died peacefully or tragically, that could not be surmised, thankfully.

The being they'd followed thus far continued on his walk until he reached the rest of his fellows, where he stopped and stared. The shimmering silver sea, crested with sky-blue waves of heads, arms, shoulders, and any other exposed silhouettes, cloistered close together. They all had their heads turned toward the beacon. Victor and Lyra followed their gazes to the black needle that shot from another castle off the steep coastline to another large rock column. This one looked older and more worn than that of the castle across the bridge. Holes and crumbled walls pockmarked the structure. The beacon went straight up and into the clouds, out of sight.

Victor and Lyra took each other by the hand. They both squeezed. The city was their goal. They knew the beacon originated from here. But this was far more awe-inspiring than even they expected. They held their breaths without realizing it. Their jaws remained agape. Their eyes scanned the shining sea juxtaposed against the blackness of the sky, battling for supremacy.

Victor swallowed and felt how dry his mouth was. It hurt as his throat caught, sticking together. He pulled his canteen out of his bag and drank slowly. He offered it to Lyra, who took it from him with trembling hands.

"Sweet gods, Victor ..." Lyra said, her voice a whisper that trailed off. "Who are these people?"

Victor shook his head, his mind trying to wrap itself around the idea of tens of thousands of silver-and-blue ghosts of every race before them. They were all there, exposed to the elements and staring at the beacon, but none moved. They covered the fields, the streets, the bridge, the tops of the walls and ramparts.

"Are they specters? Ghosts of some kind?" he thought aloud.

"Where did they come from?" she asked. "Are they—do they belong to the Inheritor in this city? Each city has had something like that, right?" Her voice trembled.

"I don't think so. They all appear to be connected to the Fifth," he replied. They talked just as much to themselves as they were to each other, combining their rambling questions and thoughts to piece together some kind of explanation. Finally, Victor was able to put his thoughts in order.

"The answer is going to be there with the beacon." He pointed to the ruined older castle, where none of the specters had managed to gather.

Lyra agreed, and they began the trek to the cliffside to see if there was a way to get to the castle alone on the rock column. Though the sea of spirits showed no open hostility or even passing interest in them, Victor and Lyra still gave the spectral gathering a wide berth. A brisk wind blew, and the waves continued to crash and echo, but the mass stood silent. It was more than off-putting. Something ominous weighed in the air. The feeling that had pressed on them during their journey was stronger than ever before.

When they came to the cliff, it was much as Victor had expected. A sheer craggy face dropped straight into the ocean. Large rocks breached the water at the base, but the fall into the water alone would be lethal. Victor looked to his left and his right. It appeared to be the same situation in both directions. The intimidating drop went on for miles down the coast with nothing but a freezing ocean between them and the tall columns.

"I remember reading about these," Victor said, the wind and waves attempting to drown out his words. "That," he continued, raising his voice and pointing toward the castle connected to the town by the fallen bridge, "is the Lord's Pillar. And the one we're trying to reach is the Storm's Pillar."

Lyra squinted and looked at both in turn. "The Lord's Pillar, I understand; the castle and all. But a second castle on an unreachable island? Why is it called the Storm's Pillar?"

Victor scoured the memories of his lessons at the Trifold. History fascinated him, given that so much was lost and left only to be remembered by those in a fortunate enough situation to be able to both read and care about what came before the Rupture. Much of his own knowledge on the subject had been buried by requisite learning of new circumstances. But scraps of information still sprouted from all the ash and gloom of recent memory.

"The Kalthavians worshiped the former gods, even after the Rupture, but they also held special regard for the greatest heroes. They were like demigods to them, if I remember correctly. The Storm's Pillar was both a keep and temple for them. Only on certain pilgrimages did people visit it, save for a handful of warrior priests tasked with the upkeep."

"Interesting," Lyra commented. "So, how do we get there? Can you fly us with your magic?"

He had the inclination she was being facetious, but to her point, he still provided an answer.

"I could, but such magic takes a serious toll. We both know that something waits over there. I won't have the power to get us back, and we'd truly be stuck."

Lyra walked as close to the edge as she dared, still staying back a few dozen feet. She lifted up onto her tiptoes and peered over the edge. "Yeah, no swimming that."

Victor chuckled dryly.

"Our only choice is the city," he said, thinking out loud. "They had to have some way to get there. We'll just have to find it."

Lyra turned and looked at the massive gathering of Fifth Sect revenants. Her mouth turned downwards and her eyes squinted. "That's not going to be pleasant."

Victor sighed in agreement. "So far, they haven't been hostile."

"So far," she echoed.

They skirted the mass of bodies as long as they could, but would were soon forced to walk through them if to get to the city outside the wall. Both of them hesitated when they reached the glowing mass. Being this close to the specters, though, revealed something else about them. Some of them had clearly defined features, right down to their hair and wrinkles. Others were merely silhouette outlines of a human shape. And there was every level of clarity in-between.

"Strange," he thought out loud.

"What is it?" Lyra asked through gritted teeth.

"Look closely at them. They all look ... different."

Victor heard Lyra's strained breathing before she suddenly huffed, "Huh, you're right."

"I wonder why that is? It doesn't seem to make a difference if they're orc or elf-kind. Some are simply more visible than others."

"I wonder if it's related to how strong their connection to Fifth Magic was when they were alive," Lyra said in a soft tone, like she was thinking aloud, as well.

The idea made perfect sense. "I think you're right," he said, sudden realization sparking many different ideas in his mind.

"I still don't want to walk through there," she added miserably.

"Nor do I," he added, and gave her a soft pat on the shoulder before moving ahead.

"Fuck ..." she cursed under her breath before following.

Regardless of the spirits' lack of acknowledgement of their presence, walking among them took all the willpower they had. Lyra grabbed Victor's forearm and squeezed it painfully hard. Victor gritted his teeth. The specters stared at the beacon, some vaguely looking toward the two of them as they passed. The worst were the faceless ones; the glowing humanoid shadows that would turn their empty faces toward them as they passed.

"So they're still somewhat aware," Victor whispered.

Lyra didn't reply. Her grip continued to hurt and bruise him as she dug her fingers into his flesh.

There were no openings in the glowing congregation. Victor and Lyra moved slowly, winding their way through and avoiding touching them at all costs. Now and then, Victor would 'bump' one of the beings only for his body to pass through, the air feeling heavier, denser where he connected with them. Lyra would let out a groan or sharp cry here and there, signaling to Victor that she just experienced the same thing.

The sight was strange for a thousand different reasons. Victor thought he and Lyra should be used to seeing anything by now, but this struck him as vastly 'other.' The city was shattered, like any other, but the houses and stonework appeared to be in good condition comparably, even as many of them lay crumbled. These structures appeared to be kept in livable conditions until fairly recently.

The contrast between the silver-lighted ghosts and the oppressive midday darkness was also striking. By his reckoning, it should be early afternoon, but it may as well have been midnight. The sky was black and bleak, the clouds' edges lined by the dullest of gray light. The combined glow of thousands upon thousands of Fifth Sect ghosts barely kept the dark at bay on the streets.

Finally, there was the overall aura of the place. It simply felt wrong. And dreadful. It only got worse whenever Victor's eyes were drawn to the beacon at Storm's Pillar. A fear that could only be described as primordial coursed through him. It occurred to him that the way Lyra reacted to the sea of ghosts could be attributed to this same fear; she had simply misplaced it. He had the sudden impression that they were both small, helpless prey animals skulking underground whilst knowing above the worst kind of malicious predator slowly made its way toward them.

They walked along the crumbling walls of the town near the edge of the cliff. A fallen portcullis allowed them to enter a tower and access the upper ramparts. Unfortunately, they found no path to the lower parts of the cliff.

As they made their way out of the towers, the one place thus far where none of the specters gathered, Lyra grabbed Victor's hand and pulled him forward. She'd obviously had enough of the lingering ghosts and wanted to find a way to Storm's Pillar as soon as possible.

Her harried pace caused them both to pass through parts of the spirits as they 'bumped' into them. Some of the figures turned to look at them, as before, but were otherwise unfazed. Victor felt the thickness of their presence where he touched them and noticed that those with the weaker Fifth Sect connection, the faceless silhouettes, had a thinner presence as the passed through them.

"Lyra …" Victor called out, softly at first. Her pace transitioned from harried to reckless. "Lyra," he repeated, louder.

If she heard him, she was ignoring him. He could hear her breathing growing louder and louder. She almost seemed to be in a different world; his arm stretched out in front of him, their hands tangled together, her arm seeming to stretch for a mile leading to her hair billowing in the wind that picked up once they reached the bridge. Silver and blue lights raced by him. So many fading bodies touching him up and down, it felt like his muscles were spasming. Suddenly, it all stopped.

He was standing next to Lyra, both of them breathing heavily. Victor felt like he'd woken from a dream. The thundering waves were louder. The wind was ice cold and blowing angrily around the pillars of the bridge, some still whole while most were broken. The gap between them and the opposite side of the wide, once-magnificent bridge yawned like a snaggle-toothed mouth.

"Ok," Lyra said, her chest heaving, "we're here. Now what do we do?"

Victor looked over at her and grimaced.

"I picked up the pace, just a little," she grumbled, looking at him from the corner of her eyes.

He pulled his cloak tighter. How were they going to cross? He took off his pack and knelt down. The ingredients from Droman had barely been used, so Victor rifled through them trying to think of anything that may help. An idea struck him, but it also caused his stomach to clench.

"I have an idea, but we will have to move fast. Very fast." He looked up at Lyra, his lips pulled into a thin line.

Lyra nodded stiffly, concern and resolution in her eyes that showed tears from the cold. "Ok."

Victor pulled out the necessary ingredients from the pack. Blue chalk from southern desert plains and a vial of distilled pine tree resin. He was missing sugar of lead, made from a distilling process involving lead and vinegar. This was the cause of his concern.

"I can make a bridge from the fallen stones, but without sugar of lead it won't last long. At all. I can try to empower it with additional Third Sect runes, but ..."

"Let's make it fast, then," Lyra finished in a firm voice.

Victor closed his eyes, gained his focus despite the biting cold, and began his work. He drew the necessary runes on the broken edge of the bridge, then additional runes on the stones he wanted to use. Victor made sure each line, each mark was as perfect and clean as possible. He added a few additional runes to help make up for the lack of the third ingredient, but it wouldn't be enough.

He stood up and walked back over to stand beside Lyra. They both approached the edge of the bridge, just behind the runes on the ground.

"When I toss out the contents of this vial, run to the very first stone you see in place. Do not stop. Do not look down." The concern in his voice transferred to her. Lyra looked even more worried than when they had to walk through the specters.

Victor removed the seal on the vial. He then spoke the incantation in a sharp, clear voice. At the moment the final syllable left his mouth, he tossed the pungent liquid out in a sweeping arc. He threw it off to the right to account for the stiff wind. The stones trembled and moved immediately, the runes glowing brightly. Before the first stone even fully settled into place, Lyra hopped onto it. The others were following closely behind, but the further out the arcane bridge stretched, the longer it was taking the stones to move into place.

Instead of hastily jumping from one stone to the next, now Lyra waited patiently for the next one to move into place. Victor followed closely behind. He tried to find the widest one possible, but most of them tumbled into the ocean. He could have made more complex inscriptions and widened the path, but there wasn't enough material—both alchemical ingredients and the bridge stones—to allow for it. The two of them were forced to make their way across the bridge one behind the other.

The wind felt much stronger here, where they were outside the protection of the bridge's pedestrian wall. Victor's heart thudded in his chest. One false step and they would fall to an instant death in the cold, thrashing waters below. He reminded himself not to look down. He focused on Lyra in front of him. From this angle, she appeared focused and steady. It had been less than a minute from Lyra's first jump.

Behind him, the sound of grinding stone made him turn his head so sharply it threatened to throw him off balance. As he'd thought, the spell was already breaking. As the light faded from the inscribed runes, the first stone fell. The next followed within moments.

"Lyra, hurry!" he shouted over the wind.

"I'm trying!" came her muffled reply. She was once more

jumping onto stones as soon as they were moving into place. She nearly slipped once, hitting a foothold too soon and nearly losing her balance. Lyra shrieked, but after a heart-wrenching second of wobbling, she stood still and steady again.

One stone after another, they made their way across. Behind them, the other slabs fell like dominoes, faster and faster. In front of them, the next stones arrived at a slower pace.

With the edge of the next bridge within a few more painfully slow jumps, Lyra stopped abruptly. Victor opened his mouth to ask what was wrong, but saw what was happening. His stomach clenched into a violent knot. Next to him, the next stone moving into place dropped out of the air. There wasn't enough power left in the incantation to make it all the way to the end.

"Fuck! Victor, what do we do?" Lyra shouted from over her shoulder.

Victor's face drooped. His eyes were wide and his face white as one of the glowing specters. "You're going to have to jump."

He must have been too deep in despair and disbelief to speak loudly, as Lyra called out to him: "What?"

"Jump!" he screamed. He took a few steps backward to give her some running room, but already felt the stone he was on wobbling as its power began to fade.

Lyra did not take time respond. She stepped back, threw off her backpack and cloak—relieving her of any extra weight or drag—and took off. Her foot left the very edge of the farthest stone. Her leading foot landed, touching by just its toes. The sound of the boot scraping off the stone and her body twisting and thudding on its side into the ground could be heard over the roaring winds, which seemed to get angrier by the moment. She crawled to her feet, holding her side and revealing just how painful the landing truly was.

Victor threw off his cloak and leaned back into his back foot. The stone beneath him was slipping downward even more. He felt and heard the scraping of the stone behind the one he was standing on fall after losing its enchantment. Lyra's eyes met his. They were squinted in pain and a rivulet of blood ran down her chin.

"Run!" she screamed. Her teeth were red. She'd struck her lip on the fall.

Victor ran. He had three stones worth of room to pick up enough speed. As his foot hit the final slab he felt it give way and begin to fall. In a last, reflexive moment, he pushed himself off into a spin. The world moved in slow motion. He turned and saw the last stones fall. He was alone, in midair, with seconds left before he would fall and die. He heard Lyra scream. Maybe it was his name, or just some incomprehensible sound. Words left his mouth but he didn't feel like he spoke them of his own accord.

Arcane power pulsed through his body, fueled by desperation and terror. The First Sect coagulated these emotions at the palms of his hands, outstretched before him, and a burst of energy distorted the air in front of him. It was enough to twist the wind around it, curl it like heatwaves disrupted by a waving hand. He felt himself hurled backwards, then pain shot through his back.

His arms shot upwards as he flailed to grab something. Somehow, his fingers found purchase. His fingers gripped a wrist while another set of hands were wrapped around his. He hung there, hurting and in disbelief.

"Climb, gods damn it," Lyra called out in a strained garble of words.

Victor looked up and saw her head and arms exposed from the bridge's edge. He must have landed against the bridge with his back and she grabbed him before he fell.

He moved his feet slowly back and forth, but he remembered through the fog of pain and fear that they were in the middle of a bridge, not a cliff. There was no foothold for him here. He gripped and clawed as he tried to make his way up her arms. She did the same, grunting as she pulled him up.

"A little further," he called out. "Just a little further!"

Her mouth opened, red teeth exposed, and her eyes clenched shut. She howled with the effort of lifting him to safety. As soon as he felt the rough edge of the bridge he grabbed it, helping her in pulling himself onto the surface. The rough edges scraped against him, tugging on his clothes. Lyra dragged him onto the bridge as his feet grabbed purchase and he scrambled away from the perilous gap.

He wanted to collapse, but he felt himself being pulled still. He braced himself on the ground and felt Lyra's arms wrap around him. She squeezed. Victor's arms rose slowly, the pain in his muscles fighting him. Once his hands felt Lyra's back, he gained just enough vigor to pull her close, too. They both remained there, on their knees, holding each other for a moment. Victor felt his eyes grow warm and wet. Then, he felt the rest of him getting wet and cold.

They made it not only just in time before the spell completely faded, but just before a vicious coastal rain arrived. His mind momentarily went to the two of them stranded on those hovering stone slabs while pelted with cold rain and he shivered down to his soul.

"Let's get off this damn bridge," Lyra spoke into his shoulder. Her voice came out muffled and irritated, yet relieved.

They put one arm around each other as they stood. Both limped and hobbled, taking care not to slip on the stones that were getting more slippery by the second. Their cloaks were already sorely missed.

Victor and Lyra looked out at the second half of the city. The buildings here weren't in as bad a condition as those on the other side. It could be because they were made of more solid material. Regardless, most of them were still collapsed in whole or part.

Lyra's armed stretched out and she pointed at something Victor couldn't see through the rain. He thought he heard her call out, but was too focused on trying to find what she was pointing at. Then, he saw it: a building made almost entirely of stone, braced with thick wood beams and iron bars. The roof was also mostly intact.

Their footsteps picked up, sloshing through puddles already formed in the broken streets. When they reached the building, the door groaned loudly as it was pushed open. Inside, shelves, desks, cabinets, and all manner of richly detailed furniture lay in ruin; their contents sprawled all over the floor.

Water fell off of the two of them in rivulets, splattering onto the floor. The sound of the rain and wind outside was stifled by the thick walls, though the few windows allowed rain to enter and created pools on the floor. Their labored breathing was much louder in here and echoed off the vaulted ceiling and walls.

They continued inside, looking for a dry place to rest. A tinkling sound caused them both to look down. They had inadvertently kicked a few coins across the floor. They had come from a small box that had broken when it had fallen from one of the collapsed shelves. Lyra looked around and chuckled.

"What's so funny?" Victor asked, nudging one of the coins with the toe of his boot.

"It's a bank," she smiled. "Old-worlders and their money. They wanted to protect it so much. Everything else is absolutely destroyed. But this bank is pretty much intact."

Her laugh infected him. It led to both of them guffawing at the ridiculousness of the situation. Victor couldn't remember the last time they had shared a laugh. It was a welcome respite.

It also hurt their respective wounds. Both of them groaned in unison.

In their search for someplace to rest that wasn't a stone floor, they found where rooms had been abandoned and wealth of all kinds—gold and silver coins, gold bars, heirlooms and jewelry —lay in piles and scattered in bits and pieces. So much wealth that in the old days before the Rupture the two of them could live an opulent life. Now, it was as useless as it was tarnished.

In one of the rooms, a lavish, cushioned couch was still intact. It looked like it was prepared just for them. The room had the look of an office of some kind. They gathered up paper and bits of broken furniture and started a fire. While Victor took care of the fire, Lyra went to find them water. After a few minutes, she returned with two goblets filled to the top.

He limped back over to the couch and sat next to her. She handed him a goblet, which was wet all over the outside.

"It's rainwater. Filled pretty fast," she said.

"That will work," he responded, taking the glass and drinking.

He regarded the goblet, which appeared to be made of silver. "These are ... fancy."

"They are. Silver I think. Found them in another room."

"Find anything else interesting?" he asked. They weren't going to be able to continue looking for a way to the pillar in their condition and with the storm, so he tried to make conversation to take their mind off their pains.

"A few skeletons. They were under some large fallen stones and shelves, so they must have died or not been able to get out when *whatever* happened to this city," she looked around the room and shrugged, "well, happened."

Victor swirled the water in his goblet like it was wine. "It was recent, whatever it was. It had to have something to do with the beacon."

"Certainly."

"Its creation must have caused an earthquake or something. The city isn't in the same shape as others. The destruction is too 'new,' if that makes sense."

She nodded and took a drink. "We should get some sleep."

"Yes," he agreed as he looked into the warm fire.

"We don't have anything to make the ward, do we?" she asked, knowing the answer.

"No. It's all at the bottom of the ocean. I wonder if we'll need it."

"What makes you say that?"

"None of the specters are here. Did you notice?"

She leaned against him, laying her head on his shoulder. "When I went to get water. I realized they weren't here."

"I think we'll be ok for a few hours." Rather, he *hoped* they'd be ok. But there was nothing they could do now. And he was tired, mentally and physically, and his body throbbed in pain, particularly his back; he had little fight left at the moment.

He heard Lyra sniffing and then she coughed. They had tea in their bags, the ones lost to the waves. Heating it over the fire with their gear would have been simple. Now, they literally had nothing. Almost nothing.

"Wait here a moment," he said, then slowly rose and walked out of the room. Outside, in the open space of the building, the wind and rain were much louder. There was a staircase leading up to another floor that ran along the sides of the building, not creating a full second story. He made his way up the stairs and checked into some of the rooms. As he suspected, one of them was another plush office. The window was broken, but facing away from the storm. The curtains were thick velvet and mostly dry. He pulled them down and took them downstairs.

Back inside the room with Lyra, the fire made the more enclosed space feel incredibly comfortable. Lyra was already asleep, sitting on the couch and laying over on one side. He put one of the curtains over her and she moaned softly, pulling it close. He gently lifted her by the head and shoulders, sitting her in his lap. He continued to stare at the fire, slipping into a habit nurtured by all the time spent traveling and not sleeping.

Exhaustion won out in the end. His eyelids grew heavy. The warmth seeped into his bones. Lyra's closeness calmed him and sleep soon took over.

His eyes opened some unknown amount of time later to the same dark skies. It would be impossible to tell if it was day or night with these conditions. The howling wind and sheets of rain slowed to a stiff breeze and light drizzle.

Lyra was still asleep. She snored softly, her head on his lap and her hair fallen over her face. He rested his hand gently on her temple. She took a deep breath, but didn't appear to wake up. He looked over at the window in this room, left exposed by the fallen curtains. It was laced with cracks. A few holes in the glass allowed rain to drip in, run down the inside in lonely drops.

A rumble in the distance. It resonated, folded upon itself and faded away. Then came another, booming against the constant patter of rain.

It's only thunder, Victor thought.

His mind had been on edge for so long, it always reflexively went to the worst places. Instead of thunder, he had imagined some extraplanar beast the size of a mountain walking along the ocean, its head breaching the water as it dragged tormented souls in its wake.

What's wrong with me? he scolded himself.

He hadn't been sleeping well for ages. He felt worn and stretched thin. Dark thoughts invaded his mind constantly.

Negative emotions overwhelmed him. Worse, his magic wouldn't be at its most potent if he didn't rest. Something was waiting at the castle on Storm's Pillar. The beacon wasn't just going to let them arrive and snuff it out like a candle. The worst was yet to come, he knew it. His magic and Lyra's blessed blade were the only things that could save them.

The rain continued to tap on the window like dancing fairies. The thunder rumbled, breaking into the performance. It must have been some kind of magic, pure and borne of nature, for it had a calming effect on him despite his troubled thoughts. He found his eyes growing heavy again. His own breathing began to match Lyra's own soft rhythm and he found himself drifting into a dreamless sleep.

VICTOR'S EYES SHOT OPEN. The last echoing peal of thunder fading away.

"That was loud," Lyra commented in a groggy voice, her head remaining still.

The rain was lighter, but another vicious crash of thunder shook the walls. The storm was still going, but changed its strategy.

"We should get moving," Victor said, his voice also heavy with sleep. "The rain has mostly let up and I can't hear the wind. It's the best time to search for a way to the pillar."

Lyra grunted a complaint, but rose to a sitting position and pulled her hair out of her face. She reached over and grabbed her goblet, which still had water, and drank the cup dry.

"Alright," she said with conviction and stood to her feet. "Let's go."

Victor stood, drank down the rest of his water, and followed her out of the room. The fire had burned down to a few smoldering coals; the only sign of life remaining after the two of them left the building behind forever.

They found a few cloaks in a closet, possibly belonging to former bank officials or wealthy patrons given how well-made they were. Victor lit a torch, fallen from its sconce on the wall, and found one for Lyra. It would help against what waited for them outside.

As they expected, the cold remained supernaturally potent. The rain was light, pecking their skin like invisible insects, while the thunder exploded beyond the clouds. The weather here was strange. It had the feeling of being alive, somehow, just as the cold did.

"Where should we start?" Lyra asked, pulling her cloak tighter around her. It was a red-dyed velvet mantle, with gold buttons and silver cords of silk. A fur capelet traced the hood and would keep her face and head warm. Victor pointed out that it was a little opulent, but she stated that, 'If she was going to die today, she would do so comfortably.'

"The castle here. The monarchy would certainly have a way over. Possibly magical, but I doubt that method is still available."

She nodded, the red hood bobbing while the fur fluttered in the cold breeze.

A looming wall circled the outskirts of the castle. The gate leading into the courtyard was still standing, but had been rendered impotent by several fallen sections. Victor and Lyra entered through one of these into the ruins of the castle court-yard. Once-detailed statues lay in pieces, lining the walkway to the entrance with their broken majesty.

They both looked up at what remained of the symbol of Kalthav during the height of its power. Like the other cities, it was naught but a corpse of wood and stone occupied by skele-tons both literal and otherwise.

"I still don't see how we haven't encountered an Inheritor of some kind," Lyra observed. "The one in Felkirk was quite possessive. And those things in Carnelia certainly wouldn't have let us get a nap in one of the buildings."

Victor grimaced. "It's more concerning than not encountering one," he said, agreeing. "Be careful, who knows how long this place will stay standing."

"Yes," Lyra replied and followed him inside.

The torchlight scarcely fought off the darkness within the castle. Holes in the wall let in weak light, but outside, the hidden moon provided little relief. Tapestries and paintings lay on the floor amid countless other amounts of detritus. Walking was perilous and they had to move slowly so as not to trip or fall over anything.

Searching would certainly be more difficult. They agreed that there was no time to bother looking upstairs, but the choice was also made for them when the weak light caught a black void where the nearest staircase had collapsed much like the bridge.

Since the castle was situated on top of the stone pillar, it only made sense to seek a door leading downstairs. After many attempts resulting in finding additional rooms, they were left standing next to a toppled throne, thinking about what to do.

Lyra walked over and sat in the throne, marveling at how thick and comfortable it was. She rubbed the arms, which were cushioned themselves, and let out a sigh.

"What was so important about this chair, anyway?"

"The king sat there. It was a symbol of their power."

"Like an elder?"

Victor smiled and nodded his head. "No. The king oversaw the entire region. The city-state of Kalthav stretched all the way to a river out west, which is dried out now, I believe. And then all the way to the east to the border of Athyl'glen, the elf-kind forest. Then north to the ocean and south to a place that's long been covered by the Wailing Ocean."

"Huh," she huffed. "All from right here."

"Basically."

"I couldn't imagine being that important. It sounds stressful."

Victor chuckled, but the discussion gave him an idea.

"We have to go upstairs."

Lyra's face squinted into a question she didn't have to ask: "Why?"

"The king and queen's chambers will be up there."

"Are you tired again?"

"No, but I'm thinking that in their chambers, or, at least, nearby, is a way to get to the other pillar."

She rose from the throne and stepped down the dais, looking like some sort of warrior-queen. "What makes you say that?"

"The hierarchy was quite stringent in the old world. Kings and queens had privileges and duties that they felt only belonged to them. If Storm's Pillar held religious or social significance for the Kalthavians, then their rulers were possibly the only ones who had access to get there."

"That makes sense," she said with a heavy sigh and looked toward the large, broken staircase.

"There may be another way up," Victor said hopefully.

There was, however, no other way up. Both staircases were broken, and the second one they found was worse than the other. Once more, they prepared to make a jump from one fallen edge to another. This time, however, there was no deadly fall involved. Victor grunted when he landed as pain laced up his back. Lyra breathed sharply through her teeth and grabbed her side. Their injuries from the bridge were still hounding them.

"This is not a good way to be walking into the mouth of the beast," she said, referencing their approach to the great, dangerous unknown while in a hobbled state.

"No, it isn't," he replied, helping her to her feet. "But we'll manage."

The top floor, they discovered, was in equally poor condition. In many places, even worse. The collapsed towers closed off areas of the castle and some rooms were fully exposed to the elements due to collapsed outer walls.

Unfortunately, they couldn't locate the royal chambers on this floor. The castle did appear to have another full story from the outside view. Towers for lookouts and protection were all that looked to be left. Victor began to grow disheartened. The chamber may have been destroyed or be blocked off from where they were. He stood in the darkness, his torch crackling feebly. The snapped frame of the broken painting beneath his feet splintered as he turned around and searched further for possibilities.

"Victor, over here," Lyra called out from the darkness ahead, the light of her own torch dancing from behind a stone column at the corner of the walkway.

As he approached her, their combined torchlight lit a section of collapsed stone—an amalgam of castle wall and tower. The rubble sealed off the inside of the upper floor from the outside, but also blocked most of the passage. That was what Lyra had to show him.

"We may be able to squeeze through here."

She pointed to a narrow, triangular crevice where the rubble led, with any luck, to a part of the castle he originally thought inaccessible. They would have to crouch and slide their way through. It would be difficult, but they could possibly make it.

"Can you move any of the stones with your magic?" she asked hopefully.

He shook his head. "I'm afraid to cause even more of a collapse. If I move the wrong stones it could seal off this part of the castle or, worse, bury us alive."

She sighed. "Or crush us. You forgot that one."

"Thank you for clarifying," he added with sarcasm. "I guess we start scurrying. You're going to ruin your cloak."

She snorted. "No, I am not." Then, she removed the cloak and tightly wound it up and place it under her arm. Carefully, Lyra crouched and maneuvered her way into the dark crevice. She was forced to attempt to slide along sideways. After a series of grunts and other sounds of exertion and frustration, Victor heard her muffled call from the other side. It was his turn.

He also removed his cloak, but only so it would not snag on rocks and trap him in the hole like a rodent. His trip was filled with far more grumbling noises, and several curses as well. His injured back screamed at him and turned a minute-long struggle into a moment of agony trapped in time.

When Victor emerged through the other side, standing up straight to the groan of a grateful back, he found Lyra standing amid a heavily shadowed stone corridor. The orange light of the torches illuminated the tarnished and faded finery more heavily marked with the royal crest of Kalthav than other parts of the castle. This must be where the royal family had their chambers and received favored guests and kin.

It was pitch black here. They walked together, slowly, down the corridor to see what they could find. Two closed doors facing opposite one another came into the light. As the two of them approached, the light caught more rubble just within the edge of visibility. This area was wholly cut off from the rest of the rest the castle by debris save for the small crevice through which they entered.

They tried one of the doors and it opened easily. Too easily. The hinges pulled away from the stone and Lyra jumped aside to prevent being toppled over by the falling iron-braced slab of wood. "Gods," she muttered.

"Are you ok?" Victor asked.

She nodded in reply and put the torch out in front of her. The room within had no windows. Everything that once stood here was now on the floor. Ornate shelves, ceremonial stands of armor and weapons, paintings—all scattered and piled on top of each other. The light slowly revealed more. Couches and chairs were clustered near the center of the room. Lyra and Victor sucked in a breath.

On the furniture, emaciated bodies sat or laid there in their final resting places. The mummified remains were still adorned in silks and furs, with gold and silver jewelry inlaid with all manners of gemstones hanging from frail wrists wrapped in skin like dry, wrinkled paper.

"The royal family ..." Lyra muttered.

"And guests, I'm assuming," Victor added, sweeping his torch across the macabre scene.

At the head of the ghoulish assembly, three corpses adorned with crowns held each other close. Undoubtedly, the king, queen and princess. The twig-like, unmoving fingers of the king gripped a lavishly decorated dagger with dark stains on the blade. They both moved closer and saw the reddish-brown blotches on the bodies of the queen and princess, starting at their chests and flowing down to the floor. The former king had a long, black gash on his throat.

"He killed them," Lyra said, her voice laden with sorrow.

"Probably to avoid starving to death," Victor surmised. "Strange. The paintings showed four members of the family. Where is the prince?"

"Who knows. Kalthav's end came suddenly. Perhaps he ... could not make it back to his family in time."

Victor shook his head slowly. The others must have used poison or some other method to meet their ends. There were no visible wounds on them. He tried not to think about any of them letting hunger or dehydration take them.

The reception room had nothing they were looking for, so they left it and its bodies behind. Victor hoped the next room over would prove more fruitful. They were quickly running out of options.

Lyra moved to open the next door, as well, but this time stood off to the side before pulling on the handle. Thankfully, it moaned open harmlessly. Victor kicked some debris blocking the door out of the way so it could open enough to let them in. Inside was much the same as the other room. Everything had been dashed across the floor. However, there was a window on the opposite side allowing in a ghostly light from outside, creating barely illuminated sections on the floor.

"Victor ..." Lyra began as though she were going to ask a question, but her voice trailed off. It was low like she was afraid of being heard.

"What is it?" he gently pressed.

"Where is this light coming from? Outside it's so dark."

Victor walked toward the window, sounds of crunching and cracking marking his movement. He feared to go too near the window, but came close enough to lean over and look outside. The rain had stopped and the clouds still hung heavy and black in the sky, gray-rimmed from the sun that fought its feeble battle beyond. That must have been the source, but it was still a strange kind of light, ethereal like moonlight.

"The rain stopped," he said, hoping it answered her question somewhat. "We need to find a way across before another storm comes."

Searching in the bedchamber was easier than the reception room. The faint light from the window allowed them to see more. It spilled across the large bed next to the wall. The mattress was covered with more detritus. Opposite the bed, barely hanging on the wall was another large painting in an ornate frame. It portrayed the royal family of Kalthav when the prince and princess were young children. They looked elegant, noble, everything that the slain corpses in the other room were not.

"Victor, here," Lyra said from across the large room.

He came over to her and she lifted her torch, illuminating a door in an alcove. Some unknown crest was carved in stone above it. The symbol of Kalthav was recognizable, but Victor did not know what the rest of the crest represented.

They tried the door, but it was locked; the first locked door they had come across in the castle. The catastrophe that brought down the city didn't loosen the stones or hinges, here. Lyra and Victor both took turns pulling on the door, but had no luck in moving it. Finally, Victor decided to try and unlock it with magic. He wasn't an expert in arcane kinesis, but his attempts proved successful. The lock audibly clicked and they were able to open the door.

Beyond the door was a room barely big enough to fit the two of them. Its sole purpose appeared to be the access it provided to a stairwell. Victor led the way and they both began their descent down the spiral stone steps one after the other, their torches held up to light the way.

The stairs went down and down, circling sharply. It almost made Victor dizzy. After an unknown number of stairs, a small landing provided them a brief rest. A few chairs allowed them to sit and get off their feet, while a table was also present for some unidentified purpose. They sat and recuperated, wishing they had water canteens, and then continued on. Another set of stairs and another landing. Finally, the scent of salt water reached them and the faint sound of thunder echoed up the passage.

The stairwell stopped at a doorless entry into another landing, this one consisting of all natural stone. They were at the base of the massive oceanside column. The large rocks jutting up nearby in the ocean provided natural wave breaks. The water here was calmer and made a lulling sound as it washed up and off the rocky shoreline. Nearby, the weak light fell on a pier, also built of stone.

A path had been carved into the large black slabs of rock and filled with gravel to make walking to the pier safer. The gravel and its surroundings were slick with ocean spray; it would have indeed been a perilous walk for the royals and guests without the aid of this man-made path.

When they arrived at the pier, Lyra pointed out a second, larger door—rather, a set of doors—set in the wall of the pillar.

"The other must be for the royal family. Escape perhaps?" Lyra observed.

"Most likely," Victor agreed. "Too bad we couldn't find that one. It was probably on the other side of the collapse. And easier to get down, too."

Lyra snorted.

Next to the pier, a small boat rocked in the coursing waves. It had a small sail and a set of oars. The pier wasn't large enough for much else.

"This is how we're getting there?" Lyra asked with concern.

Victor shrugged. "There's no other way. You grew up next to the ocean; this should be nothing new to you."

She shot him a hard look. "And I know exactly how dangerous it can be. There's just the two of us and we have to get all the way over to the other pillar without knowing exactly where we're landing."

He gazed out over the water to the pillar that seemed so very far away. "I can help with that; so long as you can get the sail up."

Lyra looked over at the pillar, as well. Her face hardened with determination. "Let's go."

They both settled into the boat and Victor immediately felt

uneasy. He never liked boats. Lyra grabbed onto the oars and then looked at Victor with a serious expression.

"This will take both of us and once we're past those rocks, the water is going to get very choppy. And dangerous."

Victor's face turned pale at the thought of rough waters. "What if I can keep the boat stable. Can you get us there?"

Lyra's face curdled. She opened her mouth to ask a question but then closed her eyes and shook her head. "Ok. Yes. Use your magic."

Victor sat as comfortably as possible, with his back straight. He looked at Lyra, whose expression was stern but not agitated, and close his eyes. He placed his hands on his knees, grabbing them with relaxed fingers. He breathed in and out through his nose with measured slowness, and listened to the sound of the calmer waves here at the pier; the repetitive roar of the waves beyond. Felt the wind lick his skin and the cold kiss of the spray. He drew all this in, combined it, compounded it. The tranquility left his body in physical form and time slowed down.

Lyra looked at Victor and tried not to let her hesitation show. His magic was marvelous, but how could he calm an ocean?

As she thought this, the air around Victor began to change. It shimmered with light the reflected on water. Then, it began to swell. The shimmering dimmed and stretched until it swelled like a bubble. Where it touched the water, the surface grew still as a pond on a windless day. The bubble grew outward several feet from the boat, then stopped. The waves did not move *around* the bubble, they simply stalled the moment they touched it.

Her lips narrowed and then she smiled. She shook her head and began to row. It wasn't difficult with the calm waters around them, thanks to Victor. When they were far enough out, she drew the oars in so she could raise the small sail. That's when she realized the problem with this particular spell. Things were so calm, it cut off much of the wind. There was just enough to get them moving. Part of the sail was outside the spell and caught the full force of the ocean surroundings, but like the waves it died the moment it rolled down into the spell's effective area.

Damn it. She grumbled inwardly.

Rowing was still in order. However, this was probably easier in the end: just longer. It was certainly safer. Lyra sighed and put the oars back into the water and began to row.

CHAPTER 4

The spell created a haze in Victor's mind. He was subtly aware of his surroundings, but serenity washed over him and held him in its trance. He did not know how much time had passed, but a sudden cessation of movement caused him to snap out of the spell's embrace.

The roar of wind and crash of waves hit him like a hammer made of noise. His eyes popped open and he saw Lyra pulling the oars in, her face covered in sweat. He stood and made his way over to help her. She finished pulling her oar in while he took care of the other.

Lyra moved past him to the front of the boat, where she hopped out onto the sand and pulled it up as much as she could. Victor jumped out to help.

After the boat was safely beached, Lyra fell back on her rump into the coarse sand. The border of this pillar was different from the other. The same rock made up its core, but a bar of this sand ran along around the side and out of sight.

Victor knelt beside Lyra, who was breathing heavily.

"I'm sorry, I couldn't help row and keep the water calm at the same time."

She waved his comment away. "It's ok. It was probably better," she said between breaths. "Looking at the waves on the way here, we might have capsized without it."

His face paled again. "Oh."

"I just made straight for the shore; I don't know if there's another pier or dock around here."

He helped her stand. "Doesn't matter. We made it safely. Thank you," he said above the rising wind.

They made their way along the shore, using the sand to keep their footing along the slippery rocks. Halfway around, the sister pier came into view. It was built on the same kind of large, dark stones as the other pillar. No boat was present here. Victor took that as a good sign. More Black Gnarl was the last thing they wanted to encounter right now.

Near the pier, a large set of double doors were set in an arch of cut and mortared stone. At least they could walk up the pillar inside, away from the storm. The doors looked to be made of hard Kalthavian cedar, braced with black iron and carved with distinct northern markings.

Victor took the lead as they walked up to the doors. He pulled on one of the large handles and the door moved only slightly. He used both hands to pull, and the door opened with a sound that reminded him of a welcoming horn.

They both stepped inside, grateful to be out of the wind and ocean spray. The sound of thunder foretold another storm incoming. Somehow, inside the pillar it felt even colder. Strangely, Victor couldn't see his breath. He expected to see it shoot out in white puffs.

That's when he noticed the torchlights. Sconces lined a wide stairway in front of them, enough for a half-dozen people to walk up astride. There was no physical way they could stay lit forever and the pier was empty. Why were these lit?

"Victor," Lyra began, her voice almost a whimper. "Something is up there. I can feel it."

He turned his head to look at her, his eyes wide and jaw clenched. That primordial terror clawed at the back of his mind again. He couldn't hear anything and the only sight out of place was the torches. But he felt something, too. Something powerful. Something old. Old and angry and evil.

The wide stairs wound upwards in a wider arc than the stairwell on the other pillar. There were easily twice as many landings, all larger rooms with supporting columns carved out of the existing stone. Smaller pillars as tall as a man punctuated a walkway from one doorless arch to another in each room. They were all lit, blazing and lighting the landings. They should have been able to take comfort in the warmth and security from the light, but the flames provided neither. The cold only intensified. The question of who lit the sconces remained.

They reached a landing that Victor thought had to be near the top, but his fatigue was washed away by a jolt of adrenaline when, beyond the archway, a gathering of the specters waited outside a set of closed doors at the opposite end. Beyond must be the top floor of Storm's Pillar.

"More of them," Lyra said. She sounded slightly unnerved, but not as terrified as she was when they first came to Kalthav. "How'd they get here? We haven't seen any since the gap in the bridge."

"I don't know. They're far more interested in the door than us, though."

"Or what's beyond it."

The closed doors and the specters weren't the only thing that Victor noted about the landing rooms. Each room was uniquely decorated. Different heraldry adorned the tapestries, rugs, and tablecloths. Different Kalthavian runes were carved into the columns, though they were similar in some regards. Among all of them, the colors always incorporated blue and red. Victor recalled these as the traditional hues of Kalthav. He also counted six landings in total.

"These rooms each represent one of the Storm Kings," he observed aloud. It was a brief but welcome distraction.

"What?"

"The patron demigods of old Kalthav," he explained, looking around and taking in the details of the current room. "There were six of them. We've made it through six floors. Each floor had different heraldry, so they must have been built in honor of the Storm King's era."

Some of the specters turned to look at him, but then turned away. He shivered.

"And the last room?" she asked, her words hesitant. The last room was their destination. The location of the beacon and gods knew what else.

"The crown of the pillar."

It was beginning to make sense.

"From what we saw, Kalthav wasn't ruined and cursed like the other cities. Something must have protected it. Since we saw the gathered specters of all the Fifth-connected peoples, I can only assume the Storm Kings themselves were responsible. That's why the city is now destroyed. That's why that beacon is here. Kalthav was the last holdout of the powers of the world before the Rupture. The powers that represented Alda's escape and defiance of the Obscured Throne."

Once again, some of the specters turned to look at them. Their gazes lingered this time before they turned back to the door. Lyra swallowed audibly. She ran a hand over the column next to her, one of the supporting structures reaching up to the ceiling.

"You think they're still here?"

Victor looked at her and then to the doors at the end of the room. "We're about to find out."

Lyra gripped the handle of her sword and they walked to the set of doors that looked so ordinary and unassuming, yet were flanked by glowing beings waiting on the edge of chaos. The closer Lyra and Victor came to the gathering before the door, the more they expected something to happen. They almost waited for the ethereal bodies to move, but nothing happened.

They were forced to push their way through the forms, feeling the thickened air all over their bodies where contact was made. There were a few feet of empty space before the door, which Lyra and Victor were grateful for. He put his hand on the ornate iron handle and pushed the door open.

Inside, the same haunting light that spilled into the castle filled this room; just enough to see and just enough to deepen the shadows wherever they lay. Before Victor was a raised section of flooring surrounded by stairs on all sides. Seven shattered thrones formed a half circle around a central eighth throne, the opening facing Victor and Lyra.

On the central throne sat some sort of figure. It appeared vaguely human, but composed of a night-black substance. No ... as Victor looked closer, the shape was nothing. A void in reality. From the top of that shape shot the same empty light that created the beacon. The twisting shape was framed by a thin, faint line of a grayish hue.

Victor didn't remember walking forward, but he felt his legs moving, his feet slowly pressing against the floor like he was stalking some kind of prey. He turned and saw Lyra gazing, mouth agape, up at the beacon where it disappeared through the roof, the stones and beams doing nothing to stop its unnatural form.

Dread, the likes of which he'd never known, coursed through his veins. His blood curdled throughout his body. His stomach went cold and his bowels threatened to loosen. This was not some arcane conjuration. This was power unknown to Alda. Victor felt it resonate painfully within him. He felt a hateful gaze upon him, like something was looking through the dismal beam of nothingness directly at them. Empty eyes glared at him and Lyra with unbridled rancor. The wretched feeling was almost palpable, so strong it sat sour on his tongue. His hands trembled and his eyes watered.

He looked back at Lyra, his head turning slowly for fear that whatever watched them would pounce on him, grab him in its fiendish appendages and rend him into pieces so quickly he'd feel every bite of pain as he was torn through the veil between his reality and that bleak, black beyond.

This image continued to assail his waking mind as he looked at Lyra, her eyes wide, tears falling freely, her lower lip quivering uncontrollably. He wanted to reach out to her, go back to her, to say some words of comfort. However, in the midst of this over-whelming saturation of dread majesty, he was powerless. The feeling that had been building upon them like a thorned mantle now pierced their flesh, found purchase in their bones and called their bodies home, their souls rendered into mourning hearths. The primordial sensation of being a small prey animal hiding from the hunters above was gone. They were now caught in the eyes of the beast, its teeth bearing down on them.

Who ... are you?

A voice cut through the awe and fear. It was young, feminine, but also strong and curious.

"Who's there?" Victor whispered. His voice broke and his breath came out in a wheeze.

Who are you? Why are you here? You need to leave. Now.

He swallowed, painfully, and his dry mouth eventually moistened enough for him to speak.

"I am Victor, from a mage's sanctum called the Trifold. We've been journeying to Kalthav to find this beacon. Who are you? *Where* are you?"

As his senses and will slowly returned to a level resembling normal, he realized the voice came from the roiling, barely human shape on the central throne.

Annica. My name ... is Annica.

The voice, Annica, hesitated as though she were unsure of her own name.

I am here. In this room ... this place. I don't know how long it's been. The beacon, the pillar of black starlight ... how long have you been seeking it?

Lyra was now standing by Victor, her own courage having returned to her. They both looked at one another, recalling the days and nights spent traversing Alda's cursed countryside. Months had passed since then.

"Several months, at least. We aren't leaving, Annica. We can't leave."

You have to.

The voice of Annica sounded urgent, almost pleading.

"We cannot," Lyra stressed, "What are you, Annica? Are you human? Elf-kind? Are you trapped?"

I am human, or I was. I'm from a fishing village; I was training as a mage when my abilities with the Fifth were discovered. I don't know what I am now. You said it's been months since the beacon appeared? I can't tell the flow of time. Everything seems to last an eternity and no time at all. Seconds ... years ... I can't tell them apart. The Herald of Storms brought me here from the castle on the Lord's Pillar. Then, I ... I met the Storm Kings. They're all gone. They were already dead, but their spirits remained; they protected Kalthav.

Lyra looked over at Victor.

"I was right," Victor said. "Now that they're gone, Kalthav was the last of the former city-states to fall. What destroyed them?"

A heavy silence hung in the air. For a moment, Victor and Lyra feared that Annica had disappeared.

She did. Janesca.

The disembodied voice trembled with anger.

She leads the Black Gnarl. They want to summon the Obscured Throne to destroy the world. To remake it.

"Fools," Victor said through clenched teeth.

She dwells within this place with me. You must leave before she realizes you're here.

"We're here to destroy this beacon, Annica," Victor said, heavy with conviction. Whoever Annica was, she had to understand.

"The world is dying," Lyra added. "Alda won't survive much longer. We fought the Black Gnarl on our way here. They're gathering up the last of the world's survivors and taking them to some city in the middle of the Wailing Ocean."

No!

Annica's voice screamed.

You can't let them take anyone there! The Obscured Throne ... one of Its Inheritors is there! Bac'thule, one of the Throne's favored. I thought I destroyed It, but Janesca told me that's impossible. I only hindered It for a while by burning Its dwelling that tied It to our reality.

Victor squinted in thought. His forehead creased and pushed his tongue against the back of his teeth. Something about this was connecting to another incident in his brain.

"Annica, where did Bac'thule dwell?"

In an aldyr. A hideously bloated one, larger than a castle. I set it on fire and it spread to the island. I swear, I saw some awful thing leave the tree and retreat into the sky.

Victor's mouth went dry again. That aligned with a nightmarish vision Nethara mentioned in her final letter.

"Do you know how long ago this was?" he whispered, unsure if Annica even heard him.

I told you, I can no longer comprehend time. If you said it's been months since the beacon appeared ...

Annica went quiet again. Victor assumed she was thinking.

Are you still there?

"Yes," he replied. The poor thing; she truly couldn't tell if she'd been thinking for moments or years.

It was at least a few years, I think. But, so much has happened.

"That sounds like a dream, a vision, my mistress had long ago. She was an elf-kind, tied to the aldyrs, so she had a deeper connection with them than we do. The timing doesn't align, though; she said it was ten years before she died, which was a few years ago when you said you burned the aldyr—the last one."

Perhaps it was a prophetic dream.

Or, perhaps, you have forgotten that time matters not to the Throne. And Its influence was strong even then.

A new voice came from the shadowy silhouette roiling on the carved throne. It was also female, but deeper and sultry, like every word it spoke was delicious.

She's here. Annica said in an emotionless tone.

Guests. The voice cooed.

Leave them alone, you bitch! Annica shouted with such fury and venom that Lyra and Victor jumped.

That's rude, Annica. After all the time we've spent together.

Victor, don't listen to her! She fooled me into thinking she wanted to help; It made me ... I let her in and she destroyed the Storm Kings. She used me!

Victor and Lyra backed away. The empty light on the throne churned angrily. Agitated sparks and flame-like tongues bounced and stretched from the vaguely humanoid-shaped figure. Screams and shouts echoed in the room and in their minds, ringing their ears just as quickly as the sounds faded out.

Your connection to the Fifth is still strong, girl. Good. The second voice, Janesca, sounded simultaneously irritated and complimentary. Lyra drew her sword. A throaty chuckle resonated in the room.

That won't do you any good here.

"It's blessed by Fifth-sect magic. I'm sure it will at least sting," Lyra shot back.

Interesting ...

Janesca sounded genuinely curious, which made Victor ask his own question: "Annica, how are you and Janesca coexisting? One of you should have destroyed the other, or your Fourth and Fifth connections should have eliminated each of you."

Victor could only assume that the leader of the Black Gnarl was potent in the Fourth Sect. Truth be told, he'd imagine someone like Janesca would easily overpower an apprentice mage. Unless, of course, something else was amiss.

Something happened along the way here, didn't it, Victor? I can taste something off about your Fifth Magic. A blemish.

It was strange hearing his name come from the faceless voice. The fact that it belonged to a Black Gnarl leader infuriated him.

"How can you feel subtleties like that in the Fifth, death mage?" he asked, glaring at the void-colored figure. Another chuckle, softer than the first, resonated in his brain.

You and I both know I'm not just a 'death mage.' Annica and I are one, now. Light and dark. Creation and destruction. Order and chaos. Reality and void. Our powers are intertwined. Her power is needed, otherwise I would have finished her off.

You would have tried. Annica's reply was steeped in loathing.

Victor took a hesitant step forward. Perhaps he was wrong

about his understanding of the Obscured Throne. Perhaps it was simpler than he thought.

"Is this the Throne your kind has been after? The amalgam of Fourth and Fifth magic? Is this where your reign begins? You rule from here, your Fifth Sect prisoner helping you mold the world to your liking with the Throne's power channeling through this atrocious joining? Is this what Jermiah Colwerth was ranting about with the windows and doors and vessels?"

Victor let his disdain be known with each word. He heard a sigh and Janesca's reply sounded like she was chiding him.

I had higher hopes when I felt such a strong arcane presence approaching. Annica, dear, you really think I let you just speak with anyone who makes their way here as I'm off galivanting around the ethereal spaces? I felt the Fifth in this one as soon as they approached the city. I wanted to listen to you. Hear what you had to say.

"You joined us awfully quickly," Lyra said.

I grew bored. Annica kept trying to warn you away, as though you would listen. Not as if you would have a choice.

"You sound very confident for a disembodied voice," Victor sneered.

Forgive me. For someone so utterly incorrect about the Throne and Its purpose, I lost my sense of intellectual civility. You think this is the Obscured Throne? This? A flickering beam of torchlight? The Throne cannot be comprehended. Not even by me, the Crown of Night. We await Its arrival, call for succor from Its Inheritors. We hope to be a part of Its long, long-awaited reclamation of Alda.

"Have you broken the remaining seals? Have you?" Victor called out in frustration. "If you had, the Throne would be here. The Fifth Sect remains, even if you've perverted one small part of it!"

Victor hoped not to offend Annica, but it was the truth. This unknown girl must have a powerful connection to the sect of creation, but by her own words, it had been twisted by the Gnarl, albeit at the hands of the Gnarl's leader.

The Fifth. Sect. Remains.

Janesca echoed Victor's words in a manner suggesting she expected his response. At the very least, she sounded prepared to throw it back in his face.

Do you know what the seals are, Victor? We do. We simply have to wait, work, and be patient. True, the Fifth does hinder the Throne's return. The First Kin were quite clever with hiding the world away and awakening a different magic. Notice, though, that it is different magic. Not new. The Fifth Sect, like all the others, still originates in the Obscured Throne. It is the source of all creation and all destruction. The Fifth Sect is merely a mutation. A disease. Once it is cut out, the world will be ripe for harvest.

Victor stood there, breathing heavily, the confident words of the Crown of Night pushing against his mental resistance. She sounded so sure. Some of her words made sense. This display of power was, despite being so awe-inspiring, not what one would think of when imagining the return of some god-like power. Stories of the old world mentioned grand magical displays larger than this.

Don't listen to her, Victor. She knows how to twist your feelings.

As though reading his mind, Annica's gentle voice rose above the hum and crackle of the magic in the room. Her presence was a complete foil to Janesca's. She could help them, if Victor could find a way to connect with her.

"Are either of you aware of the mass of Fifth-connected specters gathered outside this room? And the thousands more in the city?"

Lyra gave Victor a look that questioned his disclosure of their discovery.

I sensed you, didn't I?

Janesca answered with a smile.

"And why haven't you dealt with them, if your god has made you so powerful?" Victor growled.

There was another stretch of silence. Neither voice spoke. When Janesca replied, she sounded annoyed.

First, the Obscured Throne is not my god or anyone's god. Secondly, those gathered around the city and in this very castle are of no concern to me.

"Is that true, Annica?" Lyra asked, speaking up and into the air like she was talking to a ghost. In a way, she probably was.

She despises them. Even those just outside the door. They refuse to enter here, though.

You speak as though you know me.

Janesca's voice cut in, her reply even-toned. The silence returned, but it was different from the feeling of hesitation before. This time, the air seemed to crackle. A sense of unease built, like the moments before Victor attacked Nyla.

Perhaps I was biding my time. Like you, Annica.

Victor saw Lyra shift uneasily on her feet. Her sword wavered as though she were bracing for a strike. His own hands trembled slightly and he found himself preparing a spell, but what magic would help in a situation such as this?

I had nothing to do but think about how to separate myself from you. Flee this place. Find somewhere to hide until it is all over. But the Gnarl seems to find me wherever I go.

And we always will.

Another quiet moment. Arcs of black lightning curled from the figure on the throne to the surrounding stones of the raised floor. The aura boiled like liquid light.

You met with some of our ambassadors, didn't you?

Victor wasn't sure how to respond. Janesca already appeared to know something had happened. He didn't know the true extent of her powers, but she could detect small irregularities and large confluxes of the Fifth and Fourth Sects. If he tried to hide something, it may stoke her anger.

"Yes. We did," he replied, revealing as little as possible.

You murdered them. Both of you. I'd know that particular stain anywhere.

Victor stood up straight and pursed his lips. He took great offense at her interpretation.

"I hesitate to call the death of a Black Gnarl cultist 'murder.' How many have your people slaughtered? Tortured? Sacrificed?"

You think I'm judging you. I am not. There was a single elf-kind among our order. Such a feat, to turn one of them to our cause. Have them recant their ties to Alda and take up the mantle of the Obscured Throne—that was one of the seals, you know? When she passed, it was like a black candle was snuffed out. A dead star swallowed by the cosmos. That made things simpler.

Victor felt like he was treading a razor's edge with this conversation.

"Made what simpler?"

Run, Victor—Please!

Annica's voice called out to him, but it sounded farther away than usual. The sinister black arcs continued to strike and curl out. Victor knew he needed to have defensive magic ready. This conversation was building to a conflict of one kind or another.

I didn't need to get rid of the specters outside. Unlike Annica, I had a purpose in my time here. I was waiting and biding my time, too.

"For what?" Victor asked.

For you.

Stones, Victor learned at the Trifold, represented the earth as much as the civilization that formed them for construction. From houses to castles to fortresses, they were all built for protection. The more protection is required for the building, the more purpose—the intent, the energy, the aura—is built into the structure.

The Storm's Pillar was built to be utterly impenetrable. The Kalthavians were a strong people and relished good, quality construction; much like dwarves, every stone was crafted and cared for. Especially those used for the fortress temple of their Storm Kings. Add to that the fact that the demigods themselves were heavily tied to the Fifth Sect and there was much to draw on for defensive arcane magic.

The moment the sinister response was uttered by the husky feminine voice, a cylindrical arm, for lack of a better term, shot forth from the shape directly at Victor. He threw up both hands and barked the commands that summoned the defensive energies of the castle stones and placed a barely visible arcane shield in front of himself and Lyra. The void-black appendage exploded into countless filaments, flicking and flailing but unable to reach them.

The appendage recoiled back to the shape on the throne, and an otherworldly growl filled the room. The once-humanoid form became an unrecognizable, shapeless mass. The arcs of midnight lightning danced and curled all around the room. Churning pylons of darkness extended from the mass and slammed onto the ground, shaking the floor.

Despite having no definition, the shape gave the impression of having weight and mass. Black tendrils of varying lengths, thickness, and size sprouted from all surfaces of the quickly expanding abyss. Looking at it gave Victor a headache; it was a nauseous blend of three-dimensional form and two-dimensional shape.

Victor, run! Don't I—

Annica's voice called out to them again, but it faded away as though Janesca pushed her essence, her consciousness, aside. Was she gone forever?

Victor had no time to dwell on the idea. Lyra's voice rose in his ears in place of Annica's as she pointed at the terrible void monster.

"Gods, are those faces?" she screamed, gripping her sword in both hands.

Indeed, on the strange surface of the beast, multiple faces could be seen in various states decay, a multitudinous array of flesh-covered skulls. Some were little more than rictus grins held together by a few straps of sinew, while others appeared completely formed. All of those that were recognizable shared the same face of a woman with long hair, full lips, and large, empty eyes.

All of the faces in unison opened their mouths, and a hellish cacophony made Victor's ears ring. He could tell by Lyra's audible grunt of pain and her pinched expression she shared the same sensation.

He swung his arms wide, nearly hitting Lyra by accident, opened his palms, and splayed his fingers. His arcane commands could barely be heard above the other horrible noise. Chains, glowing with the magical energy that formed them, materialized and attached themselves to the walls, floor, and ceiling. Their free ends wrapped and tightened around any part of the living abyss they could before attaching to other parts of the room.

More tendrils and cylindrical appendages coagulated from the pulsing darkness and came at Victor. He balled his hands into fists and curled his arms inwards. The chains pulled together, bringing the captive parts of the creature with them. They joined together before Victor and intercepted the attack against him.

Lyra sprang forward and brought her sword down on some of the recovering tendrils. They dropped from the creature, who barely seemed to notice, and fell to the ground, where they materialized into boiling, smoking puddles.

She swung again and again; Victor heard an ominous sizzling as the amputated parts fell to the floor. Lyra's grunts grew into shouts and he saw the tip of her sword cutting through the larger parts held by the arcane chains. The next time he heard melting limbs, it was accompanied by the rattling of those same chains. A large pool of the strange, evil-looking substance spread before him and he looked across it to see Lyra looking back at him, breathing heavily.

Her eyes widened, and her mouth opened to match Victor's own look of shock when he reached out and grabbed her by the clothing on her shoulder. He barely yanked her out of the way of a massive shadowy pillar that crashed down like a hammer, shattering the stone floor. The momentum caused him to throw her out of the way and nearly made him fall in the process.

"Is this the power you were promised, Janesca?" Victor screamed at her. "Is this what we all have to look forward to?"

He reached up and, uttering more arcane incantations, made a grabbing motion with his hands and pulled. He felt a physical resistance, indicating his spell had taken hold, and the sound of snapping wooden beams and breaking stone preceded a large section of the roof falling on top of the abomination. Unfortunately, it had the same effect as hurling pebbles at an angry cougar.

An inarticulate, gurgling howl escaped the many faces, appearing and disappearing like bubbles in a tarry stew along the thing's surface. A large tendril stretched out and lashed at Victor, but he fell to the ground on his stomach, and it passed over his head with such force that his cloak and clothing were whipped about him.

He rose on one elbow and turned to see the door to the room being thrown off its iron hinges, tearing from the stone and causing another small collapse. A section of the adjoining room was exposed, and the shining specters all stared in with a familiar look on their faces: fear. They all began to step backward away from the room, all with their eyes locked on the abyssal shadow-creature.

The multitude of faces looked away from Victor and Lyra, who had both made their way to a kneeling position, and glared at the silver-blue figures with hideous scowls from those faces with the flesh to do so. The body of the Janesca abomination was nearly the size of the room itself. The stone throne upon which the former human-shaped figure sat was crushed to minute bits of rubble. The beacon remained intact, connected to the larger body by the flickering arcs of black lightning.

The hideous thing roared. Multiple instances of column-like legs appeared, propelled the body across the raised floor, and scurried down towards the gaping space in the wall. The specters turned to flee, but they were too late. Void-dark tendrils lashed out and coiled around some of the specters while others were crushed beneath blunt, stomping feet. The Fifth Sect aura surrounding the figures crackled and sparked like a hammer striking a red-hot blade. The power of the Fifth fought against the physical incarnation of the Fourth.

Victor and Lyra hesitated to make their escape, having no place to go but past the strange, horrifying carnage before them. He expected to see the specters fight back or at least fall free from the creature's grasp as the Fifth protected them. However, the longer the abyssal appendages held on to the specters, the weaker the sparks at their points of contact became. The first specter to be grabbed screamed, an echoing ghostly sound, as the living darkness spread over and consumed it. Another, its faint distinctions betraying a weaker connection to the Fifth, suffered the same fate in short order. A third specter followed soon after.

"Victor ... what's happening?" Lyra gasped.

They both stood to their feet, Lyra brandishing her blade.

"She's ..." Victor struggled to find the words. When he did, he was hesitant to use them. "Janesca is using Annica's connection to the Fifth and the bond they share to break through the Fifth Sect's protection. She's consuming them ..."

Lyra raised her sword in both hands and began to run for the monster, but Victor grabbed her by the shoulder. They couldn't fight this creature head-on.

"We have to run, get down to the boat," he whispered urgently. Lyra hesitated, then nodded.

They ran past the creature as it howled, groaned, and consumed its remaining prey. They barely reached the second landing when the room shook from a tremor originating above them.

"It's coming!" Lyra shouted.

The specters that fled stood in the center of the room, looking up in abject terror.

"What are they doing?" Lyra asked, her voice raised in frustration.

"I don't ... I don't know." Victor panted.

The torchlight from the sconces lining the stairwell walls disappeared. The rumbling intensified, and the abomination spilled through the open archway like black gore falling from a demon's eviscerated gut. Tendrils of roiling black once again sprang from the formless body. They struck all around the room; where they made contact with the walls, the appendage split into thin strands of weblike patterns that looked like coagulated ink. The tendrils grew taut, and the creature effortlessly pulled the walls inward, collapsing the room.

Victor and Lyra both screamed and dived into the next stairwell. They rolled and tumbled, colliding together and falling over one another in a painful, disorienting descent until they both crashed onto the floor of the next landing.

Slowly and with pained grunts and yelps, the two managed to untangle themselves and crawl away from the archway. They slouched against the wall, bruised and bleeding.

"We have to keep moving," Lyra wheezed. "We don't have time."

Victor's eyes were squeezed shut as his back shot pain through his body with each heartbeat. His elbow throbbed, and his ankle burned. He didn't even notice the many bleeding scrapes visible through torn clothing.

They both tried to stand, but Lyra slipped slightly and fell to one knee. She made it onto her feet, and they both jerked painfully when a silver and blue figure came running at a full sprint through the cloud of dust in the archway. Just as it nearly reached Victor and Lyra, an arm-like appendage grabbed it by the top of its head with fingers that looked more akin to grasping spider's legs and clutched it like a melon. The spindly spider-fingers crawled their way over the top half of the specter's head. The arm itself pulled and stretched over the top joints of the leg-fingers like a membrane until it thickened, forming a head and face of its own, the fingers now where the face's teeth should be. They both gaped in horror as it grew more defined and more detailed and morphed into a female head, the jaw stretched at its hinges like a serpent. The specter opened its mouth in a silent scream and flailed its arms. Its eyes were already covered by the grotesque stretched lips, with the spider-fingers digging and pulling, gripping the inside of the specter's mouth to pull the abyssal face further onto its prey. The mouth chewed, and the jaw rolled, pulling the panicking specter into its gullet.

Victor tasted bile, felt his stomach threaten to empty, and then felt Lyra pull on him, urging him to run. He moved his legs and forced them to take him away from the unimaginable scene.

That atrocity of hatred made manifest was consuming anything in its path. It had to be stopped, but his gut lurched, and his heart felt like it stalled whenever he thought of how to do so. The thing seemed unstoppable.

They raced down the remaining flights of stairs as fast as their beaten bodies could carry them. The void-filled abomination harried them the entire way. Howls and cries from countless screaming mouths reached out and raked their minds, leaving a scar on their sanity.

The floors leapt and cracked. The walls crumbled and broke. The ceiling buckled, then collapsed, and they dodged falling debris that threatened to break bones and crush their skulls. It felt like the entire pillar would collapse before they reached the bottom. The fiendish, otherworld nature of the beast warped reality around them, making stairs seem to shrink and walls swell like breathing lungs. Stone detritus transformed into bleeding, leering skulls before their eyes. Broken beams twisted into mangled, frostbitten limbs, with grasping and clawing fingers. It felt like they had descended far too many flights of stairs. Victor recalled what the Black Gnarl always said: time means nothing to the Obscured Throne. It is not fluid. It is not moldable. It is nothing. Were they trapped in a never-ending escape, doomed to flee this obscene evil for eternity?

He saw Lyra running with him, nearly falling down the stairs as they descended so quickly. He heard her breathing, saw the sweat on her face. She was right there next to him, but seemed like she occupied a different world, a different part of reality. Her movements looked much like his felt; mechanical. They simply had to keep moving.

When Victor thought his body could handle no more, when his mind felt ready to break and his will reduced to nothing, his feet hit another landing and he was prepared to surrender to whatever hellish fate the creature brought. There in front of them, however, were the two large doors that led to the outside, where the stone beach of the Storm's Pillar waited.

"We're here," Lyra choked out.

This was it, Victor thought, one last push and they would be out in the open. Both of them ran as a surge of adrenaline sent renewed vigor through their bodies. Victor felt a dull pain in the front of his feet. He had the brief sensation of weightlessness, then his whole body exploded in pain, starting with his chest. After a confusing moment, he realized he'd simply tripped and fallen.

A wave of ice-cold air hit him, almost taking his breath away. He looked up and saw Lyra had opened the doors. She looked back and her face contorted with shock. Lyra instantly ran back for him, her arm reaching out to help him up.

"Victor, gods, are you ok?"

"I'll live," he grunted as she helped him up. "Let's get out of this damn place."

Lyra put an arm around his shoulder, once more helping him hobble along to the door that was so very close. The rumbling of the abomination's chase melded with the muffled sound of thunderous waves outside. The door came closer and closer, the salt air touched Victor's skin, filled his nose.

Something gripped Victor's ankle. His heart froze and his stomach dropped, just before he felt pulled away from Lyra. He was wrenched from her grasp with such force that she spun and fell to the ground. He turned mid-fall and landed on his back, where he looked into the eyes of hell. A mouth with a thousand fangs like bent needles, yawned open before him. Two of the female faces, their mouths open and screaming, were in place where eyes should have been on either side of the maw. What grabbed him was a long tentacle protruding from the darkness within the mouth, pulling him toward that void like a vile tongue.

It squeezed his ankle painfully. The puckering cups on the underside were mouths—human mouths—with broken, uneven teeth. Smaller, whip-like tendrils curled out from the body and tried to grab him, some getting purchase around his waist and leg. Lyra shrieked from behind him. His mouth was open in silent pain, grunts barely escaping his throat. He wanted to tell her to run, to say goodbye, but he couldn't speak. The grip of the beast laced his body with a type of pain he couldn't describe.

A shadow passed over him briefly. He expected it to be some final blow before death took him. Instead, a flash of reflected torchlight preceded the sound of metal on stone. The tendril wrapped around his waist went slack and fell to the floor, melting into another sizzling puddle.

Lyra hacked away at the other tendrils, each falling and melting but instantly being replaced by another. The body moved forward, pulling its bulk out of the stairwell and closing in quickly. Victor tried to grab at the tendrils but soon discovered it was useless. He looked around and saw nothing but rocks and large wooden beams, all twisting into blurred images of other macabre things as the creature's reality-warping effects continued to manifest. Next to him, Lyra's foot landed perilously close to his face. He saw a knife there tucked into her boot. He grabbed it and stabbed the creature wherever he could reach it. The blade passed through like it had cut into air.

He saw Lyra's blade continue to carve away at the beast, and she landed a blow on the main body, resulting in the creature howling from its many mouths. It recoiled momentarily, possibly feeling a touch of hesitation knowing it could be wounded.

It was the blessing from the statue of Sheemra. The Fifth still worked against the creature, despite Janesca's strange bond between the two magics. His thoughts were abruptly halted by the sudden sound of a *crack*. Pain exploded through his leg as the tentacle gripping his ankle twisted and yanked, breaking it. Victor howled in pain. If felt like the tentacle was going to rip his foot from his leg. The gibbering mouths uttered words in some unknown language, neither of any Aldan origin or magical sect. They hurt to listen to. He felt warm liquid run down his ears.

The dagger from Lyra's boot was useless. Her blade continued to hack away at the tendrils, but the creature had recovered from its momentary reluctance and began to surge forward again. Two large appendages appeared and slammed next to Victor and Lyra. The ink-like webbing spread out along the stones much like in the floors above. The creature was going to rip the very ground from beneath them.

His mind numbed with pain and exhaustion, an idea somehow struck through to Victor like a beam of sunlight breaking through the clouds. The creature could be hurt by Fifth Magic, being a creature imbued and possibly created strictly from the Fourth Sect. Janesca was bound inside it somehow, so Annica may be as well. They had created some unwholesome bond between the two sects. Pieces fell into place and Victor acted.

He grabbed the tentacle around his ankle, feeling the squirming mouths attempt to bite him. It hurt to touch the foul thing. However, he felt the Fifth Magic within it like reaching beneath the surface of a murky pond and grasping diamonds covered in the muck. A low gurgle escaped the beast. Victor reached out with his own connection in the Fifth, focused on that beam of light amid an endless sky of darkness.

Victor ...

He heard Annica's voice. His magic had connected with hers, ever so slightly. The beast roared. Either it or Janesca's consciousness within it recognized what Victor was trying to do.

Lyra lunged forward and drove her blade into one of the

faces that composed the creature's eyes. A hissing and burbling noise was followed by copious amounts of the black, void-colored ooze gushing onto the floor. The thing writhed and threw its body about, causing another round of tremors to shake the entire pillar. One of the large appendages ripped up the floor beside them, causing the door to explode off its hinges and part of the room to collapse. The web-like tendrils encompassed the rock that fell near the creature, saving Lyra and Victor at the same time.

Lyra fell back, her sword protruding from the creature. Multiple snake-sized tendrils whipped out and wrapped around the handle, then yanked it free, a spray of black nothingness flowing out and landing on the floor with a series of pops and hisses. The blade was flung out into the ocean, far out of sight.

"Shit!" Lyra cursed.

The massive bulk trembled and expanded exponentially. Victor was free of its grasp as it grew too large, too fast, and he was hurled from what remained of the interior. Lyra was struck in the same fashion by the expanding bulk and they both landed in the shallows outside.

She helped him stand and practically carried him out of the freezing water. The abomination billowed from the opening and from the windows high up at the top floor. It hadn't been chasing them; it had been growing, expanding and filling the halls and rooms. Lightning coursed through the skies above, barely illuminating the darkness. The beacon still rose, black arcs dancing around the entirety of the upper pillar. Multiple faces formed from the abyssal mass. One with the spider-leg teeth, another with a half-melted face, and one with eyes forming most of the visage, bloated and empty. They all had features of the same person. They must have been twisted depictions of Janesca. Her energy, her soul powered the monster—and her power was great.

All will suffer. All will die. All will serve.

Were those Janesca's words, or were they the will of the Obscured Throne manifesting through her? It was difficult to tell. The voice was the familiar feminine tone that spoke alongside Annica, but it was warped and perverted, sounding like it came from places outside reality. The chanting persisted, irregular, chaotic, and without any notable cadence.

Lyra looked at Victor, tears in her eyes. "There's nothing we can do. We can't kill that. My sword was all I had to fight it with."

"And my magic isn't enough," Victor muttered. What could they do?

His summoning of the Fifth hurt it, goaded it into this bloated form. He turned his head and looked over his shoulder. Thousands of silver specters still lined the cliff's edge and along the city boundaries. They were pure Fifth Sect magic. All of them. They gathered here because their ties to the magic of Alda wanted them here.

His magic wasn't enough, but all theirs might be. The combined might of Alda's last defenders could put up one final battle. He would also have to take the greatest of all risks.

"Janesca!" Victor shouted. "Janesca, Crown of Night; Whore of the Throne of Darkness!"

The insults must have reached what remained of the Black Gnarl leader's consciousness. The disgusting faces all turned to him. The many eyes that appeared on the surface like blinking pustules all glared at him with open hatred. Thousands of puckering mouths all uttered the same thing: *You dare.*

"I dare," he replied. He could barely move. His ankle was completely limp. He hopped awkwardly a few steps forward. He slung out one hand, hurling a twisting helix of lightning at her. With his other hand he added a flourish and a gout of flame attached itself to the other spell. A helix of flame and lightning struck the half-melted face. He moved his hand and ran the lightning along the exposed side of the rocky pillar and onto the castle. The spell did nothing to the creature. Small fires caught along the pillar and inside the castle, lighting up the darkness.

The bulbous-eyed face leered at him, then moved closer. The hairs along the head stretched out and grabbed him and Lyra. Painful serpentine appendages wrapped around their wrists and ankles and spread them apart. Lyra struggled against them, grunted and cursing at the creature. Victor's broken bones in his ankle ground together, causing him to vomit from the pain. He bit his tongue and tried to regain control of his mind. It was difficult, given constant gibbering from the countless mouths. The strange chanting threatened to take his focus away.

I will rend you. Tear off your limbs one at a time, like a fly's wings. I will listen to your screams as your tendons snap and your bones break. I will drink your blood and feast on your shredded skin. You will die only when I am done unravelling the last agonizing nerve from your body.

Victor glared at the head that spoke, the one with the teeth like a spider's legs. They reached out for him, flicking and curling in and out in a sickening dance.

That one will watch. When I begin with her, Annica will listen. Then I will deal with her, too.

Victor closed his eyes. The spindly teeth were close, he could hear them clicking together. But, in the vast emptiness in his mind's eye, he saw an island of glistening diamonds. Silver hued and lined with blue fire. The gathered specters. He also saw the oily flesh of vipers swimming on a dark sea, many of them, holding two other shining figures. The vipers were connected to a nest, roiling like boiling black water. Inside, a soft glow. It lit the edge of the angry waters because the turbulence had joined with it, become a part of it.

Victor reached out to that glow. He conjured a small flame, smaller than a candle's last light. That flame crawled across the bending viper unnoticed. It created another flame, then another. Small flames dotted the dripping black scales like resting fireflies. The viper didn't notice. If time meant nothing to the Throne, then it meant nothing here, where these energies dwelt and manifested in things the human mind could not comprehend.

His heart raced as the last of the flames flickered into place, a chain between himself and a glow within the angry nest.

I can feel you ...

Annica's voice sounded relieved. The small flame stretched out, flickered like it was being blown out. Instead of disappearing, it touched the glow and an explosive chain reaction occurred. With the sound of dozens of fires blazing to life, the small flames erupted into silver blazes, haloed by blue light. The glow within the nest grew, but still swelled beneath the roiling void.

Can't ... hold on.

Victor physically reached out his hand in the direction of the specters. In this plane, the boundary of cliff and water stopped nothing. The figures began walking in a focused stream toward him. They reached him quickly, like there was no distance between them at all.

The one in the lead, an old woman dressed in clothing he didn't recognize, reached out and took his hand. The specters behind her either joined hands or reached out to touch one another's shoulders. Victor felt their power flowing into him.

Victor ... No.

Annica's voice sounded urgent, but he barely noticed. The vipers began screaming. The nest pulsated and whirled in a violent frenzy. Soon, all the combined power of the Fifth Sect lit up Victor's being like a beacon all its own. The silver, swirling light danced over to Lyra, then down to Annica, the glow within the wicked nest. The sound of the chanting weakened and turned to screams.

Victor opened his eyes. The hideous visage had recoiled from him. The spider leg teeth were stretched out, trembling in pain. The bloated eyes of the other face hemorrhaged black ooze. The half-melted face had snapped one of the last remaining muscles holding its jaw in place, and it now hung loose as the head flailed about.

Past all this, amid the eyes searching in countless different directions and mouths screaming countless different curses, was another face. This one appeared like a true depiction of what Victor assumed Janesca truly looked like. The visage was fading, but something else tugged at him, cast a flicker of concern in his moment of triumph: was she smiling?

It was impossible to tell. The surface of the shapeless beast began to reflect the weak light of its surroundings, taking a more solid, physical shape. The multitude of eyes and mouths were swallowed by its swelling bulk, including the face Victor thought was smiling back at him. At the same time, it began to melt with rivulets of ichor streaming down its sides and plopping onto the ground like chunks of viscera.

The sound that bellowed from the mouths of the giant, misshapen heads was less a scream and more a low bellow, like a massive horn sounding a call to war that echoed the hoarse cries of a million dying people. Victor wanted to celebrate as the appendages, heads, and extensions of the creature crashed into the ground. Despite the nausea-inducing pain in his leg and Lyra rushing over to take his arm in hers, he didn't feel the sense of victory he should have. Something felt wrong.

The spider-mouthed face that drew so perilously near to him was lying on its side. Its form sagged and the spindly legs making up its teeth curled inward, like dead arachnids do. It's fetid, black tongue fell from its mouth and began disintegrating immediately. However, Victor noticed it wasn't formed like a tongue.

It moved, writhed like the face was still alive and trying to lick the ground. That's when two arms stretched out and tried to crawl away from the open mouth. The tongue was shaped like a human—a desiccated and decaying body from the waist up. It was slick and slimy, like a half-rotted corpse coated in tar. It crawled a few inches before its face turned up to look at them. It was Janesca; or rather, what remained of her.

Her eyes were empty orbs and the flesh of her lips barely clung to her jaw.

"So close …" came her gurgled whisper. "So close …"

Janesca's head fell to the ground with a wet *splat*. A burbling gasp was the last sound the Crown of Night uttered. The beacon above flickered and died as the last of the arcs of black lightning fizzled out and spat their dying sparks.

Lyra and Victor stood in stunned silence.

They'd defeated the abyssal monstrosity borne of the unwholesome union of Fifth and Fourth Magic, empowered by the Obscured Throne. Why, then, did the unnatural darkness remain? Why was the cold harsher and sharper than ever? The sense of being watched by hungry, spiteful eyes intensified and Victor felt the sudden urge to curl into a ball and lay there on the hard, stone beach and let the freezing water drown him.

Victor, what have you done?

Annica's voice spoke to him, and he looked at Lyra, who returned his gaze as if she'd heard nothing.

"Lyra?" Victor whispered, afraid to be too loud in the heavy silence. Even the waves had calmed like the ocean itself had given up and died.

"What?" she replied.

She can't hear me. Our bond in the Fifth connects you and I after our magic combined. Where were the people gathered here, Victor?

He looked to the cliffside and the town, but they were all gone. Their power helped him defeat the creature, overcome its Fourth Sect power. He thought it was the right thing to do; the reason they gathered here to help stop the Throne.

"I combined their power with mine to defeat Janesca, that thing ... I thought they had gathered her to insulate the Fourth Magic of the beacon."

Lyra raised an eyebrow. "Who are you speaking to?"

"Annica," he returned quickly.

"She's with you?"

He nodded. When Annica spoke again, it sounded like she was close to tears.

Victor ... they were doing just that. The beacon threatened to spread and infect the land further.

"And it's gone now," he interjected. His own tone sounded desperate, but a growing dread built in him. A look of concern was beginning to twist Lyra's face.

I tried to tell you to run. You didn't listen ... you didn't listen, Victor! When she pushed my own presence down, I heard things, felt things that she couldn't hide anymore with her power swelling and her focus on you and the specters. She wanted them used up. Burned away. They were the last of the Fifth's power in the world; we are the last. She wanted you both here so she could destroy the final strands of the Fifth holding the Throne at bay. The aldyrs are dead, elf-kind is gone, and now so are the last vestiges of the Fifth on Alda save for the three of us. Once we've passed from this world, nothing is stopping the Obscured Throne from returning.

"And without the aldyrs, the magic of the Fifth is finite ..." Victor finished her thought. He fell back, the pain of landing in the shallow water and dark stone lost to the agony of this epiphany. Lyra jumped, shocked by his reaction to something she couldn't hear, and came to him. He gawked at the shapeless black mass before him. Lyra tried to help him up, but his body had gone numb.

They were the last. Victor had played into Janesca's plan. She goaded him into attacking. She became a sacrifice, herself. An abomination combining two opposing magics slaughtered by Fifth Sect power. How many seals were broken in this fight alone?

The last bit of hope lay in their three mortal lives. They were all the Fifth Magic left in the world. The only thing that ever kept the Obscured Throne from reclaiming the world of Alda. What could they do now?

"I don't know what to do."

The words hurt to say, and they resounded like death knells in Victor's ears.

There's only one place left to go.

Annica's voice sounded as defeated as his.

"Did Annica say anything?" Lyra asked, her voice soft and worried, almost childlike.

Victor nodded. Tears warmed his eyes then ran cold down his cheeks. The sound of gentle ocean waves rolled onto the rocks. It drowned out the sound of the melting abomination covering Storm's Pillar. The darkness was deep and the cold was consuming. The near-silence was the worst of all. It told him all he needed to know.

"Gods. What have I done?"

THE FINAL SEAL

Nicholas let his curiosity get the better of him. Instead of staying inside, awaiting whatever doom or salvation came from day to day, he had to find out more about the sky. It was his only relief in this world and it was changing every night. One star here, two stars there, they continued to wink out. The night itself became so dark that the Black Gnarl added additional lanterns throughout the city and began enchanting various posts with arcane light.

It did not help much. The day became a darker shade of evening, the nights almost preternaturally dark. You simply tried to make it from one island of light to the next.

The black-robed masters of the city skulked about like ghosts in the night. So far, he was the only citizen he'd spotted out. Those who ventured out into the evening hours grew less and less. Nicholas said it before, but each time he stepped out his door into the threshold of night, it seemed like a living thing. Even more so, now. The dark almost had a palpable feel to it.

He became lost at one point, the islands of light looking a bit different than he remembered. After circling the confusing, inclined cobblestone streets he found the dwelling he searched for. It was similar to every other. A marking or number the only way to tell the difference. But this one also felt different. At each visit, despite how few they were, Nicholas sensed something odd about this place, but not in a particularly bad way.

He knocked softly, as the oppressive night made it feel like any sound would carry to every street, and waited. After a few moments, the door opened and the familiar tenant answered.

The door only opened a few inches, and the wrinkled face of the old man stared back at Nicholas for a moment, seemingly needing a second to recognize him. The sunken, bleary eyes blinked and then the gray-haired head nodded.

"Good evening, old man," Nicholas muttered in a half-jest.

"Come in," came the aged, ragged voice.

The stooped old man hobbled into the small entryway and then segued into a sitting room. A small stove with a kettle resting on top sat cold in the corner. The old man started it up with a slight wave of his hand, a fire igniting in the iron-bellied contraption. Two glass cups sat on a table between two chairs. The old man poured some water into each of them and made some tea.

It was the same ritual each time. Nicholas would come to listen to stories and the old man would tell them. Nicholas would thank him for the tea and the entertainment and the old man would thank him for the company. It was a simple exchange. This time felt different. The old man looked more stooped than usual. His hobbled walk moved more slowly. Nicholas had never gotten the story about his crooked foot that turned off at an odd angle.

"You seem off, today," Nicholas asked as they sat down. "Are you ill?"

"No," came the raspy answer. "Just feeling my age."

The old man sipped from his tea. "I'm afraid I'm quickly running out of stories for you."

Nicholas nodded and cupped the warm glass in his hands. "That's quite alright. I actually came to you with a question today."

"Even better," the old man replied.

"The stars. I watch them every night. I've painted them and earned the ... meager respect of some Black Gnarl for my work. So, I know them fairly well, I'd like to think. However, lately, they seem to be—"

"Disappearing?" the old man interrupted.

Nicholas grimaced and nodded in affirmation. "Yes. Winking out, I like to say."

"They're not winking out," the old man replied casually. "They being obscured."

"Something is coming that is drowning the light of the stars. It's almost here, I'm afraid."

Nicholas put his cup down on the table. His curiosity was piqued.

"*Something* is coming? What do you mean?"

The old man sat back further into the chair. He seemed completely relaxed for having shared such foreboding information.

"You grew up on this island. In this world, for lack of a better term. It's all you've known. There used to be much more outside of Godscorn. Whole countries. Mountains. Plains. It was a broken world, but it was better than this."

"So I've read."

"The Black Gnarl are fools. They've created this infernal bastion and made themselves kings and queens of the ashes. Come with me," he said, abruptly standing and leaving the room. Nicholas followed, confused but interested.

They made their way up the stairs to the small upper floor.

Nicholas' occasional visits never warranted him getting a trip to the old man's second story. Not that it mattered. But this was a curious development.

Like nearly every other basic dwelling in the city, the upper floor was little more than a bedroom and second, windowless room for whatever purpose the tenant chose. The old man walked straight for the bedroom door and opened it quietly.

Inside it was utterly ordinary. A desk sat on one end by the window. An armoire was on another wall, and a bed sat against the other. Someone was under the sheets, Nicholas saw, and he felt uncomfortable and invasive.

"Don't worry, she's asleep," the old man said. "She sleeps a lot nowadays."

"Your wife?" Nicholas asked meekly.

"In a sense," he replied, then scoffed. "Such things have meant nothing for decades."

Nicholas turned from the sleeping figure beneath the sheets to the desk that the old man approached. He stood next to a chair and offered Nicholas the seat.

"No, you should sit," Nicholas insisted, gesturing to the chair. "I insist."

His tone suggested the old man had already made up his mind He turned, indicating he'd moved on. He opened a dresser drawer next to the desk. Nicholas sat down as the old man reached in and pulled out a book. His wrinkled hands placed it on the table with a careless flop. Nicholas sneered and recoiled slightly. It was a hideous tome.

"Do I dare ask what the cover is made out of?" Nicholas sneered.

The old man closed the drawer. "It belonged to the Gnarl. I'm sure you can guess. Don't open it."

Nicholas looked at the black, leathery binding and the crude barbed diamond carved into it. "Why would you show me a book and not let me open it."

"I won't stop you," the old man shrugged. "But you'll most likely die or go insane if you do. Or worse."

"Worse?"

"That is the source of all the misery we experience. The shit world you live in? It's from that book."

Nicholas backed away from the desk, pushing the chair and causing it to squeal on the floor. The old man never gave him reason to doubt his mental faculties.

The old, tired body walked to a chair next to the bed and laid a gentle hand on the person sleeping beneath the sheets. He grabbed the small chair next to the nightstand and pulled it over to sit next to Nicholas.

"I've told you a lot of stories. There's a few I've left out."

"You've lived a long life. I'm sure you haven't shared everything. That you have your secrets," Nicholas muttered sympathetically.

"All of which I'm about to share with you now. I don't have much time left."

Nicholas chuckled. "I'm sure you have plenty of time left. You are ... what? Sixty? A stooped, bad back and busted ankle won't shorten your lifespan that much."

"I'm two-hundred and nine, Nicholas."

The younger man was speechless. The old man had some noticeable physical difficulties, but he didn't look older than sixty, seventy at the most. He must have been lying. Perhaps a prank against the young man who visited him so late.

"I don't believe you. How could you be that old?" Nicholas doubted.

The old man looked at the book sitting on the desk. His face darkened and looked sad, but his eyes burned. "Time works differently around Them. To the Throne, it means nothing. The stronger Its presence, the stronger the effects of Its control."

"The Obscured Throne, the object of the Black Gnarl's worship? I've heard them muttering about it from time to time."

"Its name is often spoken in reverence."

"What sort of god is it? Sounds ominous, but they all do."

The only reference Nicholas had to any gods were in the books he'd read. It was the only knowledge anyone had of any place outside of Godscorn. Most citizens couldn't even read, so their entire world was the winding cobblestone streets and bleak spires of the island city.

The old man sighed and stood from his chair. "Wait here," he muttered. Nicholas heard his gentle footsteps fading as he walked downstairs.

The lady in the bed snored softly. The top of her head peeked from above the covers. Thin lines of color still streaked the mostly gray hair. Nicholas had met her on occasion when he visited. She was sweet and kind, subtly jabbing the old man with her verbal prongs. It's what made Nicholas think they were married. They certainly shared a couple's affection with each other the few times he'd seen her. Lyra, he seemed to recall her name being.

The old man came back upstairs with two cups and the pot of tea. He sat them all down on the desk and poured a cup for each of them.

"You didn't wake her, did you?" The old man asked gruffly.

Nicholas grimaced. "Seriously, Victor?"

The old man gave a rough, gravelly chuckle without much humor.

"You still haven't answered my question," Nicholas pressed.

"Which one? What kind of 'god' the Obscured Throne is or how I'm so damn old?"

Nicholas picked up his cup, smelled the subtle odor of the tea leaves inside.

"Both, now that you mention it."

Victor took a drink from his cup and sat back in the chair. His old lips stretching and contracting, like he was chewing on the explanation.

"I'm going to have to tell you all those other stories. The short version, anyway."

His head was tilted down, his eyes stared off through whatever was physically in front of him. Victor's mind was lost in the ocean of memories that comprised his life. Nicholas leaned forward slightly, giving his full attention.

"I've got nothing but time," Nicholas uttered.

Victor shook his head softly, still gazing into the past. "No, you don't."

For the remainder of the night, Victor shared the story of his life with Nicholas—all the parts he hadn't shared prior. He'd only given the young man pieces of the mosaic. The shinier portions, those unmarred by the worst of the darkness and pain. These were not tales of the road or the occasional confrontation with hostile survivors. The story of his encounter in Summer's End ended with him fighting a mage who was deceiving the townsfolk. All mention of said mage being a Black Gnarl recruiter was purposely omitted. No, these were the stories that wove together his fate and that of Alda.

He spoke of his time at the Trifold Sanctum, his former master and first lover, Nethara. How she was one of the last of her kind. He told of his encounters in towns and cities, all corrupted by the Inheritors. On that note, he explained the nature of the Inheritors themselves.

"The Black Gnarl believes them to be the Obscured Throne's children or some nonsense. They are no such thing. They are the extensions of the Throne's will. Its desire to destroy, consume, the be both adored and hated. To exist and not exist. Create, corrupt, nourish and torture. That is what the Inheritors are. Seeds of Its power. Let in by the Rupture," Victor growled.

Nicholas' understanding of the Rupture was tainted by the Black Gnarl scriptures and sparse teachings that ordinary citizens like him were allowed knowledge of. Victor shared the truth about that cataclysmic event and all that it meant for Alda.

"That was when the window was opened," Victor mumbled, losing himself for a moment. "That's when the Inheritors arrived and took this world, preparing it for the Throne."

Nicholas' ears pricked at Victor's tale of his close encounter at a city once known as Giranta. The city barely survived the world-shattering alterations of the Rupture. What remained was left on a new shoreline. A sinister presence encroached upon the newly-formed cliffs. Victor felt its presence and a mere glimpse of that shadow beneath the waves nearly overtook his mind and forced him to march to his death into the rocky waters below. He assumed that's what ultimately became of what remained of the city's people.

Nicholas took an interest in this, as that sounded similar to the waters surrounding Godscorn.

"I'd always thought that it was just the light of the sun playing with my eyes. The water further out has always appeared different. Normal, I suppose."

"Because it's what you've always known," Victor explained. "That is one of the Inheritors. It's gathered here for the moment the Throne arrives."

"How did you get here, then? Did you not say once some time ago that you arrived after the city's founding?"

Victor nodded. "Yes. We came here in a small boat we found at an abandoned harbor. It was still sail-worthy. I think our link with the Fifth protected us; that and my unique connection with the Fourth.

"The Fourth Sect? The magic of uncreation that you mentioned?"

One of Victor's stories for Nicholas was little more than a lesson on magic. "I'm getting there," Victor said. He explained one last lesson on magic he had left out: the seals. Every sect had eleven seals tied to them, as magic was an infinitesimal representation of the Throne's power. These seals were created by the First Kin, those who became recognized as the gods of the people of the old world. With these seals, they hid Alda away and so the world was allowed to flourish away from the Throne's hateful and wrathful influence.

The old man moved on to the next phase of his journey, where he met the most important person in his life. He'd had a vision that, to this day, he believes came from his connection to Fifth Magic. It led him to another haunted city, one of the worst in his opinion: Felkirk. A particularly vile Inheritor held sway there, eternally feasting upon and digesting the souls of its citizens. There, he met Lyra, whose own innate abilities kept her alive, but barely. Victor intervened and helped her escape. She lost both her parents shortly after and had traveled with him ever since.

They decided to make it their life's mission to stop the Black Gnarl. They discovered much together, though little in the way to defeat the Obscured Throne's approach to Alda. More tainted countryside, twisted denizens, and lost hopes. They did, however, discover the very source of the catalyst that led to the Rupture. An old professor and mage named Jermiah Colwerth.

He was a closeted member of the Black Gnarl. His research led him to discover secrets long sought after by his order. Those secrets warped his mind. He was ostracized by his peers and fled, leaving his family and old life behind.

Victor rubbed his eyes with his thumb and forefinger, trembling at the memory from so long ago. He took a moment to gather himself. After taking a sip from his cup to soothe his dry mouth, he continued.

"That is when we found the source of the ritual that ripped open the sky and killed the world. A small cabin on a hill at the edge of the woods, overlooking one of the greatest city states of the old world. There was a pit, small but gods know how deep. It probably fell to the center of Alda. There, the sacrifice was made to break the last seal needed to give the Inheritors their foothold and begin the downfall of ... all things."

"So, the Black Gnarl killed the world, then gathered the survivors here?" Nicholas wasn't sure what to feel. He was numb from disbelief, doubting the old man but convinced of his sincerity.

"It would be more accurate to say they poisoned Alda. The Inheritors were given a way into our world from their ethereal nether-space; to prepare it for the Throne's reclaiming. All that was left were the final seals pertaining to the Fifth Sect."

"Seals for healing magic? Why is it so special from the others?"

"Because it is unique among the magika of the world. The first three sects pertain to the world we know in all its forms. The Fourth Sect, thought for the longest time to simply be death magic and necromancy, is tied directly to the Throne. The magic of uncreation, of vile will. The Fifth?"

Victor had a glimmer in his eyes that Nicholas had never seen. It seemed like he was recalling a good memory for once.

"The Fifth Sect blossomed when Alda was freed from the Throne's influence. Without the embodiment of malice and spite and pain to twist everything around it, creation and harmony and healing were able to propagate. The aldyrs grew, one of the First Kin fostered their growth and over a few centuries the elf-kind came into existence. Alda had a soul all its own. But, when the Rupture occurred, the aldyrs died. The world was poisoned, as I said. It took centuries, but here we are. The magic of the Fifth became finite, as Annica made me so painfully aware. The less of it that was left, the more concentrated it became in those who had it. Merely the last struggling breaths of a dying beast. That is why I'm so old, Nicholas."

Victor nodded to the bed where Lyra slept.

"We are the last of Fifth Magic in this world."

Nicholas blinked, his mouth slightly agape. "I see."

"And, again, time has no meaning here, where the Throne's influence grows. You may be much older than you really are, if you were to go into the world outside the island."

"Not that I could," Nicholas said, waving the comment aside.

"I've had other dreams, visions of what remains of the continents. You wouldn't want to."

Nicholas rubbed his face with his hands and let out a large, loud sigh. "Who is Annica? Is she a friend? Another wife—not that I would judge. I've never seen anyone here but the two of you."

Victor smiled, a sad and slim smile, but it was there. "Annica was another who had powerful, innate abilities. But, the Crown of Night destroyed her body. Lyra and I met her in Kalthav. But only her Fifth essence remained. During a ... conflict there, we made an arcane connection. She lived up here," he chuckled, pointing to his head.

Nicholas looked at Victor with sullen eyes. "A ghost lives in your head?"

Victor frowned. "No, her life essence. Her soul. She told me of all she'd experienced and it made a clearer picture of what was happening in the world. More pieces in the mosaic. Her tale of this island was truly horrific. She didn't speak to me for some time when we arrived. When I first looked on that grotesque tree, I could feel her reaction. Her terror. Her pain and loss. Poor thing."

"Is ... is she here now? Can I ask her something?"

"Annica hasn't spoken to me for a long time," Victor said with a forlorn sigh. "I don't even think she exists anymore. The Fifth has grown weaker. It grows weaker every day. Her essence may have simply faded away."

For some reason, those words sparked a pang of sorrow in Nicholas. "And the seals?"

"There is only one left."

Nicholas' eyes searched the room like he would find answers there. He only just learned of all this travesty, but little surprised him, anymore. The Black Gnarl were never benevolent. He never trusted them, never thought they were keeping anyone safe. Victor's words simply piled more shit onto their list of atrocities. It didn't take an insulated, world-ignorant man like Nicholas to know that the Gnarl were wrong. Not just about their philosophies or governance—they were *wrong*, down to the core of their being.

"But all you've said about Fifth Magic, its purpose and strength—certainly that last seal can hold on as strongly as the others combined?"

"It was never so perfect," Victor grumbled.

The old man drank from his tea again, then poured more. Nicholas had the impression Victor was simply putting off the next part of his tale. Victor put the cup to his mouth but didn't drink. His hands began trembling, causing the cup and plate to clink together. He put it down on the table and then looked at Nicholas with a piercing gaze that made the younger man's insides go cold.

"*Everything* is tied to the Throne. Everything. Even the magic of the Fifth could not exist without the Obscured Throne. It creates everything, so It is *in* everything."

"The eleven seals of the Fifth—"

"Are broken. All but one, were you not listening?"

Nicholas fell back in his chair, exasperated. He wanted to help, somehow, and find a purpose. Something he could struggle for. "I want to help. I want to find a purpose."

"There is no purpose," Victor murmured.

"Certainly we can—"

"I gave up *everything*, boy," Victor sneered. He leaned forward, his teacup spilling over on the table and dripping onto the floor. "Literally *everything*. I burned up the last of the Fifth magic, defeating one of the Throne's worst creations. I thought for a long time that I had walked right into the setup the Crown of Night had prepared. But I realized something even worse. It wasn't my fault."

"Something not being your fault is worse?"

"Yes," Victor returned emphatically. "And it's there. All in that fucking book." Victor gestured to the book on the table.

"What *is* this book?" Nicholas countered, sounding flustered.

"The Dread Praises. The original. The first copy penned by the first Black Gnarl of the First Kin. Colwerth thought he had the first edition. True, it was the first made for use by the cult, bound in the flesh of the Black Gnarl's founder, but it was copied by the founder's apprentice. This was written by the founder of the Black Gnarl themselves."

Nicholas swallowed. His eyes flicked over the 'leather'-bound cover. "What's inside it?"

"Everything," Victor said, his voice rumbling. "I said the events at Kalthav weren't my fault. Because everything is tied to the Throne. It wasn't a matter of how the Black Gnarl would succeed or even if they *would* succeed. It wasn't a matter for the Black Gnarl at all. They were merely another piece. Alda was created by the Obscured Throne. It belongs to the Obscured Throne. It is a *part* of the Obscured Throne. Alda would always return to it. No matter how many eons it took. Meanwhile, the Throne would only grow more livid, more jealous; Its wroth fomenting and blackening other worlds and stars until it found us. Who knows what further hell we created for other worlds that suffered for our indignance—our defiance."

The old man spoke like a man possessed. His eyes focused on the tome; spittle flew from his mouth as his rage burned with each word.

"Victor ..."

"I could see it," the old man continued, his voice dropping to a whisper. "I could see what others couldn't. Not even him. The Fourth and Fifth combined within me? I could read the texts without my mind melding onto my skull. The Fifth kept my sanity whole, while the pages opened up to me and I could see every. Word. In. Blood."

"Calm down," Nicholas soothed. Victor was manic, falling from angry highs to sobbing lows.

"The Black Gnarl are no better off than the rest of us. The physical pleasantries they hold on to are the only thing separating them from us. They mean nothing more to the Throne or the Inheritors. They are tools. Conduits for power. Meant to be used and burned up. Do you know why they call it the Obscured Throne?"

Nicholas could only shake his head. He had no words to give.

"That's not even Its true name. It *has* no name. That is simply the only thing the First Kin who remained loyal to it could think of to call it."

Victor took Nicholas' hands in a wrinkled, shaking grip. It caused Nicholas to startle in his seat.

"Reality flees from Its presence. It is something so vast, so incomprehensible, that neither light nor darkness can exist around it. That is why it is obscured. No eye can look upon it. No mind can realize such a being. It existed before time, and It will exist after. It created time. It will destroy it. It must create so It *can* destroy. It loathes the living and the dead. It loathes existence, but It must *exist* Itself, and It must destroy so It can create ... do you understand? It is the Throne because It rules all. It creates and destroys all. It remains in a state of non-existence. Somewhere along the line of reality and void. That is the only place the Throne has solace. It exists in pain because It must. It takes joy in annihilation because It must. This is all It knows. It is everything."

Victor sat back suddenly in his chair. Tears streamed down his lined face. He placed a shaking hand over his mouth. Then, he leaned over to pick up his fallen tea cup and plate, placing them back on the table.

"I'm sorry, Nicholas."

Nicholas shook his head, waving away the apology. "It's perfectly alright."

His own hands were shaking. Victor's breaths came in raspy, staccato patterns.

"You said 'him.' You could see things even he couldn't. Who were you speaking of?"

Victor nodded sharply, visibly trying to regain his composure. "The current head of the Black Gnarl."

"What?" Nicholas gasped, accidentally interrupting.

"Yes. He knew the moment Lyra and I arrived on the island. I was afraid of such a situation and was prepared to fight if I had to. However, he was surprisingly cordial."

Nicholas had to pour himself some more tea at that revelation. The head of the Black Gnarl, knowing that the last problem keeping his order's plans from coming to fruition was on his island, was within his grasp. Yet, here that problem was, drinking tea and sharing his life story.

Victor continued to explain, telling Nicholas that Lucien, the head of the Black Gnarl, knew that the plans Janesca set forward and he was tasked with completing were not all what they seemed. She, like all her followers, thought the Throne would come and reclaim the world, setting the Black Gnarl at the top of the pecking order.

Lucien had explained to Victor that this was foolish and arrogant—the pinnacle of hubris. He knew that the reclaiming was the Throne coming to put an end to Alda. Not rebuild it. He couldn't share this with his followers, however, because it would result in chaos on their small, insignificant island. He continued to play into the lie.

When Victor asked why, Lucien simply said he wanted to enjoy the last few years of reality he had left. Even he didn't know what the end would bring when the Obscured Throne, in all Its vile, eternal malice, would bring to the inhabitants of the world that managed to escape it, if only for a time.

He offered Victor a choice: keep silent and enjoy the same courtesy, or die in a painful and public manner. Lucien never showed any sign that he knew what Victor knew: that the Fifth Magic itself was the final seal. Once it disappeared from the world, the last seal was broken, and the Obscured Throne would return. That is what Janesca wanted. That is what she meant when she uttered the words "so close." Her utterance held a double meaning. She'd hoped to destroy all Fifth Magic then and there on the shores of Storm's Pillar. However, she had still succeeded. The last of the Fifth magic dwelt in two mortals and one lingering ghost.

So, Victor agreed. For over a century, he and Lyra had lived here under the very nose of the Black Gnarl, biding their time until the end. The copy of the Dread Praises on the desk was Lucien's gift. He no longer needed it, and there was nothing Victor or Lyra could do to change anything.

At first, they tried to think of a way, of course. Annica aided Victor with her own magical knowledge and what she had learned from the Children of the First Son, as well as her time with Janesca. But, in the end, it was exactly as Lucien had stated and Victor had relayed to Nicholas. The Obscured Throne was the creator and destroyer. Scourge of Existence. And It will not be defied.

"It is only a matter of time," Victor said. "And judging by this old body, that time draws very close. Take care, Nicholas. It was pleasant having you as company."

Nicholas looked at Victor with wide eyes. This was it? He rose and nodded, thanking Victor in return. He offered to help clean up after the spilled tea, but Victor refused the help, stating it was of no consequence.

The young man let himself out, walking down the stairs and saving the weary old man the trip. Outside, the night was darker than ever before. Nicholas didn't know if it was because of all he had just heard or if something else was at work. He supposed like Victor said, it was of no consequence. Nicholas always thought of himself as fatalistic and aloof, but now he knew that nothing compared to the man in that building who had seen and experienced it all.

VICTOR WAITED for the sound of the door to close. It was quiet, barely perceptible to his old ears. Once it clicked shut, the old man stood and walked over to the bed.

"We've been through so much, haven't we?" he said to Lyra, who still slept beneath the covers. She'd become more weary in her older years, having little energy to spend. Victor thought it might be because she had a slightly weaker tethering to the Fifth than he did, as the difference was fairly small. But it was noticeable enough.

He sat down on the edge of the bed softly so as not to disturb her. That's when he noticed how quiet it had become.

"Lyra?" he whispered. Then, when no reply came, he asked again, slightly louder, "Lyra?"

His eyes grew warm. A tear rolled down his cheek, catching in his wrinkles. He crawled into the bed beside her and placed a hand on her side. She slept no longer. Finally, he was the last of those present to see the world's end set in motion.

Victor crawled beneath the covers and embraced Lyra one more time. He kissed her softly on the forehead. They did what they could in their final years, as long as they were, to simply live. He closed his eyes, hoping to see her in whatever waited beyond. Knowing what the universe was made of, however, he doubted it. He thought he was going to sleep but then felt his heartbeat slow. The dark beneath his eyes became darker, and he was gone.

As Nicholas walked home, making his way yet again from one island of light to the other, he felt a sudden pang of sadness. Not just sadness, but a foreboding malaise. He looked up at the sky and saw fewer stars than when he left. In fact, he was sure the one he was just looking at winked out before his eyes. There were so few he could count them on one hand, it seemed.

Now, only a single thing shone in the sky: an eclipse. A ring of fiendish light in the blackness. That was new.

He entered his dwelling and made his way to the second floor. He opened the drawer next to his bed and cursed at the fact that there was no wine left. He could go for one last drink.

Opening the doors to his balcony, a stiff wind had arisen. It carried a terrible stench, something he'd never smelled before. It must have come from places far offshore like Victor described. Or, perhaps, from places outside their reality.

Nicholas looked up to the sky again. Not a single star shined.

The light of the torches on the streets flickered in the wind, the illumination so weak they may have been dying stars themselves. No one walked the streets. Along the highest places of the city, the weak lights barely illuminated the silhouettes of cloaked figures. The Black Gnarl were gathering.

Seeing the black cloaks slither in and out of the darkness while the sinister circle of light flickered above sent a shiver down Nicholas' spine. The Black Gnarl coagulated like dead blood for the arrival of whatever eclipses heralded.

Nicholas recalled Victor's words. Light, darkness, and reality itself flee before the Obscured Throne. No eye can rest upon it. No mind can comprehend it. He felt as though he was looking up on it now, that great malice that neither lived nor died. He felt he was staring directly at it, but, as Victor said, reality fled. His mind could not put together what he saw. The darkness wasn't actually darkness. It was too deep. Too perfect. Light and darkness both fled before it. The eclipse was the only thing the mind allowed one to perceive of the throne. It teased the eyes with things just beyond the circular black veil, things that morbid curiosity wished to see but the soul begged to stay ignorant of, shriveling at the thought of the vile revelation.

He understood what the pang of ominous sorrow was. Victor and Lyra had passed. The last of the Fifth Magic protecting the world was gone, winked out like the stars.

Nicholas stepped onto the railing. He had half-heartedly planned this earlier but wasn't really sure if he would go through with such an end. It seemed better than whatever those black-robed bastards wanted. He climbed slowly to the top of the building. Odd-angled stones and irregular balconies made for an easier climb than expected. There, atop a townhouse filled with frightened people, he sighed, tried to take in one more deep breath while ignoring the searing odor filling his lungs, and let himself fall.

The wind whipped around his face. He tried to keep his eyes open; he wasn't sure why. There was a torch near the bottom that he watched expand as he fell. The wind continued to build, howling so loud it hurt. Just before it reached him, when he expected to feel a brief, painful moment of impact, everything went utterly and truly dark. In the brief moment before his death, when time stopped as he heard it does, he heard more than the wind. His ears did not have time to register what it was, but his soul told him to be grateful for that.

The Obscured Throne had returned.

PLEASE REVIEW

We hope you enjoyed *Shadow of the Throne*
by Russell Archey.
If you did, we would ask that you please
rate and review this title.
Every review helps our authors.

Rate and Review: Shadow of the Throne

MEET THE AUTHOR

Russell is a writer and voice actor. He enjoys all things horror and some things that are not. When not writing or building his career as a voice actor, he's playing any manner of board games, card games, and video games. Somewhere in between, he manages to be a father and husband.